HATE TO LOVE YOU

Small Town Enemies to Lovers Romance

A Whiskey Cove Novel

GINA WATSON

Whiskey
Cove
Publishing

Hate To Love You

Small Town Enemies to Lovers Romance

by

**Gina
Watson**

CHAPTER 1
LACIE (AGE 23)
May

I looked down at the letter in my hands. I'd walked back and forth in front of the mailbox five times now. To any onlooker I was engaged in a game of one-player tennis.

Lacie Ryan,
Please sign and return
to confirm your spot in the cohort for the
Louisiana State University
Speech-Language Pathology program
by the 30th of March.

If the mailbox in front of me would offer the added service of reaching out and shoving this acceptance letter into the envelope, I'd pay good money for it. I willed it to grow anthropomorphic features for a few more seconds.

"It's official, I'm losing it. Not that I ever had *it*," I muttered, and stuffed the letter down deep into the bottom of my bag.

Despite the early morning hour, my grumbling stomach, and the mailbox dilemma, I forced myself to experience real joy at the wind blowing through the drapery of flower vines at the big wooden arched

1

doors and stained glass that greeted you at the entrance of Acadian Kitchen, a little boutique grocery store this side of the Mississippi—make that the west side—in the little haven of Whiskey Cove.

Acadian Kitchen was just one of the family-owned shops on River Street in a town so cute I sometimes felt like an imposter. On the cuteness scale, I was somewhere in the middle. That meant that every day, I spent time putting on my face and tried to place my best foot forward. At five-foot one inch, I was awkwardly short, and several times per day, I caught myself making faces that were anything but cute—mostly because I only wore my glasses when my eyes were tired, otherwise, I preferred to squint.

And then there were people like my friend Kenzie who greeted me with hair as red- orange as a three-alarm fire, but who could rock a potato sack and a head full of tangles like she was dressed as the queen and ready to attend her jubilee.

"Sakes alive, Lacie, did you do your damn hair this morning?" Kenzie placed her palms on the sides of my face and pulled me in for a close inspection. "Hells bells, you've got makeup on too, and there's no doubt in my mind that this is a freshly pressed shirt." She pinched my silk top through her fingers. "My BFF is fifty years old, but that's okay, I still love you."

Kenzie could be the Town of Cute's mayor. We'd been up for hours on end cramming for finals and preparing for college graduation and everything else in between. I had no doubt she'd rolled out of bed, ran fingers through her orange curls, and then came to work in last night's attire, looking like every badass thing you'd want in your own personal pixie with wings.

I, on the other hand, took the time to wash my face, body, and hair. I applied makeup, and to confirm Kenzie's suspicion, yes, I'd put on freshly ironed clothes and finished the whole thing with a lip gloss that promised to enhance my lips by twenty-five percent. In a word, I was anal, but I respected routine and felt that I could use every bit of confidence gained when I wore a well put together outfit and was freshly scrubbed and put together.

Whiskey Cove and its inhabitants were as sweet as Southern tea.

However, surrounding myself with cuteness had its perks, TMJ for instance. But it was hard to hate cute people, and my ride-or-die homegirl was all kinds of cute. Besides, Acadian Kitchen wasn't a bad place to work, especially since I could stop on the front veranda and pick a flower for my hair before every shift, including this funky one that promised to get funkier.

Something just felt off, though it could have been the out-of-date chicken salad I'd scarfed down around one this morning.

The wind blew over my face and arms. I closed my eyes and inhaled the scent of honeysuckle mixed with manure, and well, that was the smell of home. Once summer settled in deep, you could even smell the heat. It smelled like rubber and heated concrete which, believe it or not, also smells like manure.

Inside the boutique grocery store, my footsteps made a satisfying thud against rustic wood flooring that always looked freshly sanded. I inhaled the smell of cured beef, shrimp, black pepper, and dried flowers that was signature boardwalk of a southeast Louisiana small town.

Kenzie scream-yawned while she restocked fruity truffles next to the register.

"Take a look at this," Kenzie passed me a folded square of paper she pulled from her apron pocket and I knew exactly what was on it, and *she* knew *I* knew exactly what was on it, so I was not shocked when her art was staring back at me.

She looked at me with that one-eyed squint she used when she knew she'd hear something she didn't want to hear. It was super sweet for her to design a heart from our thumbprints with our graduation year flanking the right side, but she knew how I felt about tattoos, and there was nothing she could say that would make me change my mind.

Nodding I said, "You know I think your art is amazing and you should make a big book of classy tattoos and self-publish it and retire on a yacht you buy from all your sales, but I can't get a tattoo."

Kenzie did a great impression of a fifteen-year-old who just found out there is a passcode on the streaming services for R-rated movies.

"I really don't think I deserve the hard eye roll, but I promise the first tattoo I get will be this heart," I said, holding the fingerprint art in the air between us.

"That one is mine. I didn't bother sketching yours because I knew there was nothing I could say that would change your mind, and I'm a little pissed that I picked you all those years ago to be my BFF."

I took a second look at the drawing. "Wouldn't matching tattoos be exactly the same?"

The truth was, I might get a tattoo, but I can't tell that to Kenzie because she would take the *might* and turn it into a 'right now' and within the hour I'd be sitting in a tattoo artist's chair with a needle in my arm? Ass? Thigh? Back? And we are back at the problem that has plagued me all along—where should I put the tattoo? How big should it be? What colors should be used? There is a lot to think about before putting something on my body that will be there forever.

Kenzie snatched the square out of my hand like the nuns at school used to snatch away a chorus book when they knew you had the latest copy of Cosmo hiding behind the book flap. "Did you even listen when I explained the significance of the thumbprints? I get the heart that's made from *your* thumbprint, and you get the one made from *mine*." Cue the signature Kenzie eye roll. "Otherwise, it's just dumb."

She shoved it down into her apron and returned to restocking chocolate. I had been a crappy friend lately and I promised to get even crappier which hurt my heart. Kenzie thinks we are going to college together, that we are enrolled in some of the same classes, that we will be able to carpool, and I don't know how to tell her I'm not going when I can't even tell myself.

I needed to decide soon. It wasn't a decision really. I frowned. I don't see how I can take Gramps and Mom's money for school when they work so hard for it. I'm not even sure I'm smart enough to get through a program where only half make it out.

I needed sugar, stat. I pulled a grape Tootsie Pop from my bag and then stuffed the fraying canvas bag beneath the counter while my mind filled with thoughts about Gramps handing me a lollipop bouquet in the car on the way home from church on Sunday afternoons. He'd say *for the road;* it was something he had always done.

Sniffles were annoying plus they were a dead giveaway of a person's emotional state. When you were thinking about the day your Gramps would no longer be around, sniffles were okay. I pulled the wrapper off the lollipop, the tears in my eyes distorted my vision so it looked like I was holding a small purple sea between my fingers.

"Honey don't sweat it. I'll never give up on you. We'll get our tats one day. . . we may be ninety years old, but they'll still tat us up right nice." Kenzie's warm hug was like melted chocolate, and I wondered how my mascara would ever hold up.

"It's not that." I wiped a tear away before it could run down my face and ruin my makeup. "I was up at four to help Gramps clean the plantation grounds and set up for an anniversary reception. His memory is not long for this world, and I'm worried someone's going to find out that he can't do his job." I put the sucker in my mouth and mumbled around it. "Mom didn't even tell me about Gramps until this morning when she couldn't figure out how she would be able to help him with the graduation breakfast reception set up in time for the guests to arrive."

"Can he retire?"

"Mom said if he waits two more years his income will be thirty percent more and you know he doesn't make much, so that bump is everything."

And if he did retire, where the hell will we all live? I was kind of hoping he'd retire *after* I graduate with my degree and could get a decent paying job. One of those jobs where you can go to a bank and qualify for a home loan. Mom has never qualified for any loans. Makes sense, who would give a self-employed house cleaner a hundred thousand dollars to be repaid over thirty years?

"Too bad Mr. Landry is gone."

Nostalgia pains hit deep in my core. I still remembered Mr.

Landry's enthusiasm on opening day of the pool for summer. He'd man the grill with enough hot dogs and hamburgers to feed the entire town. We'd swim all day and by the end of the day could barely keep our eyes open from exhaustion. "Mr. Landry's kids run things differently. If something is costing them money, it's gone."

"Tell me about it. I still remember that cow they slaughtered when it went cross eyed," Kenzie said while chasing away a chill.

I cringed thinking about them finding out about Gramps. Mr. Landry and Gramps had been friends. They'd been on the USS Vincennes together during the Gulf War. When Mr. Landry's parents died, he was called back home and inherited the plantation, but it hadn't been kept up. Mr. Landry threw himself into renovating the place, and when Gramps was discharged from the Navy, there was no question he'd find Mr. Landry, or Skip as he called him, and together they licked their war wounds and created an event space business that is still going strong almost forty years later.

So many people had celebrated at the Landry Plantation. It was the place people went for weddings, graduations, anniversary celebrations, baby showers, birthdays—if you could think of a reason to celebrate, Landry Plantation was where you came to get your party on.

When Mr. Landry died three years ago, Gramps started his decline. First his memory and then his physical stamina diminished. "Memory is something that can be exercised, right?" Like muscles. I learned something about the memory centers of the brain when I took an undergraduate neurology course for speech therapists, but we just learned about the brain, not the therapy.

Kenzie's mouth twisted to one side in thought. "I don't know but we'll find out in the Neurogenic Disorders course."

The letter in my bag beneath the counter that needed to be mailed was screaming at me, and I imagined it sprouting wings and flying itself into the mailbox slot. I had my doubts that obtaining a degree in speech-language pathology was the quickest way to help Gramps, but it was all I had at the moment that offered any relief to my anxiety, so I'd hold tight to it, but it meant that I had to mail that acceptance letter.

My thoughts were interrupted when Frannie Faraday Fontenot tripped into the store and knocked over the daffodils I'd set out yesterday. The whole thing was a massacre of yellow petals and a release of pollen that had Kenzie simultaneously sneezing and assisting Mrs. Frannie.

"Oh, would you look at that . . . I've just ruined a nice flower."

"You ruined quite a few—*achoo*—nice flowers, Mrs. Frannie, but —*achoo*—it's okay because I don't like daffodils anyway—*achoo*— they seem to have a hangdog expression that gives off a rather needy vibe."

After Frannie greeted me, Kenzie helped her understand and find clarified butter for whatever dish she was cooking from The French Chef cookbook. She'd watched a movie about a lady who cooked everything in the cookbook. Since then, Mrs. Frannie started her own version of the movie just after her grown son, and my Sunday School teacher since I can remember, became sick with ALS. The only problem was that Mrs. Frannie was great at making sweets but bad at making food. Her son, Steve, and my grandfather had started to decline around the same time.

I suppose that was the nature of progressive, degenerative diseases. Yet another thing I learned in the undergrad survey course on acquired neurogenic disease. And I believe that was reason number three to set my letter free. The decision wasn't an easy one to make. My mind wouldn't let me forget that this grad school was super hard—only fifty percent made it through. Mom and Gramps wouldn't let me go on my own either. They insisted on helping me with money they didn't have.

Kenzie continued sneezing while she swept up the flowers in front of the register, while Mrs. Fontenot eyed the massacred flowers with a frown. She plopped the butter on the counter, along with a pint of cream. "You can put the daffodils on my tab too, Lacie."

Achoo. "No, Mrs. Fontenot, the store can write off a few broken stems. You know Dad would never approve of charging you for broken products, or in this case, stems."

"Well, okay, darling, but don't go getting in no trouble because of me."

Kenzie shook her head. "No trouble, ma'am," and then sneezed her way to the back of the store, her *achoos* getting fainter and fainter.

"Watcha making today, Miss Frannie?"

"It's a be-your blank sauce today."

"Buerre Blanc," I corrected. Languages were an interest of mine. I had not taken French, but living in Louisiana and especially working in a gourmet food store had taught me how to pronounce French food items. In fact, Frannie would do better buying a tub of the sauce we sell in the store.

"Oh, honey, you don't need to go getting all fancy with me and that French stuff. I never could get the hang of French, too many silent letters and all that."

"How's Steve doing?"

Her face had more lines than the last time I'd seen her, and the heavy makeup didn't quite cover all the darkness beneath her eyes. "He's got his good days and bad." She sniffled. "You know he's having more bad days than good ones lately. Can't really swallow too well. I'm having to chop up his food in the Cuisinart. Still, he chokes it down." She wiped away a tear. "I'm sorry."

I placed my hand on her arm. "Mrs. Frannie don't apologize. Do you want me to come over and sit with Steve so you can go to bridge night at church?"

"Oh, honey, I know he'd love to see you."

I bagged her two items and then made her change. "Second Tuesday of the month, right?"

"That's it." She picked up her bag. "And we will see you at the blessing of the graduates breakfast."

Before Mrs. Frannie made it out of the door, Kenzie came running up with a box of Benadryl and a cup of tap water. "Ring me up quick. Between the Aquanet holding up Frannie's beehive and the flower slaughter incident, I'm about to put that *orgasm on the tenth sneeze* hypothesis to the test."

My eyebrows reached for my hairline at the thought of actual-izing Kenzie's theory about *snexing* as she called it. I rang her up and watched her down two pink pills. She was a master at taking those things and then chugging coffee or Red Bull and, on occasion, both. "Ugh, can you believe this? Are my eyes puffy?"

I shook my head no, but inside, I was keeping a big fat *yes* under wraps. In the South, we liked to use little white lies to pretend the bank accounts were in good shape, the kids weren't driving us crazy, and that we looked better than we did on any given day. Jesus forgave white lies. It was the *black* ones that could get you kicked out of a Sunday singin' with a BBQ chaser.

"I think it's time for some beignets and a café au lait." Kenzie's words sounded as lazy as the stretch she made over the countertop. "I'm going to Magnolia Diner, want anything? Do not say Dr Pepper."

Kenzie came up close behind me to tie the apron that I held to my chest. A Dr Pepper did sound good. "You know I don't drink chicory."

"And you call yourself Cajun."

Once the apron was secure, I turned to face her. "I've never once referred to myself as Cajun."

Kenzie reached across the register table to grab her wallet that rested beneath the counter. "Hmm, it may be time to rethink this friendship." With a quick motion she flipped the top up on the counter and walked through, letting it flop back down with her signature-style bang. I'd been around her long enough to pre-wince. "I'll be back, and then you can go on break." Her gum cracked like rapid-fire bullets.

Back at my job of picking through buckets of flowers, I detected Lawson's walk on the wood planks. Ba-dump. Ba-dump. If you paid attention, you could identify anyone from their walk.

Lawson was Kenzie's cousin. He also sported a head full of copper penny red wavy hair and was the cutest sixteen-year-old I'd ever seen. No acne, no awkward tooth-straightening braces, no BO. The Thibodeauxs knew how to grow them.

"If you wanna take a leak you'll have to do it at the diner or Tiffanie's Tangles. Toilet's overflowing again." Lawson snorted and pulled his phone from the pocket of his rubber hunter green apron.

"What did you do, Lawson?" I teased.

I watched red spots pop up on the apples of his cheeks. "It wasn't me," he said as he shot green daggers at me. "For all we know it's one of those feminine hygiene products again. Grandpa Jack's got Roto Rooter on the way."

"It's a great time to be alive, isn't it?"

He raised a brow as he watched me before giving up and shaking his head. "You're so weird." He walked toward the back of the store all while looking at his phone.

Meanwhile, I refilled and trimmed the dried eucalyptus and hydrangea bins that were all around the register, making everything fresh and floral. As places of work go, it wasn't a bad gig. For starters, it was impossible not to smile in this place as the Beach Boys' brand of syncopated rhythm drifted from the speakers in the ceiling. And if the Beach Boys didn't do it for you, there were individual pieces of Belgian milk chocolate available at the register. Three dollars could get you five pieces to gorge on.

. . . but sometimes . . .

The song would change, and my mood right along with it.

I set fire to the rain. . .

Suddenly, I was right back in the place I didn't want to be.

And I threw us into the flames . . .

I wondered how much it would cost to telephone the United Kingdom and how hard it would be to reach the singer, Adele. I wanted to do the impossible too . . . to throw all of the lies, the hurt, and the memories into a barrel and set it on fire.

But then, if I knew how to set the rain on fire, I would have already done that and moved on with my life. As painful as it all could be, I was still a realist. I wouldn't lie to myself and say things like *I'm over him,* because I wasn't, and this song proved it in so many ways.

A chill ran down my spine despite the eighty-degree temps we'd hit by 8:00 a.m. The hair on my arm stood up. With every millisecond that ticked by, my chest got tighter and tighter until there was no air left inside to expel.

Tell me what has to be wrong with the universe, my karma, the alignment of the stars, for Adele to play overhead at the same time

CHAPTER 1

HE would decide to waltz back into my life looking even sexier than he did four years ago. God in heaven, the man could sell a pitchfork to the devil. Even his muscles had muscles, but it was the white collared shirt with the sleeves rolled up that revealed arm veins for days that made the bottom fall out of my vagina.

Lucky for me, most people didn't come into Acadian Kitchen to buy condoms and beer as those things could be gotten cheaper at Walmart.

Unlucky for me, Robert Briggs St. Martin didn't have to worry about money.

CHAPTER 2
LACIE

Adele was a special kind of badass woman who I will never stop striving to emulate. One day, I hoped to make her proud, but right now, I was doing her wrong—along with every other woman who'd been done wrong by her low down dirty rotten filthy excuse of a man. I was hiding like a coward.

To be more precise, I had butt on the floor, back against the cabinets that held up the register counter and hoped liked I'd hoped for nothing before that I could not be seen from over the top. I reached for a Tootsie Pop. I may have a slight addiction to sugar, but in this case, I was allowed a vice.

Nerves had me agreeing with Mr. Owl for the first time in my Tootsie Pop history. Three licks to the center worked fine today. I crunched and chewed, biting down and cementing my molars together with sugar, hoping to seal my mouth shut. It wasn't like I had four years of *tell-him-off* conversation on simmer in my head.

But wait . . . that's exactly what I had. He'd left me without a word. Maybe there were words exchanged but my brain shut down to spare me a trauma response to whatever bullshit it was he had done or said to me. I did not know that day that he wasn't going to return my calls, texts, emails, or social media messages.

Ghosting is a cruel kind of special torture. Similar to grieving the death of a loved one. When my grandmother died, I remember grieving at the loss of our future together. No more lying like lizards beneath the noon day sun, getting so hot and sweaty the only way to cool off was with one of her special shaved ice concoctions. No more trips to the outlet mall the week before school to shop for new clothes. Worst of all, I'd never get another one-of-a-kind tailored Easter dress made by her special hands.

Knowing the pain of what it is to grieve the loss of someone, I have zero tolerance for people who use ghosting and I see it as the coward's way out. It's one of the cruelest forms of rejection, leaving the unwanted behind to deal with the fallout of emotions on their own with nothing to grab on to. It feels like drowning.

I crawled on my knees to the window and did my best to stay hidden while I turned from left to right and prayed for any sign of my soon-to-be *ex*-best friend. Pathetic? Maybe so, but I haven't gotten over the broken heart he left me four years ago. Since God saw fit to only give me one heart, this thing beating like a Foo Fighters drum solo in my chest wouldn't survive another break.

Where the hell was Kenzie?

I tried to calculate how long it'd been since I *hadn't* thought of him. Being busy made the task easier, but he still popped in there every night before my mind would drift off to sleep. And again, at the dawn of each day.

With cramming for finals and helping Gramps get ready for the anniversary brunch, I hadn't been to sleep yet for the night, so that means I'd managed to keep him out of my head for one day. Until Adele happened. Then he literally materialized out of thin air.

Have you ever tried to keep something out of your head? My brain doesn't work that way. The harder I tried to put thoughts in a mental strongbox and close the lid, the more my brain pounded at it like a drill breaking into rock like in the movie Armageddon. I don't know any box that strong.

Hiding was the loser's way out, but he already won the breakup, and I still had the frequent nightmares about my senior prom night that he ruined to prove it. My dreams were out of control.

I'd wondered if maybe another guy would break the hold Briggs had over me. Everyone had tried to hook me up, telling me it was best to move on. But I'd also broken up with my heart, which was an organ I think would have come in handy when picking guys to date.

I had no way to know how long me and my heart would remain apart, but she'd led me to Briggs and therefore, she could not be trusted. I gave every piece of myself to him, trying over and over to help him, to pull him out of whatever had a hold on him, but he'd bullied me instead.

One particular night featured Briggs (the bully), and me with smeared mascara face and a wardrobe malfunction (at his hands) that had my boobs still lingering somewhere in the bowels of social media; not to mention my torn to shreds favorite sea foam green prom dress. I'd skipped out on the rest of senior year.

I'd let my heart love him, and in return he'd torn my guts out.

Heart and I were no longer inhabitants of the same block. She had her own zip code and the rest of me lived on the other side of the tracks in a little town called *Reality*, a place with more downs than ups. But at least I always knew where I stood and how much life's choices would cost because in the town of *Reality*, the price tag is hanging on each poorly made decision.

Overhead, Adele ended, and there was a bit of charged air for a split-second where all the balance in the world hung. I took a shallow breath and pleaded with all that was good and holy, *God please let Kenzie come back before he needs to be rung up.*

But God was not on my side. Remember those cute, freshly sanded floorboards? Well, they weren't so cute anymore. More like the numerical countdown of a firing squad where I was the fire-ee and he was the fire-er. Each step he made thudded through the boards like a locked and loaded gun.

Thud-creak.

Shit. He was getting closer. If I had a cup of water on the counter, it would be vibrating from his *thud-creak*. The vibration would move through the water, causing rings to form on top.

Thud-creak.

Okay, it was go time, and by that I mean it was time to get the heck out of Dodge. BTW, the price on this tag was big. Like when one of the refineries in town gave money to the children's cancer center using one of those giant checks. The size of the tag related to the poorness of the decision, my brain's way of preserving our relationship so she did not become exiled like that bitch *Heart*.

On a scale of one to ten, a cashier leaving the register unattended to run across the street was an eleven. But I needed the one additional member of my posse. Theo's mom worked at the Landry Plantation so we'd grown up together. He was going to be the next big local talent. I couldn't wait to see him on the news; he'd rise to anchor in no time.

I grabbed a large basket of hydrangeas and carried them in a way that hid my face. I ran the short distance across the veranda boardwalk to Magnolia Diner and then peered inside. No sign of Kenzie. But there was Theo, his back to the crowd, slinging eggs and sausage. I entered and moved toward the long counter.

Having been a jazz lounge in the forties, Magnolia Diner retained the nostalgic flair of the bebop period. Dissonant harmonies and polyrhythms of Dizzy Gillespie could be heard above the soft hum of the patrons. Patrons who now stared at me like I was morphing into a werewolf on the night of a full moon.

"He ain't been back a week, and she's already losing it," Ray, the owner of Ray's Garage, mumbled. My mother had dropped thousands at his business over the years and so I did not appreciate the gossip on my behalf.

"I could tell by her split ends that something was up," Tiffany, of Tiffany's Tangles, said while facing her mother and shoveling a bite of buttermilk pancake into her face. At least her mom had the decency to offer up a chorus of *bless her heart*.

Cordelia, the town medium, came running up to me. "Oh honey, you must come in and let me clean your aura." She ran a shop called *Sage Advice*. I'd been in there with Kenzie who was into crystals and sage burnings. I never really thought any of that stuff worked but there was no harm in trying. "Sounds like a good idea, Miss Cordelia."

She pulled my hair into a ponytail and asked how Gramps was doing. I decided to go with Miss Frannie's response. "He has his good days and his bad days."

"You know, he and I graduated together."

"Yes, ma'am."

"Tell him I said hi, would ya."

I nodded and finally made my way to the counter, where I precariously perched the bucket of hydrangeas on a stool while I waited for Theo to turn around.

When he finally turned, he gave me a quizzical eyebrow raise. "So nice of you to bring me flowers, honey. How'd you know drangias are my fave?" He flipped fried eggs with expert wrist action.

Watching him work as a short-order cook was pretty good entertainment in these parts. Theo made great tips because he put on quite the show and he was quite handsome. Plus, he was blessed with hips that could move like the King himself. He turned and rested his elbows on the counter in front of me. "What's shaking, Lacie bean?"

When we were little, Theo always said he would plant a bunch of Lacie and Kenzie beans so that we could grow an entire circle of friends that we knew we would like. "Where's Kenzie?"

Theo pointed in the direction of the hallway where the restrooms were located. "Powdering her nose." He shook a white bag in one hand and held a paper cup of coffee high in the other. "For Kenz. And for the girl who tries very hard to reject any and all things Cajun," he pushed a twenty-ounce Dr Pepper across the counter with a diner glass of ice. "I'll need you to return this or they'll take it out of my check."

"You know I will." Thank goodness for Theo. He knew how I felt about styrofoam. And I didn't reject all things Cajun, it's just that Cajun things would eventually break your heart.

I watched Theo work the counter with the grace of a swan. When he got to his favorite customer, Xavier, the handsome guy who runs the George Rodrigue studio, he leaned in close and laughed at something Xavier said.

"Either I'm behind on more sleep than I thought or there's

something going on between those two." Back from her break, Barb, the server, pointed in Theo's direction.

I nodded and let her words sink in. It would explain all the Blue Dog paintings Theo had bought over the last few months. "Maybe this will be *the one* who gets Theo to be true to himself."

"I doubt it. His deeply Catholic mother would die."

"I think she would be okay."

Barb shrugged and went over to relieve Theo.

Theo linked arms with me and led me outside under the striped awning. "Baby girl, what are you doing?"

"I can't ring him up."

Theo looked across the boardwalk to the Acadian Kitchen storefront. "Back, and he's already sniffing around the goods," he said with disdain.

Just then, Kenzie walked out and joined us, grabbing her chicory coffee from hand. "Who's watching the store, darlin'?"

"I can't ring him up."

Theo raised his eyebrows and turned toward Kenzie, mouthing something I couldn't see while she slurped noisily from her styrofoam cup that would take a thousand years to decompose.

Kenzie made eye contact with me and then pressed her lips together. "My spidy-sense tells me this has something to do with Bri---."

"S-H-U-S-H! We don't say his name," I uttered, pleading.

Kenzie rolled her eyes and started walking toward the storefront. "It's just not healthy to carry on like this after all these years."

I shot Theo a *please help* look.

"Oh, honey," Theo made the way of the cross, "you need the kind of help only the Ayida can give."

Kenzie grimaced. "I was thinking of something a little strong. Everclear maybe." Next to her Theo shook his head and kissed his evil eye necklace mumbling something about a hedge of protection.

Of course, Kenzie was right. I couldn't go on like this hiding behind a corymb of hydrangeas. But I also couldn't look into his eyes. It's like kryptonite to Superman. Those eyes could weaken even the hardiest soul.

Once we reached the door at Acadian Kitchen, Kenzie abruptly stopped to dig through her bag of sugar-coated dough, and said, "Come out come out wherever you are; Momma needs some serious sugar." She then made a fuss of opening it and taking out a beignet, biting into it and causing a cascade of powdered sugar down the front of her apron and a bit on my Chuck Taylors. "You're going to have to face him sooner or later."

"What? No, I don't plan on ever engaging with him."

I looked to Theo for answers as he uttered something about Jesus, Mary, and Joseph. I didn't miss the way he and Kenzie talked about me through their eye gazes at one another. I smelled a rat. They knew something I didn't. It's been like this. Them trying to protect me, keeping me on the outside.

Meanwhile, Kenzie had finished off the first beignet and was licking the fingers of one hand while reaching for another with the other. "I just need to see you being okay around him and not turning into," she shook her head, "this."

"I'm pretty far from freaking okay around him. I can't do it, but why do I have to?"

"Maybe because there are three people currently waiting to check out at the counter and there is no cashier in sight."

Shit. One lady—a Karen—was already talking heatedly to someone on her phone. She said something about never shopping here again and then placed her wicker basket on the floor and walked out.

"Okay, well I'm probably going to get fired, so then I definitely won't have to check him out."

Kenzie pushed her pastries and coffee into my hand and ran over to the store while I chanced a look at Theo who was regarding me cautiously. "I just can't do it." I pressed my cheek against the basket of hydrangeas, wishing I could be one of them with no more responsibility in the world than to sit in a vase and look pretty.

As Theo and I approached the register, Kenzie was making change for the last customer in the line and apologized for the wait while giving me a look that said *you're a disaster, but I love you.*

Theo stood on tiptoes and looked over the store. "Where is he?"

Kenzie planted a sugar-coated palm on Theo's chest. "What do you think you're doing?"

"I'm here to assist."

Kenzie shook her head while pushing Theo back toward the door, "I don't think so, big boy."

"If he hurts Lacie again, I'm going to break his pretty face." Theo cracked his knuckles.

I set the basket of hydrangeas down and pulled my Dr Pepper and ice glass from inside the basket. "Can we all just take a time-out?"

Kenzie finished leading Theo to the door.

"Text if you need me."

"Just park your horse, Chuck Norris, we don't need to provoke a Texas-style shoot out."

I looked toward the boardwalk at the steaming pile of dog poo that Mr. Cole, who owned the boardwalk pet store, always left for us to pick up and cart off to the dumpster. "Looks like Baxter's been by."

Thud-creak.

My heart leapt to my throat and instinct had me crouching down beneath the register counter again, hoping I would go unseen and would continue to be forgotten.

Next to me, Kenzie crouched. "I see you've decided to play out this reunion as pathetic and lame."

My eyes grew large at her acquisition. "Whose side are you on?"

"The side that gets you off the floor and not acting like a delicate flower wilting under a one-hundred-degree Louisiana sun."

"I want to be a wilting flower. It's easy."

Kenzie met me eye-to-eye. "You can't do this every time he comes around. Look," she turned away, sighed while smoothing her apron, and then put her eyes back on me, "I happen to know *He-who-took-your-v-card* is back in town to stay, and he'll be headed to grad school in the fall with the rest of us."

I shook my head. "No . . . no . . . no—no!" My brain filled in the blanks with an image of me tearing up the envelope that held my grad school acceptance letter.

"Beans, you can keep saying no, but it won't change anything." Her lips went tight as she gave me the determined look of a scorned redhead. "I love you, but I'm not going to support your self-disparagement. Briggs is not a god. We are not servants beneath his feet waiting to be used. You're a beautiful woman with the whole world ahead of you. You can become anything you want *without Briggs.* Don't give him the power to take away your future. Leave the past in the past. On the count of three, we are on our feet, pulling our dignity back into place, and modeling Aphrodite, goddess of perfection that we are. Got it?" Her red brow arched at me.

I nodded. "Yeah, okay." As far as pep talks go, it was good. I wanted to be Aphrodite or maybe even a little Demi Moore in Disclosure or Glenn Close in Fatal Attraction, minus the dead rabbit.

I had an extensive old movie collection. DVD only. I wasn't opposed to Blu-ray, but I didn't have a player, and at every garage sale I could always find a box of old DVD movies and barter until I got them four for one dollar. That's six-plus hours of entertainment for just one dollar.

Kenzie *ahemmed* loudly, alerting me back to the situation at hand . . . *how do you look the one who took everything from you in the eye?*

Kenzie's offered hand reconnected me to the present. I took it and let her help me get my butt off the floor. "Why didn't you tell me about his return?"

"Seriously, Beans? You won't even let me use his name around you."

The pain was still raw. My chest felt cracked open, my heart was hamburger.

"You need to ease into learning to be around him."

Thud-creak.

Our reconciliation was imminent.

Thud-creak.

I walked around to the flower buckets in front of the register and took clippers to the wilted stems. *Learn to be around him.* I took a deep breath. Kenzie was right. If Briggs was back, I needed to not let his presence affect me. I could do that. I shrugged off his being in my place of work. It's just someone I knew for a moment, four years ago. Fake it 'til you make it, right?

Thud-creak.

I'd keep my head down and my focus on the crocuses and orchids that were looking particularly perky today.

Thud-creak.

I tried to copy their effortless cascade over the tall glass vase, down the vine, and reaching to the floor.

Thud-creak.

And then, *Clunk-plop.* The sound of his groceries hitting the counter.

I was still hiding and couldn't see his face, but my body knew he was there. I started to vibrate with energy, the hair on my arms stood on end, and a heat settled into my core. Visceral. How was I supposed to deal with him being near if I could not control my body's reactions?

We stood three feet apart, if that. I hid my face next to flowers while inhaling the scent of mint and fresh laundry, his signature scent.

How was it possible after all these years? Peripherally, I was aware of him speaking words to Kenzie. My body wanted to bolt, but *Brain* had my back. She stood firm, and I forced my shoulders to turn toward him.

First my eyes settled on a six pack of beer and a package of black Magnum condoms on the counter.

If I've learned anything through all the pain, it's that you can't tell your heart who to choose for love. You can't even warn her. There were signs, and I did try to make her understand, but my stupid heart wouldn't listen to anything but the sound of its own beat . . . and boy could he make it beat.

Kenzie shot the beer with the scanner gun and then picked up the box of condoms. "You certainly think a lot of yourself," Kenzie said.

Thick air made it hard to breathe. The more I turned, the more he came into view.

The brown hair turning up at his collar, the arm veins revealed by the rolled-up cuffs of his white button-down shirt, the perfect white smile, his tongue running along those kissable lips.

I faltered, my knees giving out landed me flat on my butt, my left elbow baring the weight of my fall. I grunted out an *oomph* and then rubbed my elbow. Loathing myself, I dared not look up. But I didn't have to. Trendy cognac colored Chelsea boots came into view between my Tiffany Blue Chuck Taylor-covered feet.

Adele belted out, ". . . *they say that time's supposed to heal you, but I ain't done much healing*," while I slowly lifted my chin into his perfection. Taking my last breath, I held his gaze, the one I'd held four years ago. The one that had taken my virginity. The one that had broken me apart, down to my spare parts until I thought I'd never be able to put myself back together.

"Lacie." Watching the sound of my name form on his lips was nothing compared to the raspy deep voice that set my core throbbing.

The air was suddenly sucked from the store. Briggs lowered to a crouch using long fluid movements unlike my ungraceful meeting with the plank flooring.

He extended his hand, but I was too lost in his aura to take it. The air molecules crackled like lightening around us, some visceral connection that time could not still.

When his pupils enlarged, I knew he felt it too. It had always been this way between us. Our minds and words, the things we thought and said to each other had been horrid and unhealthy, but our bodies knew how to react to one another.

Like lost and lonely friends who had come back together after years apart, my pulse raced and thudded against my rib cage, the hair on the back of my neck stood up, and breathing ceased.

His hand reached for mine, and this time, I grabbed onto it and let his strong arms pull me up into his chest. I could feel his breath against my neck. The feel of him, after all this time, had me right back where I'd been when I was 15 years old.

CHAPTER 3
LACIE (AGE 15)

Who has their own lake? The St. Martins, that's who.

At the water's edge, I put my towel down on a clean patch of grass and toed off my shoes.

Thick air laced with humidity and heat wrapped around me, almost suffocating in its cloak thanks to an unseasonal heat that had held the gulf states in its clutches for the greater part of three weeks. Gardens bloomed early and flowers drooped.

The State's motto was Sportsman's Paradise, but Theo thought a better way to capture the Louisiana atmosphere would be to call it Satan's armpit.

I missed my friends, missed my grandmother, and I missed being a kid who never knew what death really meant. Death was finite, static, bounded. Not even kings nor the Messiah could escape it.

Dusk settled, quickly turning the colors from bright greens and blues to shades of gray. I took in the remote setting and then divested myself of everything but undies and slipped into the lake.

Sighing appreciatively, I let the cool water envelop my hot skin like soothing aloe after a sunburn. I turned on my back to float and greet the moon as he made his position more prominent in the sky. I liked night better than day because at night, things could hide, and people didn't pry as much after the sun went down. Vices became more acceptable.

One bright star twinkled at me, and for reasons I couldn't understand, I whispered, *"Hi Grams."* It was nice to think of her as a star, bright and shining in the night sky, free from anything that wanted to hurt her ever again.

One day, a long time from now, I could join her, and we would play Candy Land with real candy as playing pieces the way we used to do. For now, she watched and twinkled to let me know she saw me, and I smiled back.

Trusty, the Landry barn dog who'd followed me onto St. Martin property, barked in warning using the growl-bark he did whenever a stranger came near. Immediately, I let my body go under the water, regretting my decision to strip down to my underwear. I watched for someone to appear from the grasses and when Briggs did, he wasn't alone. Some of his school buddies that I knew were with him.

Attached to his hand was the Super 8 camera he always carried. Most of the time, if I was around, he had that damn thing aimed at me. Like he did now. I could hear the motor whirring, indicating it was running. "You enjoy filming me when I'm at a disadvantage."

His head cocked to the right. "You're so right, I do enjoy watching you squirm."

So *not* a gentleman. He squatted before my clothes, lifted my sports bra, and showed it off to his friends. He rifled through the rest of my clothing while Trusty growled next to him. "Lacie Ann Ryan . . . by my calculations, you're in nothing but your underwear." His cartoonish smile was thin and toothy like Red Riding Hood's wolf.

Briggs's friends laughed, egging him on. Things played out in slow-motion as he tossed my clothes and then my towel to his buddies. "Take them into the field."

Something bad had happened to Briggs. It wasn't anything anyone had done to him but something he had done to himself. I didn't understand it all really, but whatever demon was inside of him that caused him to act this way was a demon that he could not exercise.

"I'm glad you came out to play, to be honest. I was so bored I was going to go caterpillar hunting."

I bared my teeth and lunged forward, bringing myself closer to the shore. All I could see was red. Chum in the water. "My grandmother's funeral was today, you asshole."

He remained squatted at the water's edge, watching me with those beautiful eyes that I knew to be blue but looked black under the moonlight. "Did I say you could use my swimming hole?"

My arms lifted and came down, creating a big wall of water that drenched him. I couldn't deal with his teasing and bullying right now. I was tired and confused, but mostly angry. "Give me my clothes, and I'll leave."

He shook his head. His friends had returned to his side. "Not without paying the toll, Lace."

"What toll?"

He smiled that wolf-like, toothy grin at me, but this time, there was blood and guts on his teeth. "You're the entertainment tonight. I'm not leaving until you get out of the water."

I looked from him to his other two friends. "Parker, can you get my clothes?"

His eyes moved to meet Briggs's where they conducted an inaudible conversation. Parker's chin jutted down to his chest. "Sorry, Lacie."

"Tex, you still got that flashlight on you?" Briggs asked.

Tex pulled something from his backpack, and then the pond was flooded with so much light that I could no longer see their faces. I waited in the water, hoping they'd give up and take off. To be fair, it seemed like Tex and Parker wanted to, but every time they made a move to leave, Briggs redirected their attention onto me.

Time passed, and the boys talked about the best types of lures for catching certain kinds of fish. With the sun gone, the heat was also going down. I estimated it had been thirty to forty minutes that I'd been in the water. "Give me my clothes." My voice was weak, defeated. He'd surely hear it.

"I have no control over what these guys do," he pointed to his friends, "but I will not leave this spot until you emerge from the water." He shined the light on me, and I knew he was telling the truth.

I would have to walk out of this body of water in white, wet panties and nothing else. I was out of options.

"Do you know what kind of flashlight this is, Lace?" Briggs cocked a challenging brow. The light bobbed in my face.

I wasn't going to answer a Robert Briggs St. Martin rhetorical question. I'd done that before and lost. It was another one of his games.

"I'll answer for you because I can see you're dying to know. It's a BBE 130 tactile military ballistic LED torch. Just for reference, a 100-watt bulb burns at around 1,750 lumens, but this bad boy clocks in at 58,000 lumens. With this light, you can see an egg yolk sitting perfectly inside its shell. You can also see the bottom of this pond. I know because I've done it, and right now, all that power is pointed at you."

In that moment, I hated him, but I also knew that I still loved him. How strange when the two existed so strongly side-by-side. And yet, I knew it was possible to love someone so much you also hated them because I was experiencing that right now. I also knew he wanted me to hate him. He fed off the negative energy. When he was down, he wanted everyone down with him. It was the same when he was up.

Unfortunately, he was down more than he was up. It was exhausting.

Five more minutes passed. I had music to face. I would walk out of the pond, but I wouldn't do it like someone who had been defeated. No, I'd do it proudly with my shoulders back and my chin up. Balls to the wall, as they say.

I swam toward the shore, closing my eyes to deflect the light in my face. When I felt the sandbar, I went down to it on my knees so that I was still covered by water that appeared black under the Louisiana moon. I took a deep breath and then stood, the water hitting my calves. I didn't walk forward though. No, I stood, planted firm, letting them all get a good look.

"Is this what you want? You're pathetic. All of you are so hard up just to look at some tits you'd let this asshole lead you past the gates of hell. Well, get a good, long look because it's the only pair you'll see this year after I tell your parents what you've done." I raised my arms in the air and charged like an angry bull.

"Get the hell out of here!" I yelled. Tex and Parker cut and ran but Briggs sat, stone cold watching me with that fucking flashlight. And then I heard it . . . the damn whirring motor of that camera.

I charged at him, scratching and grabbing for anything I could get. I ended up ripping the light from his startled hands. "Let's see how many lumens it can light up from underwater." I ran toward the water.

"Lacie, don't! That's two thousand dollars," Briggs yelled.

I heard him, but I couldn't stop. I threw it with all my might. The light remained on and gave an ethereal effect as it sank, smoky and casting an eerie glow as it lowered. In Louisiana, the water is murky. You can't see through it, so it was weird to be able to see the light. Until it died.

Under the full moon, we stood next to one another. Me, soaking wet in my underwear. Him, in a tank top and athletic shorts. Our eyes did that standoff thing that we'd done so many times before.

The emotion from the last few days ran up my arm, and I reached up and slapped him clear across his too-handsome face.

He lunged for me, and then we fell into the grass, my fists punching his chest, until he grasped my wrists and clasped them together. With his strength, he turned us so that I was beneath him and then drew my arms above my head.

I'd never been this close to him. I could smell the mint on his breath from the gum that he always chewed. I wiggled, but his strong forearms held me down.

He lowered his face close to mine and looked down at our bodies, so close together. His skin touched my bare breasts. As breasts go, they weren't big, not yet, but I was sporting a B cup and thought what I had was nicely shaped and attractive. I was pretty proud of them. I wanted him to want me, to be driven mad by me, to tell me anything about my breasts that I'd bared for him.

And then I caught myself. I was in bed with the enemy.

I hated this boy.

I loved this boy.

I struggled, fighting him off, squirming out of his hold, crawling away, but he was too strong and pulled me by the ankles until I was right back under him. He blatantly stared at my bare chest. I fought some more, but this time I wasn't so lucky and only succeeded in brushing my right boob against his cheek. Instant heat pooled in places I'd never felt come alive before. I groaned and writhed.

He smiled slightly, and then I felt the length of him between my legs. I knew what it was and felt my face and chest bloom with heat. I'd known this boy for eight damned years and not once had I ever seen him smile, smirk sure, but not smile. His lips parted to reveal a set of straight white teeth that could melt the spandex off a porn star.

"I like this." His voice was raspy and deep.

"What do you like?" My voice sounded grown up, breathy and affected.

"You, beneath me, with no top on."

"Don't get used to it." I squirmed and almost got a knee up, but he deflected it with his thigh muscle.

"Do you want to play, Lace?"

Another rhetorical question. I loathed this blue-eyed devil.

He moved to hold my wrists in just one of his hands. The fingertips of his free hand feather touched the skin of my neck, and then my collarbone, getting closer to my bare chest. And God . . . I hated myself, but I wanted him to touch me there.

But he didn't. I kept squirming, trying to wiggle free of his hold, not because I wanted to be free but because I wanted him to touch me.

"Does it feel good? Because I love to watch you struggle beneath me." He was a monster. So what did that make me? I couldn't deny that it felt good to struggle against his strong, athletic body.

And just like that I figured out why he was such an asshole. He could manipulate people because he understood them so well. At the age of fifteen, he already knew how to read the subtle cues given off by people and how to interpret and use them. He could bend you to his will. He knew I liked rubbing and struggling against him. He knew it was helping me release all the fucked-up shit that happened that day.

He let me squirm, giving me the perfect amount of struggle until I was just perfectly exhausted and knew I'd sleep like a baby.

"Are you done now, sweet Lace?"

Oh, that voice and my reaction to it. I nodded. But also, *Sweet Lace?*

"Good." His lips met mine, and if it were possible to die from one kiss, I would have. His hot kiss melted down my walls, and instead of squirming, I was now coiling my body around his. Our connection, the one I had suspected all along, had ignited electricity in us like a fork in an outlet.

Maybe this is what we needed to do, maybe we needed to be physically connected.

His tongue slipped past my lips, and I was now engaged in my first French kiss. His dominance over me was acute. I brought no knowledge to this dance; he had all the power and I let him take it. His kiss wasn't soft or sweet. No, like him, it was hard and rough, and with an urgency like he needed to jump inside my chest in order to survive.

We suddenly broke apart, but I held him with free hands that had been released sometime during our kiss. His eyes stared into mine, unyielding.

My chest heaved up and down from the endorphins of our kiss. My arms went around his neck. Ready for more, I lifted my upper body slightly to meet his lips, but suddenly, he pulled away, jumping up and taking flight.

From the ground, I watched him climb out of the sand banks that surrounded the pond and fade under the light of the moon.

My first kiss, in a Brazilian nutshell, had been incredible but equally awful.

CHAPTER 4
LACIE (AGE 23)
Present Day

I could tell Briggs was just as affected by our reunion as I was. His warm smile and lingering stare took me in. Our bodies seemed to vibrate, a low-key thrum that was the music our bodies make together. He pulled a flower from my hair, and my body revved at his gentle attention.

He looked the same but somehow different, and it wasn't just the longer hair or the added muscle; his entire demeanor seemed more relaxed than he'd ever been before. The guy before me had a casual style and a kindness in his unspoken body language, while the Briggs who left me behind was dark and moody.

I guessed the thing I liked about him the most was that I never knew what he was going to do. It was exciting but exhausting at the same time. It was also not sustainable as a relationship. I knew that now, and I vowed to enter this new realm, if there were to be one, with the wisdom born of my past.

Standing there in this moment, I could almost imagine us back together, as if one little elegant action on his part could undo a lifetime of the pain he'd inflicted.

His scent was an old, familiar friend, and his jaw moved as he chewed gum. His hand reached for my elbow and rubbed the wound I could no longer feel. "Are you okay?" he asked, concern etched on his face.

"I'm . . . I'm." I was definitely not okay. I searched his face for answers, confused as to why he was standing here before me.

"Why are you here?" Kenzie's voice made my brain skip the track, but Briggs was a hundred percent present.

Without taking his eyes from me, he answered her. "This is a grocery store. I'm buying groceries."

"No, you're buying beer and condoms, and it's out of the way to buy those things on the boardwalk unless you're staying nearby, which you aren't."

My eyes were drawn to the offending items that Kenzie spoke about. When Briggs noticed my gaze on the condoms, he said, "Those aren't for me."

"That's what every guy would say," Kenzie said.

"It's always so nice to catch up with you, Kenzie," Briggs said.

"I imagine it is, but you haven't answered my question. My Spidey sense thinks your presence here today has something to do with Lacie."

"I came in to invite you to a party," Briggs offered.

His grip on me loosened, but he still held onto me with one hand, leaving tracks of fire on my skin from his touch. This one little connection made all the emotions come screaming back. Like a break in a dam, my system was flooded. They say time heals all wounds, but they don't say how much time is needed.

Gone was the intensity and the eyes that always read too much. The man standing before me wore a genuine smile, the glad-to-see-you kind that lit up his eyes and gave him a pleasantness that drew you in.

Four years ago, he'd either been super wired and short on focus, or he'd been completely aggravated and unwilling to engage with anyone. Mean. He was all kinds of mean. Looking at the gentleman across from me, it was hard to see the teen that had been. The slight curls at his collar also served to soften his appearance, and I wondered how silky it would feel to run my fingers through it.

When he was up and took you with him, it was the best time you ever had. I remember finding new joy in simple things like the blossoming of a flower or the smell of rain on hot concrete.

Through his photography, he'd taught me to stop and relish in all that was around me, to find beauty in chaos. But when he hit the dirt, he could rip your heart from your chest. There was no in between.

Now, he existed somewhere in the middle space where we all lived our day-to-day. It was a little weird because I was used to seeing him through big emotions and grandiose verbalizations. Running sixty-five miles an hour in a thirty-mile zone until he hit the wall. When he was down, he was almost catatonic. Feast or famine.

His thumb rubbed circles into my palm. It was a little thing that no one else could see, but it meant something. I didn't know what yet, but as my brain mapped the path of his thumb, it was clear my body wanted more of him.

A cough from Kenzie's side of the room brought me back to reality. "Did someone mention a party?"

By now we had a reunion of hot guys taking place right in front of the registers.

Briggs's cousin Parker had come inside to ask what was taking so long and to confirm the purchase of the box of condoms, which Briggs tossed in his direction, which came with the added bonus of watching Parker turn a color that matched the primroses we sold.

"Lacie, you remember my cousin Parker."

When had Briggs become so fancy with his introductions? I nodded. Sure, I remembered Parker. He'd been around on prom day, an innocent bystander, and he was there when Briggs had stolen my clothes when I was in the lake.

It was Finn, Briggs's slightly older brother, loitering at the door that worried me more than seeing Parker, an acquaintance who had seen my boobs on more than one occasion.

Since I couldn't begin to process the whole *Briggs is back in town for college* thing, I excused myself and made a beeline for Finn.

"You no-showed on me," I said, aware of the placement of my

hands on hips that completed the transformation of me becoming my mother.

Finn shook his head and then pulled a notepad that had a putt-putt sized pencil in the spiral end from his pocket. He used the pencil to write the word *sorry*.

This primitive form of communication was all that was left after he'd gotten into a bad wreck. He'd piled behind the wheel of his father's truck when he was a little too young to drive after his mom announced she was leaving his father.

In his anger and turmoil, he'd wrecked, careening off into the Atchafalaya Swamp, where he was stranded for several hours before anyone could get to him. He'd hit a cypress tree before he landed which was how he damaged his larynx. He was lucky to be able to breathe but the accident had cost him his voice.

He hardly left his family estate these days, only venturing out with Briggs, or one of his other brothers, or his father.

There were some surgeries that could help him, at least that is what Jenna, the speech pathologist I'd met at a student conference, had surmised based on the information I'd emailed her. She worked at the hospital in Baton Rouge and had said she'd speak to Finn about his options for communication.

"I set that meeting up for us with a professional. You promised you'd show. I was pretty embarrassed."

His writing movement became jerky. *<u>SORRY</u>! I changed my mind.*

"It's fine to change your mind but at least call me next time." I realized my mistake after I'd said it.

If only I could SPEAK<u>!!!</u> He punctuated each exclamation point with his pencil stabbing the pad, a clear sign he was agitated. Parker walked past us to exit. Briggs stopped next to me, and Kenzie next to Finn.

"Everything okay?" Briggs asked.

My heart broke for Finn. Without the use of his voice, he was like the early homo sapiens who used drawings and symbols to record early records of their everyday life.

Of course, Finn had the alphabet system at his disposal to form words and messages, but considering how long it took him to write a sentence, he may as well be drawing.

Finn and Briggs had always been together. Which meant that I knew Finn about as well as I knew Briggs. When Briggs left us to attend the University of Texas it didn't help with Finn's temperament or socialization, or my emotional scarring.

Briggs's leaving had brought Finn and I closer as we had occasionally met out at the lake to nurse our wounds and discuss communication options for Finn as I learned about them in class. We also communicated about Briggs and his decision to leave his hometown for college, but Finn always just told me it was something Briggs had to do.

I didn't understand, and there was no way Finn could explain Briggs's leaving me the day after I gave myself to him that would suddenly make understanding dawn on me. I also got the feeling Finn blamed me a little for Briggs's leaving.

The day Briggs left was the day after prom and the day after I gave him everything I had to give. The fact that he was here now, asking if things were okay, made me mad. It wasn't an emotion I wanted, but it was the only one coming to the surface.

I thought about school and the decision I'd yet to make. Maybe it was for the best, if my inability to persuade Finn to try a computer talker was any indication of how bad of a therapist I'd be, I should just bow out now.

There was a time when I'd tried to help Briggs communicate. I'd been unsuccessful there too. But here he is, big as day, communicating just fine without my help.

I looked at Kenzie. "I'm going to start stocking. Please turn off Adele radio. I need Christina, Kelly, Alanis," I whispered so only she could here.

She nodded at me with her downturned eyes that I'd always thought alluring and expressive. Right now, they were sadder than I'd seen in a long time, "I know what you need."

I walked away feeling dizzy and defeated. If Briggs was going to LSU for graduate school, I'd need to add another line to the con column on my list entitled: *Grad School yes or no.*

CHAPTER 5
LACIE (AGE 5)

When I was five years old, we had to move in with Gramps because our beach house was destroyed in one of the Gulf storms. Except Gramps didn't really have a house. He had an apartment with the other workers who tended the Landry Plantation. Mom was helping here now, and occasionally, a rogue wedding guest or 50th anniversary patron would wander back here to the workers' apartments, stumbling and falling. Mom said those people had had too much fun.

One day, Trusty, my old gray lab, and I were in the breezeway that led from the eight-bay garage. It was made of stone and had concrete floors. I triple-counted the garage doors to make sure. Eight stalls. At our tiny beach house, we had just parked somewhere in the yard. It didn't matter because at dusk, during low tide, the only thing anyone saw was the sun setting over the ocean while the seagulls flew and honked overhead. When it was especially windy, saltwater sprayed on your face making it sticky and a favorite attraction of Trusty's tongue. That was home. This was not.

I wandered over to the fence that separated the Landry Plantation from the St. Martin estate. The fence was broken down and rusty. Drawn to the promise of a lake, I'd wanted to climb over the fence many times, but Mom had told me I had to focus extra hard on not being seen or heard so that we could continue to live in the apartment with Gramps.

My home had washed away two months ago. I lost my extensive collection of paper dolls and Vogue magazines in which I had used craft snips to cut out pictures of current couture to create custom clothes for my dolls. The organization of these clothes is where I'd put in extensive time designing storage bins out of cereal boxes and cross-referencing the types against the styles of garments. I'd had eight boxes fully packed and was working on two more: summer wear and day into night styles. My mom lost her watercolor paintings and about a million Highlander romance novels.

Next to me, Trusty gave his warning huff, and I turned to find Theo, another child who lived in the apartment next to us. His mom cooked for the plantation.

"Easy, boy," Theo said as he tossed pieces of cooked bacon right into Trusty's mouth. Theo was two years ahead of me, but due to being diagnosed with ADHD, he had repeated kindergarten, so was just one grade ahead of me. The fence careened toward my shins when Theo climbed over it. "I'm gonna take a dive in the lake. Come if you want." He started walking away, fading the further he got in the tall grasses.

"This is where you and I part ways," I told Trusty and then climbed over the fence, running to catch up to Theo who was tall even at seven years old. "Are we allowed to be over here?" I asked, between heavy breaths.

"If we don't get caught."

I stopped dead in my tracks. Next to me, Theo followed suit. "I can't risk getting caught. Mom said Gramps' job will suffer if I'm bad."

Theo raised his hands in surrender. "I was only joking. The St. Martins don't care if we're on their property or if we swim in the lake."

It was hot and overly green outside due to the monsoon rains we'd been having. My denim overall shorts clung heavily to my body as the sun beat down. I used to visit Gramps and Theo, and I would swim in the big plantation pool, mostly after the plantation had closed for the day, but Theo and I swam during the day on the slow days when Gramps said it was okay to do so. We played hours of Marco Polo and shark, which was a game we created, but lately he hadn't been around to play in the pool. It wasn't as much fun on my own so I hadn't done much swimming.

I pulled a grape Tootsie Pop from the center chest pocket of my overalls and unwrapped it. Gramps was always giving me a Tootsie Pop cluster. He said there wasn't a lot that couldn't be made better by a sucker with a chocolate center.

Grandpa knew a little something about everything.

With the lollipop in my mouth, I walked until my feet padded over dusty, sand-colored rocks. I thought about turning back since the terrain had turned rocky, and I wasn't wearing shoes.

Looking down in the tall grass, I couldn't see the rocks; they'd snuck up on me, but I did see something interesting. I bent and picked up a shiny red rock. I was especially good at picking out that which didn't belong with other things. This rock was one of those puzzles. How did it get here? Someone must have placed it here before or after the white ones.

I turned the rock over and gasped when I found a green caterpillar crawling over the surface. "Hey, little buddy." I let him crawl onto the fingers of my other hand and then put the rock in my chest pocket for safe keeping. Mr. Caterpillar and I decided we could follow Theo a little further on the over-the-fence property with the bumpy white rocks.

The caterpillar crawled up my hand, and I brought it close to my face. "How'd you get all the way out here?" I knew caterpillars like this one lived on trees and plants, not in grasses. "I think I should call you Scooter." I was already making plans to build Scooter a house to make his chrysalis—which was probably all he thought about. If I were a caterpillar, all I would think about is becoming a beautiful butterfly.

I imagined what it would be like to be born as a furry green caterpillar, which is not really anything special. Maybe he even wore glasses and had scars on his face, or pimples. Pimples were ugly.

And then one day you would go to sleep and wake up as one of the most beautiful creatures on the planet. It wasn't a bad existence at all.

"Looks like we've got company," Theo said

Looking up, I saw him. He stood barefoot and bare-chested at the banks of a pond. Wet jean shorts and a camera of some kind in one hand, pointed at me.

Theo and I continued our advance toward the lake slowly. I recognized the camera operator. At school, he was in the sister-class next to my class. Sometimes, our classes would combine by opening the big divider wall at the edge of the room, and we would become one huge classroom.

The closer we got, the more I could see of him. Ice-blue eyes exposed his inner thoughts. Behind the ice was a storm that churned within. I wasn't making this up, you could see the white clouds reflected in his eyes. A mirror image of his thoughts.

I was aware that Theo dove into the lake mumbling something about it being hot and wanting to cool off. I, on the other hand, could not take my eyes off the boy from the other kindergarten class.

He had the expression of an adult and, from what I'd seen at school, all the problems to go along with it. He didn't smile or talk; just intimidated me with those eyes and that gaze that could get intimate without asking.

Scooter and I walked toward him.

He had a magnetism that drew me in like a bear to honey.

His face told the story of a raging storm, a mind conflicted, emotion always leading. Eyes the color of ice. Cold and distant. A color that said stay away. It was easy to recognize now, but back then, when I had his attention on me, I did everything in my power to keep it there.

We stood, no words exchanged. Scooter held steady on the back of my hand, between us. The beautiful boy with the stormy eyes took Scooter between his thumb and forefinger, held him in front of his face, his eyes focused on the caterpillar until they moved to me. What I saw in them sent a line of chills down my spine. I knew as sure as I knew I'd never again see my father that he was going to hurt my new friend.

I reached for Scooter, but Beautiful Boy pulled his arm up and the caterpillar out of my reach.

I jumped for him, but it was no use. Beautiful boy was tall.

"Give it back." The caterpillar squirmed between his fingers, clearly under distress. "Come on, give it."

"How bad do you want him?" His voice was low even by five-year-old standards, with perfectly enunciated words and an undertone of aggression.

"Just give him to me." My voice had a sense of urgency to it and a quivering break that his narrowing eyes said he'd zeroed in on as soon as it happened. The smirk on his face said he enjoyed teasing and taunting me and my caterpillar. Pleasure from pain. That was a dangerous game. I sensed then I was out of my league with this boy.

"What would you do to get him back?" Laced with hope, his voice was snappy and higher than it was before. He'd caught something on his hook and enjoyed the challenge of reeling it in.

I decided to play it cool. "He's mine. I don't have to do anything."

The beautiful boy tilted his head and stared at me without blinking, his lips moving ever so slightly.

Why does our heart choose to love the one who will make us suffer?

If love was a choice, then I was making the wrong one. To love is to suffer. But not loving also leads to suffering. How can anyone win in this game?

Locked in a toe-to-toe, eye-to-eye stare down, he made his next move.

Over my head, he pulled Mr. Scooter in two.

My heart stopped, and I felt the blood drain from my face. I didn't say anything. The evil inside him threatened to smother the life in my veins. And yet, I felt connected to him by a thread that I had no control over.

Next to me, his camera motor fluttered as he surveyed me through the lens. "Who are you?" he asked, all traces of his former smirk gone. In its place a mask of grimness that no five-year-old should know about.

"Hey," he said, putting a finger beneath my chin and lifting my head to see my eyes, "I asked who you are?"

"Lacie Ann Ryan. I live next door."

"Next door?" he questioned. I guess the concept of next door was funny, given that there were so many acres between us.

"I recently moved to the Landry Plantation to live with my grandfather," I clarified.

I could see his mind working behind the gray clouds in his eyes. "Your parents don't want you or what?"

My father had walked away while making eye contact with me. That stung, and I swallowed down heavy grit pieces of sandpaper. At five, I hadn't even known to ask why he didn't want me. Mom loved me and took care of me, but she was alone, except for Gramps. It was the three of us against the world. "My mom lives with us."

"What about your dad?"

I swallowed around a lump in my throat that I was sure was made from cotton. "I don't have one." I'd been quick to reply, hoping he'd drop it.

"Everyone has a father. I think what you mean is your dad doesn't want you."

My mind flashed to the image of a black Lincoln driving away, getting smaller and smaller, and my four-year-old self powerless to stop it. The night he left, I knew he wouldn't be back. My dad never said things he didn't mean, and he'd said, "Goodbye, Monkey."

My gut felt like I'd swallowed a bowling ball. I turned to walk away from those tormented blue eyes, but before I could get very far, he pulled me back.

"You want to lie to yourself, fine by me." He shrugged. "You don't have a dad."

I couldn't figure out if I liked his straight-talking, cut you to the quick brand of conversation.

"And your grandmother?"

"I have one grandmother. The other one is no longer with us."

"She had cancer or what?"

"No." She had something that sounded like old-timers that made her forget my name. It had been hard at first to accept that she didn't know who I was, but mom had told me that her old self was trapped inside a shell that had a malfunction like the time our freezer made ice that wouldn't drop on its own and we had to stick a knife in the top of the ice maker to get the ice out. Except with people, you couldn't poke at them with knives, or you shouldn't. Mom said our memories were safe because once a memory goes in, it never comes out. However, a memory could become misfiled. "Grandmother's files need to be organized is all."

Beautiful boy picked up a rock and threw it. I watched as it skipped across the top of the water. Theo must have walked back, which was a relief since the blue-eyed devil was now impressively tossing rocks.

"Hey, how did you do that?"

He searched the rocks beneath our feet, reaching for a particularly flat one the size of his palm. "You hold it between your thumb and middle finger, then hook your pointer finger around the edge." He held the intricate hold before me, letting me get a good look before he tossed it.

"Do you live with both your parents?" I asked.

He huffed out a breath. "Yeah, but they fight all the time, so I stay away."

It was hard to tell how he felt about his parents since his expression hadn't changed, but his distant look affected me. I felt blue right alongside him. And yet, I hadn't forgotten that he was the boy who had ended Scooter's life just a few minutes before. "Why did you kill it?"

He huffed. "It was just a worm."

"It was a caterpillar, and one day it would have been a butterfly."

He thought for a second. "His death makes all the other butterflies more valuable because now there are less of them."

I frowned. "What's wrong with you?"

He grabbed me by the arm and squeezed. "Don't ever ask me

that!" he yelled and then ran away, crushing buttercups under his feet. I was frozen in place. The shock of his intensity made my stomach flutter with nerves.

Theo materialized out of nowhere, wet and swift. "What's with him?" he asked, hitching a thumb over his shoulder in Beautiful Boy's directions.

I couldn't tell him because I didn't know. One second, we were talking, and the next, he was flipping out. He was hot and cold, fire and ice, but one thing was for sure . . . beauty around him was doomed, destroyed until it was as ugly as he was on the inside. Even as a child, I sensed his pain. I would become his caterpillar . . . a girl with the potential of growing into a beautiful woman, as long as I could steer clear of Beautiful Boy's clutches.

CHAPTER 6
LACIE (23)
Present Day

Kenzie wanted to go to Tiffany's Tangles to get her nails done. To be honest, Tiffany was fine, but she knew everything about everyone and was full of gossip that she couldn't wait to repeat, even if it was the kind that could ruin families. Mom had said for years that Tiffany had quite a sense of humor, but I'd never been able to see it.

Tiffany's place was small, and we could hear everything she and her current client talked about. Evidently, there were ten sex tricks that could drive a man wild. Top of the list was for a woman to demand to be taken from behind and a variation of that when he lies on his back and you sit facing away from him.

Kenzie stroked her neck, looking very deep in thought. She nodded. "That'd do it."

My mind conjured up the image, but instead of using a place-holder for the part of the guy, my brain inserted Briggs. I shook my head and let the image dissolve while I looked around the shop and admired the cute lace curtains and possibly too much hot pink décor. Even the floor mats at Tiffany's were hot pink. I loved the nostalgia of her shop and the fact that it always smelled like baked apple pie and bleach. Sun shone through the bay windows in the part of the room that was designated as the waiting area. I stuck my hand into the candy dish that Tiffany kept stocked with Peanut M&Ms.

Kenzie said her nails looked like they'd been put through a meat grinder, which wasn't untrue. She chewed her nails, a trait that was endearing but made for stubby fingers worsened by nails chewed to the quick. Once, she tried shaking some drops of Tabasco on her nails not realizing it would burn since her cuticles were gone. I'd helped her wash the pepper sauce off with the first thing I grabbed, which happened to be Paul Mitchell shampoo.

We sat waiting for Miss Kitty to arrive so that she could work on our pedicures because Tiffany only did hair. She didn't like touching people's feet.

"I want us to go to Briggs's party."

I sighed. I knew this was coming. I'd seen her eyes light up when she'd asked about Briggs's friend Tex, and he'd confirmed that Tex would for sure be in attendance.

"I'm busy."

"I know you're not. You just want to sit on your bed and binge old movies and cry about Briggs."

Two years ago, I acquired the movie *Ghost* from the antique store in town that sold more junk than high-end furniture and lamps—which is what I think of when I hear the word antiques—but to be fair the name of the shop is the *Time Traveler's Trunk* so you could find pretty much anything there.

Once, they had a trio of stuffed Boston Terriers that had belonged to Mrs. Macintosh, who ironically taught keyboarding at the middle school back in the day. The dogs were her companions. After they crossed the Rainbow Bridge, she'd had them stuffed. When she'd died, she'd left all her money to an artist who only painted dogs. The same dog actually, but in different colors and doing different things like gardening or riding a motorcycle. He's really famous now, so it turns out Mrs. Macintosh had an eye for art, which is shocking.

One of his paintings sold for ninety-thousand dollars—usually they go for somewhere around five. But, back to the movie *Ghost*. After Kenzie and I watched the movie, she enrolled in any and everything clay pottery related. Also, after watching *Ghost*, she made us watch *Dirty Dancing, Roadhouse*, and *Point Break*. The first two were good, *Point Break* not so much.

"I can't go to a *Briggs* party."

"Well, good because it's not a party, it's a bonfire."

"I haven't slept, and I'm working tomorrow."

"No, I made that schedule and was certain to give us the night off."

"Mr. Thibodeaux called and asked me to work."

Kenzie turned those big downturned eyes on me. "Tell me you didn't say yes."

"I already told you I'm working, so what do you think?"

Her sigh could fill an airplane hangar. "What's wrong with you? They only call you to take the crappy shifts because they know you won't say no."

"It's fine." I wasn't even tired. Well…my body was exhausted, but my brain was like a runaway train. I couldn't slow it down, and I knew there was no way it would let me sleep.

"How is it fine? You promised me we'd go out tonight, and I want to go to the bonfire."

"I promised you Uber and bars with putt-putt to finish off the night." Which sounded horrible given my current state of exhaustion. "Since when do you want to hang out outdoors anyway?"

"Since Briggs came back, and that means Tex will be there tonight."

Right. While I had my troubles with Briggs, Kenzie had her own problems with Tex. "You still want to be with Tex?"

Kenzie held a bottle of dark blue nail polish in the air between us. I wrinkled my nose. "No. I want the opportunity to bring him to his knees."

"How will you do that?"

"I don't know. I've imagined tying him naked and spread eagle to his bed and leaving him for his mother to find."

I frowned. "Is that a big deal?"

"It'd be a big deal if he was on his stomach and had a dildo in his ass."

Sometimes Kenzie could really paint a picture. "Wow, okay." I wondered how she could so easily want to be around Tex after he'd hurt her, how she could be so badass about getting even; but her expression didn't match the words coming out of her mouth.

"I'm worried about getting lost to Briggs," I admitted what had me avoiding him, and the party, at all costs.

Kenzie took me in with those eyes so blue they seemed to be liquid like the sea. "Awe. Lacie, you can't avoid him forever. You need closure. You need to find out why he took off after you had your perfect night."

It was perfect for me, but I was afraid that what I thought was perfection was no big deal to him. My biggest fear was that I was not memorable. I could recall every detail of that night, every sigh, every single heartbeat. What if he didn't even remember that we'd been together?

"You need to be alone with him. Have sex with him, but this time take the reins. Leave while he's still wanting more. It's clear he's changed. Show him you have too." She shrugged one shoulder.

Had I changed? I wasn't as certain as Kenzie was. She made it all sound so easy. However, about tonight, if I was being honest, my body was more bonfire speed than loud, syncopated rhythm and fighting off sweaty bodies speed.

"I'll go to the bonfire." I had no way of knowing if I was ready to be alone with him again, but I would let a little of my resistance go. "But I'm not having sex with him and you have to clear things with Mr. Thibodeaux."

"Done." Kenzie nodded that kind of one-and-done nod that people did when they confirmed what they already knew—that she'd be able to talk me into the bonfire.

CHAPTER 7

LACIE

Kenzie and I arrived at the bonfire together. That's where our togetherness ended.

She saw Tex and he saw her. She told me she was just going to say hey. Tex had moved here when he was ten. His parents moved their vet practice from Houston to Whiskey Cove to avoid big city life. Still, given his lazy lowland drawl, he couldn't avoid the nickname. To this day, I don't know his real name.

So here I was, alone in front of the big fire after Kenzie promised she wouldn't leave me. Whatever. Now I could just walk home, but first I felt like having a drink. The thud of bean bags hitting plywood permeated the air as partygoers played lawn games, whistling and whooping.

I hadn't seen Kenzie in over an hour. It was worrisome to me that she had been with Tex all this time. Their breakup tore her in two. We'd nursed each other through the hellfire that these men had put us through. My hell came a few weeks before hers.

The way of it was, I did not return to school after prom due to the stress I'd been put through. Poor Kenzie and Tex broke up right before he left for the University of Texas around the first of August. She hadn't known he was leaving. He'd planned to attend LSU with her, until his plans changed when he got kicked from the football team for vaping weed and then arguing with the coach.

The air shifted, and my body seemed to know why, but my searching eyes never found him. About one mile was all it would take to walk to the property line fence that was still broken down and easy to climb over. Couples paired up kissing and smiling, their content glowing from the firelight and that three-beer buzz.

My bones felt heavy from exhaustion, so I decided to have one more beer from the keg and then start the trek home, hopefully with Kenzie in tow. I took a red solo cup full of beer and sat on a hay bale, sipping and watching, wondering which of the paired-off couples would still be together two or three years down the road.

"Is this seat taken?"

Boy-next-door cuteness hit me square in the chest. I moved to make room for him on a bale of hay and said, "not at all," which I then hated. Why couldn't I just say "no" like a normal person?

My new neighbor smelled like gasoline and sawdust. "Last bonfire I went to, a yeti ran out from the middle after the base was lit," he said.

"A yeti?"

"A guy with a long beard and shaggy hair. Was naked too, out in the snow. Where I'm from we call that a yeti."

I laughed and took him in. His hair was brown and short, his face sported at least a few days' worth of beard. His eyes were gray and reflected the fire light.

He didn't have much of an accent. "Are you not from around here then?"

"Originally from Colorado, though I've lived here six years. Other than the lack of mountains and snow, I don't really see much difference."

I'd never lived anywhere else so I couldn't relate, but Louisiana had its own culture, as I'm sure Colorado did, but with the voodoo, alligators, swamps, Cajuns, jazz, and crawfish, just to name a few of the differences, I couldn't agree with his *not much different* viewpoint.

"I'm kidding," he chuckled, "they're worlds apart. You don't think

Coloradans would eat ditch bugs, now do ya?" He winked at me and smiled a slow, sexy smile that had me thinking about how it would feel if he smiled against my skin, maybe my neck during a make out session.

He sipped from his own red solo cup, and I watched his throat work as he swallowed. I suddenly felt too warm next to the bonfire's flames.

My brain presented a myriad of wonderings all at once. For instance, what would have become of me if this handsome stranger had been the one who took my V-card. What if me and Mr. Boy-Next-Door continued our little verbal dance for a few minutes more? Would he ask for my number? Would we leave together and go get coffee and talk late into the night?

The rest of our conversation was easy as he told me about taking online classes to get his bachelor's in criminal justice.

As he spoke, my mind started to drift. With his legs out in front of him and crossed at the ankles, he had an easy way of communicating and just existing in a space.

His voice was soft, and oh how I wanted to find him interesting and a contender for something that was so much more than sitting by a burning pile of dead wood.

I willed the devil from my mind, but it was difficult since he was back and living among me, migrating into my circles. I hate to admit I'd read Cosmo's *How to Forget a Guy in 10 Days* while waiting for my toes to dry back at Tiffany's.

The article recommended closure rituals that included burning anything of the offender while doing breathing exercises and meditation. Cordelia would be perfect in that capacity, but come on, was I really going to start acting like some crazy old lady with smoking sage wands? I might live in Voodoo country, but that didn't mean I believed in all that black magic trickery.

Remove reminders . . . another Cosmo suggestion and one I dearly loved. Unfortunately for me, the entire town of Whiskey Cove would always remind me of Briggs St. Martin.

As a child, if I was at the library, he was there pretending to be interested in books. If at the River Park, he'd bring his lab and throw a tennis ball back and forth, and then always at me, usually after it had reached peak slobber.

He'd even come into Tiffany's Tangles when Mom and I would go for pedicures. . .the one thing my mom refused to go without during sandal season, no matter how tight the money got. He'd feign needing a trim or come in to pick up something for his sister and wouldn't leave until I'd been good and well teased. Once, he asked Tiffany's manicurist if she wanted to borrow his dad's belt sander for my toenails. She snort-laughed more than was necessary.

Those teases were always milder than the ones he'd adopted as we got older. Mom used to say if anyone was ever looking for Briggs, they could just come find me, and he wouldn't be far behind. Of course, that was until he up and left without a word.

I went after him once and learned my lesson well. With his words, he'd cut me down so deep it took a year for me to recover. I'd missed the last few weeks of high school. I also missed the first semester of freshman year of college. I busted my ass for two years to make it up. Now it was time for grad school, and I still had so many decisions to make.

"Well, you're either a graduate or somebody's girlfriend. Wanna set my mind at ease?" The guy next to me had finished his part of the conversation. He'd asked the question with a certain inflection that said he was repeating himself.

My mind skipped and started to work again. "I just finished a degree in Communication Disorders."

"What do you do with that?"

"Get a masters."

"Ah." He nodded and sipped from the red cup. "Name's Matt, by the way."

"Lacie," I offered and then stuck my hand out for a shake. He chuckled and then grasped it. I needed to answer one burning question. Was there a spark?

SPARK
noun
1.

> *a trace of a specified quality or intense feeling.*
> *"a tiny spark of passion flared within her"*
> *verb*
> *1.*
> *ignite.*
> *"the explosion sparked a fire"*

The short answer was no. There was no ignition, no intensity, and definitely no passion.

Matt started talking about his college experience again. I got the feeling that criminal justice was about as exciting as a bag of hair. Thankfully, I had yet to finish my recap of Cosmo's recommendations. Next up was cleansing the aura—a physical purging of the guy and his thoughts from your body.

Have you ever thought about something so much, you made it happen? When I was little, I wanted a Green Machine so bad I could taste it. My mom, however, was against it because she'd heard one of the neighborhood kids broke his clavicle the first time he'd taken his out. The commercial would come on, and I'd drop everything to run to the TV.

I still remember the music and the overhead voice talking about a racer that was for guys who liked a ride that was really fast . . . *"Six shift steering. Twist, turn, and spin like wild."* I talked about it so much that my mom made a rule that if I could go a whole year without talking about the Green Machine, I could get one.

One thing you need to know about me is, I'm very goal-oriented and can be really determined. I used a combination of those two things to create a plan that put me on a path to earning Green Machine ownership. It was my Christmas gift that year. It took me seven months to acquire my very own Green Machine.

Alas, if I could have purged Briggs and his words, the memory of his touch, the feel of his breath on my skin, the warm glow that popped up in certain places when I thought about prom night, well let's just say I would have given up a limb to remove all the lingering memories of him.

My body does not work that way. Case in point. . . my body's

Briggs response centers just lit up like I'd hit the center shot on a pinball machine and knew his body orbited close to mine.

Sitting on a bale of hay catty-cornered to mine, he wore jeans and a fitted white t-shirt. The ever-present Super 8 that seemed to have grown as an extension of his hand whirred and clicked as he pointed it at me. Occasionally, friends and family would approach him with a chorus of congratulations for graduating. He'd smile, looking younger and more carefree than I'd ever seen him. So much about him was different. It made my body yearn to know if anything else had changed . . . the intensity of his love making, the words he whispered as he took me, his ability to go from perfectly happy to intense anger and destruction.

The day after the greatest night of my life, he'd been admitted to *Bayshore Behavioral Hospital*, a place he'd been in and out of several times in his young life.

When I went to visit him, he'd been maniacal and cruel. And so cold that a shiver raced down my spine at the memory of it all. That day four years ago was the last time we'd shared words—until he'd come into the store. I still didn't know what happened, what I'd done to set him off. In my memory, the night we shared had been magical.

Next to me, Matt cleared his throat, and I was reminded of his handsome face that had a *Jim from the Office* quality that I found adorable. Even his hair curled nicely around his ears and neck. "Are you a friend or a graduate?" I asked.

"Neither, really," he said while popping the top on a local IPA he seemed to produce out of thin air, or I really was bad at paying him attention. "I was here doing some work on the master bathroom. Installing a steam shower and some other spa features."

Mr. St. Martin owned a commercial construction business. I wondered why he'd hire out for a bathroom remodel. I guess it was a cobbler's shoes kind of thing. "That sounds nice. I hope he went with sea foam green for the tiles."

"A classic, but no. Smoke gray glass."

I feigned a pout. Though there was some real merit to my frown. Everyone in town knew sea foam green was my favorite color.

If it wasn't my shoes or clothes, my eyeglasses gave it away, not that I was wearing them now. But the blouse I wore was my color.

We continued to talk, but every now and then, my line of vision would connect with Briggs as he intently watched our interaction. I shored up the idea of a quest to find *Mr. Safe Guy* and felt my eyelids slow blink. It was my tell, a warning that I needed to be cut off from alcohol.

I was three beers in, one more and I wouldn't be so good at keeping thoughts of Briggs at bay. Or keeping my body at bay. My Safe Guy Matt passed me beer number four. Seriously, where was he getting them from?

". . . that pretty much sums up the major differences between steam and regular showers."

Dang. I totally wasn't paying attention. And, let's face it, I couldn't keep my gaze from the little tormented boy cattycornered from us and filming our every move. I cleared my throat. "Well, it sounds really nice."

Matt nodded. "I think I need to take a break from the smoke and beer. Wanna go for a walk?"

I glanced over toward Briggs yet again and spotted those blocks of ice on me. Good to know he still had the smoldering intensity thing down that I used to love so much.

His presence and attention made me a little mad. Nothing from him for four years, and now he wouldn't take his eyes off me. He was being weird.

"Actually, a walk sounds nice."

Before I could even get both feet under me, Briggs was there. "Going somewhere?"

"For a walk." And far away from you, I thought.

"I don't think so." Briggs pulled at my elbow, forcing me to slide up close to him.

I strangled off a laugh that threatened to rumble free. I heard Kenzie's voice in my head . . . "If something is not funny, don't laugh. Men are stupid. They don't understand nervous or anxious laughter. A laugh is also consent to them, so just don't do it." *Okay Kenz, I'm not doing it.*

I pulled my elbow from his grip and took a step that put me back on Matt's side of our standoff square. "You can't tell me not to go for a walk."

"I can and will." Some of the old Briggs was evident now. The twitching jaw, the hand ruffling the hair in frustration, the challenge in his eyes that was set directly on me.

Matt tucked my arm into his side.

Briggs set his camera down on the baled hay. The fact that he'd spent the night drinking Smart Water meant that his focus was more acute than most who were here. That didn't stop the camera phones from making an appearance. Many were aimed at our love triangle, or whatever this was.

I needed to be the kind of woman who could stand up to Briggs. I squared my shoulders, placed my hands on my hips, and leaned into him. "I'm going for a walk and there's nothing you can do to stop me." One of my eyelids came down slowly but the other one stayed open. I swallowed a burp. Pretty sure I looked anything but confident, but I didn't care. Briggs wasn't just going to waltz into town and start dictating what I could and could not do. It was important that I emulate Aphrodite, Goddess of Perfection, that I am. Kenzie could come up with some real good shit.

Suddenly, the earth flipped on its axis, and the ground moved. Arms like heavy blocks of stone banded around me.

"Put me down, you overgrown ape!" I yelled, but he only walked faster. I focused on keeping down Taco Bell and four beers. It was a bouncy ride that had me screaming when suddenly I was sliding down his body, and then he released me.

The sense of falling had me reaching for him, but the glowing lights and smell of chlorine zapped in my synapse, and before I broke through the surface of the water, I knew what was happening.

When I hit the water, my head went under, my nose unprotected and burning almost on impact as I sank to the bottom. When my feet hit the concrete, I used the inertia from my plunge to spring-board myself back to the top.

Erupting from the pool like a bullet from a gun, I screamed and flung water at him, cursing the day he was born. "You asshole. I hate your fucking guts!" I pushed against him, putting all the hate and anger into it. He may as well have been a big boulder for all that I was able to move him. Now we were faced off like Colonel Travis and Santa Anna, his arms crossed, my body dripping and eyes wet, not just from pool water. He held his chin high, but his gaze cast low to reach mine. It was the smirk on his face that radiated enjoyment at toying with me like a cat pawing a mouse to death. I just had one question for him . . . "Why?"

People stood around us, phones held high in silence as the fire crackled just feet away. "I told you not to go."

"Letting you dictate what I do and don't do is a privilege I will never give you."

He shrugged. "Doesn't need to be given. You're on my property. You obey my rules. That means I'm telling you what you can and cannot do."

Leaning into him I couldn't believe what I was hearing, "Obey?"

It was the smirk that decided my next move.

I slapped him.

I'll never forget the shock on his face, and even though it was there for only the tiniest of seconds, I still play it on repeat in my head because it was the first time I'd ever seen Briggs out of balance when it came to me. For our entire history, he always knew what I would say, what I would do; he was always one step ahead of me. But he hadn't predicted that slap.

Except for the fire, it was dark. Cameras flashed. I stepped forward. "Do whatever you want. You'll be doing it without me."

The walk toward Landry land would be shortened to eight minutes if I could keep my current frenzied pace, but once I got closer to the lake, I had to slow my pace due to crawfish hills. As far as hills go, they weren't very big, but they dried as hard as concrete, and there were hundreds cloistered close together, making it hard to walk.

Slowing my pace was good for regulating my body. It wouldn't do to drag this anger across the property line and risk upsetting Mom and Gramps.

I willed my feet to stop and took a deep breath. Suddenly, the ground shook like I'd roused the hounds of hell, and given the fury running through my veins, I expected to turn and see actual hell hounds.

Instead, Briggs bounded toward me in an off-road Polaris contraption on four wheels. He took the crawfish mud hills too fast and got actual airtime between the ground and tires, putting the axels to the ultimate test.

It was the thought of my purse that had me stopped in my tracks. I checked my hip, but the crossbody bag wasn't there. Where had it ended up? Probably at the bottom of the pool. Damn, I'd need a new cell phone.

The commotion stopped, causing the quiet to permeate the air. Then, the unmistakable sound of whirring and clicking incinerated any calm I'd engineered. Incendiary rage struck as I thought of that damn Super 8 camera filming me at this moment, looking like a drowned rat and still raw with hurt if the tears falling from my eyes gave any indication.

Would he watch it later and get off on the pain he'd caused me yet again?

"Get in the mule."

Like hell I would. My patience snapped, and I charged him, took advantage of his fiddling with the gear shift on the mule, and wrenched the camera from his grip. He lunged but was too slow.

Ankles be damned. I ran using the moonlight to mark the way. With any luck, I'd avoid slamming my foot into any crawfish holes and shattering bones.

I ran so hard and so fast the only sound that could be heard was that of my own breathing. I wouldn't turn to see if he pursued because the only thing I had against him was a small head start.

I focused on two things: not breaking an ankle and keeping my lead. Crab grass bit at my ankles, but I fought to stay ahead, focused on the distant glow of the Landry property.

When I made it to the broken-down fence between the properties, the speed I'd built up had me practically flipping over the fence. I landed on my side, and an *oof* escaped my lips, but I'd managed to hold onto the camera. Using my one free hand I pushed up from the earth and pushed my legs as fast as was safe given the mini crawdad mud mines.

Under my feet I could tell the landscape was smoothing out as I reached the edge of the tended lawns. I high tailed it past the pool and headed for the barn. Once in the barn, I flew past the horses who had been put away for the night and headed for the stairs that led to the loft.

I still wouldn't turn around.

I climbed the thin stairs and walked across the wooden planks to the open hayloft doors. I stood in the shadows and watched for him to appear. My breathing slowed as I waited for any sign of Briggs. Suddenly, the thin wooden step ladder creaked. My eyes adjusted to the dark shadowy figure as he emerged, but I sank deeper into the darkness, hoping to hide from him.

I'd forgotten Briggs was part tiger. He made a guttural growl when he found me and slowed his forward advance.

A fissure of excitement set my belly alight with nervous energy. I knew I would give away my location, but I set the camera to record because watching Briggs prey on something he wanted was like watching a god take a soapy shower.

I swallowed and parted my lips for air. My heartbeat and breathing were out of sync. I darted out of his line of sight, but in two long strides he pounced on me. Leaning forward, I pulled the camera into my body and held it there with all my might, wiggling and worming to prevent Briggs from reclaiming it.

When the camera fell and landed in hay, Briggs was so close to me I could feel his breath.

His fingers reached for my arms, attempting to hold me, but still I wiggled free, sliding from his grip.

In my retreat, his arms banded around my waist and took me down to the hay so that I was beneath him. His hands held my wrists above my head as his knees went down on either side of my hips. His boyish smile incinerated any lingering anger I had.

This Briggs was the one in my dreams, the one who put everything he had into foreplay and could love you like you were the last woman on earth. His focus on me was acute, and yet I still bucked against him, pretending to get free but in no way wanting to. We loved to play this game.

I jerked my hips, twisting from one side to the other, but Briggs's made-of-steel body tightened, rendering me immobile.

His head lowered to mine until his whispered breath tickled my lips. "Are you fighting me, Lace?"

Breathless, I returned his call. "I'll always fight back."

He nodded. "Good." And then his lips descended onto mine. I let him kiss me for a moment and then bit his lower lip hard.

The surprising move had him lifting his lips from mine, which then revealed the shocked spark in his eyes that caused an ache to grow between my legs. His look right now, that anger mixed with sex and raw male virility, was the hottest thing I have ever experienced in my twenty-three years on this earth.

Wet lips.

Dark, smoky eyes.

Swollen bite.

Slight smirk.

The bite extended the challenge of roughness that Briggs was only too happy to accept.

Bras that clasp in the front are easy.

Strapless bras are even easier.

Briggs held both my wrists in one of his hands and started to unbutton my top. By some magic of the roundtable of hot men everywhere, he managed to pull my bra out of my shirt before all the buttons were even undone.

With his focus back on the buttons of my shirt, I slammed the heel of my foot into his back and used his stunned reaction to turn us so that I was now straddling him. His growl of approval spurred me on, and I ground myself against him.

His hard length hit me in all the right places. I powered through this thing that I think was called a dry hump.

When I leaned forward, Briggs made the most of it by reaching strong arms around me and holding my chest to his face, teasing my nipples through my seafoam silky blouse, the wetness from his sucks causing the shirt to cling, bringing my chest into full bloom from the abrasion and temperature changes. Anatomy was so wonderfully sensitive. And traitorous, but wonderfully sensitive nonetheless.

We kissed until my lips stung, and I could feel his arousal between my legs. Animal instinct had me rubbing and grinding and grunting from my position on top of his lap. And he was with me, for a moment in time, he was with me. I saw the passion in his eyes when he licked his lips and thrust in time with my grind. We were in tandem. I cried out his name, and he called to me, "Lace," the nickname he'd given me so long ago.

I knew I had him at my mercy when he made the most manly, beastly growl of frustration-laced satisfaction. It was the kind of sound you make when you've finally caught something you've been chasing. He made that sound because he'd looped his legs with mine and flipped us again. My time on top was short-lived, and now I was at his every whim, a wonderland for his amusement.

He lowered his head, his lips on mine. I turned and presented him with my cheek, irritated that I no longer had control. His soft giggle melted my insides. "You're no good at this game, Lace."

"What?"

"Pretending you don't want it when your entire body is beating in time with mine."

So he knew? Didn't matter. I'd still pretend I didn't want anything of his touching me, biting me, next to me. I'd do it to see how hard he'd work to get me. I lifted my chin and doubled down on turning my face away from him.

His giggle turned into full-on laughter. "The scent of your arousal is also a dead giveaway."

My nose crinkled at his words. God. Cue the instant mortification.

"Alluring and driving me wild," he said.

His hands still held my wrists above my head. Our lips crashed together, tongues dueled, I lifted my head and neck as far as I could to gain more of him, wanting all of him, but he moved just out of my reach, his smoldering smile setting me on fire. His fingers parted my shirt and his appreciative groan had me answering in kind.

When he reached for the Super 8, his erection pressed heavily between my legs.

I let him film me. . . my breasts, my arm coming up to shield my smiling face. He looked sleepy and like he was right where he wanted to be; anywhere else and he'd be trying to get back to this moment right here. I knew he felt that way because it's how I felt.

With the camera in his hands, he leaned further and further back, messing with the angle, until his hips leveled with mine. "I've missed you. Your blonde curls belong on film."

What a charmer. With one hand up my still-damp-from-the-pool skirt, he massaged my hip while he filmed. He'd always been skilled at waking up the secret parts of me. Now, even more so. I wonder how many women there had been since our night under the silver moon. He knew the ins and outs of a woman's body and everything in between. Kenzie had said everyone has a number and I wanted to know his.

"How many women have you been with?"

His hand on my hip froze, his eyes narrowed as he looked into my eyes. "Do we need to talk about this now?"

I lifted one shoulder. "I'd like to know."

Slowly, I pitched forward and came down, causing a moan to escape his throat. "Why?"

"Just wondering how I measure up is all." I sighed. "Do I rank in the top ten, or is my rank lower?"

He sat up, his arms closing around me, his lips sucking ever so lightly on my neck, his breath at my ear. "You're my only number, Lace."

He feathered kisses on my earlobe. "The number is one."

His lips sucked lightly on my neck. "*You.*"

He released a long breath against my skin. "You're all I've ever needed."

He confused me.

"I don't understand. Just tell me what number I am in the line of women you've had sex with."

"There are no other women. I've only ever been intimate with you."

Holy Christ. I sat up next to him. I couldn't think, couldn't breathe; his words immobilized all thought and action. I couldn't believe what I was hearing. "But you've seen you, right? And you're so good at it...how can you be so good at it?"

"*It what?*" he asked.

"Sex."

He chuckled. "I believe the word you're looking for is *porn.*"

If porn made you great at sex, then I needed some porn stat. I'd consider it.

His head went back to the lump of hay, and he cleared his throat. "So, what's your number?

It was a tit for tat situation. I considered teasing him. He certainly deserved it given all of the teasing he'd done to me in the past. But it didn't feel right to use our intimacy against one another. "My number is the same as yours."

He pulled me into his side and kissed the top of my head. His hand rubbed my back, and we lay content for several minutes, knowing each other's numbers. We'd spent four years apart only to come back together, the same but different somehow.

The trust I'd placed in his hands on prom night was the hardest thing I've ever done. That night was the thing dreams are made of. There was no denying that the day after prom changed us.

CHAPTER 8
LACIE (AGE 18)

Prom night was always a big deal, especially in the South. People planned for them like they planned for weddings. However, since my home was full of happiness, not money, so Mom sewed a dress for me in sea foam green tulle material we'd found on the sale rack at the back of Chateau Sew & Sew on Magazine Street in New Orleans. We'd eaten oysters from the half shell, Mom and Gramps washing them down with beer and me with Ginger Ale. I could eat my weight in oysters, any way they came.

Making an A-line silhouette, the dress had a plunging V-neck that cinched at the waist, empire style, with a three-inch sequined band of delicate crystal flowers before flowing to the floor in waves of sea foam. I'd worn a fair amount of padding to fill in the top. Luckily, I didn't have to afford much more than the dress and a pair of sea foam green Chuck Taylor's that gave me a collection of ten. I liked nice round numbers.

Kenzie and I had spent prom day at the St. Martin Estate, engaged in the usual spectacle of teen frivolity that accompanied prom. The St. Martins practically lived on their backyard deck that was the size of some people's houses. There were couches that curved in an S shape, complete with pillows and blankets. A large television and stereo system with cooling mist fans and even gas heaters for the winter. A kitchen, off the kitchen, had everything and more, including a pizza oven. Beyond the deck was a hot tub and pool that I (*and the guy who did not ask me to prom, but I wished he would have*) had spent endless hours in.

Memories assailed me. The summer my grandmother died, and he'd taught me how to French kiss, and then we spent the rest of the summer in this pool. Laughing, frolicking, and causing general mischief. My friends, his friends, my family, his family, all of us together, spending lazy summer days making pizzas in the oven and snow cones in the shaved ice maker, getting so tanned my skin was the color of pralines. Poor Kenzie just burned, and that was the summer I realized what a gift my French blood was. I liked keeping my color up because it made me feel close to my Grams who was caramel all year long.

I sighed. For some reason, Briggs had asked big-breasted Natalie McMahon to prom instead of me. I kept telling myself I wasn't jealous of her bra size. If I repeated it enough, I'd believe it.

At this point, Natalie decided to walk over and dive into the pool. I really hoped her top didn't fall off. I knew CPR but didn't want to have to use it on any of these guys when they fainted at the sight of her huge, uncovered boobs. Alas, I knew everyone in the yard and would save their life if need be because that's just the kind of person I am.

It seemed, as it usually did, that people filled in the space around Briggs, who was at the center of the circle of our high school peeps. Some of them floated around the pool while me and Kenzie sunned ourselves off to the side. Tex was next to Kenzie, playing Angry Birds on his phone that he shaded, mostly unsuccessfully, with his towel.

Theo lounged on a chair beneath a tree, saying his bronze was the perfect shade and he didn't need any more color. His date, one of his mother's bridge club daughters who attended Saint Catherine's of Alexandria Parish School, was oiling herself with baby oil and soaking up as much sun as possible.

Reese, my date and the quarterback of the football team,

couldn't seem to find a happy full spot in his gut and was picking pieces of fajita steak straight off the platter and putting them right into his mouth. Finn was there and the only one of us that didn't seem to have a date. But he did eat fajitas and sip margaritas with Briggs, who was there with Natalie and her huge boobs and curvy hips, and let's face it, who was light years away from me in the full-figured woman capacity, and I had to think that if Briggs liked her, he couldn't very well like me. And, well, I guess he didn't, or I'd be his date instead.

Reese was okay, and I really tried to tolerate him, but he had meat burps from eating so much that it turned my stomach. That didn't mean that I wasn't going through the motions. He brought me food and drink and made sure I didn't want for anything. We exchanged bites of things we thought were extremely tasty, like the tres leches cake, and shared a poolside lounge chair when all of the others were taken. To any spectator, we seemed in sync, like boyfriend and girlfriend. That's where it ended for me.

I couldn't get comfortable with Reese for feeling like I constantly had to be aware of where his hands were going and trying to stay three steps ahead of his intentions so that they didn't go anywhere I didn't want them to. It was exhausting.

When Natalie emerged from the pool, wet and ready for her porn shot in a string bikini that was two sizes too small, I started to believe Theo may be on to something. Looking around, every guy's jaw was on the ground, eyes bulged, drool slid down chins. Every guy, that is, except for Theo and Briggs. Reese was standing right next to the table that was closest to the ladder that Natalie used to pull herself from the pool. Reese glanced at the movement of her body, and his eyes did that cartoon wolf thing where they practically popped out of their sockets and went *awooga*. The steak fell from his mouth, and for a moment, his interest shifted from food to something else.

Briggs's eyes, though, those blue blocks of ice were on me and only me. We connected and stayed that way, while in my peripheral, Natalie's butt cheeks bobbed up and down as she walked over to the lounge chair and bent to pick up her towel.

His eyes stayed on me even when Natalie turned around and did a little walk over to the food table, the underside of her boobs uncovered by the scant material of her top two triangles that covered her nips and nothing more. It was vulgar and sexy at the same time. Throughout the day, Briggs had his camera out and pointed at me. Theo said this meant something.

"If I were naked, I'd be showing less. Jesus Christ," Kenzie said while watching Tex.

Having been caught red-handed, Tex coughed and looked away from the peep show. "What's that? You want to go get naked?"

Kenzie scoffed and threw her scrunchie at him.

Tex caught the hair accessory in his fist. "What? You're beautiful, let's go. I'm game."

They went inside. Most men were easy, but not the one I liked; he still had his camera pointed at me and his face down in the viewfinder, and it struck me that Natalie and I were night and day. Let's just say, Natalie wouldn't need any padding to fill out my prom dress if it fit her at all. She'd worn a string bikini that was two to three sizes too small. It wasn't lost on me that Briggs wasn't doting on her, not that he doted on anyone, but the guys who were here were doting because the rumor was that prom night meant sex, and they all seemed to be hopeful that the rumor was true. All except Reese, who was still eating, Finn, who had no one, and Briggs, who still stared at me.

***

BRIGGS (AGE 18)

I walked out from the shower with nothing but a towel around my waist intent on getting dressed for prom.

To my surprise, Lacie was in my room, waiting for me. A present wrapped in a big bow, waiting to be ripped open.

The dress. . .*the dress would kill me.*

That skin. . . it glistened and smelled like vanilla.

My brain interpreted: For him, not for me. She'd worn this for him. Her warm skin was for him.

Not for me.

He'd have her tonight, if he hadn't already.

I closed my eyes tight.

Couldn't think.

She did this to me.

She stood frozen, staring.

Clothes. I should dress.

But wouldn't.

Beautiful. *She was beautiful.*

My head felt like it was on fire. Couldn't breathe. Hard to look at her.

She walked over to my bookcase. "Candid's of your family. Did you do these?" She picked up a framed photo and stared at it. "They're beautiful. I've always loved how you capture people in their natural state. Real and vulnerable. A true expression of life."

He was going to fuck her.

Mine!

He was a fuckboy. She wasn't that kind of girl.

She looked to the bed and what was on it. I froze. Shit, my work. *It was shit.* I could do better. I only wanted her looking at perfection. I tried to move. Tried to talk. Couldn't.

My eyes traveled over what she saw. Dozens of photographs of local landscapes and people, strewn haphazardly across the bed. Her hands padded across them. The photographs had mats around them and a number in each corner indicating they'd been on display. Black and white.

"Earl's Cajun Market." She smiled fondly. "And Big Earl front and center in the picture, smiling big as day with that crooked front tooth of his." She chuckled. "He was old when I was a kid. Always had that big ole' pot belly and the best sausage in all of Louisiana. Non-locals drive for miles to buy his seafood boudin. Did you know it was featured on Food Network? They seemed fascinated that instead of pork he uses crawfish, crab, and shrimp."

Her soft words and smiles breathed new life into my veins, and I let her goodness wash over me. I knew she could save me. If only I could be good enough to be the man she deserved. Reese didn't deserve her. He would fuck her, but she should be mine.

"During the holidays, me and Gramps make the trek to Earl's to get several pounds worth of boudin. We eat all we can on the ride back and share the rest with all our friends on the estate." Her face morphed into an appreciative smile. "God, Briggs, the amount of nostalgia in this one photograph alone has my eyes swimming in tears. This is my life in black and white." Her eyes moved to the logo at the bottom of the matting. "Did you enter these in the art contest at the rodeo?"

I covered the photos with the comforter. "They suck." I couldn't even look at her anymore. The images my mind conjured up of her spread out naked on some altar for Reese. The images of her on his social media page, like all the other girls Reese had fucked.

"You're wrong. Your work has always been amazing, but these shots are incredible. Makes me hungry for Earl's seafood boudin. I can even smell the inside of the place, like lemon Pine-Sol and smoked meat."

Fucking Reese. Anger funneled through me, seizing my spine with pain. I tried to keep it harnessed tightly so I didn't do something I'd regret.

Abnormal. That was my identity, and I needed to remember it. "They didn't place. Guess that makes you a liar or a shit art critic," I said, and then regretted speaking to her in that way.

She shook her head. "The rodeo, Briggs? These don't belong at a rodeo. They belong in a gallery. You just need to get them into the right hands, somebody who will take you where you deserve to be.

Anger simmered across my skin. The shower I'd taken wasted as sweat incinerated my forehead. "What do you know about it?" I let the towel fall and walked to my dresser, searching for boxers. "You and Reese seem to be hitting it off."

"Why is that any of your business?" she said in a huff.

In my briefs, now I turned to see Lacie aglow in a wash of red on her face and neck, down her bare chest and swallowed the lump in my throat. I could so easily take her and mark her as mine . . . a little wood elf that happened into the wrong forest. I was the big bad wolf, fangs dripping with digestive juices that would help me eat her whole. "You're in my room, that makes it my business."

Her face transformed with confusion. "I don't think it makes my relationship with Reese your business."

Relationship! I growled like the animal I was. "Does he fuck you?"

Lacie puffed out a hot breath, her eyes simmering with untapped rage. "What's wrong with you?"

I shrugged, trying to display that it didn't bother me that she had or would give herself to Reese. I needed to punch something now! "So do you? . . . Let him fuck you?"

She set her palms on my chest and pushed with a force I wasn't expecting, but I was the boulder of Sisyphus, always coming back to her for more.

"Just stop, Briggs. You're disrespectful, and if you care so much, why didn't you ask me to prom?"

I loved watching the blood rush through the vein in her throat, that pulse undeniable in her rage. So beautiful. I imagined grazing my teeth over that spot. I wanted to tell her so many things. Things about her dress. Things about asking her to prom. But I couldn't think clearly, couldn't form coherent thoughts about her. It happened a lot when I was in the middle of an episode. I suffered from episodes of spiking and crashing. My therapist wrote a book about it.

When I was ramping up, I couldn't organize my thoughts with the motor planning of speech, so sometimes I couldn't communicate. I explained this to Lacie once. A few days later, she led me through a guided meditation that was something she'd researched about my condition. She was always trying to help the people in her life.

"Because you don't have the balls," she spat.

"What?"

"You heard me," she said before passing me by, the material of her dress and the beads scraping across my bare chest.

My arm reached out, my hand squeezing around her upper

arm. "Don't let him." I sensed her head turn back to regard me, but I stared straight ahead, careful to avoid her eyes.

"Briggs, please just leave me be. I can't understand you when you're like this. You don't want me, but you don't want anyone else to have me. It doesn't make sense."

I wanted to tell her about Reese and his videos. The ones he took and shared around the web. I wanted to tell her we could blow off prom and just stay here. But couldn't. "Please, Lace, don't let him," was all I could manage.

And she was dead wrong. I wanted her like I wanted oxygen to breathe.

Deserving her was another matter.

And I didn't deserve her.

**

LACIE

I left Briggs's bedroom knowing full well I'd recognized the heat in his eyes when he'd looked at my body. I'm almost certain he had feelings for me that, for some reason, he denied. I'd known him longer than most girls had, and we'd French kissed under the silver moon when I was thirteen. That kiss was *everything*. No one will ever convince me that the emotions coursing through my body during that kiss were one-sided because there is no way a one-sided kiss could be *that* good. We belonged together. That kiss proved it.

The sound of glass clanking together pulled my attention away from the sadness that was *Briggs and Lacie*. I walked toward the noise and soon I found my people all doing shots, dressed in their finest duds, getting drunk and altogether rebel rousing before the night had even really begun.

Reese put his arm around my waist and lifted me off the ground, spinning us and squeezing the breath from my lungs. "You look amazing."

Reese looked dapper in his gray tuxedo. "As do you." Over his shoulder I caught sight of Kenzie in her royal, deep purple gown.

She was a queen. I blew out an imaginary fire on my fingers and then pointed to her. She smiled. Tex's tuxedo bowtie and cummerbund matched her shade of purple to exact proportions. They were beautiful.

A beautiful girl in a red strapless gown had joined the group while I was MIA. Her skin was bronze, and her hair thick and dark. I found out from Kenzie that she was one of the St. Martin cousins and here to be Finn's date. She looked like them. Tall and confident, with a smidge of attitude mixed in around the edges.

Finn stood off to the side just a tad, like he didn't want to commit to the circle of friends and frolic but instead watched every movement like a hawk. He looked so handsome and so tall in a classic black tux with matching red accents to accompany his date, or cousin.

The whole thing with prom meaning sex made up a lot of the conversations Kenzie and I had, and I suspected the guys too. Kenzie said the guys *had* talked about it, and she and Tex had even taken the pressure off the night by declaring to each other that they would be carrying out the tradition.

Thinking about Finn's situation, bringing his cousin, he wouldn't be in a position to engage in all that prom had to offer, and I wondered if he was sore about it. Finn was a year older than us, but he'd been out for a year after his accident. This group of seniors wasn't his class, but surely there must be someone he liked from our group.

Logan, another of Briggs's friends, and his date showed up dressed to impress and ready to shoot tequila. Impressively, Logan shot two tequilas down his throat without so much as a wince.

I took a step back, hoping to avoid any sort of shot taking, mainly because I was a lightweight and hated the taste of all the hard alcohol I'd ever tried.

"Finn told me you helped him. I think it'd be cool if he'd learn sign language. I just wanted you to know we all appreciate what you're trying to do." Finn's date smiled a genuine smile, and it had my guts twisting with the revelation that I was unable to help Finn the way she'd thought.

"I don't know, he doesn't seem to want to do it. It may not happen."

"Don't give up on him. He's a stubborn fool. I know we're only cousins, but he's like a brother to me. He saved my life. Let me know if there is anything I can do to help you. I'm Francesca, by the way."

"I'm Lacie." It was then that I noticed the scars along the side of her right temple. "Since his wreck, it's been hard to get him to communicate at all. Does he communicate with you?"

She nodded. "I think it's because we're both broken. I still have panic attacks from the PTSD. He's so kind. He invited me to prom even though I know he'd rather not go. I tend to get panic attacks in crowded, loud spaces, but I trust Finn to guide me through them. I think because he can't talk, he's extra intuitive and just knows when I need his focused eyes on mine to get my breathing under control. He's helped me so much, I'd like to help him in return, but it's not easy to help someone who doesn't want to be helped."

I twisted the bracelet on my wrist. I thought back to a few years ago when Finn was gone for an entire summer. Briggs said he was with their cousin in New Orleans. Francesca, of course, this was her. It was a horrible, fluke accident on the coast during fair month. Her long, thick hair had gotten caught in the Ferris wheel ride and instead of ripping out her hair, it ripped the skin from her scalp.

"I don't intend to give up, I just need to figure out how to help him," I said.

"Giving him his communication back would help restore a part of him that was lost. He's suffered so much. He is afraid of sleep. Imagine that. He has night terrors from the accident."

"I had no idea." I knew the accident kept him from being able to finish school on time. He homeschooled with tutors and then missed prom. That was a couple of years ago though.

"Catch up." Kenzie passed me a shot glass so full of golden liquid that a little sloshed from the rim.

"What is this, like two ounces?" I asked.

"One and a half. Don't be a snit, just drink." I did not want to get drunk. I wanted to be able to remember this night.

I sipped the whiskey—maybe it was tequila. It burned and I grimaced, but Reese tipped the glass up to my lips, forcing me to drink or spill. In the end, a lot of both happened, and the whiskey even went up my nose and had me coughing and wheezing for air.

Suddenly, a fist went flying and the sound of skin on skin preceded the sick cracking of bone. I continued to cough, my world going dizzy as I heard the scuffle and shouting between Briggs and Reese. The other guys ran to intervene, more fists flew, Kenzie and Nicole screamed. Theo grabbed me around the waist, pulling me free of the fighting, while I kicked and screamed for Briggs to stop.

Theo, reached for Briggs, trying to pull him off of Reese, but ended up getting punched by Briggs so hard that blood gushed from his nose. The sight sending me scrambling and I pushed into the counter with my feet, knocking myself to the floor between the guys, blood splattered across my face and chest, I was between them when Briggs's fist went flying, his eyes locking on mine, his face morphed into an animal-like grimace.

"Stop." A raspy voice, a protective hand blocking the out-of-control fist headed for my face.

"Finn," I whispered, my voice raw and lacking volume. Briggs's hands opened, fell to his side, and then reached for me like I was a life ring. It all happened so fast I didn't realize my dress had been torn and my bare breasts were out. Natalie's phone pointed at me, and Theo's date had two phones pointed at me.

"Accident," Briggs whispered. "Accident, Lace." His voice was so strained it cracked.

I shook my head and pulled away from him. Moving required effort. My limbs moved like they had to pass through thick mud, making it hard to hold the top of my dress against my chest.

Ice-blue eyes froze the burning anger in my stomach, turning that flowing lava to a heavy ice block right in the middle of a full combustion, halting every and any action I could take. It felt like my body was chained to the back of a runaway train, heading for a mountainside.

One big fat tear slid down my face. He reached for me, but I turned away. *Say Something* played in the background. How appropriate.

. . . and I am feeling so small . . .

Sometimes the soundtrack of my life could be a real bitch.

. . . and I will stumble and fall . . .

Bloody, tattered, and torn, I sat on the kitchen floor, friends standing around us, Reese holding his nose, laid out and groaning on the floor.

Briggs had lost control. He'd ruined everything. Prom, my dress, Reese's face, Theo's nose... But it was that feeling of safety and security that I missed the most, the feeling that no matter how mad he got, how upset I made him, he'd never let that tight control over the animal inside of him loose.

So many men in my life displayed quiet control. Men like Theo and my grandfather. I'd seen them get blood-simmering mad, body-shaking mad, but never once had they turned that anger on me, never once had I felt in harm's way in their presence when they were angry. Even Reese could get mad, and sure, what he'd done to me with the tequila was a dick move, but Briggs was out of control.

In Briggs's moment of rage, I was terrified. He was the only person who ever made me feel that way. My mom had told me a few things about my father when I'd asked. She would always make sure to pair something negative with something positive. I could tell she didn't like to talk poorly about him because he was my father. She'd say, "He had many wonderful qualities; just look at you." But I knew they had some pretty bad knockdown, drag-out fights before he left us.

I was four years old when he left. Mom said he had to because they couldn't get along. "The heart doesn't tell you who to love, it tells you who you're attracted to; it's the brain you should be listening to," she'd say.

Theo came to my aid with his tux jacket, placing it over my shoulders, drowning me in a scent that immediately took me to the comfort of home. Pine and lemons, pure Theo. I tried to offer up a weak smile to him. "Take me home," I whispered.

***

LACIE

The blood from Theo's nose had stopped. There was still some swelling, but he said he knew it wasn't broken. Not wanting him to miss his senior prom, I demanded he drop me off at home and then intercept the limo.

"Let me stay with you."

"No! I just want to be alone, okay?" I got my phone out and texted Kenzie.

> Me: Can you get the limo to stop by the Landry apartments and pick up Theo?

> Kenzie: Of course. Be there in 15. Let's you and I hang back, you can get cleaned up and put on another dress.

> Me: Like I told Theo, I just want to be alone.

> Theo: Please let us help you.

> Kenzie: Sorry Beans.

> Me: I was iffy on prom BEFORE the tequila fiasco. Now I'm a hard no-way-in-hell am I going. Please leave me be. I need to think!!

> Theo: Love you.

> Kenzie: Okay hun. FYI, Briggs is MIA.

***

LACIE

Thankfully, no one was home. All the tension I'd felt for the whole day compressed into a red ball of fire in the pit of my stomach that decided to release at that moment. I let out a scream and then the tears came. I ran into the bathroom, and when I saw myself in the mirror, I went numb.

The elastic that was holding my hair had snapped sometime during the commotion. My platinum hair was all over my head. My mascara had run down my face and my dress was completely ruined. And soon my boobs would be trending on social media.

This is what happens when you spend prom day with Robert Briggs St. Martin.

I don't recommend it.

CHAPTER 9
LACIE (AGE 18)

Under the silver moon, on the edge of the black water, I sat in my favorite place and cursed his name. Prom was officially ruined. I'd never get a chance to have one.

It wasn't enough that he bullied me for thirteen years. I'll say it again, I never knew which Briggs I'd be presented with on any given day . . . angel or devil. That he destroyed any confidence I ever had in myself, that he would rather beat up the poor, unsuspecting guy who asked to take me to prom and one of my best friends did not sit well with me.

"God Theo, I'm so sorry," I whispered to the moon goddess. His poor face had been so messed up.

I sat there, on the water's edge in my torn dress, holding the side in place with my hand. I knew the fight and my boobs would be all over social media but honestly it was hard to find the will to care. All I cared about in that moment was getting to the bottom of this thing with Briggs. What had I ever done to wrong him so much? Why did he hate me?

I thought I was done hating him, but after tonight, I had a newfound anger, and it was directed all at him.

Warm wind cascaded across my skin. I inhaled the scent of wet earth and grasses, the full moon reflected in the water, slight ripples rolled across the surface. Crunching pebbles behind me had me sighing. It was him. I knew this with absolute certainty because I could hear the whirring of his camera. I remained frozen, staring out at the pond, whose dark water matched my heart.

He sat down next me on the sand bar. Gone was the tuxedo. In its place he wore gray sweatpants and nothing else, even on his feet. We didn't talk. What would be the point? Between the anger coursing through my veins and his presence so close to me, I wouldn't be able to communicate more than a few words at a time anyway. And yet, even though I could have killed him for what he had done, I knew I'd bow down to him; all he had to do was ask.

Hatred and love coursed through my body, both passengers of the same vessel, at the same time. It made me crazy. I wanted to hurt him as badly as he'd hurt me, but I also wanted him to quench my body's desire for all things Briggs.

A heaviness pushed against my diaphragm, making it difficult to breathe. We shouldn't be this calm. We should be fighting, kicking, and screaming. Discontented with his quiet fortitude, I punched him in the arm. It felt so good that I brought up my other fist. Before I knew it, I was hitting him hard, and then I slapped his face.

Somewhere deep down I thought to ask myself *why am I doing this?* It wasn't like me. I hit, bit, pulled his hair, and screamed in his face. It was a culmination of every mean thing he'd done to me or had done on my behalf, starting with Scooter the caterpillar and ending with ruining my prom.

Never had I been like this. Not even when he torched the American Girl doll I got for my birthday. I had run away crying. But I was done crying—or was I? I felt moisture in my eyes. Maybe I was still crying, but I was also fighting.

He took my abuse somewhere far away from this place; his eyes were glazed, his expression stone. When he took me in his arms, I kept up my fight, pushing my palm into his chin, trying to rip his face from his neck so I'd never have to see it attached to his body again.

Still, he didn't try to stop me. My bites along his skin left marks, my scratches on his cheek drew blood, I had his hair in my fingers, but I kept pounding. I pounded until my muscles seized up. I cried until tears could no longer form.

Loving Briggs had driven me to the brink of my sanity. This is who I was now, driven crazy by the man I loved and who was incapable of loving me how I deserved. It was maddening. And now I looked like the unstable one.

I stopped fighting and let him pull me into the cradle of his arms. My breasts were uncovered; I knew this because I felt my nipples get hard from the breeze blowing across them. I did not care. With a tender caress of fingers, Briggs pulled the material of my broken dress over my exposed skin and then bent his head and placed a kiss on the cloth that covered my nakedness.

Something so tender from someone so damaged and cruel. From my position across his lap, I watched his face, and what I saw there not only confused me but scared me a little too. He was repentant, which didn't at all match the Briggs from earlier who was so angry he bruised and battered the faces of our friends and then almost hit me.

"I'm sorry," fell from his cut lip. Tears rolled from his eyes. His body shook. Briggs had never been vulnerable around me.

I knew his anger, I knew his indifference, but I'd certainly never heard him apologize. Frown lines on his face smoothed into something clear and untethered, he almost looked younger than his eighteen years.

"I snapped when I saw him forcing that shot down your throat causing you to choke." He scratched his eyebrow. "Lace," his eyes seared into me, "he's done some bad things; he's not a good guy."

I scoffed. "And you are?"

He broke our gaze, breaking our connection to look out over the water. He sat for several seconds, silent and seemingly deep in thought. "I want to be. For you I want to be. I'm so sorry I ruined your dress and your night."

My heart was breaking. He'd never apologized for anything he'd ever done to me, and he'd done a lot. I'd certainly never seen him cry. He was Briggs, my bipolar neighbor who I secretly obsessed over, but who could drop me into a world of hurt in two-seconds flat.

Briggs, the kid next door who killed my caterpillar for no reason. Briggs, the guy who taught me how to skip rocks. He was Briggs, my first kiss. Briggs who had adult-level problems and demons he couldn't shake.

"Isn't that why you exist?" I smiled.

"Are you saying I exist to ruin you?" His expression had changed again, aloof and something else, anger maybe. "How can you think that?"

I pushed away from him. "You ruined prom, you ruined Scooter, you ruined my Gram's funeral, and on account of you, over one-hundred thousand people have seen my boobs, but what hurt most of all was when you burned that American Girl doll my dad left for me. It was all I had to remember him by." I felt my blood pumping, stuttering really, as it tried to restart my heart. "If hurting me's not what you're about, then do you want me to hate you, is that it?"

His fingertips lightly traced my jawline, making their way to my lips. "I really don't know. In the moment by the pool when your head was on his shoulder, I wanted to hurt him . . . even wanted to hurt you for letting him do that to you, for letting him touch you." He forced a swallow, his Adam's apple bobbing up and down. "I wanted you to feel what it was like to want something for so long and know you'll never have it."

What was he talking about? I wanted him like that, but I didn't think he felt the same about me.

It took me a few moments to sort through what he was saying, to realize whose shoulder he was talking about. I'd had my head on Reese's shoulder today at the pool when we were on the lounger together. "My head on his shoulder made you beat him so badly."

He hadn't wiped his tears away, and one particularly bold tear that had clung to his chin fell onto my neck. "I didn't like seeing that you were so comfortable with him."

"He's just my prom date."

"Seeing you with him like you were, my head filled in the gaps. Put in images of the two of you in positions that I didn't want to see."

"You could have told me that earlier, when I was in your room."

"I didn't know how. I tried. The words wouldn't come out."

"You're doing it now. What changed?" Maybe if we could figure out what had changed, we could figure out the key to unlocking his communication.

He shrugged, looking so hopeless my heart punched into my throat. "I wish I knew, Lace. I'm so clear right now, so much so I can see the words in my mind before I speak them."

"Has that ever happened before?"

"I don't know. Maybe the last time they changed my medication." He took me in his arms, pulled me tightly into his chest, and sighed. "There's something wrong with me, Lace. I feel like sometimes I'm not in my own body, like I'm somewhere else. I can't always remember things that have happened."

That would be so confusing and scary. "Do you remember doing those things I mentioned?"

"Yes, that I do remember, but I can't remember why." He pulled me back by my upper arms so he could look into my eyes. "I know you've devoted a lot of your time trying to help me. It's not lost on me that you've been punished for it. I don't know what's inside of me that makes me do bad things, but I promise I won't stop trying to get better. I want to be a better man."

His voice broke on the last word. I wanted to comfort him but didn't know how. "Hey, it's not all bad. Because of you I know what lumens measure. And I can skip rocks whenever I want. I know how to skin a buck," and I saved the best one for last . . . "because of you I know how to do a really good French kiss."

His eyes watched my lips and I willed him to kiss me, but it didn't happen.

I decided then and there that to be Briggs's girl, I needed to help him communicate during those times when he spiraled and couldn't. Since I could still communicate during his episodes, I could help him, like Virgil guiding Dante through the nine circles of hell. *When he's spiraling, I'll guide him through to the other side of it.* I would have to learn to overlook his anger and his saying the most God awful shit. This wouldn't be easy. His body language toward me during those times is the thing of nightmares. How would this even work? There was one question I still longed to ask him. "Can I ask you something?"

He shrugged. "Sure."

"Why didn't you ask me to prom?"

He took a deep breath and exhaled slowly. "I don't know. I didn't think I *should* ask you. I didn't know I was going to react the way I did when I saw another guy's hands on you."

"You didn't know you had feelings for me?"

"No." He shook his head. "Yes." He let out a pained groan. "I've always wanted you." He picked up a rock and threw it in the water. "I haven't always deserved you."

Oh God, I couldn't breathe. Fresh tears welled in my eyes and my hand went up to cup his scratched cheek. "Hey, I don't think people can stay in the space of deserving one another. If we all played that game no one would ever get together and the human race would perish. Inevitably we are selfish and mean."

He was listening intently, so I continued. "In a relationship, some days one person is giving ninety percent because the other can only give ten. It's okay. People can ask those they care about for forgiveness and mercy and those they've asked can choose to give it or not. But deserving? No. In Sunday School I was taught that I'm not deserving of God's love, but he gives it to me anyway. Relationships ebb and flow. I decide if you're deserving or not, and right now I say you are."

"When did you get so smart?" His smile radiated. He was so beautiful. Since it was so rare to see him like this, I picked up the camera and rolled the film like he'd taught me so long ago.

"Oh, I thought of another thing you taught me, how to operate a camera."

"I don't want to watch you dance with someone else. I don't want you to be with anyone else." His eyes were on my lips again.

"Then be the one who's with me," I pleaded.

He lifted me, placing me in his arms, our mouths close enough to breathe each other in. In one movement, his lips descended on mine in one crushing blow. It was five years of pent-up tension emanating from the very first kiss. That kiss we'd shared when we were thirteen had ignited a fire inside of us that had continually smoldered, sparking when we had been in close proximity to one another.

We were so desperate to be connected that our teeth knocked together, but it didn't slow us down. His hand closed around my neck, guiding me closer so his lips could bruise mine, and when I opened, his tongue licked inside. I tasted him and fumbled, my mouth not used to the intrusion, my tongue confused in this move-ment, my breath, the inhale birthed from his expired life force.

I thought this kind of kissing would be kind of gross, but I was so wrong. The earth around me spun, but I held on to his kiss. I was swimming in the deep end of the pool, where my feet could not touch, but Briggs's arms were there to catch me. It was the first time I'd felt safe around him, the first time I trusted him with my body. I simmered there, in that moment, memorizing the feeling of it.

It was my second kiss with him but the first that expressed all we'd left unsaid. His kiss consumed me, and I let him take my mouth at a frenzied pace. When his palm closed around my exposed breast and his fingers squeezed my nipple, I broke away, needing to find a way to get more air. I could have fainted from his complete attention and devotion.

He let out a deep, throaty groan while slickened lips traveled the column of my neck, sucking lightly, ending at my breast and sucking me into his hot mouth. My core pulled even more than it already had.

It seemed like words would be unnecessary, or even taint the cloud of intimacy around us, plus I knew Briggs could have a hard time accessing spoken words when other senses were heightened so instead of telling him with words that I wanted, that I *needed* more, I leaned up and removed the seafoam green and torn dress, leaving myself only in a thong.

His eyes traveled down my body, stopping to stare between my legs and then his gaze came back up to settle on mine. No words were exchanged. He laid me down on the sand and kissed between my breasts.

He bit the top curve of my right breast. I let out a groan while he almost smiled at his artwork. I wanted to ask him why he did this, but I still didn't think he'd be able to put it into words. The skin there burned, and when I looked down, I saw the perfect imprint of his bite marring my skin, starting to bruise.

A mark. His mark. I bared it and was beginning to understand his obsession with bruising me. Our existence, in love and life, was predicated on pain. I literally burned for him. Through his ministrations on my body, I learned that intimacy between two people could leave one untethered; pain had a way of bringing gravity back in, pulling our bodies back down, anchoring us so we didn't float away.

How could I think I wouldn't get incinerated by him? He shined brighter than me and breathed fire. I wished on a star that I'd survive his all-consuming assault, hoping I didn't end up engulfed by the flames.

I ran my hand down his chest. In case he was unsure, I cupped his hardness, tilting my chin up so he could clearly see me licking my lips. I untied the drawstring on his sweatpants and then slid my hand down his hard abs, getting lost in his peaks and valleys.

His length was hot in my hand, branding me in a different way than his bites on my flesh as he sizzled and burned in my grip. So hard and still growing. This was a man. Intrigued, I moved my hand deeper, to where his dick met the rest of him, and then I gently squeezed. His eyes closed, and the hard set of his jaw twitched in time with the throbbing between my legs.

His audible slow exhale in my ear undid me. "Can I?" He looked out toward the lake and then came back to me, a groan on his breath. "Touch you?" he whispered.

This man.

I had my hand down his pants, and he ask for permission to touch me.

In case he had any question as to how much I needed him in this moment, I set out to make him certain, grinding my hips up and into his thickness, letting out a long, throaty moan of desire. "I want you, Briggs." I spoke in breathy tones.

His hand slipped beneath my panties, finding the place I'd kept secret from everyone. His fingers touched me softly, sliding through my wetness. His groans and heavy breaths against my skin let me know he was just as needy as I was. "So wet."

Heat bloomed across my neck and chest, but the embarrassment never came. I'd read several of Grams' Highlander novels. Wet and sex went together.

His head went down on my shoulder, and then the burn from his bite bit into my skin. I didn't mind; I wanted to bear his marks all over my body. He moved to my lips, biting the bottom one before letting me have his tongue.

His strong palm fisted me, gripping me almost too tight, the lace straining under his invasion. "Take them off," I managed through a gasp. By the pull of his fingers, they ripped, and in seconds I was completely bare beneath him, and wanting to grind my core into his fist, but he took his hand away to bring my panties to his nose, closed his eyes, and inhaled deep to memorize my scent, like an animal.

So far, sex had been wet and animalistic. *Noted.*

I noted other things you needed for sex too, like trust. Here I was trusting Briggs, my mortal enemy, with my body's deepest secrets. For a second, I thought it might be a mistake, but he was different tonight. Beneath the silver moon, he worshipped my body, and suddenly I understood all those songs like *Sex On Fire* and *Closer*. "Do you have a condom?" I asked, wanting more of him everywhere.

His fingers were between my folds, his eyes dark and glinting with need in the moonlight. In one swift motion he plunged his finger to the depths of me, and I cried out from the fullness.

Briggs buried his face into my neck; his hot breath on my skin drove me wild and sent delicious shivers down my spine. He was everywhere and touched me not as a teen touches a teen, but as a man touches a woman. When and where had he learned to do that?

The stroke of his finger, combined with the thrust of another, had me panting his name. The intensity was too much. I closed my legs around his hand for leverage, but he forced them open. "Need to see you." His face looked pained, his cock thick, hot, and heavy where it rested on my thigh.

I watched him watch as he fingered and pushed me as high as I could go, crying out for him to ease up when it started to hurt after I'd climaxed. As he pushed his sweatpants down, pulling a foil pack from the small pocket, and held out his cock, his eyes met mine, he fisted himself, holding himself steady as he rolled on a condom.

He readied himself while looking at our bodies, his tongue darting out and running over his lower lip just like the Big Bad Wolf right before he devoured poor Little Red Riding Hood.

In one fluid motion, he moved me closer, my legs spreading farther. I took a deep breath as he pressed into me, steady and smooth. The pressure was worse than the stinging bite of pain, but that only lasted for a moment. I was stretched beyond comfort but didn't care because we were connected; he was inside of me, and in that moment, our union was all that mattered.

In the moonlight he pumped, his hips turning slightly as he alternated between deep and deeper thrusts. Taught muscle caught the starlight, mesmerizing in all its sinew and veins, its dance held my gaze as he pulled me onto him. When had he become this rugged creature of strength and skill? I missed the moments from when we were children, when he'd only hurt my worms and not my friends.

He watched where we were connected, and I wished I could see but the transcendent look on his face said what words could not. I knew he wasn't with me; he'd gone somewhere, and I needed him back. I called his name, but he was entranced, pumping with even strokes, getting deeper with each thrust.

He wasn't responding to my calls of his name, so I reached my fingers up to his hips and scratched him deep.

Laser blue eyes shot to mine and stayed there. "Hurting you?" he asked, his face morphed in concentration.

"No, Briggs."

His thumb touched my core. "Touch yourself like this while I'm inside you," he panted.

My finger replaced his thumb. Within seconds I was coming again.

Over the years, I'd heard Briggs make lots of sounds. . . growls, huffs, grunts, yells, and on the rare occasion, I've even heard him laugh, but the sound he made when he came was by far the sexiest sound I'd ever heard. His Adam's apple bobbed up and down as he let out a raspy moan and some semblance of my name. It made my insides sizzle because I was the one who made him make that sound. Raw male mixed with unbridled passion. I wished I could record it and have it always to listen to whenever I touched myself.

We stayed as we were for a moment, a little snapshot of time that I will always cherish and remember.

I did everything in my power to imprint the smell of the moisture from the lake and the earth from the grasses, his scent mixed with mine, the sound of crickets and the water lapping the shore; the gray-silver moonlight on his sweat slickened skin, the taste of mint on my tongue, the feel of his rough stubble against my cheek, his teeth in my flesh.

I bottled it all up tight, hoping it would be enough if, for some ungodly reason, this was all there was ever going to be.

He dressed me, tying off the broken strap of my dress with deft fingers, kissing the mark he'd left on my chest as he did so.

The whirring of his camera motor sounded louder than it ever had out here in the quiet of the still night beneath the heavens and the stars. The Super 8 pointed at me, as it had been so many times, made me wonder how much footage he had of me.

If I were nearby, it seemed to be pointed at me, and I usually pushed it away, but tonight I watched him move this way and that, playing with me, laughing softly, taking in my afterglow. When he was satisfied with his shot, he balanced on his heels and moved in a slow, fluid motion, panning and scanning, creating a world all about me.

I was only covered by my ruined gown. It wasn't exactly on me, but I let him have some time with the scene. At some point my giggling went out of control, and I attempted to cover my face with my arm, but he was all around me, exposing me through film.

The wind blew and so did my dress. I could feel the coolness across the bare skin of my breast and let the heat bloom across my chest and face at what I knew his camera captured.

Who knew how long we'd been out there but at some point, it had to end. Everything moved forward. Time would never move back. The memory of this moment was all we'd ever have. Anxiety settled low in my gut. His memory was sometimes affected by his mood swings. On one particularly twitchy star, I made a wish . . . please don't let him forget how he'd turned me into a woman tonight.

We walked hand-in-hand, and I marveled at how much bigger and coarser his hand was when compared to mine. Tomorrow would bring a new dawn. I hoped, God, how I hoped, he'd be like he is right now in this moment.

I stared at him, memorizing exactly how he was. When he gave me a funny look, I guess I'd stared a little too long.

"What?" He asked.

I shook my head. "Nothing."

We rounded the large plantation and continued to walk toward the apartments.

The little complex that we referred to as apartments, a name that stuck from days long ago when the housing was all one unit. That unit had been destructed, the land cleared, and individual houses built. Cute little cabins, each with its own screened-in porch, the houses created a semi-circle around a gravel drive with a garden and large pecan tree grove in the center.

With three bedrooms, our unit was the largest, but Gramps had earned his place in the ranks after thirty-five years working the property. I loved it here, this earth was part of me, the dirt in my veins was as much a part of me as it was the Landry children, maybe even more. I'd definitely spent countless hours more than the Landry's on this land.

Briggs's hand remained linked in mine as we ambled toward the pecan grove. We walked slowly like we hoped our pace would slow down the ticking of time, my head on his shoulder, his arm around me, caressing my bare lower back. I led him under a particular favorite pecan tree of mine. June bugs were already out and fluttering under the lights, but it was dark and private beneath the tree.

He hadn't said much, and it had me worried, but on his face was the truest look of contentedness I'd ever seen in him over the past thirteen years. When I looked at him, he gave me a sexy, shy smile that hit me right between the legs. Messy hair flopped down over one eye, the tight jaw, the half-lidded eyes, those swollen lips. I started to combust under the tree.

"Penny for your thoughts," he said in a soft whisper against the skin at my neck.

There was one thing I wanted him to know and decided to tell him. I took a fortifying breath and said, "I wanted it to be you." I hugged him like I'd never see him again and added, "You're the other half of my heart."

Utter adoration was the look he gave, and I willed my brain to memorize the way he seemed to only have eyes for me, the way his eyes stayed right with mine like he couldn't tear his gaze away. I didn't think I imagined the extra moisture in his eyes. His smile as breathtaking as it was rare, his mind was clear, I knew it, and I memorized what he looked like free of his demons. "Lace, you're half of mine."

I exhaled and closed my eyes to let his emotion wash over me. I'd waited a long time to hear him put our relationship into words, and I let the sentiment fill my pores to the brim.

Opening my eyes, I knew I had to find a way to end the night. Letting the real world in had me feeling a little embarrassed about the events of the evening, but it was Briggs, and he had been so perfect. I leaned forward and kissed his cheek. "Goodnight, Briggs."

When I finally fell asleep, it was to the memories of my evening at the lake with my beautiful boy. Realizing he was no longer a boy, but a man, did things to my insides. Nothing that happened before tonight mattered anymore. The only thing that mattered was that I had the love of the other half of my heart. Maybe we didn't say the L word, but we'd showed it in our actions and emotions.

I loved him.

He loved me.

With that, we could get through anything.

CHAPTER 10
LACIE (AGE 23)
Present Day

"There are no other women. I've only ever been intimate with you."

"My number is the same as yours."

Boy am I glad I ran into this barn. The smile on my face started to get sore. I was in a dream starring none other than Robert Briggs St. Martin, my arch-nemesis and the greatest love of my life. Boy was I in trouble. How could it be that he'd not been with anyone in over four years?

I rolled into his side, letting his warmth seep through him and into me. Even though I was damp, the barn was warm and cozy.

One day I would tell the story of Briggs and Lacie's day after prom, but not right now.

I had not thought about my horrid little prom story in months. Reflecting on it while Briggs softly snored next to me in the barn-yard loft made me realize I wanted him to apologize for that night, the next day, and everything in between. I wanted him to address what had happened the next day and to explain away all the tears I'd shed over that twenty-four-hour period, and then the next four plus years as I fought hard to purge him from my system. The short answer is I didn't.

Observing all the differences in him now made prom seem like a lifetime ago. But it wasn't, and I knew that given a few seconds of searching on the internet, I'd be able to find all the evidence from that night in video format. It was just the cruel, hardened world we lived in now.

The cuff of his T-shirt sleeve revealed a black band around his upper arm. Pushing it up, I could see that he'd inked himself with a tattoo that looked tribal. With his facial stubble and what Kenzie called sex hair, the addition of a little ink made him even sexier somehow. I couldn't stop looking at him. How would I ever stop thinking about him now? Did I even want to fight that battle? He'd clearly changed. Would it be so bad to do the friends with benefits thing? Provided we discussed prom night and the next day and then closed that horror movie of a door.

An idea formed. A bad, incredible, genius idea. I slid my arm out from underneath him and lightly walked in search of some rope. One thing about growing up in Louisiana was that, between the shrimping, crabbing, and farming, everyone learned to tie a few basic knots. Good little Girl Scout that I am, I was no exception to this rule.

BRIGGS

Realizing I'd dozed off had me worried until I saw her climbing over the top of the ladder. "Where'd you go?" I sat up, but she pushed my chest back down and straddled me. A long rope in her hands tickled my bare chest.

"Put your hands up. Wrists together."

She knew what she wanted, and I delighted in the playful look on her face. I did as she commanded and she tied the knot around my wrists using a handcuff knot, which impressed me greatly. She then knotted the ends through the slatted boards that made up the loft. Tricky and tighter than necessary for foreplay, but I wouldn't stop her. If she wanted to play, I would never stop her. I would never stop giving her anything she wanted, even if my well-being were at stake, which it wasn't.

She shimmied down my body, her hands reaching up and

undoing the hardware of my jeans and then tugging them off. My dick was already hard enough to cut glass so when she freed it and slid off my briefs, I was feeling completely exposed to her. Being on display, watching her eyes darken as she perused the skin I was in caused me to harden even more before her eyes.

She was entranced, as was I, as she began to trace the muscles around my abdomen with her finger. The action tickled, but it was her own movement that had all my senses on high alert. Her every touch was a sweet torture that I endured, waiting for the moment I could let go and fit myself fully inside of her.

There were thoughts in the back of my mind to wait until we'd talked through all that needed to be said, but I rationalized those thoughts away. I'd longed for her for four years. Screw it, we could discuss everything after sex.

"You got a tattoo." It was a statement not a question. "A tribal tat? I never pegged you for one who followed a trend." Her fingers raked up and down my chest to my abdomen as she watched my face for every reaction.

"Not tribal. Waves."

"Like sea waves?"

"Lake waves." *Our lake.*

"But they're black."

"Because they're lit by moonlight." *Our moon.*

She leaned over to reach for the camera, and I missed the warmth of her hands and the scratch of her nails on my chest and abs. While she filmed me, I used my hips to push my erection against her core. She fumbled, dropping the camera. "Don't stop," I said.

Something snapped in her, I saw it reflected in her eyes. Suddenly she was standing, taking the blanket with her—and my clothes. "Actually, I do have to get home to help Gramps with the preparations for the grad breakfast." She smiled. "You understand. But I'll see you bright and early tomorrow." She started backing away.

"Lacie Ann Ryan, don't you dare."

"Sleep tight." She waved goodbye over her shoulder.

I was in a right good predicament.
Deservedly so.
I laughed until tears ran from my eyes.
Lacie Ann Ryan had bested me.
And I hadn't even seen it coming.

CHAPTER 11
LACIE (AGE 18)

Lacie (Age 18)

I woke up feeling sore in all the right places.

I was happy. No, I didn't get a prom, but what Briggs gave me was even better.

He invaded my dreams, and I was only too happy to let him.

Flashbacks to images from our lovemaking last night assailed my brain—sweat-slickened abs, flexed biceps that held my hips in place for leverage, rocking thigh muscles, blue eyes that held mine. He was savage in his possession of my body, filling every pore and taking over all my thoughts.

I stretched, remembering the sweet, stinging ache and pressure when our bodies became one. Would it always be this way? I felt a strong urge to be around him, so I put on a pair of shorts and a tank top and hopped on a Landry Estate golf cart.

The wind was hot as it blew across my face, through my hair, not unlike his breath across my skin last night.

When I was eight, I started a journal simply titled *Him*. It chronicled all my interactions with Briggs. Last night, I dug it out and wrote about every detail of his touch, hoping I would always be able to remember. I wanted more, needed more. He was my caffeine in the morning, my bubble bath in the evening, and now that I knew him in that intimate way, I wouldn't be able to think of anything else.

The morning mist rose and huddled somewhere between the ground and the sky, giving a mystery novel feel to the warm morning. Birds chirped and answered each other while grasshoppers jumped against my calves.

When I parked the cart, my stomach did a flip, and I felt like my skin had been set alight by candle flames beneath my skin. Maybe there was something to that whole after sex glow.

The St. Martin house was quiet and cool, causing gooseflesh to rise on my skin. A home full of six kids and two adults, plus one adopted sibling should be full of fluttering activity in the morning, and there's usually was. Walking through the large home, I searched through multiple living areas, the kitchen, the bathroom, but gave up and climbed the stairs to the second floor.

Finding his door closed, I knocked. When he didn't answer, I turned the knob and whispered a *hello* in case he was still sleeping or showering. A smile spread across my face in the hopes that it was the latter. I peeked around the door, my eyes going large and my gut going heavy like it was filled with liquid metal.

Holes, the shape of fists in the wall, had my arms hugging my body. The mirror on his dresser was broken, and the French doors to the terrace were off the hinges and letting in a good bit of heat. My guts seized, but I walked toward the balcony, stepping over broken mirror pieces to get to the threshold. It is then that I spotted Finn on the balcony, holding one of the French doors upright, investigating the damage. The room had all the makings of the aftermath of one of Briggs's episodes.

When Finn saw me, he leaned the door against the jam and locked eyes with me, a frown on his face. Back inside, I took in more of the damage. A wall shelving unit had been broken, and Briggs's plasma screen TV had been cracked.

The destruction was total and more than I thought one man could manage. It looked like one of those bar brawls you see in a movie where one guy throws another guy onto a table, and then it shatters into pieces while more guys join the fight. Broken glass was in every corner of the room. Had our night led him into an episode? I wanted to use denial here, but it sure seemed like being with me had instigated this destruction.

Tears immediately stung my eyes.

"Where is he?"

Finn's throat worked with his desire to speak, his face morphed into a grimace, and esophageal sounds from deep inside his body were expelled, but it wasn't really sounding like it was anything close to speech.

Our eyes locked and then a sound came out that was strained and possibly painful. When he closed his eyes, embarrassment clouded his features, his face turned red. I turned to give him some privacy to regroup. I turned back around moments later when I heard him rummaging through the nightstand. He pulled out some paper and a marker and wrote on a pad.

Hospital.

My hands automatically went up to cup my cheeks as my breathing hitched and my knees threatened to drop my weight. "Hospital?" He wrote some more, but that medium was too slow for my liking. Anxious, I began to pace.

Bayshore.

The behavioral center. "When?"

This morning.

"What happened in here?" I couldn't fathom what could have happened between the moment he left me at the Landry estate and now. While Finn wrote, my brain went into overdrive thinking of scenarios.

Had Reese come over here to settle the score? What about Briggs's father? Could they have had a fight? They could get into some pretty good arguments about Briggs's interest in film instead of the family business. It was a sore spot with Mr. St. Martin that only one son wanted to understudy for the part of head of the company that had provided so much to his family.

You caused this. Can't you see, you two can't be

together. It will kill him. You bring out the worst in each other!!

Finn dropped the pad and went back to working on the doors. My skin stung like I had a bad sunburn. Finn just cut out my heart and left me to bleed out. "Finn?" How could he be so cruel? "Last night we did not bring out the worst in each other."

I couldn't exactly go into our every move from last night, but our relationship was changing, and for the better. I sat on his bed, staring at the horrible scrawl of words glaring up at me from their place on the hardwood floor. Thousands of thoughts poured through me as I struggled to process that Briggs was an inpatient at the behavioral center after he dropped me off at the plantation last night. But he'd been all smiles, cute even. . . a Briggs I've rarely seen.

Finn didn't move from his position at the door, but he did pause in his movement to take in my words. I kept talking; if he wanted to say something, I was sure he wouldn't hold back.

"What actions from last night would have led him to the hospital?" I rubbed my shoulder where one of the bite marks was turning darker in the morning light. Was it wrong that I liked the beast in him? Even now my core pulled at the thought of him rabid and needy like he was last night. It was like he was Adam, and I was the forbidden fruit, a situation that lent itself to all kinds of dark fantasies.

Last night I'd given myself to him and he'd taken. The intimacy connected us, our relationship transformed into possession and surrender, leaving us somewhere mixed up in the middle.

"I just don't get it. It's hard to know what we are to each other." But he'd gone to Bayshore. My brain couldn't process it. Briggs could get impulsive when he was in a good mood. . . driving too fast, drinking too much, and not sleeping.

When the canon ball dropped, he was the opposite of good, which in this case wasn't bad—it was destructive. In one second, he could say something that would undo years of friendship. Worse were the things he'd do, not just to little girls with grape lollipops but to his family, friends, and to girls who had been around over the years.

One time, I came to the property and found one of my classmates in a heap, unable to function, on the St. Martin's back deck. Briggs had done and said horrible things to push her away.

Still, none of what he'd done to others ever added up to the amount of shit he'd pushed onto my plate. For some reason, he seemed to hate me the most. My heart wouldn't make this easy on me, and for that, I hated myself.

My hand brushed across the softness of his pillow while tears fell from my eyes. God, the boy could sleep, I guess that was the price he paid for all that physical DNA perfection . . . it was also how he made up for the lack of sleep during his highs.

The night we shared played on an endless loop in my mind. It seemed so long ago now. "Emotionally he was with me, we'd been connected. He'd been clear."

Finn frowned from the threshold of the balcony. He could lie and call me crazy, but there was no denying the possession in Briggs's stare, the love in his gentle caress of my cheek, the reverence when I gave him everything I had to offer.

Now he was in the hospital, and I couldn't shake the feeling that it was because of what had happened last night, when he was different. He'd given me so many smiles, and those words he'd said had given me the biggest hope I'd ever had, which was something for a girl like me with no dad. He'd said it, *you're half of mine.*

"We are each other's half." It had to mean something. I know it seems naïve to think I could somehow be different to him, but it was all I had in this world, and I'd hold onto something fierce if it meant he'd one day come back to me. Something happened between the moment he left me and this morning. I had no way of knowing what it was, but I was going to find out.

CHAPTER 12
LACIE (AGE 18)

Lacie (Age 18)

It may seem weird, but I couldn't remember ever being in a hospital before. I assume I was born in one, but Mom had never explained my birth, I think because it had been painful for her when my father's family walked out on her. On us.

My grams was taken care of out of our home at the Landry Plantation. Nurses would come every day to take care of her.

I walked through the doors and was a little worried I'd gone to the wrong place. Thick maroon carpet and homey lounge furniture had the place looking more like an upscale hotel than a hospital.

Jazz music lilted through the air, and a lady who greeted me with the enthusiasm of the girl who worked at Dylan's Candy Bar smiled falsely at me from behind a large, curved wooden tower of a desk.

"How may I assist you today?" Her high-pitched, sing-song voice poured an animated surrealism over the setting.

And what was with the "How may I assist you today?" *Today?* Like the whole entire day. This place *was* a freaking cartoon. "I'm here to visit a friend."

"Absolutely. What is your friend's name?"

"Robert St. Martin."

The hesitation in her movement where before she'd been so willing wasn't lost on me. The smile drooped, telling me instantly that she knew him. "And you're his . . ."

"Friend," I quickly answered.

"Girlfriend?" Her lips twisted.

This was a distinction that mattered to her. I swear everywhere we went women, even older women flirted with him. "Yeah. Girlfriend." I gave him my virginity so I felt I could claim it. She passed me a badge and watched with intent as I pinned it to my chest. Like, how old was she anyway? She shouldn't be flirting with teenagers. . .I mean *my boyfriend*. She should not be flirting with my boyfriend. It felt weird to think of Briggs, my childhood nemesis, as my boyfriend.

"I'll show you to the reception area."

I followed behind her swinging ponytail. When she walked her hips swayed way more than necessary. Either she'd sustained an injury, or she'd practiced the walk thinking it could get her something a regular walk could not. Three-inch heels lifted her even taller than her already above-average height. In white Chuck Taylors, I wasn't giving my five-foot-two inches any kind of a boost.

From somewhere in the wall, she opened a door out of nowhere. "Please wait in here. Help yourself to water and refreshment."

I gave a single nod. Wasn't water also considered a refreshment? This place was freaking weird. Floor to ceiling windows did a one-eighty around, looking out over the landscape. The view was breathtaking, all green trees and hills. I guessed the windows were at least twenty feet tall, lending to the feeling that I was in a bubble in the middle of a forest. Unfortunately, the recirculated air made it artificially cold and dank. The ginormous table could seat twenty people.

I should be able to hear the industrial lawnmower right outside the window, but it was dead quiet inside except for Benson Boone singing softly about slowing things down. I rubbed my arms, now laced with chilly bumps, and looked around, all the while recognizing this place was into curves, in its workers and its design. On a marble console table sat large glass water canisters with flavors in the core. One watermelon, one cucumber. Tiny blue foil bags of macadamia nuts sat in a basket next to the water. The basket next to that offered Famous Amos cookies.

"Who told you?"

His voice behind me, barely perceptible, sleepy like he'd just woken up, had me dropping a bag of cookies. I wet my lips and then turned to face him. I couldn't read anything in his beautiful face. Gone was the boy from last night with the kind eyes, the one who'd held me like the greatest treasure he'd ever owned. My eyes welled up with tears. His facial hair was a few centimeters longer, his hair messy, his eyes unblinking and focused on me.

He stood before me in jeans and a white T-shirt. His intense eye contact was getting me more nervous by the second, so I looked away, out through the panes of glass that made life within the hospital akin to being in a fishbowl. "Why are you in here?" I simply asked.

He scoffed, pulling my gaze back on his pained face. "Are you really that stupid? Or are you pretending not to know in the same way you pretend you don't have a father?"

My intestines twisted, causing intense cramping in my gut, but I kept my face pokered. I picked at the bag of cookies I'd rescued from the floor. I hated when he was rude, but I could let him cut me. If it helped him to get better, I could do it. Swallowing the hurt, my throat felt like it was made of hot concrete. "I know why. I want *you* to tell me why."

He shook his head while he walked to the long, curving table. S shapes were a thing here at Bayshore. He huffed out a long breath and pushed his hands through his hair. "I can't control my fucking emotions. But you knew that already, so why the fuck did you come?"

My eyes closed and I lost one tear. I hated shedding my layers in front of him, but only someone carved from stone wouldn't cry for him like this. "Are you here because of me?" I asked from a scratchy throat. Needing something in my hands and cool water down my throat, I grabbed a paper cup, opting for the cucumber water.

Sitting across from him, I took in his demeanor as he leaned back in the chair, watched me, stared at my lips while licking his own. I felt we were in the fairy tale. So many times he'd looked down at me like this and licked his lips, anticipating his snack.

"You'd love that wouldn't you, Lace? You'd love for me to go mentally insane over you, for my love for you to be too much, your beauty to be too pure." He laughed, a maniacal sound that came through too loud and lasted too long.

I couldn't stand the sound, so I covered my ears and shook my head to rid it of his mocking screams. It was sad because to some extent, I thought it was true. Last night changed things; something was brought to life between us. I felt it and knew he did too.

We sat in silence long enough that the sun moved up higher in the sky. Birds left their chirping posts to go do whatever birds did all day.

He picked at his hands.

I couldn't stand the silence any longer and pulled two Tootsie Pops from my small purse. I slid one across the table to him, not knowing if he'd accept it. I even let him have the grape.

To my surprise he unwrapped the sucker and put it in his mouth.

I did the same. We sat in silence again, except for the sounds of sucking on lollipops.

He pulled his from his mouth. "I can't believe you still eat these things."

I shrugged and spoke around my candy. "When they stop being good, I'll stop eating them."

"Still playing with worms too?"

"It was a caterpillar," I shot back with a defensive tone.

"What's the difference?"

There it was . . . his inability to see the difference between something ugly and something beautiful. Could he really not see it? "Worms are ugly, butterflies are beautiful."

"Wrong again," he said. It was my turn to let out a manic chuckle. "Worms eat organic waste matter and then shit it out leaving behind nutrient rich soil without which those butterflies would have no flowers."

His smug look said he thought he'd won this one.

"Butterflies pollinate which helps plants reproduce," I countered.

"Plants need soil to grow."

"Are you seriously arguing soil is more valuable than seed."

"No, you are."

Fine, I could give fuck all about soil or seed or worms or caterpillars. He could have this one.

"Why are you here, Lacie?" His sober voice and zero affect put me on high alert.

"We need to talk about last night."

I thought he'd get mad. Shut me out. Tell me to leave. But he didn't.

"So talk." He simply said with a shrug of his shoulders.

"It was my first time." I blurted it out, best to just get that out in front of us. It was hard to look directly at him, but I would. I might be crumbling to dust on the inside, but I squared my shoulders and kept my chin up.

He gave nothing away and my frustration grew to unhealthy levels. I fisted my hands in my lap to keep them from shaking. "Can you please just . . . just talk about it. How it felt to you. Did you like it?"

The smirk on his lips and twinkle in his eyes alarmed me more than any neutral position he could have given.

"What's not to like." He shrugged. "You have a greedy little cunt that's been begging for my cock ever since you started to bleed." He reached down between his legs and did what I imagined to be, holding his cock in a provocative gesture. My mouth went dry. "I'm the drug you want and need. Guess that makes me a dealer." He shrugged again.

My face melted from the heat and my stiff spine gave way. His vulgar words fizzled to ash in my stomach. I pushed my thoughts down and pressed on. "Tell me about us." I had to know.

"About us?" he repeated, brow cocked.

"Are we together now?"

He leaned back and rocked on the heels of the fancy velvet chair. "How long have you known me?"

I grimaced. "I don't like this question."

"Here's one you might like. Have I ever been exclusive with anyone?"

I turned my head away from him so he couldn't see the fresh tears head on. He'd know though, because he just knew people.

"I'll give you this one. Sex is an innate, animalistic act that doesn't need to be defined. It happened. It was good. That's it."

Forget tears, I was a waterfall. "I HATE YOU!" My voice broke and I was fighting to keep the snot in my nose. Not how I imagined the day after giving the man I loved my virginity.

His lips tightened. "I know, baby. Always say that. Never let me in. Promise me," he said, his voice now full of anguish.

He was serious. But it was too late. He was in deep, lodged places I didn't know how to reach. "I promise I'll always hate you." Here is where I wanted and felt my body gearing up to lunge at him, claws out, breaking skin on contact. But instead, I took a deep, fortifying breath.

I had made a promise to myself, and I guess in a way to Briggs, even though he didn't know about it. I was definitely in my emotional brain now. I forced my thoughts to move to the thinking side of my brain.

It's Briggs, he has problems. He can't communicate correctly when he is in an episode. I thought of his bedroom back at home. Broken glass. Fists through walls. Relationships destroyed. His current mindset had all the earmarks of an episode. I'd vowed to help Briggs communicate through his episodes.

"Briggs?" The silky sweet utterance of his name took that attention of his I'd worked so hard to get but couldn't keep, even though I'd given him everything I had.

"I'm gonna take a walk on the trail if you wanna join me," the woman cooed. Her voice was husky like she was deliberately trying to sound sexy. I turned to see the front desk girl licking her lips and standing with her chest out.

Briggs stood and started to walk away but turned back. "Don't ever come here again," he said, his voice direct and unwavering.

If he'd slapped my face, it would have been less humiliating. At least I could have slapped him back, fought for myself. When I was upset, I wasn't good with words either so all I could do was look blankly at him while Adele sang fiercely:

And the games you'd play, you would always win.

I watched him walk away, an older woman by his side, all kinds of wrong for him. I couldn't feel, numbness had taken hold of my fingers and toes—my body's defense against his brutal assault. It was time to end my connection with Robert Briggs St. Martin.

Like Adele I knew this would be the last time.

I didn't want to, but it had to be done.

I had to purge Briggs from my system.

So how did I do it?

For starters, I didn't return for the last weeks of school. As it turned out, I had a doctor's note. The stress of graduating, coupled with exams, had caused me increased anxiety. Or that's what the doctor had said, and that's what I'd told everyone. I'd also developed a severe case of eczema, which worked to stave off Theo's interrogation regarding my current state, but he remained skeptical.

I didn't even attend graduation. At this stage in the game, were I to look upon his ridiculously handsome face, I'd probably burst into tears.

I felt a small measure of success in that I managed to not go flailing at him like I did the night before, right before I let him do things, so many things, to my body.

Some nice things.

Some not so nice things.

I'd spend the next four years trying to get over him.

What I failed to realize is that it's impossible to live without half your heart.

PART TWO

CHAPTER 13
LACIE (AGE 23)
Present Day

It was five in the morning when I rolled over and heard metal banging on metal somewhere in the distance. I made my way to the bathroom, recalling the visit to the bottom of the pool that had brought Briggs and I together in the barn. Heat bloomed on my head and chest when I recalled how I'd left him. I chuckled, wondering if he'd be on time for his own blessing of the graduates breakfast.

I followed the sounds of metal on metal out to the pavilion. That's where I found Gramps standing among a circle of chairs on the ground that seemed to have fallen from the dolly.

Some chairs were out but had yet to be unfolded and draped in satin and ribbons, the usual attire for event chairs in these parts. Stones slicked with morning dew made a footpath to where Gramps stood in the middle of all the tables, shaking his head, fiddling with ribbons from the satin chair covers. Satin chair covers that were still hanging in their plastic bags like little soldiers on a clothing rack.

"Gramps?" I called as I walked toward him, my stomach sinking as the realization that he hadn't finished the setup that we discussed yesterday dawned. People would be here in less than two hours.

There was no way to get everything up in time. "The chairs aren't setup."

He had on tux pants and cummerbund with a white T-shirt and leather sandals on his feet. "Chairs?" He looked at the ground around us, where a rack of chairs had slid to their death, littering the lawn. "I don't know. They're folded shut." He leaned a chair against his hip and tried to attach a satin cover to it.

Footsteps on the stones had my spine stiffening with tension. I turned to see who was there.

"What's going on?" It was just Theo with bed head hair.

"Oh, sorry. Did we wake you?" Theo's mom was born and bred in Guatemala and believed in the healing properties of a sleeping deck. Only here in Southwest Louisiana there was no such thing, but they did sleep with the windows open.

"The sound of crunching metal worked itself into my dream. I jolted awake from a head-on collision." He looked down at the metal chairs that littered the ground and then lifted a satin cover from the rack. "You're going to need help if you're gonna make it by eight." He unfolded a chair, ripped the plastic from a cover, and tied it onto the seat. "Let's assembly line this."

God bless Theo.

A half hour later, we'd made a good dent in the work. Theo didn't ask questions, just worked efficiently like he'd always done. At some point in all the commotion, Briggs had found me, or rather he found us. . .Theo, me, and Gramps must have looked like a colony of bees working to satisfy the queen.

"What's all this?" he asked as he took in our haphazard team of Theo with the bed head hair, Gramps in half a tux, and me sweating it out still in my pajamas, pulling a piece of damp hair from my forehead.

"We're just putting the finishing touches on the breakfast," I offered. Briggs frowned, and he threw a questioning glance over to Theo who then looked to me. I don't think I imagined Theo's slight shake of the head that worked to shut down Briggs's tendency to ask questions.

"Looks like more than *finishing* touches, but whatever," Briggs grunted under his breath as he walked around.

While I tied off ribbons, I kept a close eye on Briggs. He walked over to the table that had been set up with a fountain for sparkling water and large silver platters for food. At least Gramps had understood that. It worried me that he had become so confused so quickly. He'd forgotten our entire conversation about how to dress and arrange the chairs.

"What's this?" Briggs asked.

While in my own head worrying about Gramps, I'd slipped in my duties of keeping an eye on Briggs. He stood next to a large box, a fist full of shrimp in his right hand, questioning like he always did. I felt confusion crease my forehead. "Is that shrimp?" I walked toward where he stood.

"*Was* shrimp. The ice has melted and the shrimp is room temperature." He fisted more shrimp in his free hand while I grew dizzy at the thought of all that wasted shrimp. Menus stood in stands atop all of the tables. I grabbed one and read *David Gulf Shrimp* front and center like a light shining in the dark. Looking up, Briggs had his phone in hand and was tapping out a number.

"What are you doing?" I asked, more breathlessly than I'd intended.

"I'm getting my cousin Parker to come get this shit and leave some fresh shrimp." Briggs's unwavering look predicated my next move of grabbing his phone and ending the call.

I shook my head. "Please, you can't."

He frowned. "This is inedible."

People were going to find out about Gramps and his waning memory. If word were to get out that he was confused and inept at doing his job, he'd be let go, and we'd be homeless. I handed Briggs his phone and then folded the shrimp box up. "I know we can't serve this. I'll handle it, just please let me deal with it. I don't need your help."

Briggs threw his hands up in a frustrated gesture. "I'm not trying to upset you. Why won't you talk to me? Last night, I thought we were cool with each other. You hiding my clothes and leaving me tied up naked was fair play. I was hoping we could use this time before the breakfast to talk about everything between us."

"Look, I don't want to talk about the shrimp right now." I didn't have time. I had to figure out what to do, and I couldn't think clearly in front of him. Plus, Parker couldn't know about Gramps. He'd no doubt tell his father, who would call Landry Plantation to express that Gramps had signed for the shrimp order. No, Parker David couldn't know what had happened. No one could.

"I don't want to talk about the shrimp either, I want to talk about us. If you'd let me call Parker, he could have a fresh case of shrimp here in twenty minutes."

"No," I said, my pitch higher than normal." I picked up the box of spoiled shrimp. "Look, Briggs, if you call Parker, or if you tell anyone about the shrimp, I'll never speak to you again."

He froze and stared into my eyes. I thought he was going to throw down like he used to. Get angry and destroy anything in his path, but suddenly the lines in his face smoothed and his jaw loosened. He let out a breath and then spoke, "You don't have to threaten me, Lace. I don't know what the hell is going on, but I trust you're handling it. I'd like to help, but I can see that'll have to wait until you can trust me, which is fair. I'll leave you to it but promise you'll seat us together at breakfast."

Okay, now I was almost about to cry. I nodded and with a quivering chin, I held on tight to a box of eighty-degree shrimp if the temperature outside had anything to do with it.

He started to walk away and then stopped. "I know I'm asking a lot from you, and you have no reason to trust me when I tell you I've changed. My hope is one day you'll see the difference in me.

My eyes blurred with moisture. I nodded and whispered a *thank you* to the man who I'd already recognized had changed, even if I wouldn't admit it to myself. New Briggs was empathetic and even kind, something I'd never said about him before. Where he usually caused me problems and pain, here he was trying to solve my problems and help me.

My head was racing at the thought of putting my trust in Briggs.

Thoughts of the day after prom flashed in my mind. His words had crushed me, and I still had not recovered.

***

LACIE

After running around to big box stores all over town, I'd managed to get my hands on a large amount of smoked salmon to supplement the measly ten pounds of shrimp that I found, but it felt better knowing there was actual shrimp on the buffet table, since the menu specified shrimp. Maybe no one would notice it wasn't David Shrimp, though they are well known for their quality and taste in these parts, so it was a gamble.

Gramps was conversing with the kitchen staff, telling them about the addition of the smoked salmon. It was seven-fifteen and time to think about getting ready, but I wouldn't budge until Gramps came back out from the kitchen, and I knew things were okay for now. Luckily, he emerged and was laughing with Mrs. Gulch, Theo's mom, who was the head of the kitchen. She gave me a knowing look, and I knew she had his back for now.

I'd been so busy worrying about the fish that I hadn't looked over at the tables that were perfectly setup and complete with polished silver centerpieces with petite pink and cream roses on a bed of baby's breath. When had they done this? Across the way, I saw Briggs trimming stems to put the finishing touches on the arrangements and Theo rolling the last of the silverware. Walking toward them, Briggs caught my eye and then held his arms out, complete with clippers in hand. "I hope you approve. I think I finally got the hang of it. Doesn't look half bad." He stood back, admiring his work on the flowers.

Moisture flooded my eyes. Without Briggs and Theo's help, none of this would have been possible. Theo came over and stood next to me. "I see a floral shop in his future."

I laughed and took one of each of their hands in mine, "I don't know how to thank you."

"Just see that I'm seated next to you. I've gotta go get showered."

"Same here. See you soon." Theo left but I held on to Briggs's hand.

I didn't want to let go. I felt like I desperately needed the lifeline to get through the next couple of hours. He pulled me into his chest and let me pull from his strength. "I'm glad you aren't mad that I helped."

"Of course not." I closed my eyes and shook my head.

Briggs leaned into me and with a crooked grin, said, "Cause you seemed mad earlier when I was trying to help you."

"Not mad. I have to watch out for Gramps. If it were to get back to the Landry's that he can't handle his duties. . ." I couldn't finish and instead swallowed the lump in my throat.

Briggs rubbed my arms, making circles at my shoulders. "I know." We walked, and Briggs continued to hold me, his arm around my back. "How long have you been covering for him?"

"About a year."

He walked me to my apartment and said he'd see me back at our table. Before he left, he turned back, "Hey Lace?"

"Yeah?"

"Parker discretely dropped off fifty pounds of shrimp for my graduation party. Theo helped me haul it over in the mule. You don't need to worry when you see it. No one will ever know."

I watched him jog away, wondering when he'd become a man. Where was the boy who couldn't speak for being so eaten up with anger that he couldn't communicate, let alone be aware of the needs of others? It was all too much, too soon for me. I couldn't process this new Briggs.

I just kept thinking the old Brigg's would rear his ugly head in the near future. Maybe Briggs had found a way to suppress his demons even better than before but the one thing I knew about demons was you could not outrun them no matter how hard you tried. Eventually, old Briggs would emerge and unlike last time, this time I might not survive him.

Survival was hard. Compartmentalizing ideas made surviving

easier. In my head I created a box for new Briggs, making sure to place this new box away from the box that held old Briggs. I put Gramps in another box, and my grad school letter and decision in yet another. While I was at it, I decided Finn deserved his own box, and so did Steve LeBlanc.

I took a deep breath and felt the morning dew and haze settle on my skin. With any luck, I'd be dressed and seated at the breakfast by five to eight. With even more luck, no one would miss the exotic tropical fruit mix that was replaced by balls of watermelon, kiwi, and pineapple chunks. Yet another thing Gramps had left out in the heat.

***

LACIE

I showered, did some semblance of hair and makeup, and dressed in a sea foam green wrap dress with brown leather wedge sandals. When I made it back, it was five *after* eight, and the pastor was up on the outdoor stage, talking about child rearing and what an important job it was. My eyes locked on Briggs and he made an almost imperceptible grimace, but I saw it. His jaw tensed and his body stiffened. These were the little movements that made me more uncomfortable than the large grins he'd given me in the barn. I'd been interpreting them since I was five and knew what they meant. To that end, I'd been thrown off kilter by his new stuff.

Walking toward the table I saw Parker, Paisley, Theo, Tex, Kenzie, empty chair, Briggs, and Finn. I took in Briggs's attire of black dress slacks and white dress shirt with the sleeves rolled tightly up to above the elbow. His bronze skin glowed under the morning outdoor light, and I swear to God above he had that dang Super 8 camera rolling and focused right on me.

I took a shallow breath and pulled out the empty chair. The wind decided to tease me with Briggs's clean mint scent mixed with a masculinity that was all him. Maybe I couldn't do casual with him. I was a hundred ways of turned on right now just from his smell.

On my right Kenzie leaned over and whispered, "You're in big trouble."

I locked eyes with her. I knew I had plenty to worry about: had she found out I had yet to return my grad school acceptance letter? Had people found out about Gramps? Did Briggs have a girlfriend? Okay, that last one came out of nowhere. And I what did I care if he had a girlfriend or not because I was just his childhood friend.

My number is the same as yours.

I looked over to the family table right next to ours. Mom and Mr. St. Martin were talking about something that required a visual as Mr. St. Martin was drawing on a napkin. Kenzie's parents were smiling and focused on the stage. Moving my eyes from table to table, I recognized almost everyone.

That was the thing about Whiskey Cove, even acquaintances were like family. These people kind of took care of each other. I knew that Mrs. Gulch cooked for anyone who had suffered a loss or who had barely sprained a finger. My mother, an avid gardener and seamstress, offered her ragtag group of services to monetarily challenged brides all over town. Tray, the town mechanic, had been known to offer free services to distressed women and grandmothers. And Mr. St. Martin, well, he took the cake.

When I was five, we lost our home. The only thing left were the stilts where the home had sat. It was bad enough that we'd lost everything, but mom was still paying on the home. With nowhere to live, and no way to pay for a new place, we had to move in with Gramps.

After Hurricane Alex, Mr. St. Martin took on the insurance companies, even hired his own team of attorneys. He'd even rebuilt our home for free. Scared, living on the coast as we were after experiencing three hurricanes, we put the beautifully redone home up for sale, and it sold quickly. Mom put the money into the bank. She'd used a lot of that money to put me through undergrad.

Kenzie passed me her phone with a preloaded video. I hit play and all of the events of last night's pool fight came screaming back. The angry words spoken between us, our feet squared off in stances that communicated we were ready to fight, the push/pull of our exchange, and then Briggs picking me up and tossing me in the pool. The slap, my escape, his following close on my heels.

It wasn't just the video but the comments from people I now knew were gossiping about me, people who I thought were my friends, or at least positive acquaintances.

Briggs's back and they've picked up right where they left off. #hatetoloveyou

No boobs this time. #boobocalypse

Good for her, I would have brought him to his knees. #3totheknees #eyesthroatballs

She's not even that pretty. #fuglybitch

Nausea settled in my stomach. All of it was too much and suddenly I hated this small town very much. I longed to run off to New York City where no one would know me, and if they did, they wouldn't care.

I passed the phone back to Kenzie. I'd been in this position before when the whole prom fiasco had been uploaded to social media, and along with it, my boobs.

But this Briggs wasn't the Briggs from prom. I watched in awe as he seemed to know just what to do while in contrast I was dying inside and just wanted to run into my bedroom and pull the comforter over my head.

Once the prayer ended, we made our way through the buffet line. The shrimp was the star of the show, with choruses of *David shrimp is the only reason I got out of bed* and *This is the best Gulf shrimp money can buy*.

A few attendees made note of the not-so-exotic tropical fruit options, but when I made eye contact with Mrs. Gulch, she pushed my Costco fruit, and I thanked my stars she was just as intimidating as she was. Maybe there'd been a reason for that all along, maybe it was to help out my little family, to protect my Gramps. I mouthed a *thank you* to her, and she winked. *Winked!* If I could have known on that first week at arriving on the Landry Plantation that Mrs. Gulch would have been my ride-or-die, I would not have been so afraid of her in my youth.

Grandfather crisis averted, my ears were clear to focus on the gossip going around the tents that housed the tables. People had seen the video and the fact that I was seated next to Briggs was baffling to the masses. Not only that, but several people brought up the prom video.

"I remember that. Her boobs all over social media. God, could you even imagine."

"She's got that voodoo blood in her that drives the men crazy, best to stay away from that one."

"I heard she's been with five of the St. Martin brothers."

I chuckled. Only five? I'd had four years to blunt my skin against this bullshit, but I still couldn't understand what made people talk about other people who were in the same room with them. Granted, we were outdoors, but I'd had years of practice at pretending I didn't have ears. It was growing old, and I was tired.

When I took my seat at the table, Briggs wasn't far behind me. "Rumor mill is going strong."

"Yay for us." I took a huge gulp of tepid water and contemplated how I'd ended up on social media again, and in a not so great light again. I turned to look at Briggs.

He lifted his glass. "Hey, fuck'em all."

I laughed, if only I had his ability to not care about anything. Or anyone. To be honest, I didn't want to fuck them all. These people were my friends and family; plus the community members I'd grown up with.

I wanted them to place themselves in my shoes and understand what I needed from them. I needed to figure out a way for my body to see Briggs as a road sign that read: *Slow down, dangerous conditions ahead.* I needed to find a way to stay away from him, but here I was seated right next to him, our shoulders and thighs brushing against each other.

In the distance, the pastor of the local Baptist church droned on about communities supporting the futures of its young people. Normally, I would have followed along, but I was so exhausted from helping Gramps and my unbelievably weak moment with Briggs that I could barely keep my eyes open.

I opened the internet tab on my phone that had the application for a coffee bar manager opened. I'd been working on finishing the application when the cute guy Briggs had pulled me away from at the bonfire had asked to sit next to me.

I thought the coffee bar manager would be a good shift for me, not that I knew anything about managing a coffee bar or even drank coffee, but it was a new addition inside Acadian Kitchen, and it appealed to me since I would be able to continue on at the store in some form. It's just now that Gramp's memory was affecting his job, I needed to have a plan B for our living situation. To move required money that we definitely didn't have. The management position came with a large raise.

I groaned. It was that time in the program for show and tell of the graduates. I loathed myself in pictures, especially from my youth. I was in my caterpillar stage. Theo was first to present his slide show. Sure enough, he had all the pictures of me in denim overalls, with dirt on my face, black feet from my refusal to wear shoes, and a lot of grape lollipops.

"To know Lacie, is to laugh because if she is around, she is infectious. Her light shines bright, her insight can be unnerving, but above all she is the best friend a guy could ask for. Please, raise your glass to Lacie. I love you Beans."

The show and tells continued until it was Finn's turn at the podium. He'd asked me to show him how to use text-to-speech on his computer. I'd helped him of course, but he was not happy with the quality of output the computer offered. The voice didn't sound real he had said. I suggested a three-hundred-dollar program to him that had many real voices to choose from. He'd said he didn't want to get it because it would get my hopes up. After the presentation, he didn't plan on speaking in public ever again.

It just wasn't true. He didn't know if he would desire to speak again or not. What about wedding vows? Emergencies? 911 calls? Let's hope he never had to use that feature on his phone since he wouldn't set up any accessibility features.

When Finn finished his presentation, a girl who had been a year ahead of me in school started to clink her butter knife against the glass at her table setting. *Clink, clink, clink.* "Speech, speech."

What the actual eff. I swung my head around to find Finn. He stood at the podium. All color drained from his face. People joined the little witch in courses of requests for Finn to make a speech. I jumped up and dashed to the podium. I wasn't going to speak for him, but I did open a blank document and started to type . . .

Finn understood as he was a quick study of pretty much everything. He punched the microphone button, and the message was spoken through the speakers in a robotic computer voice.

THE PRESENTATION IS OVER.

"*Encore*," the little witch shouted, getting the crowd all riled up and looking to Finn for more words.

I watched his throat work, if from reflex or because Finn was actually trying to speak, I didn't know. He wouldn't look at me, but I was trying to mouth words to him, to let him know that I would speak.

Finn has pride. A lot of it. He doesn't accept help very well, so I stood back and waited with the rest of the patrons as he played the final slide and message about Briggs yet again.

BRIGGS HAS WORKED EXTREMELY HARD TO BECOME THE MAN HE IS TODAY. HIS FRIENDS AND FAMILY ARE PROUD THAT HE HAS COME HOME AND DECIDED TO PURSUE HIS MASTER'S DEGREE IN VIDEO EDITING FROM LOUISIANA STATE UNIVERSITY. PLEASE JOIN ME IN A ROUND OF APPLAUSE FOR ALL HE HAS ACCOMPLISHED.

Before the crowd had finished clapping, Finn shut his laptop and walked off the podium, heading toward the inside of the building. I followed, calling after him, but he wouldn't stop.

I ran to catch up to him, tugging on his arm to get him to slow down.

Finn stopped and looked me in the eye, his face hardened. "Are you okay?"

Holding the computer, he threw a hand up and shrugged while staring at me. With jerky movements he opened the laptop and typed with his index finger.

I CAN'T SPEAK.

THE PEOPLE WHO KNOW I CAN'T SPEAK KEEP ASKING ME TO SPEAK.

I'M FRUSTRATED, MAD, AND WANT TO BE LEFT ALONE.

Once the computer finished the lines, Finn slammed it shut and walked on through the building and out the front door. I didn't try to go after him. When he was like this, nothing could move him. Presenting my research to him about his options would need to wait until he was open-minded and calm. I would wait.

Back outside, the pastor encouraged the congregation to swing by the graduate tables and wish us well. Slowly, people trickled by. Cordelia brought coupons for free tarot card readings at her shop and placed a sage wand in front of me, along with some literature about how to cleanse your aura. Who knows, it may be worth a shot I told her.

The last time I'd been into her shop I was twelve and on the prowl for a magic wand, which I found and used for a good solid two years before turning my sights onto the world of vampires. With it's purple and olive-green lights, ornate wood designs, and boxes of multiple wands of different shapes and sizes, Cordelia's shop was straight out of *Diagonally*. Mom went into the shop on the regular to purchase essential oils and herbs.

After Cordelia had made her rounds, Mr. St. Martin swung around in his chair to face us. "Maybe you two can shed some light on this. I received this video from Coach Boudreaux."

Great, the video had made it around to my old high school volleyball coach.

"It's nothing, Pops, Lace was just teaching me a lesson." He took my hand in his, locking eyes with me. "I didn't handle my emotions well, and she let me know."

Swoon.

Mr. St. Martin put his phone away while smiling at me. "Good girl, Lacie, you give him hell."

Briggs rubbed circles into my palm, leaving tingles in his wake.

"Um, what are you doing?" I asked, if a little breathless.

Briggs cocked his head at me like I wasn't getting the right answer on a math problem. "I'm diffusing a bomb."

Kenzie leaned in, whispering, "Oh wow, did I mention, when they get all *perfect* it's damn near impossible to keep sex and emotion in separate parts of your brain."

I eyed her coolly. "You're the worst friend in the world." She had the audacity to laugh.

More people passed us by, dropping gift cards and packages on the table. It felt like one giant birthday party shared with friends and family, which wasn't a bad thing. That is, until Professor Beauregard stopped by. Every time someone mentioned the video, Briggs defused another bomb.

This situation was so much different than the last time I'd ended up on social media due to an argument that included Briggs. This time Briggs was here, fighting in the trenches, supporting me and slowing the gossip train. Last time, I had been alone and humiliated.

It may seem a bit extreme, but at eighteen, giving yourself to the boy you loved who the next day turned a complete one-eighty while your video, complete with breasts out, was making rounds all over town was a lot for a teen to process.

"Lacie Ryan, I'm glad I got the chance to speak with you today." I nodded and felt my lips spread into a tight smile. "If there is anything I can do to encourage you to turn in your acceptance letter for the graduate SLP program, let me know. The deadline is fast approaching, and I wouldn't want you to miss out due to an unanswered question."

Shit. Shit. Shit. I nodded and tried to say thanks, but it came out whispered and the only one who would be able to hear it would have been Trusty since my vocal cords were so tight I was speaking in frequencies too high for the human ear to discern.

"I knew you hadn't turned in that letter." Kenzie's voice was loud and not surprisingly rough as her eyes filled with tears. She stood, pulling Tex with her. "You lied to me."

"Hey Lacie," Tex frowned looking all kinds of uncomfortable as he held Kenzie close to his side, rubbing her back in comfort.

I called her name, but the sounds of my voice met their retreating back, Tex looking back just as lost as I felt.

My mom took Kenzie's empty chair. "Lacie, what's going on? Have you not mailed your acceptance letter?" She swallowed back the hurt I knew was crawling up her throat. "We celebrated that night you told us you had accepted. Your grandfather treated you to Willie's so you could get your favorite fried popcorn shrimp."

Shit. Frustrated I squirmed in my chair all too aware of Briggs's eyes taking in the secrets that my mother spilled. He sat with a leisurely lean, watching me with x-ray eyes that saw everything. "Yeah, Mom, not here, okay?"

"Okay, honey, you've got me really worried."

Double shit. A tear fell down her careworn face as she stood and walked back to her table. I exhaled a frustrated sigh, looking over at Briggs with narrowed eyes.

"What?" he asked, laying a butter knife across his plate.

"Aren't you going to ask me why I lied?"

"You didn't lie to me. We haven't talked, despite me wanting to sit and have a discussion with you." He put his hand across his chest. "If I may, you seem to be avoiding me." He wiped his mouth with the cloth napkin. Why was that move so sexy? "If I could get penciled into your busy schedule, that'd be great."

Maybe I should just leave. And I would have, but at that moment, Mrs. Frannie drifted into the table area, holding the hand of her thirty-year-old son who looked ancient. He looked so frail I gasped, my breath catching in my throat while I attempted to calculate when I had last seen Steve. It was around Valentine's Day. I remembered because after I'd demonstrated to him how the personal voice amplification system worked, he jokingly said, "What every woman wants for Valentine's Day, a guy with a mechanical voice." He'd held the contraption in his thumb and index finger as he spoke through the cheap speaker. But it had done the job. His voice was loud enough to be heard, and he didn't have to exert much energy. It wasn't working now. His lips moved, everyone watched him, but no one could hear what he had to say.

Steve had been thin back in February, but now he was frail and looking like a strong wind could knock him over as unsteady as he was.

I had helped him, or tried, with the amplification of his voice when the clinic he went to had nothing to offer him. I'd researched that eventually he'd need an expensive augmentative communication system. But Steve had no insurance and, given his age of thirty years, relied on Medicaid disability that paid diddly squat for conditions that were terminal.

Amyotrophic Lateral Sclerosis, I'd learned in my undergrad neuro course, was a progressive, degenerative disease. The prognosis for Steve wasn't good.

I watched Steve as his lips moved, and he chuckled silently like he'd said something funny. His eyes moved around from person to person waiting for a reaction, but there was none because no one had heard him.

Knowing Steve, what he had said was hilarious and on point for the occasion. When he could still talk, he was usually the funniest guy in the room. Even one of the most handsome guys in the room. I recalled watching him with his wife when I was younger; she was a looker too. I always felt a fissure of hope for myself, watching how easily they had perfected life.

And then one disease, three little letters, took all of it away.

Steve was a roughneck. He owned his own drilling rig that companies would contract. He drilled out in the Gulf of Mexico. It was brawny work and the guys who did it looked like the guy on the paper towel rolls. But it was hard, backbreaking work, the kind of work left for those guys who are rebellious, don't go to college, and don't grow up with a privileged spoon in their mouths, according to what my father had said to my mother.

I watched Briggs carry on a conversation with Steve. Briggs had let Steve put the amplification system right on his ear. Briggs was saying something about the free point and torque, and as I leaned in to hear more, I wasn't prepared for Steve to tell Briggs, "You were the best damn floor hand I've ever had. A natural. You want more work, you let my buddy Tim know."

When had Briggs worked as a roughneck? I locked eyes with

him, his lips spread in an expression like the cat that ate the canary, only I was the canary, and he was an overly large smug cat, a cheetah really. "You have secrets," I said.

"That I do." He lifted his iced tea and took a sip before placing it back on the table. "Wanna tell me why you haven't accepted your spot in the program?"

Roughneck work was dangerous, and the thought of Briggs out on a Gulf drilling platform had my jaw tensing. I took a sip of water, being deliberately slow, trying to think of something to say. "I have secrets too, Briggs." If he'd wanted to know, he should have been here. We were nothing to each other, just acquaintances who had good sex. Unbelievable sex. Mind-blowing sex.

Only problem was, it wasn't just once now. I'd given myself to him four years ago, and last night I took from him what I'd needed. I felt something stir at my core. I needed him again now. Everything was just so messed up. Briggs was back and I was as confused as ever. Gramps was not going to be able to work much longer. Steve's disease was progressing rapidly. Kenzie was pissed at me.

I'd opened an old high school wound and poured salt on it. But sex with Briggs was good. It was the kind of sex that made you forget everything except what was going on in the moment. Briggs's ability to obsess over things worked in his favor when he was completely devoted to consuming me. He was a *ladies first* man in bed.

Sex connected us, in more ways than one. Recalling the feel of him moving inside me had my old dusty dried out heart sparking and trying to come back to life. I watched him with the breakfast patrons, animated and happy as he worked the crowd and filmed with his Super 8. It left me wondering what happened to him and at what point in whatever happened had he worked on Steve's oil rig?

I sat and let people buzz around us, knowing I wasn't interacting and should start so I didn't seem unappreciative. With so many things out of order and exacerbated by this breakfast, I couldn't think straight and needed a breather.

I excused myself to walk inside the inn and use the restroom when it was really just to take a break from all the hullabaloo masquerading as a potty run. That's when I saw Steve in the lobby with his two girls, one in kindergarten and one not yet in school. A handful. They ran around a large cherrywood entry table, playing chase. Steve's body and face displayed a stern expression while his lips moved, but in all of their excitement, the girls couldn't hear him. It was hard to hear him in a quiet background when he was standing right next to you. The vase of tulips on the table teeter-tottered before crashing to the floor.

I ran over. The girls stood frozen in place, eyes as large as red-hot fireball candies. Steve tried to shout some words to the receptionist, but all that could be heard were the background sounds in the room.

I put my hand on his shoulder. "It's okay. Let me get Mrs. Gulch. Take the girls outside. Really, it's fine." He thanked me as a look of relief washed over his face.

Within minutes, a fresh vase was on the table and the glass and water had been wiped up. Penny, Steve's wife emerged from the bathroom looking more haggard than I'd remembered. She'd been one of those debutantes, her family big in the carnival atmosphere, Krewe of Athenians. A princess, she is Krewe royalty. She looked around, searching for her family, no doubt. "Steve took the girls outside. They were getting a little rambunctious."

"Oh God, what did they do?"

"It wasn't a big deal, just knocked over some tulips. Mrs. Gulch set it back to rights within minutes."

"Oh no, please give her my apologies."

I nodded.

Her lips pressed tightly together, the grimace on her face had me swallowing a lump of emotion. "It's the most undignified disease." Absolutely, it was. Penny needed someone to talk to and I wondered if there were any support groups in the area.

"You know he can't talk, and he was always such a talker." A smile lit up her face, her eyes glazed over in memory. "He types into the laptop, and it talks, but the girls are so hyper most of the time he can't get them to stop and wait or listen."

I nodded my agreement with her words. Typing everything you

wanted to say was cumbersome. I knew of some other options that used symbol-supported communication that could be exchanged much quicker than typed words delivered text to speech. Only thing was, those devices were in the thousands and I knew the budget was tight for the LeBlancs. Penny's parents had bought a wheelchair and Mrs. Frannie a motorized bed, but they didn't have ten grand to blow on a speech device.

"Doctor said the next thing to go may be the swallow muscles." She let out a harsh chuckle. "Can you believe it? I didn't even know there were so many muscles for swallowing food."

I wanted to do more for them. "If you need a babysitter or just a break, let me know. Steve has my number from when we texted about the voice amp system. I don't mind coming over to spend time with the girls or with Steve."

Penny slumped forward a little and started to cry, though it wasn't my intention to upset her. "Penny?"

"I'm sorry." She covered her mouth with the fingers of her right hand. "It's been hard, and I feel shame for wanting to just run away from it all." She paused and took a breath. "A break would be nice."

"Done. Let me know when is best for you."

We left things open, with the commitment that I'd come sometime in the next week to sit with the girls and with Steve so he and I could talk about options for communication. Only I didn't know what the options were. I decided then and there that I would submit my letter, securing my spot in graduate school for speech-language pathology.

CHAPTER 14
LACIE

Lacie

After the Blessing of the Graduate's fiasco of a breakfast, I walked to the apartment, ignoring Briggs's request to sit out at the lake and talk. I was bone-deep exhausted, and I had unanswered questions to get all kinds of obsessed over, and since I'd yet to go through that process, I couldn't discuss Briggs and me today.

The one person I couldn't avoid was my mother. I had enough time to shower and get into yoga pants and a Myley Cyrus Bangerz tour T-shirt before my mom was in my room, picking up clothes from the floor and putting them in the basket under her arm. "I saw the video from the bonfire. You and Briggs haven't grown much in the four years you spent apart." She picked up the panties I had on from last night and put them into the basket. I was one shallow breath away from fainting to the floor dead.

I stood in front of the vanity in my bedroom and combed through my wet hair, wondering if I was old enough to tell my mom I didn't want to discuss anything about last night. "I know. . .but we are different, last night notwithstanding."

"You can't get derailed right now, mais cher, you've got too much going for you." Did she think I didn't know that? Besides going to school, I'd have to carry this family and figure out a way to help Steve and Finn with their communication, and there was the added bonus of Gramp's cognition that something would need to be done about.

If I decided not to go to school, I wouldn't be able to help Steve and fulfill the promise I'd made to Penny and Steve. Plus, Kenzie would kill me if I didn't attend grad school with her. I also wouldn't be able to help Gramps and Finn and Steve without access to the knowledge I'd pick up at school and from training with therapists. But not going to grad school meant I could work more and save more and move us all into a house so that Gramps could retire.

Mom put the laundry basket down and was now onto making my bed, which I thought a waste since I was about to sleep for ten hours straight. "Quitting him almost undid you. You won't be afforded so much time to recover from him the second time around."

Wow, right to the gut. I could say this for my mom . . . she didn't believe in beating around the bush. "I know, Mom. That's why I'm not going to get involved with him."

She harrumphed and fluffed my pillow before placing it at the head of the bed. "Make sure he stands where you stand, that he walks with you, not behind, or in front, but beside you."

Braiding my hair, I turned to her and gave her my best bug-eyed expression. "Mom, I don't know what that means, but I have to get some sleep." I walked over and let my knee rest on the bed.

"Not until you come clean about your acceptance letter."

Oh, that. *Shit*. I looked down, shamed for lying to my mother about something that meant so much to her. "Mom, I . . . I'm sorry I lied it's just that I'm worried I won't pass the fifty-percent mark, and I know you and Gramps don't have the money to waste on someone who might not make it. I haven't been able to help Briggs, Finn, or Steve communicate any better," *and now Gramps can't organize his thoughts*, "and I'm scared and . . ." I took a deep, quick breath and squeezed my eyes shut, willing back tears.

Mom's hand lifted my chin. "Honey, no one will fault you for trying. Money spent on you for anything is never a waste, no matter what happens." She kissed my forehead. "Giving you this money is more about showing how much we love and support you. You taking the money allows me and your grandfather to love you through our actions, not just our words and affection." She squeezed my arm. "You're going to give yourself high blood pressure worrying about all that. Briggs, Finn, and Steve's problems with speech aren't your utter responsibility. Finn made his own decisions, and Steve's prognosis isn't good; that's hardly your fault, honey. You need to find the will to go a bit easier on yourself. Promise me."

I nodded. "Okay, Mom." After seeing Steve, there was no way I wasn't going to send in my acceptance letter. I just needed to make sure I didn't give anyone false hope. I wanted to help him have as much quality of life as possible toward the end of his life. God, were twenty-two-year-olds supposed to be carrying this much mental and emotional weight? It felt heavy.

"Get some sleep." She picked up the laundry basket and turned off my light. "And you misunderstand me about Briggs. I'm not saying ignore your destiny. He's your guiding light, and you're his. I'm suggesting the two of you need to figure out how to walk together through this life. To figure it out, you'll need to spend time around each other, existing in harmony."

"Okay, Mom." Her words were crazy. She could sometimes be too much into the Four Noble Truths, but I agreed with her that we needed to figure out how to be around each other without fighting since he was going to be attending the same school.

I didn't get the chance to tell her about Gramps.

Before walking out of my room she turned, looking back, "you're wrong about Briggs, you know. He has changed. His communication is light years better than it was when he left."

His communication is all better.

He only got better once he left me.

***

LACIE

When I woke up it was five o'clock in the evening. I'd been asleep for seven hours. As the first threads of alertness hit my brain, memories of Kenzie's disappointed face hit me. Steve's emaciated body made a connection somewhere inside, along with Finn and Briggs and the unmailed letter. God, I wish I was one of those care-free people who just didn't care about anything.

I reached for my cell phone and checked to see if there were any missed texts, but there wasn't.

First, I sent Kenzie a gif of the cutest cat I could find who had an apologetic look on its face. Then I group texted with Theo and Kenzie:

> Me to Theo/Kenzie: I'm sorry, I'm a shit friend.

> Kenzie: Not going to disagree with you.

Ugh, okay that hurt.

> Theo: You should know, I'm the one who found Mr. Sex on a Stick in the barn.

> Me to Theo/Kenzie: God

> Theo: Yes, he is

> Kenzie: WHAT!?! I need deets! TALK TO ME. I'm still mad at you tho

> Theo: Hey now make that ME into an US.

> Me to Theo/Kenzie: Yes

> Me to Theo/Kenzie: 🤍🤍🤍🤍🤍🤍🤍🤍🤍

I sent ten hearts in alternating pink and green, Kenzie's favorite color combo.

> Kenzie: Common Grounds. 6:00.

> Me to Theo/Kenzie: I love you guys.

> Kenzie: You're lucky I love you too.

> Theo: 😊

At least she was willing to hear me out about the unmailed letter.

Anyone who has never made a mistake has never tried anything new. The quote by Einstein was my new life motto. I wouldn't get anywhere without taking the first step, which meant I had to mail in my acceptance letter.

> Briggs: Hi

> Me: Hey

> Briggs: Are you gonna ever talk to me again?

> Me: Yes

> Briggs: I want to tell you something, but I'm afraid you'll freak out

> Me: Wow, that really doesn't make me want to talk to you

> Briggs: I want to say it in person, but you won't let me

> Me: There is a lot going on. I'm sorry

> Briggs: After last night I just want you to know . . . I have always loved you.

> Me: You mean as a friend.

> Briggs: Friend, lover, life companion, and everything in between.

The bottom fell out from under me, and I had to lie back on the bed. My body was shaking. I read his last text five times and still couldn't write a response. How could he do this to me now when I needed to focus on school, work, Gramps, Steve, and Finn?

> Briggs: You freaked out, didn't you?

> Me: No. I'm processing. It's going to take a while for me to respond

> My heart thumped bass lines in my ears.

> Briggs: How long?

> Me: IDK

My hands shook as I typed.

> Briggs: Why? You either feel the same or you don't. What's there to think about?

> Me: I'm just doubting a lot right now

Like can I even trust my body's reaction to his words? Or just frigging trust him. Last time I did, I lost my favorite dress, my dignity, and my virginity.

> Briggs: I'm going to make you feel it so deep you'll never doubt it

Gah . . . WTAF was going on? I'd waited for him for four years. Was he really doing this now. Now, when I have no time for it. Now, when I'm not even sure I want to open that door.

My mother's words from earlier came screaming back in my head: *Quitting him almost undid you.*

It didn't almost undo me, I was flayed.

I put on jean shorts and left on my Miley Cyrus because I had a mood going, and it was definitely *Wrecking Ball.*

Because Mom was a savant at all things gardening and flowers, we kept tons of vases and baskets around for her hobby of making arrangements. Our apartment might be small, but there was a fresh flower arrangement on all flat surfaces. The cheeriness was boundless, and it wouldn't be home without those smiling flowers.

On my way out of the apartment, I'd picked out two square glass vases from Mom's stash. I then stopped at Acadian Kitchen and purchased some delicate green pompom button flowers, sunflowers, green hypericum berries, and green trachelium to surround the sunflowers. I sat at a bistro table on the front patio of Common Grounds. This place was located on the boardwalk just a few stores down from Acadian Kitchen. I sat and used the wait time to arrange the flora in the clear cube vases—one for Kenzie and one for Theo—accented by curly willow. The sunflower bouquet shined bright and fresh among the luscious greens. If this didn't say friendship, I didn't know what did.

Kenzie walked up to a free chair at my table but didn't sit quite yet. "I'm on my lunch break. I want details and I want em' fast." She was texting on her phone. "Also, Theo's parking." It was then that her eyes landed on the flower arrangements. "Wow, they've really upped the tablescapes in this place." She plopped her purse down on the table and then pulled her chair out to sit.

"I made that for you," I told her.

She folded her hands in front of her. "Beans, are you okay? I sense something is going on with you. Why are you not talking to me?" She pulled the flowers closer and smelled. "These are beautiful. Sunflowers are my favorite."

"I know. Well, I really don't want to talk about Briggs. I haven't even had time to think about everything that's happened with him. He wanted to meet, but I told him I had a bad headache, well I did have one earlier, but I told him that so I could stay in tonight and think about it all. That was before I got your text. And the truth is my head feels fine now, but my heart is breaking."

"Why is your heart breaking? Are you not back together?" Her eyes held mine in question.

Back together. There was no previous togetherness. "Not really."

Theo showed up looking all kinds of hot in white jean shorts and a purple tank top. He pulled out a chair next to me. "Damn girl, I thought you'd be all smiles after your sexy barn time with Mr. *Sex*Martin."

"Uh." I put my head in my palm. "You've got to stop calling him that."

Theo turned the other flower vase this way and that. "Are these for me?" he asked placing his hand over his heart. I nodded. He gasped, "you shouldn't have, but I'm so glad you did."

"Let's circle back to you and Briggs having sex in the barn." Kenzie pointed a finger at me. "Right now, I'd like to hear why you lied to your best friends."

I talked while Kenzie and Theo ordered from the QR code menu. I told them all of the things I'd said to my mom about how worried I was that I'd fail since I'd failed at helping my friends and family. I told them about the money from Mom and Gramps and how I felt nervous that I'd waste it if I were to flunk out. Then I told them about Gramps, though I think Theo had figured out Gramps was getting dementia.

The drinks were delivered, and Theo passed me a green tea Frappuccino. "Elixer of the gods." He'd ordered a drip for himself.

Kenzie sipped her drink and then made a dissatisfied face. "Excuse me, no, this isn't what I ordered." She rolled her tongue. "Yuck, what is that? Blueberry?"

"Blueberry crumble latte."

"No. I had the dry cappuccino with an extra espresso shot."

"Right, sorry," the server said.

Kenzie nodded once, looking smug as an all-star quarterback. I envied her confidence.

"You're awfully confident she won't spit in your drink," Theo teased.

"Nah, Amanda knows I'm a good tipper." Her hand came down on my forearm. "Look, just like that blueberry crumble abomination," she pointed toward the server and retreating tray, "there will be mistakes. In fact, wasn't it Madonna who said if you weren't making them, you weren't doing anything?

"I believe that was Einstein." Theo pulled four packets of sugar in the raw from the caddy on the center of the table. "But I get what you mean."

"No. It definitely wasn't Einstein," Kenzie retorted.

I chuckled at how confident Kenzie could be even when she was wrong. "Of course, I know I can make a mistake. I am just wondering how I can look after my grandfather, Finn, and Steve." And manage whatever this thing was between me and Briggs.

Kenzie waved her hand in the air. "My entire nursing program is endless hours at the hospital. I'll help you keep an eye on Steve."

"But you'll be too busy to leave your own caseload," I answered, watching Theo and Kenzie share a knowing look. "What's that look?"

Theo's hand came down over mine. "Honey, Steve went inpatient today."

I froze. "Inpatient." My thoughts started racing as to the many possibilities *going inpatient* could mean. "Is he . . ." I couldn't finish the sentence.

"He should be okay," Kenzie offered. "Frannie said he was having trouble swallowing."

And he would continue to have trouble swallowing, breathing, and speaking as those muscles further weakened.

"They want to keep him for a while to run tests on some other stuff," Theo said.

My two best friends watched me; the look of compassion on both their faces made me want to cry. They were here for me after I'd lied. No matter what I did to them, I knew these two selfless creatures would be here for me. That knowledge, plus the updated news about Steve, solidified my decision. "I really am sorry I lied to both of you. I should have just come to you. Forgive me for being stupid and an all-around bad friend. I'm going to turn in my acceptance letter."

"That's the girl we know and love. And while we are on this subject of lies by omission, I happen to know from my uncle that a certain someone is going to be promoted to coffee bar manager. Yet another thing you forgot to tell me."

I smiled as relief stirred in my chest. "Really? I got the job?"

"You sure did," Kenzie nodded. "I of course provided a glowing recommendation but left out the part where you don't drink coffee."

"Oh wow, thank you. I'm so relieved."

"Didn't know you were so into making coffee," Theo said.

"I'm not really. Forgive me for not telling you. It's just that I need the money that comes with this promotion. If word gets out about Gramps, we may have to move. This job will allow me to save up money for a plan B."

Theo placed his hand on my arm. "Beans, you know we will be here for you if it comes to that."

"Absolutely, you do not have to worry about where you all will stay," Kenzie added.

I wasn't so much worried about myself. It was Mom and Gramps (plus me) that worried me.

Kenzie pulled up her shades and looked over my shoulder while her body prepared for an incoming threat. "Oh, Jesus."

I tried to turn but my vision was blocked by the umbrella on the table behind me. "What is it?"

"Now, honey, wipe those eyes and stiffen up that spine stat." Theo was being weird.

"Why are you guys being so strange?"

"Lace?"

God, that deep voice, the questioning lilt in his raspy voice had me wondering if I could orgasm just from hearing him talk. I turned. "Hey. Um, Briggs."

"So when you said you had a headache and didn't feel well enough to go out, I think you meant you didn't feel well enough to go out with me." He held quite a bit of takeout in his hands like he'd ordered for his entire family, which he probably had.

"Ouch," Theo whispered.

Was I just going to piss everyone off today? "I uh . . ." I looked at Kenzie for help.

"I threatened her within an inch of her life, Briggs. She had no choice but to crawl out of bed, no matter how ill." She kicked my shin.

"Yeah, I owed her one, but I am feeling bad, well, my brain is, or it was, I'm better now." *God, just shut up, Lacie.* "I don't have an illness per se, but I don't feel like myself."

"Eloquent," Kenzie whispered in my ear.

"You don't owe me an explanation, but I do appreciate it." He nodded to Theo and issued a goodbye greeting to us before turning on his heels and walking away.

"He sure is different now. And he's gotten like ten times hotter, which I didn't think was possible," Theo said while fanning himself with a coaster.

"Even his muscles have muscles," Kenzie added.

"Hey," I said in a warning tone.

"If you're not into him, he's on the market. I wouldn't wait too long to decide what I'm doing where he's concerned, or you might find he's no longer for sale," Theo threw out.

"He's not bi," I pleaded.

"Maybe I can change that." Theo winked.

"All right you two." Kenzie snapped her fingers. "I'm willing to be late returning from lunch to hear about this barn thing that Theo seems to have the upper hand on."

I groaned. I really didn't want to unpack this right now.

"Don't give me any bellyaching. It's not fair that Theo knows and I don't."

"Jealous much?" Theo taunted.

Kenzie frisbee threw a coaster at Theo's neck.

"Ouch. So violent."

Kenzie glanced at her watch. "Spill it, Beans."

I told them most of it, including how I'd hidden his clothes as part of my revenge plot and how different he was since I'd last seen him. He'd stuck around and was there for me this morning. He'd tried to help, but I wouldn't let him. He'd wanted to talk but so far, I'd pushed him away. But the biggest change in him was that instead of adding to the teasing where I was concerned, he sided with me and protected me.

"Wow, Lacie. Forget that thing I said about sex with no emotions. That's dangerous here."

"Great, now you tell me."

"Wait, you told her it was okay to have sex with him?"

"Only if she could leave her emotions out of it. Which would have totally worked if he hadn't gone and gotten all perfect on her."

Theo shook his head. "Hmm, I don't think sex without emotions ever works."

I threw my hands in the air. "I'm right here, guys. And last night we blew way past being able to debate on sex without emotions."

My friends went radio silent. "Uh, guys? A little help, please?"

Kenzie's head tilted to the side in thought. Theo scratched at his head.

"I think you've gotta talk to him, boo." Kenzie said.

"Wow, well I already knew that part. What I need to know is what to do about the sex part. Specifically, the having it, or not having it."

Kenzie, "Have it."

Theo, "Don't have it."

They spoke in unison.

"You two are no help at all."

"I'm just saying, you're already emotionally entangled so why not enjoy yourself a little," Kenzie said.

"And risk the emotion getting out of hand?" Theo questioned.

"I don't think her emotions are going to get any bigger; they may change, but she's a big girl."

"Don't talk about me like I'm not here," I demanded.

Kenzie stood. "I think the main question is, have you forgiven him?"

"Forgiven him?"

"You know, for all the bullying, and ruining your prom, taking your V-card, killing your worm, hiding your clothes - - -"

"It was a caterpillar," I cut Kenzie off. "Besides, forgiveness is an act, not a request. I'm the forgiver, he's the forgivee, therefore he's the seeker of my forgiveness, making me the one who chooses to forgive him or not, but only if he asks. Forgiveness is given, not sought."

"So, it's in your hands," Kenzie said.

"Basically."

"But you can't unless he asks," Theo added.

"So, tell him to ask for it," Kenzie ordered.

"I can't. Asking for forgiveness is the same as admitting you did something wrong. If he won't ask for it, then he doesn't feel he did anything wrong. Even if I forgive him already for all the things he's done, if he doesn't seek my forgiveness, then he doesn't believe he's done anything wrong, and if he doesn't believe he was wrong, then we have a real problem."

"Because he thinks what he did was okay to do to someone," Theo clarified.

"Right, or he's so narcissistic that he doesn't perceive of his actions and how they hurt others," I retorted.

"Whew, remind me never to get on your bad side," Kenzie said while motioning for the check.

"Am I really that bad?" I questioned Theo.

"No. You deserve the best and you know it. Nothing wrong with that."

"Briggs already paid for everything. He said order anything else you want." Our server picked up our empty glasses.

"Thank you, Amanda." Kenzie cleared her throat. "Well, at least you don't have to worry about him being a narcissist." She kissed my cheek and hugged Theo. "I gotta jet." Kenzie took the last sip of her cappuccino. "I'm glad we will be together at school." She squeezed my hand and took off walking down the boardwalk.

Theo leaned back in his chair. "Any idea when you'll talk to him?"

"When I figure out what I want." I still hadn't told my friends about his *I've always loved you* text. Not because it wasn't something I wanted to hear, because I did. I wanted to run around Whiskey Cove shouting *I love Briggs Dean St. Martin, and I don't care who knows.* But I couldn't. Not yet. Not until I could be sure he would never pull another prank on me as long as we both shall live.

"Earth to Lacie. Should we go pick out the wedding China now or wait until it's official?"

I tried to frisbee my cardboard coaster at Theo, but I wasn't as smooth as Kenzie. Instead, the coaster zipped right past his head and hit the old man eating behind him in the back of the head. Cringing, I ducked and let Theo make apologies.

"Time to go, Pete Rose."

"But I still don't know what to do." I let my forehead plop onto my arm on top of the table and groaned.

"I think I'll stick with the baseball theme here and say . . . don't let the fear of striking out hold you back."

I raised my head. "Who says I would strike out?"

"You won't, but you might not get exactly what you want, but don't let it stop you from going for it."

I thought about what he said and tried to apply it to my current situation. What exactly did I want? Looking a bit into the future I saw myself as a successful therapist, but was that all I wanted? I forced my mind to conjure up a date night. I saw myself clearly, dressed in a gold jumper and beige wedges on my feet, a slim gold necklace around my neck, next to me a guy with an undefined face and dark, thick hair and lashes. It could be anyone except for that band of tattoos around his upper arm. I took a deep breath and let it out slowly.

"I'm scared, Theo."

He smiled compassionately. "I know." He leaned forward at the table. "But aren't you the one who told me if I didn't apply for the internship at WCAM that I'd be throwing away a perfect opportunity to show all of West Baton Rouge Parish how talented I am?"

"Well, you are uber talented. The station manager would be a fool to pass on you. Plus, the collective age of the WCAM team is sixty-five; you'd bring that number down into the fifties, which is a start. They desperately need you, and they're going to call, I can feel it."

His smile grew into a playful grin that reminded me of Theo when we were kids. "Your gut was right, they called."

We high-fived. "I knew it." Pointing to my gut I said, "the gut knows."

"The gut knows," he repeated. "What is it telling you about grad school?"

I tried to tune into my body. I listened and waited for any kind of response be it hunger pangs or intestinal cramps. Instead, I got absolute stillness.

"My gut says *Green Light Go!*" Theo cheered.

I chuckled. "Green Light Go. God, we haven't played that game since we were ten."

"Think it'd look bad if we played a game of that on the front lawn of the estate. We could pull guests over in their garden attire, the ladies in floral cotton dresses, wedges, and big hats, with us forcing laughter and grass stains."

"Probably get our families fired but what a great way to go." We laughed until the moment faded. "Theo, I'm so proud of you. You've accomplished your dream."

"It's just an internship."

"There's no way it won't turn into everything you've dreamed of." Once they got a look and a listen at Theo, he'd probably become the newest anchor. He was an incredible debater. He took our high school team to the national stage. Not to mention, he had looks to kill. "When did you find out?"

"This afternoon, and I've been high ever since, but you know what would make this day perfection?"

"Hmm?"

"Mailing your letter. Together."

We left the bistro, but not before I ordered a chocolate scone on Briggs. My fingers shook as I brought the letter up to the slot. Theo put his arm around my shoulders and said, "Carpe diem, Beans."

I let the letter go.

"I'm going to carpe the hell out of this mother-fucking diem."

"That's my girl."

I've always wanted to say that.

CHAPTER 15

BRIGGS

July

The fight with my dad this morning had me driving faster than usual. I needed to regain control of my body before I lost it altogether.

It's taken me twenty-three years to be able to control my body's reaction to my emotions. Through the consistent practice of meditation and controlled breathing practices, and a tight focus on my diet, I'm now completely unmedicated.

It was the toxic cocktail of psychotropic medication given to me in my youth that fought against my body's overabundance of certain chemicals and not enough of others, which had my system flooded to the point of insanity.

Now, I used a combination of yoga and cognitive behavioral techniques to regulate my emotions. It's been no bed of roses but at least now I'm able to remain in control during bouts of chemical imbalance instead of blacking out.

I pulled into one of the parking spots at the marsh, a particular favorite place of mine to practice yoga. I grabbed my mat, Super 8, and a towel and locked up the SUV. I could already hear the wind blowing through the marsh reeds and started timing my breathing with it.

These walks were medicinal for me now . . . my body craved them. I tuned out all thoughts and for a moment only heard birds answering each other, frogs croaking, cicadas dancing, and reeds scraping each other. In the center of it all was a large marble plat-form with columns and a covering that provided much-needed shade. I unrolled my yoga mat and then sat down in the lotus posi-tion and started the process of clearing my mind.

My life would have been a lot easier without the chemical imbal-ance in my brain. The strict diet I followed could be a buzzkill just because caffeine and other stimulants weren't allowed, but it was the right formula of nutrients that kept me balanced. Without that balance, I couldn't be in control, and I'd learned to love control.

I hated arguing with my father. But worse was arguing over the phone. Fighting was personal and emotional, but on the phone, you couldn't get into that vibe. Not to mention the yelling my eardrums had endured.

He didn't understand me. I stretched and coordinated my breathing as I was taught. Once I'd completed the exercises and my breathing was in check, I picked up the Super 8 and set about finding some cool footage. Before long, I was filming a great blue heron chowing down on a redfish. His face was nearly white but there was some black and white streaking down his front. He used his orange beak to crush the fish.

Pop didn't want to fund this side gig any longer. He'd said he'd be cutting me off unless I got a dual college major. Good thing I'd been looking for work.

Currently, I mow lawns. Most of the people I mowed for were elderly church members who lived on social security so I mowed a lot of acreage for free, but I couldn't bring myself to charge them the going rate. I had a few commercial gigs that were lucrative, and I made do with that. I also mowed for the Leblanc's, since Steve could no longer manage it.

My entire life I'd been working on one thing and one thing only . . . video. I wanted to get recognized, and my professors had told me I was a visionary when they'd viewed a portfolio of my work during my grad school interview. If only I could organize my thoughts into a film project with merit, I'd finally have a chance to get some recognition. To get started, I needed a thesis idea, but I'd yet to get one of my ideas approved. I breathed through the frustration trying to take hold.

It pissed me off that my father didn't recognize all the positive changes I'd made in the past six years. He just kept pushing me to be more like him. He wanted all us kids to go into the family business.

But you know what?

I could spend twenty-four-seven curled over a drafting table looking at blueprints and building with him, but it wouldn't change a thing.

And you know how I know this?

My brother Camp does it, and they still don't get along. Instead of pestering Camp about his life choices, he gets to listen to Pop grind on all day about what a poor contractor he is.

Fuck that. I'd done all the things he'd asked of me. Apologized to all the people I'd let down . . . except for one, but she wasn't interested in what I had to offer, so I planned on changing her mind.

I was working on a plan that would afford me a lot more time with her. It wouldn't be all roses, she'd have my head on a platter at first, I was sure of it. Hopefully, it wouldn't be fully severed, and I'd be able to reconnect it at some point.

I took as much video footage as my reel allowed and then switched to still pictures. I'd been developing them in black and white. I didn't use digital for this one, but old-school sheet film developing.

Sometimes, after just barely waking up in the morning, my fingers would twitch, and though I wanted to roll over and get a few more hours of sleep, my body had awakened me for a reason. My subconscious didn't want me to miss the sunrise. I *had* to capture it. My father just didn't understand; film wasn't a choice for me, it was in my marrow and I had no choice but to set it free.

CHAPTER 16
BRIGGS
October

By the time fall had rolled around and school started, I still had not been able to persuade Lacie into having dinner with me.

Or to hang by the pool.

Or hell, just step outside and sit beneath her favorite pecan tree that made up the circle in front of her apartment.

I knew she was busy, but I couldn't shake the feeling that she was avoiding me. It was now close to Thanksgiving, and I was starting to get restless, something I tried hard to avoid.

I was clean of stimulants of any kind in my system through the tight control I kept on my diet, exercise, and mental focus. My body did continue to occasionally produce additional chemicals, or not produce the right ones, but I'd learned to listen to my body and make adjustments to my diet, sleep, and exercise to get it back into balance.

"Sup?" Parker dropped his backpack and took the seat next to me in the advanced editing course we were taking together. He was getting a degree in Television and Media Management and was using this course as one of his upper-level graduate electives. He didn't really want to go to school but his family wanted him to have an interest in something besides the family businesses. They supported him fiercely. I wondered what that would be like.

"You get your thesis topic approved?" I asked.

"Nope. Grabassy said I need an original idea. It's my fucking family tree. How much more original can I get."

Our professor's name was Grabassy, pronounced grab-ausie, but because he liked to sleep with young college coeds, he'd earned the nickname Grab-assy. Parker's project was about his family and their settlement story, being one of the first families to live in West Baton Rouge Parish. He was a McIlhenny on his mom's side and part of the family who has made Tabasco on Avery Island for over five generations. On his father's side he had the David Shrimp success. He was Baton Rouge's most eligible bachelor. Too bad for single girls everywhere, Parker was a love 'em and leave 'em kinda guy.

"Grabassy said it had been done already and so I asked him if it had been done by a McIlhenny, and he said no, but that it wouldn't make any difference if it had."

"Did you give him the Saints tickets?" I asked.

"No, man, I don't wanna prostitute for it."

"Give them to me. I don't mind showing a little leg for an approved thesis project."

He passed me the tickets. "I don't think it's the leg he's after."

"Maybe not, but that's all he's gonna get." As Professor Grabassy lectured on the four advantages of using digital over film, which was something I'd learned when I was seven years old, I postulated how being a grad student was way better than being an undergrad. For starters, the parking was light-years better. Case in point, I'd pulled into a reserved slot directly in front of the cinematic arts building. As I'd walked into the building, I focused on finding that satisfied, sated feeling I'd felt before.

The act of being content in oneself was harder to come by than you'd think. If you could find it, you'd be home because there's nothing like bone-deep satisfaction.

I'd felt it twice in my life.

Both times with her.

CHAPTER 16

Once, when I was eighteen and we were at the pond, Lacie had given me half her heart in exchange for half of mine. I felt it again the night of our graduation from college, in the barn, when she'd satisfied me like nothing ever had.

I aimed for that feeling on a daily basis and because she let me experience what it felt like to be completely full on all levels, I now knew what I was aiming for. With lifestyle changes and therapy, I'd come close to the feeling of contentment that I had with her, but it still wasn't exactly right.

I had gotten better. I was holding on now. My grasp on reality didn't require a tight, white-knuckled grip. In fact, I was able to loosen that grip a little here and there and have some fun. Something I never thought I'd say.

Learning my system couldn't handle stimulants of any kind and coming clean, I had been completely stable and without a blackout episode for two years now. I used to think the fact that I couldn't process stimulants made me weak, but I wasn't starting where other people were.

I had a chemical imbalance. Dopamine, serotonin, norepinephrine. Labs had confirmed it. With my lifestyle changes, I mostly felt in control of my actions and thoughts. I couldn't always say that.

Then fucking Matt had to show up at the bonfire, his sights set on her and slowed me down. I didn't know what to do to get her away from him, so I'd told her not to go walking with him.

Matt is not a good guy, to say the least. He may actually be a criminal. Verdict is still out on that measure, but he had a lot of videos on social media of his conquests and even some local police reports of possibly drugging women.

He'd worked for Dad's construction company. I know it's hard to get help these days, but why was Dad hiring criminals? He'd told me Matt was innocent and that it was God and the courts' job to place blame. That's all well and good, but as soon as I saw his interest in Lacie, that's where our ties had ended. Dad said he would no longer use him. It was either that or I was going to fight the fucker.

Next to me, Parker had dozed off, a slight snore emanated from his body, so I nudged him awake. He woke on a gasp and then rubbed his hands over his face, straightening up in his chair.

Filming and editing had a special corner of my heart. Detailed focus on all the little aspects required to produce a movie are what helped me when I was down with my dick in the dirt.

I'd worked hard as an undergrad, and my professors told me I was talented, said I had the drive and the skills, even the insight necessary to make a name in the field, but my father wouldn't know anything about that.

He preferred to have no interest in most of my projects, and when I invited him to the academic awards banquet, he turned down the invitation flat out. When I invited him to my undergrad graduation and told him I was graduating with honors, he chuckled and asked what honor there was in making videos. He didn't attend that night, but I did let him foot the bill for the party.

During my meeting with Professor Grabassy, I noticed the guy had thinning hair and a shiny forehead, but he was a genius at editing and an excellent mentor. I had been lucky to snag him, but lately I felt bad because I couldn't give him what he wanted.

"Bottom line, if you don't bring me a fresh thesis topic within the next week or two, I see you prolonging your program." He lit a cigarette and walked over to open the window.

"I just brought you an idea." I didn't understand what I was doing wrong. He wanted me engaged in a project, I gave him ideas, but he wouldn't let me get started.

Professor Grabassy picked up the blue notebook I turned in and read, "Teachers' Use Of Audio-Visual Media In The Classroom." He slapped my notebook down on his desk. "It's been done. Hell, I just co-authored two of these last semester. I'm bored. Bring me something that hasn't been done and I'll approve it like that." He snapped his fingers.

I was frustrated. This was the third idea of mine that he'd put down before I could even get it out of the gate. I ran fingers through my hair and stood. "All right, I'll bring you something that cooks."

"Two weeks tops," he said as I was walking out the door. Coincidentally, he'd taken the football tickets, noting that they wouldn't sprinkle magic dust over my program. Fair enough.

A thesis advanced editing project that hadn't been done before. I didn't really care what I filmed. Editing was the money shot that could turn ordinary into extraordinary and it's where I excelled. I could tell a story about anything.

I walked the campus, racking my brain for a thesis idea that Grabassy would accept, but every time I came up with something, it had already been done. But hadn't everything already been done? Especially anything that would center around my interest in classic Super 8 film. I was thinking local historical, but Grabassy said the Super 8 was holding me back. Looks like I'd be shooting 16 millimeter for this project which I already wasn't excited about, but it had to be analog and not digital so I was stuck.

I felt my phone vibrate against my leg and pulled it out of my pocket hoping it was a text from Lacie inviting me over to talk. Instead, it was Finn asking if I'd pick him up an order of fried shrimp and rice from Crazy Cajun.

Since he'd lost his voice, Finn didn't go out much, and when he did, I had to go with him. Which could be the reason why he didn't date. He hadn't ever had sex with a girl because he was so embarrassed by his inability to communicate. I'd wanted to hire him a hooker when he turned eighteen, but he freaked out so much at the idea that he'd punched me and made me give him my word I wouldn't. After that I never tried to intervene on behalf of his dick, but I worried about all the hours he spent alone.

Crazy Cajun was right next to Acadian Kitchen. I could feign needing a coffee from their new coffee counter and wondered if by any luck, the new coffee bar manager would be working. I returned Finn's text letting him know my plans and asked if he wanted a latte.

Finn: I'm good, thanks. Lacie's there.

Me: Interesting that you know her schedule.

Finn: She texts me every day.

How was it Finn could get her attention, but I couldn't, and how could I be so out of touch that I never recognized that she was more into Finn than she was me. But Finn wasn't interested in anyone. And I couldn't be sure, but I kinda thought Lacie got on his nerves because of all her prying and pushing where his communication was concerned.

Me: I can't even get her to talk to me.

I walked toward my car careful not to run into a pole and become yet another texting while walking fatality.

Finn: I've been a favorite project of hers since I lost my voice. Was hoping grad school would change that but she messages me more now than ever.

Me: What does she want from you?

I plugged in my phone and used my hands-free auto feature to communicate with Finn while I drove to Whiskey Cove.

Finn: She knows an SLP at the hospital. They wanna stick a camera down my neck and look at me while I try to talk.

Me: Yikes.

I mean the process sounded awful, but if there was a chance she could help him I guess I couldn't understand why he wouldn't let her.

Finn: Tell me about it. I'd rather stick hot needles in my eyes.

Me: But is there a chance you'd be able to talk again?

Finn: That's just it, no one knows for sure so why even go through that stuff.

I parallel parked at the boardwalk and got out to put coins in the meter.

Me: What kind of odds would make you consider letting Lacie help you?

Finn: 100%

Me: *audible groans*

Finn: Feel free to let her stick a tube down your throat.

Me: Be home in a few.

I slid my phone into my pocket and then walked into Crazy Cajun to order two orders of shrimp and rice. They were slammed and I had twenty minutes to kill so I hoofed it over to Acadian Kitchen with extra bounce in my step that did not go unnoticed by Mrs. Doucet who was the founding member of the Whiskey Cove Quilting Club, a group of ladies who sat around and made quilts for people when they fell on hard times or became ill or lost a loved one. Mostly, I think the club got together to gossip about everybody, but no one could argue with the caliper of quilting that went on in that circle.

"Good afternoon, Briggs. You're looking particularly happy today." Mrs. Doucet waved.

I shot her through with my most adorable smile, or so I'd been told. "Acadian Kitchen now has its very own coffee shop, and if there's one thing I love, it's a good cup of joe." White lies never hurt anyone.

I held the door open for her. "Thank you, don't mind if I do. I'm so glad you're back in Whiskey Cove." She crossed the threshold, and my nose tickled at her rose-scented perfume. "Are you and

Lacie getting on all right? I thought I saw you sitting together at the blessing breakfast."

"We're just friends, Mrs. Doucet," I said as we walked to the back of the store.

"Oh, of course darling. You know the Mimkins over on Route 7, the church has been after them for years to marry, but they won't because they too are *just friends*." Mrs. Doucet giggled.

"I see, Mrs. Doucet." The Mimkins also had eight children. I shuddered.

"My granddaughter sent me a video of you throwing that poor child into the pool. Don't look like friends to me. Well, I guess two kids who can't get along probably shouldn't date."

I wasn't going to argue with an elder. "When you're right, you're right."

As we approached the back of the store, there was a crowd huddled haphazardly around the coffee counter. Expletives flew and the sound of metal hitting the floor had me squinting my eyes to counteract the loudness on my nerves.

Steam hissed from a La Pavoni Espresso machine while espresso spewed out in all directions with who else at the center of it all but Lacie. The espresso machine blew a loud hiss right into her face and she screeched. My guess was the brew valve wasn't properly seating and may have worn the gaskets down.

I'd had a little barista job during my rehabilitation. When going through rehab, it's good to have somewhere to put your focus. I walked up to the counter and stood to the side, watching Lacie finish off a sloppy rosette decal on a large latte and slide it to the pick-up area. "Cassie!" she yelled.

"It's Casey," the man countered.

Lacie turned and used her arm to push hair from her eyes. "My apologies. Be glad it was in the ballpark, and I didn't call you Jason."

"I'm still waiting for a dry cappuccino. Large." A testy gentleman in an expensive suit shouted over the abandoned coffees that no one had picked up. Shit, did they leave after paying?

"Coming right up, sir." She pointed to the cappuccino machine and got to work on his drink, burning her finger in the process. From where I was standing, it didn't look like the usual surface burn but was an intense pain that stole away her concentration, and her ability to make his drink.

I could no longer remain a silent observer. I stepped behind the counter, washed my hands and then grabbed a towel, filled it with ice, and nudged Lacie aside with the ice pack.

"Wh . . . what are you doing?"

"Quiet. Put the ice on your hand." First thing I did was take a moment to get organized by putting dirty spoons and mugs in the sink. Then I wiped the counter free of coffee granules.

Lacie called out drink orders, and I filled them. Americanos, cappuccinos, and lattes with flowers, rosettes, hearts, combo designs in perfect crema. I adjusted various hardware on the machine until I had it preforming almost to perfection. I was aware of Lacie watching me like a casino owner watched someone who had won every hand at a blackjack table with the best dealer in the house.

Once the rush was over, I inspected Lacie's hand while she regarded me with suspicious eyes.

"You cleared the lobby in ten minutes, and your latte art is better than mine."

I placed the ice back on her palm. "I wouldn't brag too much about your latte art, Picasso." I grimaced, and she punched me in the shoulder.

"So what gives? You had a secret life as an off-rigging barista?"

"Actually, *there was* a cappuccino machine on the rig. It was kind of a condition of my employment." I winked at her. "But I had a job as a barista in a coffee shop for a while."

"Why didn't you tell me?"

I wiped the counters down, folding the rag when I was satisfied. "You didn't ask and every time I try to suggest dinner, or hanging by the lake to talk, you give me some lame excuse like a fake headache."

"It was a real headache, it just subsided by the time Kenzie texted me to meet her at the bistro."

"Headaches are funny that way." I chuckled.

"I'm going to get in trouble if you get caught back here."

"No, you won't. I know Kelvin."

"Kelvin?"

"The guy who signs your checks."

"Mr. Thibodeaux?"

"The one and only. He's good friends with my father."

"Of course he is." Lacie jumped off the stool where she had been sitting and emptied the now-melted ice into the sink.

"How's your fall going?"

"About as well as my ability to make cappuccinos."

I followed her out from behind the counter to where a few bistro style tables had been set up under an indoor pergola draped with climbing roses that seemed to be real but at the same time were almost too perfect. I plucked at one and a few soft petals fell into my hand. "Classes going okay?"

"Lots of studying to keep up, but okay I guess. I just wish I had enough time to devote to my projects and internship." She collected dirty coffee cups on a tray. "I feel like things are piling up, and I'm at the foothill of a ginormous mountain that I can't climb because I don't have the tools. I keep having a dream that all my teeth are falling out. I just feel like I'm on a runaway train that's on fire and I can't get off."

I wasn't going to offer to help her. I'd done that time and again, and she just wouldn't trust me with anything. It hurt. Now I know how it felt. Sometimes, I wondered if the things from our past could be forgiven. How could she not understand that I was a different person now? That before, I had been affected by a system flooded with chemicals and no way to filter them?

My body was making chemicals to counteract the chemicals the doctors kept feeding me. It was actually Steve's rig that I'd turned to for help. I spent a back-breaking summer there, hauling meters, gauges, pipes, and hoses up and down stairs and scaffolding until all my body could do was pass out. That was how I cleaned my system of the pharmaceutical cocktail prescribed by the good doctors of my youth.

I held her elbow. "Lace, I understand. Life can be a sprint sometimes. It takes great stamina to keep up the pace. It may not seem like it when you're in it, but every little piece you chip away at, every step you take up that mountain, is one less that bars your path to the pinnacle. Take the steps one at a time."

"You make it sound easy."

I shook my head. "Not easy. It's about taking the first step. After that, it's about the second step."

Her smile could melt even the most hardened heart. She was beautiful, and no one delighted in the little things quite like she did. She'd get this look on her face, this little gleam in her eye, and an angelic little smile would curl up the corners of her lips. It could be anything; even when she cleared the tables of trash and dirty mugs and dishes, you knew she took enjoyment in the task.

She sat at one of the tables that was piled high with flowers and vases. Observing the tables now I noticed a beautiful floral arrangement in the middle of each table, all made by her hands I was sure of it. She always did love to have her hands in a flower bush.

God, I wanted her. I remembered one thing I loved about her was the way she could make you feel like your words were the most important to her in the world. She was right there in the moment with you when you were retelling a story or felt your emotion when you were down in the dirt. In a way it was a curse. I remember my moods could so easily affect her own. She'd cross onto our property all bubbly and licking that grape fucking lollipop, and I'd tear into her. The tears would roll, but then she'd eventually become as angry and as dark-hearted as me.

I know it had been hard to be friends with me, or whatever we were. The worst thing I ever did to her I did the day after we shared a piece of each other under the silver moon. It was her turn now to empty her dark onto me. Maybe after she emptied the tank, we could refuel it with something else. Something that made the edges of her mouth curl up. This would be the one shot I'd take. If she still hated me, if she was unable to recognize the change in me, I'd let her go, and as the Disciple Paul, I'd roam the earth alone until my last breath.

It was time to go pick up the shrimp and rice, but I found myself not wanting to leave. I could watch her wipe tables down forever and still not capture every nuance that was Lacie Ann Ryan. "See you around." I hoped. As I walked away, I thought about asking her to dinner again, but I'd asked several times already. She knew what I wanted. Ball was in her court now.

"Hey, Briggs?" I stopped and turned around. "Thanks for your help." Her smile was more of a look of relief that washed over her face.

"You're welcome, Lace."

CHAPTER 17
BRIGGS

Several hours after I'd helped her at the coffee bar, my phone lit up with a text.

> Lacie: Can you come out back?

> Me: On my way

When I walked into the sunroom off the patio, I saw Lacie standing at the French doors, holding a loaf of bread in one hand and a bottle of juice in the other. Were those things for me? To say I was intrigued would be an understatement.

I opened the door and invited her inside, stopping her at the threshold to remove a baby's breath flower from her hair.

Her cheeks turned rosy when she spotted the flower between my fingers. "I was making floral arrangements."

"I can see that." I smiled and then led her into the kitchen. She seemed quieter than usual and yawned into the countertop; her low hanging eyelids gave away the exhaustion she felt.

"This is a nice surprise." I smiled and willed myself with self-talk to be chill while my insides were being tickled by all the promises of a future with her floating around. "How did you know where I lived?"

"I went to the estate. Your dad told me you'd rented an apartment in the city." She pushed the loaf of bread across the counter toward where I stood, along with the juice and I found it interesting that she came all the way back into the city. "Cinnamon bread loaf. It weighs five pounds. When you eat it, you'll know where it went." Her forehead wrinkled and she shook her head. "I don't know what I'm saying. I realized today that I don't even know what your favorite coffeehouse drink is. You said no caffeine. There are a lot of good teas without caffeine. I personally love matcha lattes, though I'm not sure that's caffeine free so instead I went with grape juice."

"It's one of my favorite drinks."

She smiled. "Really?"

"Yeah." Whatever she'd brought would have been my favorite. I didn't give a fuck about the drink. However, I hadn't had a stimulant in four years and couldn't drink coffee. Juice was thoughtful but that was Lacie.

Behind me footsteps and the sound of dishes clanking could be heard. Lacie's face morphed from tired, agreeable kitten to anxious tiger in three seconds flat. "Is that Finn?"

"Uh, not exactly." I guess it could have been anyone, but it wasn't. Rylie and Sarah, Steve's daughters, were here for the night.

"OMG, I'm sorry I. . . " she slid off the stool, "I never meant to interrupt anything." She started to back out of the kitchen, but I wasn't letting her go anywhere without bringing her into the living room so she could see all the fun I was up to.

I reached for her, balancing the five-pound loaf in one arm, and leading her through the house with the other. "Briggs, let me go."

"There are girls here that you need to meet." I countered.

"I'd rather not." Her body tightened in my hold.

We rounded the corner into the living room where Rylie was finishing up her ice cream that lay half-melted on the coffee table and Sarah was morphed into a pretzel as she tried to keep her limbs on the proper squares of our Twister game. They were in jammies, as they called it, and Sarah's hair was still wet. I'd been able to blow

Rylie's dry, but Sarah had refused to give up her lead in Twister when I called her over to the dryer.

Lacie let out an audible breath of air. "Sarah and Rylie."

Rylie, the youngest at five, greeted her first. "Do you live with Briggs?" Rylie squealed when she fell off of her colors. Sarah joined in the squealing and giggling.

Lacie's eyes grew large and round, their hazy green color prominent. "I . . . I don't. No. No, I don't live with Briggs." She giggled. "I'm just visiting."

God, she was so stinking cute. I had to grind my teeth to keep from reaching for her. I wanted her in my arms but knew I'd have to wait, for more reasons than one.

"You should stay over with us?" Sarah chimed in, then fell into a fit of giggles when she literally fell from holding her pretzel shape.

"I work with Briggs. I only came by to give him. . . snacks."

"Snacks?" Rylie questioned with hopeful eyes.

"Yes, cinnamon bread."

Rylie's nose wrinkled instantly.

Lacie turned to me. "I wanted to thank you for your help today. I couldn't have been successful without you."

"You're welcome but I wasn't expecting snacks." Leaving Lacie's gift on the coffee table, I motioned to the couch and sat, watching her look around for a better spot, and probably one that wouldn't have her sitting next to me. "Kenzie tells me you've been promoted to assistant manager."

Lacie cleared her throat. "Well, I don't have the title yet. I'm on a thirty-day trial. I hope I get the position. It comes with a raise, and I could use that money." Her eyes searched the room, moving from ice cream to the Twister board. "I didn't know you were keeping the girls."

"I don't believe we ever discussed it."

"Do you do this often?"

"Briggs, you have to spin," Sarah said from her position on the Twister board.

"When Penny works her one night a week, I keep the girls." If she wanted to know what I was up to, she should have answered my texts. "If you'll excuse me, it's my turn at Twister."

"Bedtime Twister," Rylie corrected.

Lacie gave a skeptical look in Rylie's direction. "What's bedtime Twister?"

"We wanted to do one more thing before bed, so Uncle Briggs let us pick, and Sarah picked Twister," Rylie yelled.

Lacie looked me in the eye. "Is this supposed to calm them down before bed?"

I shrugged. "I'm Uncle Briggs, I don't bring the rules. I only bring the fun." The girls fell down in a fit of giggles and agreement. Lacie chuckled too but then offered a story.

"What kind of story?" Rylie asked.

Lacie looked off into the distance in thought before turning back to answer. "The best kind. It's about Mr. Mouse's family and their big move."

"I want to hear about Mr. Mouse's family," Sarah said.

Lacie sat on the coffee table, hunched over the girls who were on their knees in front of her. She had their full attention. Lacie was magical in that way; she could command the attention of an entire room. I'd seen her do it on different occasions.

"Mr. Mouse lived in a cottage by the Atlantic Ocean. At night, he would come out of his home in the walls to get food for his family. They liked certain things like the cherry from the top of a sundae or the marshmallows out of the cereal box. Even the butter left out to soften for the breakfast biscuits. These are the types of things Mr. Mouse would come out to forage."

"Fow- ed." Rylie tried.

Lacie pointed to her lips. "For- age."

"Fow-age."

"Hmm. We'll have to work on that R at some point, but I like your effort." She bopped Rylie on the nose with the tip of her finger.

"What else did Mr. Mouse get?" Sarah asked.

Lacie cocked a brow. "Well, if you want to know, you'll need to get into bed, and we'll finish the story there. The one rule Mr. Mouse has is that I only tell his story once you're in bed."

Sarah stood. "Come on Rylie, let's go get in bed." They were down the hall in a flash, leaving me to wonder if Lacie wasn't an actual magical unicorn this whole time and I was just figuring it out.

I followed the girls, Lacie followed me. "That's some skill you have." I directed my comment at Lacie.

"It's all in how you spin it. I'm not giving away my story for free."

In the past, she had been confident around me, but it was usually after I'd provoked her enough to work up her nerve. I won't pretend I don't like her dominant side. I fucking loved it. For once, I was glad it made an appearance without my intervention. I can't change the past, but I do know that I'd always loved her, even when my actions made her hate me.

She continued with the story, and I just felt lucky to be along for the ride. ". . . and in this way, Mr. Mouse took care of his family and Mrs. Mouse took care of Mr. Mouse until one day Mr. Mouse had to leave."

"But why did he have to leave?" Rylie asked, worried.

"Daddies have to leave sometimes." Maybe Lacie was thinking about her own situation with her father, who, as far as I know, she had never met. Or was she preparing the girls for something?

"Did he come back?" Sarah asked, hopeful.

"He wanted to, but he couldn't, and this was a troublesome thing because the cottage the mouses lived in was being torn down, which meant they had to move."

"But how would the dad know where they went?" Rylie asked with a hint of worry laced in her little voice.

Lacie kissed the top of their heads. "Well, you see, dads have magic, the good ones anyway."

"How do you know if he's a good dad? With magic?" Rylie asked.

"Oh, there are ways to tell." Lacie placed a finger on her lip and looked up in thought. "Does he make you laugh? Does he hug and kiss you? Those are all things the good ones do but the main way to know he's good is if he has always been there when he could. And if he says he loves you. That's how you know he's really good."

The story went on for ten more minutes. The house got moved with the help of all the dad's friends, and the dad never came back, but the house had been moved to a tree that the dad had lived in when he was a child, and it even had his name carved into it. In this way, the dad was always with them.

The girls snuggled against Lacie and fell asleep. In the end, she was trapped. "I guess you'll just have to stay there all night," I whispered.

"Not a chance. I have to study for an exam I have at eight in the morning." I helped her make her escape. The girls shuffled some but didn't fully wake up.

I led her to the kitchen and offered her a glass of wine that I kept for company. "I would have a glass, but like I said, I've got a long night ahead of me still," she said. It was closing in on ten thirty.

"Thanks for your help with the girls," I said, wishing we had more time for just us, but our lives were filled to the brim with others.

"It's nice of you to watch the girls," she said in slow hushed tones. Her mind was still going but there was no way her body was going to let her stay up and work.

She rubbed her eyes, the exhaustion settling in. I wanted to offer her the couch but knew she wouldn't take it. I walked her to the door, where I was glad she lingered. I liked her all soft smiles and gentle, like she was ready to curl into a ball and fall asleep. She looked at me with those tired eyes. "This was a good night. Unexpected but good. I really did come over here to thank you for all of the help at the store. I still can't believe you can make latte art."

"Well, believe it. I hope you can see that I'm trying to make it up to you."

"Make up what?"

"All of the things I've done in the past. That wasn't the real me." I put one hand to my heart. "This is the real me."

She watched me, focusing on my hands. "I recognize the

change, but I'm not ready to jump into something with you based on the fact that you haven't had any . . ." Her lips pressed together as she looked away.

"I know what you want to say. You're right to say it. I haven't had any episodes. I hope that's what you were thinking, because I'm able to manage those now and I'm glad you can see it."

Her brows furrowed in thought. "But how?"

"It's a combination of breathing techniques, meditation, and cognitive behavioral therapy. I also follow a strict diet to keep my labs in check."

Her intensity when she looked into my eyes and at my body had me wanting to duck and run. What was she seeing? How far into the past would she go before she let us have the future?

"Isn't it hard to constantly manage yourself?"

I shook my head. "No. I don't want to hurt the people I love. When put in those terms, it makes it easy."

She nodded. "I get that." She pointed to the room beyond. "You should try the cinnamon loaf while it's still warm. You haven't tasted heaven until you've had warm cinnamon loaf."

I tilted my head and regarded her, contemplating her words. Oh, I'd tasted heaven, but I knew it would embarrass her if I told her I'd found it between her legs. "That right?" I stepped back and opened the door for her. "I'm glad you came by."

"Me too."

She lingered, her eyes dropping to my lips. I wanted to reach for her. Kiss her. Touch her. I also didn't want to end up being any kind of regret to her. She'd said she had to study. If she wanted to stay and have sex, she'd need to be the one to make it known.

I didn't have to wait long. Leaning in, she placed her warm lips on mine. Remnants of cinnamon and tea on her breath. It was chaste right down to the little sigh she made in the back of her throat as she lifted her head from mine. *Come at me hard, baby.* I willed her to take what she wanted. Hell, what she needed.

Lacie's lips crashed into mine. Need and desire coursed through us. I kissed her back with the same fierceness she brought, needing to be inside her already. Her tongue swept across my lower lip and I sucked it into my mouth. I growled, scraping my teeth across her tongue, showing her how I wanted to treat her body.

Her low moans had me getting hard. I tore my lips away from hers to kiss down her neck, sinking my teeth into her carotid artery, making her take my mark. Sucking with my lips and scraping with my teeth, excited by the bruises to come.

She tilted her hips and then wrapped her legs around my waist, her heat resting right over my growing cock. I pulled her inside, over the threshold and decided to carry her to my bed before she came to her senses. With one swift move, I flipped her body into my arms and used my foot to close the door.

A peep escaped her mouth. "Briggs, what are you doing? I have to go home."

"You can go home once you have the taste of me on your tongue."

***

LACIE

Oh. My. God.

Please let him say more filthy things like that.

I was going to let him do this. I wanted to forget all my responsibilities and just have the awesome, mind-blowing sex that I knew he could provide. He'd make demands of my body and I'd let him.

We had no business doing this. Not until we talked about . . . well everything. But here, in his room, as my body responded to him stripping out of his T-shirt, I had no reserves and was fast losing control.

My eyes traveled the length of his torso, my lips trembling. I didn't want to think anymore. I only wanted to feel. When he approached me, I jumped at his first touch. He peeled my shirt off and then reached back to unclasp my bra. I wondered what he thought about my body, different from what it was when we were eighteen.

When he touched me, I forgot all about being nervous with him.

He softly skimmed over each hard nipple. When he sucked the nub between his lips, I cried out.

He backed me up to his bed, his head lowering to my chest to pull my other nipple into his mouth. He clamped down with his teeth and a whimper caught in my throat. Why did I like it when he bit and nipped at my skin? His knowing smile said he knew I enjoyed it.

More bites resulted in my mind clearing until the only thing I could think of was the heightened arousal of my sex. If I didn't get relief soon, I'd die. My hips writhed beneath him as he reached to undo the button and lower the zipper on my pants. He pushed his hand roughly past the waist of my panties. Maybe I should be embarrassed about how wet I was. Maybe he would laugh.

His moan was my answer. "God, you're soaking hot." His fingers plunged into me deep and I shrieked in surprise at the invasion.

He released my nipple to watch my face, backing off to stare down at me. "You're so tight. Are you hurt?"

"No. Don't baby me. I want more and I think I'd like it rough."

He inhaled deeply and then exhaled slower, more controlled. "I want to give you what you want. If you need me to stop, tell me."

I nodded. Something went off in him. I swear his overall demeanor darkened as his hand closed around my throat, maneuvering me so that my head hung off the bed. His zipper went down and then his cock moved across my lips and then down to my chin and across my cheek.

He pushed into my mouth in one fluid motion, filling me so fully I couldn't breathe. I should have been scared. I should have push against him. Fought. So why didn't I?

"Lift your chin for me."

I complied. Truthfully, it felt good to let go of every thought and exist at the mercy of his hands and body. No thoughts about school, or Gramps, or Steve. Even the decision to breathe had been conquered by him.

"Turn off your brain, Lace. Let me have control."

I closed my eyes and escaped into the gray, my mind completely voided of all thought, my nervous system on a pilot light, I was focused only on existing. Complete peace washed over me and my body started to go numb.

Briggs released the hand he had on my neck, and I gasped sharply, a rude awakening from the calm of seconds before. I wanted it back, but he'd started thrusting in and out of my mouth. He hit the back of my throat, then went deeper until I pushed against his thighs.

He didn't let up. Over and over, we played a game of push-pull until I lost my mind. I sucked, swirled, and tried to hold on. Tried not to black out. My vision went spotty, and then he released down my throat, violently pushing into me with each pulse.

When he pulled from me, I sagged to the side, the only thing in my thoughts was the ache between my legs. Squeezing my thighs together, I moaned for a release that never came.

Holding my thighs, he spread me wide, watching while revealing my core. Briggs dragged his fingers through my lips, "you're wetter now."

I met his eyes but couldn't admit what he already knew to be true. His finger slid inside me. Over and over, he thrusted in and out. The sounds were embarrassing. "You liked me fucking your throat so much you almost came."

He curled the now two fingers inside me and I shifted as his digits stretched me.

He added another and then leaned forward, tasting me. A moan followed by another lick, then he put all his focus on making me climax. The fingers inside me never stopped moving while his lips nibbled on the bundle of nerves between my legs.

My core clenched and then I spasmed all over his fingers. Whimpering, my back arched off the bed, my nipples tightened. Shivers wracked my body as wave after wave crashed over me.

Suddenly, Briggs pulled his fingers from me and then his cock rammed into me so hard my eyes flew open. The intrusion was foreign and my body raced to adjust. My core clamped down on his dick while one last spasm played through me, setting my nerve endings on fire.

When his hips rolled, I answered with a groan. This was so much more intense than anything we'd done so far. His third time inside of me. The first time reaching the absolute depth of me.

His head lowered to mine and he placed a kiss on my lips, brushing his tongue inside, so that the taste of him and me mingled together.

Breathing was a struggle. His thrusts were so hard I was resolved to gasping while he pounded and bottomed out inside of me. *Was it possible that I was coming around again?*

"Oh God," I rasped when he traced his fingers over the knot where everything begins and ends. His movements were deliberately slow and feather light, toying with me. Driving me mad.

"Briggs," I reached a hand between my legs, pushing against his, or trying to. He immediately seized my arms and held my wrists aloft so that I writhed with the need of my release.

He resumed to slowly stroke and thrust. "Briggs. Why?" I whispered, not able to find my voice.

He smirked on one rather wild push that had him stretching even further inside of me. "I want to make you as crazy as you make me."

I knew it. "Whom the gods would destroy, they first make mad."

"Are you calling me a god?"

"Let me come and I'll call you whatever you want."

He drove home, pounding into me while perfectly massaging me into oblivion.

"Let go. I've got you."

I shuddered and writhed, mumbling something unintelligible.

Before I left, I made it clear to him that this night did not mean I forgave him for everything. I wasn't going to forget just because he had a golden cock and knew how to use it. Really well.

Really, really well.

CHAPTER 18
BRIGGS (AGE 24)

Have you ever had to block your father's number from your phone? For the last few hours, he'd been texting me invoices of all the purchases he'd paid for over the last few months. Purchases that were for my *hobby*.

Breathing strategies and meditation could only carry me so far, proactive tactics were also necessary to remain sane. Hence, I blocked his number so I could focus on remaining calm.

The thing is . . . my father was a good person. No one could argue that. Case in point, here I was taking an envelope of cash to Penny LeBlanc, something I did every two weeks, to help her and the kids while their father, Steve, was in the hospital. He'd been in here for a while but wasn't getting any better.

On the other hand, my father had money. He'd come from money, as did my mother. They wanted for nothing, and they used all they had to help everyone in their vicinity live a better life. It was one of the things that made me proud to be a St. Martin. So I couldn't understand why he was singling me out.

I clipped the hospital visitor pass to my shirt and walked to the elevator. It never got any easier to see our family friends going through so much pain. I patted my shirt pocket, ensuring I'd brought the envelope with me. Penny had told me so many times what a lifeline it was to have help from friends. I exited the elevator and smiled at Angela, a nurse who always flirted with me.

"Bout time you show that pretty face up here." She was older than me by probably twenty years, but she was a fucking great nurse, so I always played along. She deserved to have a little fun.

I walked over and stepped behind the counter to land a kiss on her cheek; if I didn't kiss her, she would just demand it. "You know nothing can keep me away from my favorite nurse." And then it happened. . . you know that feeling you get when the hair on your arm stands up, and your body goes on full alert. My body was suddenly aware that there was something in the immediate vicinity that it wanted. I scanned the area, turning until I found it.

Her.

The one whom my soul loves.

Suddenly everything fell away. The only thing left standing was the two of us. My body hummed with the energy of holding back instead of reaching for what it needed. All I wanted in the world was to be given a second chance with her, one chance that I wouldn't fuck up like so many times before. She wore sea foam green scrubs. Of course she did, it was her favorite color. I saw that color in my dreams. Her hair was pulled into a ponytail, exposing the long column of her neck that I loved to bite and soothe. I recalled the marks I'd left on her three times now. I wanted her to always bear my mark.

When we came together it was intense. Before my turning point, it would have been too much. Now I could handle her. Learning what she needed was becoming my favorite hobby. The night she'd brought cinnamon loaf to my house, she'd needed to empty her mind, clear her head. Lacie wasn't someone who could just shut everything off. She'd needed to be brought to an altar so that she could lay down her burdens. Some rough handling helped her enter that space. She'd trusted me to bring her there. If she could trust me with her body, surely the mind wasn't far behind.

I took a breath to control my intense want of her. I counted with pacing. I pulled out all the tricks so she wouldn't know how affected

I was. "Lacie." It was no use. My voice came out husky and affected.

Her eyes almost bugged from their sockets. "What are you doing here?" Her voice was cautious. Her face was turning red. I hated that I caused that reaction in her. I wanted her to feel comfortable and safe around me.

"I'm here to visit a friend. What about you?"

Her forehead furrowed in thought. Her eyes darted around the nurses station like she was looking to spot this mysterious friend of mine. Watching her problem-solve the situation was a thrill for me, and I smiled, deeply happy to just be breathing the same air as her.

"I intern here." I knew that, of course. Truth is, I'd been coming here a lot lately, recording intimate family moments for Penny and her girls to keep Steve's memory alive once he was not longer part of their lives. I always came in the evening because that's when Penny and the girls were here. Actually, I knew Lacie's internship schedule by heart. That led me to know that her presence here right now was outside of internship hours.

"She's the best speech pathologist I've ever worked with; don't run her off." Angela put in her two cents and then passed a clipboard to my girl. Of course, Angela, being the one who had given me Lacie's schedule, was playing both sides of the coin right now.

"I wouldn't dream of it." Quite the contrary, I'd like her to stay around forever. She'd also been adding videos to Penny's collection. There were videos of her treating Steve and videos of her teaching him how to use various equipment for speech. I'd watched hours of footage. One particular video was taken right after Steve was brought into the hospital as an inpatient. He'd asked her to help him find a way to vocalize so that he could tell the girls he loved them and say goodbye to Penny using his voice. The whole thing had gutted me.

Lacie took the clipboard and then buried her thoughts deep into whatever was on it, leaving me to flounder like a fish out of water. I wanted her to engage me, but I didn't know what to say or if it was even worth trying. God knows I've tried but to no avail. I get it. Across the nurses station, Angela caught my eye and shook her head, sending me off. I needed to give Penny the envelope anyway, so I walked away with Lace never far from my mind. In fact, it would be easier to compute the amount of time in a day I wasn't thinking of her.

I rounded the corner and walked into Steve's room. Penny saw me and set the book she was reading on the hospital table and came over to hug me. Steve was a rigger by trade, but he did odd jobs during off-times. He'd worked in construction with Dad before he came down with ALS. To look at him so small in his chair, sleeping like a child, he seemed at peace, but also like he'd already ascended this world, angelic and child-like. He'd been in the hospital for over six months. At first, I couldn't understand why he wasn't getting any better. Then I learned that his disease was progressive and would end up killing him.

Mother fucker.

Penny was quiet as she watched his chest rise and fall. "He's been sleeping for the better part of the day. Therapy really takes it out of him, and he wants to be rested up when the girls get here."

"Oh, before I forget. . ." I passed her the envelope. She took it but started sniffling. I hated to always be the one to make her cry, but I knew she appreciated every little bit of help she received. I think Dad was paying their bills. Through it all, she never once missed church on Sunday. I wondered how she could still humble herself before a deity that had turned its back on her family. I was pissed at her God for her, even if she wasn't.

She went to speak but then covered her mouth and squeezed my upper arm. I pulled her into my arms and let her take her time with the grief. The thing about me was, I didn't fear death. It was one of the side effects of my psychosis. A lack of fear. In fact, were I laid out in the bed like Steve, I'd have taken the steps necessary to end it all.

I said I didn't fear death. I never said I wasn't a coward.

The lights came on, and then I heard her sweet voice. The voice I heard in my dreams. A voice that stopped stone cold when she saw me.

"Briggs?" Lacie asked in a what-are-you-doing lilt.

Releasing Penny from our embrace, I smiled to bring down the intensity in the room. Penny and I moved apart, but I was aware of an intense energy in the environment, given my newfound skills of listening to my body and tuning in. "I'm here visiting Penny and Steve—if he can spare an ounce of beauty rest." Speaking of Steve, he was coming to, waking from his slumber. He seemed to like my teasing, so I'd kept it up whenever I came to visit him.

Lacie carried an old VHS camcorder, immediately piquing my interest. She set it up in the corner of the room on a tripod and hit record. She bent to look through the lens. "Briggs, you're in the shot."

I moved, wondering what all this was about. She sat on a chair next to Steve and held up a small round device. "I've got something that I think we should try." She held the device in front of Steve's face so he could see it. "It uses EMG . . . electrical activity produced by skeletal muscles. Your thoughts will get it started, and then the barest movement of your finger will pick up that electrical activity. That little millionth of a volt is all that's necessary; the device will amplify it, condition it, and then send a signal via Bluetooth over to whatever device you're controlling. Best thing about it . . . assistive technology controls the equipment. I've got trials on both units until Thursday."

It was Monday.

"Care to play around?" Lacie asked.

Steve blinked once.

She smiled and looked genuinely excited about the possibilities the little device would afford Steve. "Using your computer, the program will scan line by line until you see the word or predictive text you want to say and then it signals, through your muscles, when the software should stop. It may take practice, but we can work on it."

She did what amounted to a seated jig . . . like his own personal communication cheerleader.

THANK. THANK. THANK.

The words came out repeated and fast. Lacie jumped in, stopping him and directing him to look at her while she explained something. "Show me what you want to say." She watched something happen on the screen. Steve watched her for cues as she pointed and taught him how to maneuver the words with the new device. "Ready? Okay, with me." She opened and closed her fist while he used the device to make words. She was beautiful in her confidence and ability.

The whole thing was a symphony and she the conductor, guiding him through the intricate details. They went through many more trials. I grabbed the camera so I could zoom in and get some better angles. Suddenly, I was inspired. *This could be my thesis project.* A documentary featuring the LeBlanc family and their particular path through diagnosis and progression of ALS and all the pieces in between. If there was going to be a positive side to any of this, it would be exposure. The world needed to see the devastating effects of the disease and work together to develop a cure.

THANK YOU FOR GIVING ME A VOICE.

"I only brought the means; you provided the end," Lacie said. "I know you said increased overall independence was your main goal, but I may have found something that can help you at mealtime. I've signed up for a trial and spoken to the representative. He'll be here Friday, and we can try the new equipment. It could make it possible for you to self-feed."

Steve struggled with the new device; words were repeated and then phrases came fast but he couldn't make a coherent statement. Lacie used trial and error to determine different ways to control the device.

SELF-FEEDING. A LUXURY.

Filming them was just the beginning. I'd need tons of footage in order to put together a movie.

"The thing about this new voice output device is. . .it's just a loaner." Lacie twisted her lips after she delivered the news. "We only get to try it out until Thursday, and then they will come take it back. I will put in a recommendation to order one for you, but insurance has to approve it, and we haven't been so lucky in the past."

"How much is the device?" Penny asked, worry evident in every word she spoke.

Lacie looked down to the floor, no longer meeting Steve's eyes. "It's an unbelievable amount. I didn't realize it would be so expensive when I asked the company to set up a trial. I'm so sorry."

"It's okay. It was nice to hear Steve, even if for a while," Penny said, wiping tears from her eyes.

Lacie nodded her agreement. "I'm actually hoping the hospital will purchase one for the rehab department. I have made a presentation to present to the board. I have an appointment with them in about an hour. If the hospital owned something like this, it could be marketed as part of the therapy services for strokes or other patients who struggle with speech." She shrugged. "I feel like we have a really good case here. I'm hopeful."

A swath of hot pink and green swirled into the room. "Uncle Briggs." Squeals filled the room, and then there was a LeBlanc daughter on each of my legs; my knees were rendered motionless. To their delight, I walked like a robot, and more squealing ensued. It wasn't long before they hopped up onto their father's chair and hugged and kissed him. Their resilience always astonished me. They weren't bothered by their father's inability to hold them or speak to them with his voice, though he tried to speak using the new computer equipment.

WHERE? GO?

"Bounce Zone," Sarah said with excitement.

"There's a bazillion trampolines for bounce, bounce, bouncing," Ryley said, jumping in the air three times.

"It's only like twenty trampolines, Ryley," Sarah corrected.

"How do you know? Have you counted them?"

"Dad, will you tell her it's not a bazillion?"

KAJILLION.

Rylie giggled.

"That's way more than a bazillion," Sarah said with exasperation.

The girls continued to talk with their dad when Penny reached for me. I leaned over to hear her whispered thanks for the money and my help with the girls. I hated when she cried, and I always hugged her and told her everything would work out. Why did I say this crap? It made me feel better, but no one could control Steve's prognosis. I apologized for saying it.

"Who's ready for liver and onions?" I asked.

Both girls expressed their dislike through fake gags and coughs.

"We want pizza," Ryley pleaded.

"Pizza! I bet we can get liver and onions on pizza," I teased.

"That's so nasty," Sarah scoffed.

The girls said their goodbyes, and then we walked from the room, but not before I caught sight of Lacie, who regarded me like I'd grown a third eye. I wanted to ask her to join us but knew she was busy with her presentation to the board. I told myself to play it cool. "It was nice to see you."

"Yeah, you too." She looked like she had more to say but only stared blankly at me before saying her goodbyes to the girls.

Life felt weird. I'd gone out of my way to force a connection between us, and as it turns out, it wasn't even necessary. Fate brought us together here at the hospital; our separate lives weaved together all on their own, provided I could get permission to make the documentary.

The more I thought about it, the more amazed I became. Sometimes life had a way of working itself out.

I just had to figure out how not to fuck it up.

CHAPTER 19
LACIE
November

Walking from the billing clerk's office, I recalled my visit with Steve over the summer before school had started. He'd had just enough voice support left that if you put your ear up to his mouth, you could make out some of what he was saying. Now, he couldn't even move his lips, among other facial muscles. That day, I promised to help him fulfill a wish. He wanted to be able to tell his family he loved them, and he wanted to leave some recorded words for Penny. It seemed like a goodbye with words to get her through the year after his passing. It was gut wrenching, but I'd recorded a message for him every day.

It was now six months later. We'd accomplished the *I love you's*, but he still had things he'd wanted to communicate to Penny. Today, he was able to communicate with me using the loner equipment. He told me he'd been too ambitious in his initial plan to make one year's worth of videos. He said he knew he was about to be called home.

I agreed to help him. I promised to do so many things that I haven't been able to deliver on, but I've learned something now that I wasn't aware of six months ago: As an intern, I don't have a lot of power. I had thought that the SLP who worked on the rehab unit might have some sway over the budget that's used to order special equipment, but he told me that Steve no longer qualified as a rehab patient due to his progressively declining status.

I inhaled the deepest breath I could and exhaled slowly. When I decided to become a therapist, I didn't know I would have to fight for the tools I would need to help people communicate. It was frustrating and disheartening to learn that people were just numbers.

Easy to spot with her red, curly hair, I walked toward the table where Kenzie waited for me by the mini-Starbucks inside the hospital. She looked as cute in her nursing scrubs as a basket of puppies in red bowties. Being in different fields of medicine, she and I didn't see each other that often during the day, but we always coordinated our breaks together.

I worried for Kenzie's safety as she texted with both thumbs, not looking up from her phone while she walked toward me. "Tex got Ed Sheeran tickets for winter break." She finished texting and then slipped the phone in one of her many scrub pockets and stood in line next to me. "There's still time to add two more if you want to have some fun before you turn eighty."

"You know I'm going to use that time to catch up on my graduate project."

"Yes, I know." She rolled her eyes.

"So, what were you doing in the billing office? Did you forget to pay your cafeteria bill again?"

I regarded her suspiciously. "Are you in the matrix? How did you know I came from billing?"

"I saw you through the window when I passed by."

I guess that made sense, although her internship assignment didn't go down the billing office hallway. We moved up in line. When I told Kenzie about the augmentative speech device that Steve needed and how much it cost, she said the hospital would never go for it. I'd wanted so badly to prove her wrong, but as it turned out, she was one hundred percent right. "I presented the need for the EMG equipment to the rehab manager and the billing manager, who I was told had grant money to use up, and the budget director. They all managed to turn me out in less than five minutes."

"I'm sorry, honey, I know you had high hopes for that."

"I know. The clerk said Steve doesn't have insurance, and his prognosis doesn't warrant such an expensive device. Can you believe that?"

"Actually, I can."

"It sucks. I wish I had more money saved up from my new management position job." With the raise I'd saved up over three-thousand dollars.

"Girl, you've gotta set some boundaries. You can't do this for every patient you get."

"But Steve is a family friend and a member of my church."

"So what? You probably have a relationship with half of Whiskey Cove. You can't go giving away all your earnings whenever one of them is in need. You need to think of another way to help them. Aren't you already sitting for the girls for free?"

Kenzie could be direct, so much so it hurt. I swallowed the huge cotton ball in my throat and coughed. At the counter, Kenzie ordered a green tea, which was odd. One thing I knew about Kenzie was she drank coffee like camels did water. I placed my order for a vanilla latte and then asked, "What's up with the green tea?"

"I just stuck a tube up a guy's urethra, and now I can no longer unsee that. Kidney disease. I plan to learn to love green tea."

"I don't think taste buds work that way."

We moved down to the established pick-up area. Kenzie selected a packet of stevia from the sweetener options. "I need to tell you something about Steve's case that's going to be hard for you to hear."

"Sounds bad." I knew someone on Kenzie's team was assigned to Steve, so every week she got updates about his case.

"Yes. They talked a lot about him in rounds today," she said while emptying the packet of dried leaf crystals into her tea and then taking a sip. "Bleh, I do want to be kinder to my bladder, but I want a cappuccino with a double hit of espresso more."

"So, what is it about Steve?" I took the lid off of my own tea and dumped in two packets of sugar.

"His prognosis isn't good. As in, he doesn't have much longer. The disease has innervated his swallowing and breathing musculature. He's getting an n/g tube placed tomorrow, along with supplemental oxygen. He may be on a ventilator soon, Lacie. What kind of learning curve is there for that augmentative communication device you want? He may not even be able to learn before he'd be gone."

How could she be so heartless? The timeline had moved up is all. I needed to move quickly to obtain the device so he could tell his family what he needed to say. "I'm not going to give up on him just because some doctor has made a prognosis based on averages and progressions of other cases. Steve's case might be different. Did your doctor account for that? He has a strong support system and God on his side."

"You're right, he does, and so did a lot of the patients who came before him, and it didn't save them. I'm worried you're getting overly close to this case. You need to step back. Right now, you should be preparing the family for palliative care, not getting their hopes up about Steve regaining the ability to communicate. He's struggling to swallow. Focus of speech therapy should be on managing his dietary intake, a system without which he can't survive."

"I am focused on swallowing and dietary intake, but I can also help him communicate. It could help in the days to come if he were able to describe how he is feeling. Doesn't he deserve the dignity and right of communication during his last days?"

"Of course he does, Lacie. But there are yes/no boards and simpler augmentative devices that can be used to achieve that."

"Why are you so against this?"

"I'm not against it, honey, I just think you're being unrealistic. Steve doesn't have much time, nor does he have any funding."

My jaw clenched, and I threw my tea in the wastebin. "As long as there is breath left in his body, I'll be there by his side, helping him communicate. He deserves that basic human trait that separates us from being animals." I was so angry at her flippant attitude I couldn't think of the right words to say. "You're . . . heartless . . . and . . . a coward . . . and a bad nurse."

I wanted to take the words back as soon as I'd said them. Kenzie's light darkened, and her demeanor got small. But it was true that nursing school wasn't teaching her about compassion. She wasn't any different than the budget director. How was there nothing anybody could do? Without realizing it, I'd started walking away from Kenzie. When she called my name, I didn't look back.

Arriving back at Steve's room, I heard a commotion coming from inside. Peeking inside his room, I was not prepared for what I walked into. It wasn't sad, but cheerful. His girls were back from lunch and on the bed tissue paper flowers, petals, and stems littered the blanket and floor. Rylie ran the leaves of her flowers over the arm of her father, while Sarah twirled her deep purple flower between her fingers. Penny stood over them, smiling and singing *Build Me Up Buttercup*. In the corner of the room was Briggs, holding a high tech video recorder, capturing their private moments.

I walked toward him. "What are you doing here?"

He moved the camera from in front of his face but left it rolling, his expression dubious. When he didn't answer right away, I said, "You can't just take video of the family like this. You have to obey the HIPPA privacy laws." My voice had gotten louder than I'd intended, but I was irritated about how everyone was ignoring the rules. During my internship, I'd learned that first and foremost, patients had rights, and to not abide by them was breaking the rules. Not only was he ignoring Steve's rights, but he was jeopardizing my internship. Just last week, one intern was placed on probation for putting a picture of a patient on their social media.

I fumed while explaining the HIPPA laws to him. It was also important for me to stay mad at him for the infractions of his past that he'd yet to apologize for and for what he might commit in the future. I know it seemed mean, but I had known old Briggs for eighteen years, whereas I'd only known new Briggs for four months. Staying mad at him was the only way I had of protecting my heart when she wanted to do something stupid, like fall in love with him again.

I've always loved you.

Gah, shut up, Heart, you stupid bitch.

"Lacie, can I talk to you for a moment." I followed Penny out into the hallway. She cleared her throat and gave me a sincere look. "You know how much Steve loves to help people." She looked away and swallowed. "He said he doesn't want his life to be a waste and he'd like to record his experience with ALS to help shed light on the disease and to help others who are diagnosed so I've asked Briggs to help take some family videos. I don't want Steve to be around any bickering. He should have as much peace as possible in his last days." Her lips thinned as she looked into my eyes. "I know you and Briggs have some bad history and some things to work through but please, I have to ask that you not do it around Steve."

My guts seized. God, she was so right. I had been immature. "I'm sorry, Penny. I'm completely at fault. Please forgive me."

She squeezed my hand. "Forgiven."

Of course she forgave me. I followed her back into the room, suddenly feeling petty and stupid. My face flushed with heat. What had I been thinking? It was Briggs. He always made me act irrational, crying and even scratching and hitting him. He was my drug and when I used him, he wasted me.

Briggs's eyes froze on me, his expression stoic. I guess the videos I'd taken weren't good enough. Last month Penny brought in the vintage RCA VHS camcorder, I'd operated it when I could between patients and charting. Suddenly, the room was too small, I needed air.

On my way out of the room, Penny called my name. She smiled. "I just want to keep things as calm as possible."

"Of course you do. Again, I'm sorry. And you're in good hands. Briggs is the best."

I delivered the words and then moved toward the door. I stared at Steve, my own muscles feeling weak as recognition of Briggs's new role settled into my psyche.

Watching Steve like this was strange because while his eyeballs moved to track the action before him, nothing else did. Even his breathing was imperceptible. Zero body language to gauge his reaction to things. It was especially hard because I'd known him before his diagnosis. He had always been animated and fun. Now he was a passive observer in his own life.

I thought about what Kenzie had said. Once I'd gotten over the initial anger at her black and white view of things, it was easier to consider what she'd said about simpler communication aids. A yes/no board would help Steve answer questions about his care and his wants/needs. I decided to get started on fashioning one that would be easy to grab in an instant, making communication like a second skin, as it had been for him before ALS.

Once I was done making the board, I wandered back to Steve's room. The commotion had settled down. The girls were asleep, and Briggs and Penny were softly talking.

"Briggs, can I talk to you?" I felt guilty about my rudeness earlier and wanted to tell him. After a long exhale, he set the camera on the corner chair and followed me out the door. At the nurses station, Briggs stood with crossed arms and tight lips. *Shit, I'm going to piss off everyone today.* "I'm sorry about getting short with you earlier. Do you want to get together tomorrow?" I cleared my throat, wanting to fill the silence between us.

"So now you're ready to talk?" He forced a laugh.

I blinked, dumbfounded. He'd asked me about fourteen times to talk over dinner or a walk. "Yes, I would have contacted you sooner, but it's been a little crazy learning a new job while going to classes while completing an internship." Not to mention taking care of Gramps and trying to figure out what to do about Steve and talking Finn into coming to the speech clinic to get a videofluroscopy of his throat.

"Yeah, okay, I guess we can talk."

Feeling awkward and suffering from where to put my hands, I fidgeted with the pen I wore around my neck. A necklace pen Briggs had left for me at the nurses station one day because he knew I was always losing them. "So, do you want to meet somewhere for dinner?" I asked.

"What, like a date?" he questioned.

Frustration settled in my hardening stomach. "You've been . . . you've asked me to dinner half a dozen times."

"That was before."

"Before what?"

"Before you turned me down—exactly fourteen times. Ball's in your court. A man can only take so much rejection."

"Why don't we . . . couldn't we…" Damn I didn't know. I shook my head. This was too much in addition to everything I was balancing.

He leaned toward me, offering a genuine smile. "Come to the estate. Saturday at seven. I'll make dinner."

"You'll make dinner?" I wasn't aware he could cook, though if someone had asked me if he could make latte rosettes, I'd have said no. "What should I bring?"

He squeezed my earlobe. "Just bring you, Lace."

CHAPTER 20
BRIGGS

It had been Thursday when I'd last seen or heard from Lacie. I had no idea if she'd even remember to show, but if she did, I planned to be prepared to impress her. I'd been planning this dinner all week. Several times I caught myself humming or smiling like a fool. I had not stopped to eat lunch today, and my energy was through the roof.

I envisioned calm lake water and a fishing rod. Stupid since I didn't fish, but something about that mental imagery calmed me when I added deep breathing, so it remained my go-to façade.

In truth, I was worried about Lacie. She just seemed off. The way she'd taken me to task for shooting video was strange, especially since it occurred in front of Steve and Penny, who didn't need any additional negative energy around them. Of course, I'd gotten the go-ahead from Penny to shoot video and edit the film into a sequence for a documentary. Lacie would have no way of knowing that and had been fiercely protecting her patient. Whatever was going on with her, I planned to get to the bottom of it over dinner.

The kitchen in my childhood home had been remodeled within the last few years. In fact, it was Steve who had done the custom subway tiles in a herringbone pattern on the backsplash in gray and white. The floors and the ceiling had been done in bamboo by Finn, who was a savant when it came to wood and paint. He'd white-washed the whole thing, so it matched the light gray on the back-splash. The new look just felt refreshing on a hot summer day, like an ocean side cabin, except that the kitchen, with its full table for eight and six island bar stools, was the size of some small cabins. My favorite feature was the windows on the east side that opened to the outdoor kitchen on the largest home patio I'd ever seen, which I used to its full potential when I was younger and had the time.

Finn stood in front of the refrigerator with the door open, blocking my ability to get the ingredients I needed to make the second course of my dinner for Lacie. "If you're going to stand there, I'm going to put you to work."

Finn turned and signed, "You can't afford me."

"Hand me that bag of lettuce and the block of feta cheese." From the counter I picked up a pomegranate and googled how to get the seeds out. Finn and I had started taking sign language classes together on the internet. I promised I wouldn't interfere between him and Lacie. They had an ongoing battle of the wills. He didn't want to talk about surgical repairs to his voice, nor did he want to talk about computer talkers. Both things Lacie kept pushing.

When he'd asked her about sign language, she'd told him it was just as laborious as other mediums of communication, if not more so, because it placed a lot of burden on his communication partners since they would have to know sign language in order to converse with him. The thing Lacie failed to realize was that this was the only communication medium that interested Finn.

To me, it was a no-brainer. High interest equaled more benefit, but again, I wasn't going to intervene. I had my own problems to work out with Lacie. Though it would be fun to watch when she learned he'd been signing behind her back.

Finn placed sandwich ingredients on the counter while I made the first cut in the pomegranate– the result of which had deep violet juice flowing in every direction. "Shit."

Finn passed me a towel. "What the hell are you doing?" he signed.

I wiped up the mess. "I'm making dinner for Lacie."

"Since when do you cook?"

"I don't really, but how hard can ravioli be?"

"I think it's hard," Finn signed while chuckling at my plight.

"I've got the video queued up on the fridge. I'm going to watch and do exactly what they do."

Finn slapped an assortment of Italian deli meat and cheese between a sub roll. His next move would be to drench it in vinegar and oil. I cut more of the pomegranate, using the towel to mop up the liquid while Finn lifted some of the butter lettuce from the container I'd bought for tonight's salad. "Hey, that's for my dinner."

Mouth full of sandwich, he shrugged. I decided I should lay down some ground rules about tonight. "If you give me the kitchen tonight, the wooden spoon carving set is yours." I thought the kit might sweeten the deal. I hadn't used it since my rehabilitation days and thought it was a good time to pass it on to Finn, who whittled on a daily basis; mostly woodland animals, but he had started to do spoons and butter knives, and to be honest, I liked using them more than the stainless.

Finn fingerspelled d-e-a-l and walked out with his sandwich wrapped in a paper towel. For things we could not yet sign, we fingerspelled. Then Finn would write that word down for the next class and ask for a demonstration. He was smarter than I was and was already light years ahead of me. Luckily, I didn't have to be fluent at the act of making the signs, I only had to read what Finn signed. Finn said my signing was shit. An opinion confirmed after receiving a low D on my first sign quiz.

"Hey, Finn?" I called, and he turned back. "Lacie texted about fifteen minutes ago that she's bringing the LeBlanc girls with her tonight. Do you think this is still okay?" I was clueless about feeding kids. Finn looked over the thin strands of pasta I'd laid out on the counter for the girls and then gave me a truly clueless look before shrugging.

"On second thought, I can make the girls grilled cheese." Finn used his sandwich-free hand to give me a snap-point gesture that said I'd nailed it. "Thanks, man, and if you do come out of your lair, put on a shirt."

He flipped me off and then was gone.

By six-thirty, I had the crostini appetizers in the oven, the salad cooling in the fridge, and the ravioli water simmering. Around seven, Lacie walked in carrying a bottle of red wine and a bottle of grape juice. The bottles clinked together when she set them on the counter. "The door was open, so I didn't bother to knock."

She stood looking sexy in short cutoffs that had frayed and a gray tank top. Her lips and face look dew-kissed from the heat of the day. I tried not to focus on the gooseflesh that prickled her arms or her nipples that began to harden beneath the tank. I guess it was cold in here, compared to the humid heat outside. It took all the strength in me to focus on the drinks she'd brought as I walked to the fridge. "You know you're always welcome here." When I moved the salad to place the bottles of wine in the fridge, I noticed the lettuce had started to wilt. Badly. "Shit."

I pulled the salad bowl from the fridge while Sarah and Rylie poked their heads out from behind Lacie, their eyes large and set on me. "Oh, you said shit."

"Err, sorry."

Lacie put a finger over her mouth and shook her head at the girls. "What's wrong?" she asked.

"The lettuce has wilted," I said.

Lacie walked over and took the bowl from my hand. "You dressed it?"

"Yeah," I said, reaching for the dressing. "It was the first thing I made."

She grimaced. "You can't put the dressing on until you're ready to eat it."

"Well, that's ruined." I felt a fissure of anger open up at the base of my spine and willed it down using breath control exercises. I wondered if she noticed. If she did, she'd either get used to it or hate it enough to keep us apart.

She shook her head. "I'm sure it still tastes good." She popped a green, wilted leaf into her mouth. Well, she tried, but it landed on the side of her lip where she used her tongue to guide the rogue lettuce into her mouth, but it kind of disintegrated in the process. "Hmm, on second thought, maybe it is inedible."

I went over to her, lifted her head, and wiped the offending greenery away. "Good as new."

Rylie held her arm out toward the oven. "Is something burning?"

"Fuck!" I leaped over to the stove and pulled out a tray of blackened garlic crostini. "That's two out of three. Shit, I really thought I could do this."

"One fuck and two shits. That's five dollars," Sarah said.

"Girls! We don't repeat foul language," Lacie chided.

"Five dollars?" I questioned.

"Each," Sarah countered.

Lacie pulled Sarah against her and giggled. "The ravioli looks amazing," Lacie said with a big smile on her beautiful face.

"Yeah, I guess I could do the ravioli and use a couple of Finn's sub rolls for garlic bread."

Lacie slid onto a stool at the bar, looking worried as she chewed on her lip. The girls were at the window, admiring the pool.

"Don't worry, I'll get us all fed one way or the other," I comforted.

"I'm not worried; it's just the filling is coming out of your ravioli in the water."

"Oh shit."

"Six dollars each," Rylie yelled.

I grabbed the big spoon and tried to scoop a ravioli out of the boiling water, but it kept slipping off the utensil. Lacie ran over with a colander and set it in the sink nearest the stove. "Stand back, I don't want to burn you."

When I poured the ravioli into the strainer, the ravioli fell apart, and most of the filling fell through the holes. I placed my palms on the edge of the sink and bent over the carnage, taking deep, slow breaths. In rehab, we'd made ravioli with a visiting chef. The whole process seemed so easy with his guidance. I rubbed the area between my eyes and then turned to lean a hip against the counter.

Lacie started to laugh, the kind of laugh where your eyes water and you can't breathe. I joined her. The whole laughing episode was cathartic and something I desperately needed at the moment.

Sarah was at my hip. "Do you have the blue box mac and cheese?" She squealed and added her joy to our laughing party.

"I don't think so."

Her big eyes blinked up at me and she surveyed the kitchen carnage. "Six dollars would buy a lot of blue boxes."

"What's with the six dollars?" I asked.

"That's the fee for swearing in front of me and Rylie. Daddy always carries singles around. Not for strippers, but for swears, he always says."

"Oh, right." I pulled out my wallet and counted out twelve dollars.

"Girls, why don't you go set up the game in the living room." Lacie pointed in the direction she wanted them to go. "And leave poor Briggs alone for now."

Sarah took the money I offered and did as Lacie asked.

Lacie seemed to be trying to hold back a laugh, but she wasn't doing a very good job, which made me chuckle. "I was trying to do something nice for you, and honestly," I exhaled, "I hoped to impress you tonight, but that's out the window unless you like water-logged ravioli."

She pulled out her phone. "How about I order takeout from Lorenzo's?"

So much for my big effort. She ordered while I cleaned up, admiring her legs in the frayed jean shorts she wore. The days were still hot, topping out around eighty-five degrees, and her skin had tanned, giving her skin a succulent caramel color. "Delivery or pick up?"

"Have them deliver it," I said.

I heard her rattle off the address and smiled. When you knew someone as long as we'd known each other, you just knew those mundane things about each other. I'd learned other things in the last few months. Lacie's hair smelled like strawberries, and when the sun caught certain strands, they lit up like gold. The freckles on her nose and cheeks were darker after she had been outside. Her green eyes changed colors depending on what she wore. She picked her nails when she thought about Steve. She hated cappuccino machines. Perhaps the best thing I've learned since being back was . . . I can make the fire in her eyes ignite by sucking on her earlobe.

"Okay, food will be here in about an hour." I had the dishes all cleaned up, the evidence of my ineptitude gone.

"What can we do while we wait?"

I cocked a brow and caught her gaze, her cheeks stained red within seconds.

She cleared her throat. "I mean, should I pour us some drinks?"

"Yeah, drinks are good." I used the time to adjust myself and take a few deep breaths. *Grandma St. Martin's false teeth.* Grandma loved to wrap them in a napkin and forget about them until the next morning. It was disgusting.

"Hope you like white grape."

"Whatever." I didn't really drink grape juice all that much, but since she bought it, I was going to drink it like I'd been in the desert for three days. After the first sip, it really wasn't that bad. "Mmm, good."

She sipped her red wine, closing her eyes and licking a drop off her bottom lip, sighing. "It's Cabernet Sauvignon, my favorite."

Christ. I'd be buying an orchard just to watch her take erotic sips until the end of time. Plus, now Lacie had a favorite wine. Adulthood looked good on her. I wondered if she saw any differences in me.

"You're so different now. I feel like I don't know you," she said, reading my mind as we walked toward the living room.

"I think we got to know each other pretty well a few months ago in the barn." I lowered my chin, feeling the unruly piece of hair that curled slightly come down over my right brow and let my eyelids lower with it, basking in the afterglow a little more. "Didn't we?" Her blush deepened to a nice rosy color; the bastard in me loved to get her all hot and bothered. "You hid my clothes, payback for when you were thirteen?"

"It's only payback if people saw your nakedness."

I chuckled. "The stable workers saw the dark side of the moon as I came down from the loft ladder, so you got your wish. Plus, Theo was there."

Her laughter was infectious, high and giddy, pure enjoyment. I liked her like this, liked being the one to put that smile on her face. I followed her into the living room.

"What's the dark side of the moon?" Rylie asked.

Something I was learning was that kids heard everything. "Who's this?" I picked up one of their dolls, hoping to change the subject. I sat on the couch, and Lacie sat next to me, putting her between the girls who sat on the floor and had every inch of the larger-than-normal coffee table covered with dolls in bright neon colors and glitter. "That's Princess Aurora."

"Oh, yeah, from Cinderella?"

The girls fell into a fit of giggles. "That's not Cinderella."

I turned the doll this way and that in my hands. "It's not."

"No! This is the Princess Cinderella." Sarah handed me a doll with the same face and blonde hair but in a blue dress. "I thought Cinderella was a movie, not a princess."

"It is a movie, but she's a princess too."

"Why would anyone be named *Cinder*-ella?"

"Oh my gosh, he doesn't know anything about princesses," Sarah said to Lacie.

"That's because he's a boy. He only knows boy stuff," Rylie said.

"Daddy's a boy, but he knows girl stuff and boy stuff," Sarah countered.

"The way I see it, there is only one solution here." Lacie set her wine glass on the end table.

"What's that?" I asked.

"We watch Cinderella," Lacie said with an apologetic look.

The girls jumped up and danced around the coffee table.

An additional twenty-eight dollars, and we were streaming the new live action movie, and later, a promise of the animated version loomed. This was not the way I imagined the night going. I'd hoped to talk things out with Lacie. I'd wanted to apologize for how I'd left things four years ago.

The girls sat in front of the large flat screen and ended up watching both versions of Cinderella before Penny arrived to take them home. By the time they had left, I had seven blue ribbons in my hair, and Lacie had the nails on her hands and feet painted pink and purple.

We landed exhausted on the couch.

"How ridiculous do I look?" I turned toward her.

"I think this could be your knew look." She pointed to my hair and yawned. Her eyelids hung lower than usual and that was her third yawn.

"Tired?"

"The four a.m. mornings are taking their toll. Not to mention my classes, the internship, and my new management job at the coffee bar."

"Four a.m.?"

"I've been getting up early to help orient Gramps. It helps if we go over his schedule, and he writes it down in his own shorthand in this little pocket notebook he carries around, something he did in the Navy. This morning, he seemed more confused than usual. He started talking about Grams. He said she'd made pancakes and eggs and couldn't I smell the maple syrup? I'd just poured his Cheerios in a bowl and was cutting up a banana to go on top–the same thing he's eaten every morning for as long as I've been around, even when Gram was alive."

She shook her head, looking confused. "After breakfast, I got him started on his schedule for the day, which included mowing the grounds. We went out to the storage shed, and he'd forgotten his keys, so I went back to the house to get them and returned to find him MIA. Thankfully, Theo texted me that he was at the main house."

"That's a lot on you, Lace."

"Yeah, it is. But if the Landrys find out he's forgetting things, I don't want to think about what might happen to the three of us." Her eyes filled with tears.

I put my arm around her. She was so unselfish she gave every-thing of herself to her family and friends, but I worried she was trying to make the impossible happen here. The day of the blessing breakfast, Gramps had been completely lost. He didn't seem to know what he was looking at. Like the folding chairs–when unfolded, he seemed confused about what they were. That wasn't forgetfulness entirely. At least, I didn't think so. You forgot phone numbers or where you left your keys. You didn't forget how to use a chair.

"What about retirement?" I shrugged, hoping she wouldn't get upset at my asking. "Could he retire?"

"Retirement would be good, but he isn't old enough yet to collect full retirement. Plus, we are saving for a place to live." She rubbed her arms and looked away.

"Oh, right." I also looked away to focus on my thoughts. I'd give anything to help her and her family. Would she let me? I remembered her house getting washed away during one of the storms. Dad had helped them with some legal stuff, like he'd done with so many, but it was hard squeezing blood from a turnip, as he'd say. Those days my veins were flooded with whatever prescription meds the doctors wanted me to try, plus all the added chemicals from my brain's imbalance made a lot of the details fuzzy.

"You know Dad got a bungalow on the river for Finn, hoping he'd use it, but you know Finn's got a mind of his own. It sits empty. I know dad wouldn't mind if you and your family needed to use it for a while. He's always offering it to people. I know he'd like to see it put to use."

The awkward silence was my cue to shut the fuck up. Maybe she thought I'd expect something in return, but I expected absolutely nothing. The thought of her not having to worry about where her family would live was return enough. I loved her. I wanted her to have everything and I wanted to be the man to give it to her. I wanted her to let me. "I'm sorry, I didn't mean"—

Just then she smiled. It lit up her entire face, making the wear dissipate and her beauty shine. "That's actually a really nice offer."

I exhaled in relief. "Yeah?" I questioned.

"Yeah."

"How bout we open that other bottle of grape juice and talk?" I didn't wait for an answer but went straight into the kitchen and walked back to the living room with glasses, and wine and juice to find Lacie on my laptop that I'd left propped open on the end table next to the couch. I liked turning off the screensaver and sleep features when I edited video because I didn't want the screen saver popping up. Now that little irritation seemed silly.

"What am I looking at, Briggs?'

I froze. There was no mistaking the overhead narration leading into a commentary about Steve's bout with ALS. "I was just messing around," I said as I set the drinks on the coffee table and pulled the laptop from her lap. Not sure why I didn't tell her about the thesis project or the documentary, but I just couldn't bring the words up. I didn't like not knowing how she would react. Before I'd gotten better, I engineered my behavior to get the actions and words I wanted out of people.

Now, I feared if she were unhappy with any part of what I was doing that I might drop the whole project. I didn't want to stop the forward momentum that had been created that had Professor Grabassy approving my project and had breathed new life and energy into my program. I wanted this so bad I could taste it and I didn't want myself or Lacie to jeopardize the project.

She frowned. "Please make sure that's all your doing."

I struggled to bring up such a sensitive subject, but I'd gotten the permission forms from the major players. It wasn't her place to tell me I couldn't use the footage to make a documentary about ALS that may help thousands. Except that I needed a permission slip from her too, since she was in almost every video working with Steve on his communication and swallowing. "This was one of the things I wanted to talk to you about."

She slammed the laptop shut.

"One of the things?" She raised an eyebrow in question.

"It's just, I want to make a film that chronicles his journey with ALS."

She leaned forward and placed her elbows on her knees, her hands rubbed her face as she sighed. "It's not a journey, Briggs. Steve is walking the course that leads him to the end of his life, like the green mile, but he's completely innocent. It's not fair. He can't even talk to his family in his last days without a device that costs thousands of dollars, which may as well be a million given his ability to obtain it."

"The hospital isn't going to get one?"

She let out a long, frustrated sigh. "No, the hospital isn't going to get one." She steepled her hands and rested them against her mouth. "I don't want his pain and lack of medical insurance exploited." She shot her eyes over to me. "Can I think about the film?"

"Yeah, think about it." I sat next to her, my mind burning up with words left unsaid. It didn't really matter if she wasn't on board. I already had signed consent forms from Penny and Steve's lawyer, who acted as his guardian. My mind kept going back to Steve's need for an expensive speech generating device. "I think we should do a fundraiser to get the money for the communication machine."

"A fundraiser?" She cocked her head at me.

"Why not? He has a lot of friends in town, and beyond. People are opening GoFundMe accounts for much less. Steve has a story to tell. Friends and family, even strangers, will be moved by his story and donate to his cause."

"You wanna open a GoFundMe?"

"No. I think we do a classic fundraiser like a casino night."

"Casino night?" She shook her head. "Sorry I don't mean to sound like a parrot this is just a lot."

"I can bring Cash in."

"Isn't he in Vegas?"

"Actually, he's in Morocco for a no-limit hold-em tournament, but you know my brother . . . he'd come home for Steve."

She nodded. "Yeah, he would," she agreed, and then let out a long breath. "I don't know."

"Do you trust me?"

She swallowed and sat up straight. "I've got so many things going on right now that I'm trying to hold onto, and I can feel them slipping away. I feel like I'm holding the strings to a bunch of kites, and the wind is picking up; the lines are getting tighter and starting to cut through the skin on my hands. At any moment, those lines are going to break. I can feel it. It's just too much to hold on to."

I reached over and grabbed her hand. "Let me hold some of it. I can do this." She nodded, but I could see the doubt in her eyes, doubt in me from the trust I'd broken. "I know I haven't given you much reason to trust or believe in me, but I'm hoping to change that and for you to see some semblance of the man that I am." My voice broke at the emotion I felt at all the shit from our past and the broken bonds. Could they ever be mended? "I'm sorry, Lace. For everything. Sorry for Scooter the Caterpillar, sorry for taking your clothes on the day your Grams had died, sorry for the day after our prom." A tear slid down my cheek and I left it there, a symbol of an hourglass of all the time I'd waisted.

I saw her tears as she leaned into my side so I could put my arm around her. "I want to be the man you run to and I know you're not ready to hear this, but I can't stop saying that I love you." I placed a kiss on her forehead.

"Briggs," she whispered, "I think I want that too, but I need time. I'm so scared."

"I know, baby, but Steve doesn't have time."

She sat up, and I wiped her tears away. "Say you'll let me throw him a fundraiser."

She nodded. "Yes. That would be incredible."

I shook my head. "It's nothing. What you do for Steve, that's something incredible. What you do for everyone is incredible."

"And you really think your brother would come all the way to Louisiana to do this for us?"

I wondered at her question. "People do things for their family. That's how it works. All I have to do is ask him." I guess she didn't have any real family except for her grandfather, and he couldn't do much given his age. She would learn how families worked. In good time, she'd learn. I'd make sure of it.

She shrugged. "I thought he didn't get along with your dad. Isn't that why he left?"

"No one gets along with Dad, even Camp, who works with him

daily. It only works between them because Camp knows how to keep his mouth shut."

"Cash's twin? The one who works with your father. Didn't Cash work with Camp at some point?"

"Every one of us, except Finn, has worked for Dad at some point. Even Clara. My father has high hopes of grooming someone to take over the business."

She nodded. "And Camp will do that."

I shrugged. "Not sure. Finn, however, enjoys woodworking and construction, but I think Dad dismisses him as someone who could run the business since he can't talk, and Cash uses all the money he earns from gambling to put back into his 3D printing construction business. I know he has approached Dad about collaborating, but Dad is a stubborn ass and untrusting of new-fangled technology."

"Wow, Cash must be a really nice guy to put his life on hold and help Steve. If we can raise enough money, it would enable me to have cash available for his medical needs, and that would be one huge worry that's gone for Penny. But it would need to come together fast."

I smiled. This gave me yet another thing to work on with Lacie. I was pumped that it may also help the LeBlanc family and even the ALS community.

Somewhere in the distance, a phone chimed, alerting a text had come in, but I wasn't ready for the world to intrude, and Lacie didn't seem to be ready for that either. We sat, our heads together, my arm around her shoulders. I felt like we'd taken the first step forward in our journey to the peak of the mountain top.

If she was scared, I was terrified.

I could do with a reset here, but life was no movie set, and there was no director calling the shots.

With Lacie, I'd used up all my mistakes already and now I had to be perfect.

Thing was, I wasn't sure I could do perfect, but if I could, it would be for her.

CHAPTER 21
LACIE

Shit. I had three texts from Mom. Gramps was in some kind of trouble. I quickly called her, and she picked up on the first ring.

"Oh my God, Lacie." Her voice was raw with emotion.

My own throat went tight. "Mom, what's wrong?"

"There's been an accident. The tractor was upturned in the bayou and there was a trail of blood leading to the forest. Gramps is nowhere to be found."

My stomach turned. I placed my hand over my mouth when I thought I was going to vomit. "Oh, God."

Briggs rubbed circles on my back. I passed the phone to him and ran to the bathroom to relieve my body of the dinner I'd eaten. When I returned, the front door was open. I grabbed my bag and hurried outside to find Briggs in the mule with several high-powered lights and light bars attached to it as he continued to snap more on, a spotlight-looking lamp and a rack to the top. "Get in, Lace. We're gonna find Gramps."

Thank you God for sending me Briggs. I boarded the mule, reaching up for the pull-up bar with shaking hands. As we roared over to the plantation I thought about our morning. I'd gone over the poster board with Gramps. Pictures of the plantation lawns with definitions such as driveway lawn, rear acreage, and bayou side yard to make clear the mowing job he had to do today, which seemed easy. We'd even walked out to the stables where the lawn mower was kept and problem-solved how to start it up and operate the controls. He'd seemed fine and calm, like he'd done it a thousand times before, which he had.

Briggs focused on avoiding large holes. I wish I could do something that would actually help someone. I thought the pathfinding aids would help ease Gramps mind but evidently, I'd failed him. "He should be enjoying his retirement. Not worrying about having to work to pay for my college and keeping a roof over my head."

"Lace, you have to know that your Gramps would still be trying to work on things that he shouldn't, even if he weren't housing you or sending you to school. He can't sit still. This would have happened no matter what you were doing."

Thinking about Gramps working even when he was supposed to be on a holiday or during his vacations, I realized what Briggs said was right. "That's true. He won't stop." And me and Mom not living with him wouldn't have made this situation better. It probably would have been worse. At least we are right here with him. Mom was there. I'm here. Briggs's here. We would find him.

When we arrived, everyone was outside including some unwanted quests. "Oh my God."

"Lace?" Briggs questioned.

"The Landry kids are here. That's not good." I got out, and Briggs had walked around the mule to sidle up next to me.

"Don't say anything about your grandfather's issue. For all they know the zero-turn had a malfunction. Doesn't mean your grandfather had anything to do with it."

I look at him in disbelief. "But he had everything to do with it."

He shook his head as we walked toward the scene. "We don't know that."

"What if we can't find him."

He stopped our ascent and squeezed my upper arms. I looked down to let the tears roll. "Lace, please look at me." I did as he asked, my face a mess. "I know I haven't given you many reasons over the years to put your faith in me, but I'm giving you my word here . . . I will find your grandfather and bring him back to you."

He placed a kiss on my forehead and then turned to walk away, leaving me looking after him. My uncontrollable and disturbed little boy had grown into a confident and concise man capable of taking control in intense situations and even have control left over enough to comfort me. I truly did believe his words, and I let them guide me and carry me. It was the only way to keep me from freaking out completely.

I entered the fray of people who had gathered around the pecan grove near the front of our apartment. The benches surrounding the trees set the scene for the recovery crew. I saw Police Chief Fontenot and three deputies, including the one who played Texas Hold'em with Gramps in a local monthly game. His nickname was Sturgis on account of his yearly trips to the bike rally every summer. It could be raining cats and dogs, but Sturgis would ride around, unfazed, patrolling on his motorcycle like it was a sunny summer day.

Mom and Sturgis spoke while Theo headed my way.

"How you doing, Beans?" He reached in and gave me a tight hug lasting several seconds, which was exactly what I needed. I sighed into him and let him hold me.

When he released me, I saw the tears in his eyes. "Thanks for being here, Theo."

"Beans, where else would I be?"

I was grateful for him. "Do you know what happened?"

When he pressed his lips, his jaw locked, which I did not take as a good sign. "I came out to run some Advil to Maw and saw the lawn mower in the ditch. I went over to kill the engine and saw the blood, but Gramps was nowhere nearby." Hands went in pockets, and then his head went down. His classic body language when he was just as lost as I was. "I'm sorry, Beans."

Mom approached, her arms already open in need. I leaned into her, taking whatever energy she could give. "I'm sorry, Mom, we'll find him."

She lifted her head from my shoulder. "I know we will." Her smile was more of a crooked line.

God, I'd failed them. Mom, Gramps. I should have told him not to mow. At least not until someone could watch him. What had I been thinking? Someone who can't remember what day it was shouldn't be operating large equipment. Had I taken the keys to the mower, he'd still be here with us.

"Don't do that," Mom said. "I know what you're thinking, Cherie, and I want you to take those thoughts from your mind right now. Everybody ages, and you can't stop the process. All you can do is be there when he needs you, and he will need you as soon as he comes home." She squeezed me so tight I could feel her heart beat against my own, in tandem. Mother and daughter, carbon copies, with only a few individual differences. Life was a gift, no more controllable than the rain or a raging angry fire.

"Come on, Beans, let's go into the woods." Theo shined a spot-light in my direction and then handed me a government issue one of the same.

I wondered how many lumens the light measured and felt a smile spread across my face. Briggs was in the woods. "Let's go."

As we walked, I spotted Kenzie, speaking with the Landry brother-sister duo. She hugged herself, her hands rubbing her arms like she was cold. Only it was hot outside even though it was November. My stomach went nauseous with the pang of seeing her here, supporting my family, even though I'd said those mean words to her when she'd tried to tell me about Steve's prognosis. Her gaze came to me on the wind. Her face said it all. She was here for me, even though I was mad at her. I swallowed back the tears.

At the edge of the forest, we were stopped by the sheriff. "Only law enforcement allowed past the tape. We'll find your Gramps, Lacie. No need for you to cause more worry for us by being in the forest."

Theo grunted. "Not a lot of faith in our skills, Beans."

"But Briggs and Mr. St. Martin were allowed past the tape."

"They've been deputized, ma'am."

They had? What the hell did that even mean? "Can we be deputized?" I pointed between me and Theo.

"I don't think that would be a good idea." Chief Fontenot tipped his enormous hat at me.

I looked at Theo. "You gotta love the South."

"Aye, and you know we do."

Just in the distance, Cordelia was heading this way with a large box and her entourage of followers. "I sense trouble on the horizon. This has all the makings of a voodoo ritual," Theo said.

"Theo! Don't say things like that." He shrugged and I shivered. While I may not believe in a lot of the spiritual mediums in these parts, I still respected them and gave them a wide berth.

Cordelia lit something that started to smoke. She waved it around and chanted while the ladies that had come with her set out blankets and golden pots. They all sat in a circle while Cordelia danced around, waving the smoking wand. "I'm getting a strong pull to the Northeastern energy." Her eyes opened starkly, and she seemed to look straight into my soul. "Lacie, Theo." She motioned that we should come closer, and so we did, albeit cautiously. "Theo, run and tell Fontenot to search GPS coordinates 29 degrees 54 minutes 12 seconds north latitude and 91 degrees 38 minutes and 58 seconds west longitude."

"Uh, Miss Cordelia, can you say that again slower so I can type it into my notes app."

Miss Cordelia opened one large dark-brown eye and aimed it at Theo. "Harness! Your inner power, Theo. You can recall the coordinates using your brain's energy. Go forth and receive!" Her intonation made the words have a hysteric quality.

Theo walked toward the Chief, looking confused and a bit scared.

If someone had told me that I'd be giggling while my Gramps was lost and possibly badly hurt, I wouldn't have believed them. But that's exactly what I was doing. In fact, a giggle turned into full-on belly laughter that had me laughing through the tears. Peace washed over me, and I knew that this rag-tag team of friends and community members would not stop until Gramps was found and brought back to safety.

***

LACIE

In the hours that followed, Gramps was found. He'd lost his way and was quite confused, but his confusion cleared right up when he spotted me and Mom.

He was diagnosed with the beginning stages of Alzheimer's, and I worked with my SLP mentor at school to provide him some additional pathfinding clues. We worked out his brain with exercises just as one would work out a muscle group in the body.

The exercises were helping and the pathfinding cues that I'd hung around the apartment and yard seemed to help his confusion the most. However, those successes were not enough to keep him from being let go. To be fair, the Landry family did allow him to retire instead of firing him outright. There was a big party that seemed to include everyone who lived in town, and Gramps seemed to thoroughly enjoy.

Mom and I had been looking at apartments in town, but three bedrooms made the rent too high for us to afford at this time, so we didn't really have a plan, and that's how we ended up accepting the bungalow on the boardwalk that belonged to Mr. St. Martin. He said we could just stay there until we were able to find something. I told him we may never find anything, but he said we could stay as long as we liked. Mom had said, "God bless Mr. St. Martin."

Yes, God bless him. I still didn't understand how he and Briggs never could get on, but I hoped one day they would.

Gramps was going to be fine and coincidentally he was found at the exact coordinates Miss Cordelia had given.

Maybe I was starting to believe in the voodoo power that existed here in the little bayou town of Whiskey Cove.

Maybe not, but I was definitely starting to believe in Briggs. For he was the one who'd found my Gramps and brought him safely back to me just like he'd promised.

CHAPTER 22
BRIGGS
December

Exactly four weeks after Lacie had given me the go-ahead on the casino night fundraiser, the event had come to actualization. Tonight was the night.

I got to the hotel early. I wanted to get my bearings and make sure I was ready to do my part, which was basically MC the event. I was the co-project manager with Lacie. She was wining and dining the bigwigs while I was overseeing the operations end and trying to throw a net on Cash, who could sometimes be a loose cannon. I was hoping that the fact that he'd not been home in years wasn't going to cause any problems with the family. I had both Cash and Dad entered into the game but not playing each other. Actually, I purposefully seated them as far from one another as possible.

The hotel ballroom was loud and chaotic with set-up in progress. The bar was set up along the side wall, the tables were down the middle, and cameras were everywhere. There were people from local news, national news, and World Poker Television. The accounting firm we were using had security and an actual booth they were setting up, and hotel security had their own cameras. It was madness. To add to the chaos, Finn was here dropping off the poker tables we'd commissioned him to make. He had Dad's crew and was using Logan as his wingman since I was too busy to be his voice.

I walked over to the two of them engaged in making adjustments on the feet of the tables. Logan had a drill in hand, and Finn was using a level. The tables were incredible. Made of cherry and polished to perfection. The tops were green velvet, and the leather edge was made from St. Martin cattle-hide. I ran my hand across the soft leather, marveling at Finn's skills. "The tables are a work of art."

Finn kept his focus, but Logan popped up to his full height.

"Not bad for a boy from Whiskey Cove." Logan clapped Finn on the back and then nodded toward the bar. "The hotel is serving my beer tonight. You have anything to do with that?"

I nodded. "I wanted to support local Whiskey Cove vendors as much as possible since Steve grew up there and your beer is the best around, so it's a win-win from where I'm standing."

When we'd put pen to paper on this idea four weeks ago, I never dreamed it could be pulled off in so little time. But time being the one thing Steve didn't have, Lacie and I pulled the trigger and never looked back. We had thirty-six high rollers pay into the pot. That's a lot of money for Steve's equipment needs, Penny and the girls, and ALS research. The entire pot would be for Steve and ALS research if Cash won.

I wasn't worried. Cash had never lost a tournament. It's why he was the reigning world champ.

I spotted Lacie from across the distance of the ballroom. She looked adorable in an LSU sweatshirt, denim shorts, and flip-flops. She was touching the fabric of the tables and speaking with one of the hotel managers. I was learning how detailed Lacie could be about things. She wasn't wrong. She and I'd had a hard time reading the layouts on the cloth-top poker tables, which were important when dealing with serious tournaments, and we were every bit as serious as Las Vegas. Even more, since the money made from this event would help so many people. She was having the hotel swap their tables with Finn's.

Four weeks was a long time. Twenty-eight days to be exact. I'd seen her each day. We'd had so much to work on that we didn't have time to think about our past or the future as it related to Briggs and Lacie. But we were working on the future, and it felt good. I sensed that her walls had come down; if not all the way, they had at least come down to waist-high so I could see over them. You better believe I wasn't taking any chances. I wouldn't make any mistakes with her this time around. We'd been so busy that we hadn't been able to get that close physically. We'd kissed and made out a little, but we always had some place to be, or the girls with us, and it just didn't feel right.

We agreed to book ourselves a room for two nights at the luxurious Rio Hotel in Baton Rouge. It would be an easy transition after the game. We could just take the elevator home. We wanted to take some time after everything died down to relax and be with one another. I sensed tonight might be the night, and it was almost all I could think about. First, I had to make it through this poker tournament fundraiser starring none other than Cashel Gray St. Martin.

When I caught up with Lacie, she seemed a tad stressed. "Hey, have you talked to Cash?"

"About what?"

She frowned. "I don't know. I'm just worried. He should have stayed the night here in the hotel. Then we wouldn't have had to worry about getting him here. We'd already have him."

She'd been worried about this for a week. Mainly because Cash hadn't been home in so long, but also, she was against having Cash and my father together under the same roof. Nothing I said comforted her enough to not worry. "I spoke with his driver. We're all set. He'll land at six. He'll be here by six-fifteen."

She nodded. "That sounds good. Archie Manning, Dr. John, Trombone Shorty, and John Goodman have all paid in. Last minute additions, but feasible if we move a few people around—that includes moving your father closer to Cash." She cringed.

"It'll work out. I'm not worried." That was a lie. I'd be worried until I had my brother in my sights. When I'd tried to speak to Dad about Cash and the Texas Hold'em game, he wouldn't engage and shut down my every attempt at a discussion, but still he said he'd enter the tournament.

A lot of what they fought about was Dad's mentoring of Camp over Cash. I'd seen Cash die a little each time Dad would say, *"Why can't you be more like Camp?"* or *"I would have given you the reins if you'd turned out more like Camp."* Dad had always been extra hard on Cash, though no one knew why—even Camp—as he and Cash were identical twins. They were close and the favoritism from Dad didn't seem to come between them, but I was always worried it would.

Lacie nodded and ran her hand over the felt tabletop. "I'm not worried, Briggs. Just updating you. Are you worried?"

I pulled her into me for a hug. I whispered into her ear. "Not worried, just wanting things to get started so they can end. The only place I want to be is room number eight-thirty-three." A blush crept up on her cheeks. After all this time. It was the cutest thing I'd ever seen.

We had work to do, and it was time to get our game faces on. It was too early to call Cash. Not by my standards, but then he kept long hours into the night, and I didn't want to do anything to disrupt his sleep. I needed him to be on his game today of all days. The game started at seven tonight. I had Cash's driver's number. I'd already checked in with him this morning, and everything was looking good for arrival time. Plenty of time to get wired up to his poker network and to interview with some of the news channels who were already here because I had promised exclusive access to Cash.

First, the hotel caterers arrived, followed by the two bartenders. Then the dealers showed up, dressed in their Vegas best. We considered having the event in Vegas, or Cash country, but it was actually Cash who suggested he come to Baton Rouge to honor the life of Steve LeBlanc who was somewhat of a hometown hero. During hurricane Katherine, he'd formed a rescue operation consisting of speed boats that would go around and rescue people from flooded homes and apartments. They called themselves the Cajun Navy.

Once Penny arrived, I watched her walk up to the large picture of Steve that hung from the ceiling. It was more of a banner, and it displayed pictures of him pre and post ALS. I walked up to her expecting tears, but she was smiling. She pointed. "I remember that suit. It was my favorite. He looks good in blue."

I felt the urge to ask something I probably shouldn't . . . "Would you do it again? Knowing how it all would end, would you fall in love with him again?" My mind wasn't quick enough to stop the thoughts from escaping.

She looked off in the distance, her mouth opened, and she took a small, shallow breath of air. "I had no control over falling in love with him. He swept me away." She pressed her lips together and thought some more. "I don't know how I'll live without him, but I know that not loving him would not be possible. To know him is to love him. There is no doubt in my mind. One hundred percent yes, I'd do it all again."

I felt my throat close up and my eyes start to water. I was raised in a land where men don't cry, but I was never afflicted with such an unreasonable request. I cried. Even before rehab, with my emotions all over the place, I cried.

It's true, I'd never seen my pop cry. I can't recall my brothers crying, though I can remember them making fun of me for doing it. I'd like to see my siblings and my father stand witness to Penny's words and not shed one single solitary tear.

I wiped away the drop rolling down my cheek and said, "If you need anything, you know my family is your family. We'd be happy to have you and the girls join our gang."

"Thank you, Briggs. You've been like family to me throughout this whole ordeal. I honestly don't know what I would have done without you."

A commotion behind me had me turning into the face of hotel security. "Excuse me, Briggs, your father's here, and he's asking for you in the lobby." I glanced at my watch. What the hell was my dad doing here at noon? I left Penny and followed security, hoping that this wasn't the first sign of trouble. I spotted the irritation in my dad's stance before I even heard the first word come out of his mouth.

"Briggs, tell these guys I'm with you. What's the big deal? All this security for a poker tournament."

"The security is for Cash. He's got fans, and a lot of them are aggressive."

He scowled as he processed what I'd said. "Aggressive poker fans? Are you shitting me?"

"I didn't say they were poker fans. Women love him. Come with me."

"Women, ha." My dad huffed and grumbled but followed me to the ballroom.

"If you want to see how much women love your son, walk around to the outer door and look through the window. They started lining up early this morning."

He looked beyond the crushed velvet, wine-colored curtains. "These women are here for Cash? Is he famous?"

"The Nevada Times described him as charming and smooth talking." Did he really not know? Cash had single-handedly done more for poker than Doyle Brunson. He made it famous. Shows were sold out a year in advance. Primetime television now aired the games. You could buy books and games at big box stores that had Cash's face on them. Wayfarer made a line of sunglasses just for him. Yeah, he was a tad famous. Even more so in Asia, where there were social media accounts of people who dressed and acted like Cash. "Yeah, Pop, he's famous."

I needed to get my dad involved in something or I'd be playing nursemaid until seven o'clock rolled around.

Penny headed our way, and I recalled her telling me about her mom's house. After they said their hellos, I introduced a topic. "Hey Dad, Penny received some insurance money after the flood. She was wondering how to go about getting set up for contractors to come out." It wasn't her house, but the house needed to be repaired so she could sell it. "She wants to fix it up at cost because she'll be looking to sell it. I wanted to get your advice on who we should get to do the contracting."

Pop folded his arms across his chest in thought. "Well now, Penny, I don't think I'd be looking to trust anyone for the project.

Lotta scams out there, and those girls are gonna need a nest egg you can count on." Steering Dad's focus was like taking candy from a baby.

"Thank you, sir, the house actually belongs . . ."

I squeezed Penny's elbow to get her attention. "Let Pops take care of you." I winked at her. I knew Dad well enough to know he would be taking the project on himself. He'd save her the most money and see her through a fair sale. I checked my watch again. It was closing in on one. Cash should be up by now. I excused myself and then dialed him, but his phone went straight to voicemail so I left him a message to call me once he headed this way.

When three o'clock rolled around and I still couldn't reach him I was wiping sweat from my upper lip. It didn't help that Lacie had asked again if I'd reached him. I wouldn't lie to her. I told her the truth. She freaked out a little, which I didn't appreciate because I was already freaked out enough for the both of us. I had the pressure of this night on my shoulders. The weight of Steve, Penny, the girls, and my future with Lacie at stake. I was putting my breathing techniques to the ultimate test. I managed to calm Lacie down even though, inside, I was a lit fuse whose timing for detonation was in Cash's poker hands. I wished he'd call me, or even better, I wished he'd walk through the door.

My dad was back by my side, asking for a computer to use to show Penny some of the new options out there for flooring. "Dad, can't it wait? I'm kind of busy."

"What can I do to help?"

"My computer is right over there on that table." I pointed.

"Is there a password or anything?"

"Yeah, Dad, the password is . . ." Well shit I didn't really want to tell my father that my password was LACIEBEAN. "I'll type it in for you."

"You afraid to tell me your password?"

"Nope, I'd just prefer to keep this one to myself." I set him up on the computer and hoped his attention would hold for another few hours.

By five o'clock, Kenzie and Tex showed up. Lacie and Kenzie

were still at odds with one another...something I knew was wearing on Lacie. My constant suggestion to Lacie that she send Kenzie a text or a call resulted in zero attempts.

At six, the World Championship Poker network was shooting footage for their pre-game show. Everyone was breathing down my neck asking when Cash would show up. I pushed my fingers into the back of my neck and twisted this way and that. Then I put in another call to Cash.

"My brother in Baton Rouge, how's it hanging?"

I let out a hot ball of air. I'd never been so glad to hear from Cash. "It's hanging low, man. Where are you?"

"We'll be landing in Baton Rouge around seven."

I lost it a little and raised my voice into the phone. "Around seven? The game starts at seven."

"Chill little bro, those things never start on time. I'm building demand. Trust me, by the time I get there, those cocks will be locked and loaded and ready to place careless bets. We will take the house."

Jesus. Hopefully my heart would last until then. "I'll chill when I set my hands on you."

I hung up and stretched my shoulder and neck, closing my eyes for a bit to picture the marsh where I meditate. I took a few breaths and then opened my eyes to find Lacie standing before me in a sea foam green dress that made her eyes sparkle. The dress shimmered in satin and was the sexiest thing I'd ever seen her wear. No bra. No backing on the dress that was cut extremely low. God, this would be the biggest distraction of the night. I leaned in to whisper in her ear. "You're gorgeous and way too sexy for me to keep my hands to myself."

"I didn't think there was such a thing as too sexy," she teased.

I turned my pelvis into her so she could understand my meaning. "I'm already getting hard."

Her mouth made an 'oh'.

"I like your shoes." I imagined sucking on her red polished toes which was torture at this point.

"These are not shoes, they're Jimmy's." She corrected. "I'm here to relieve you. Go take a hot shower, take some time for you, and then get into that suit." Her eyebrows waggled, and I laughed, but it wasn't just a laugh with my mouth; I felt genuine relief in my bones and gut.

I grasped her hands, pulling her into me, and we laughed together.

"Everything is going to be fine. You can breathe now." She came up on her tiptoes and placed a kiss on my lips. "If I forget to tell you later, thank you for this."

While Lacie held things together in the ballroom, I held myself together in our hotel room. I'd sprung for the suite, so we had a balcony hot tub that I made use of to relieve some tension in my shoulders. After some meditation and breathing, I did as she said and took a hot shower. By the time I had my suit on, I felt better and refreshed and ready to start the evening.

When I returned to the ballroom, it was six o'clock, and things were picking up. Some of Lacie's VIP guests were being escorted to their seats. Dad was still on my computer, and he and Penny were acting strange. I walked over to them and saw they were watching the documentary video that was my thesis project.

The blood in my veins turned to ice. I had not yet told Lacie about my thesis which was a documentary feature film starring her. If she found out here tonight, I sensed it would all be over between us.

Penny was crying, and Dad was . . . also crying. Okay, so I was right about Penny making all the men in my family cry but fuck, this wasn't the venue nor the vibe I was going for.

Penny's arms went out to me. "Briggs," she cried. "The video is incredible. There are no words to describe how well you captured everything he is to us."

Dad stood and joined our circle. Hugs from my dad . . . I can't recall the last time it happened. "You should show this to the world." He pulled back and looked me in the eye. "I was wrong, son. You have a gift. I'm glad you didn't listen to your old man. Your skills are infinite. The world needs you and your voice in it."

I was speechless. It was the first compliment my dad had ever given me. Now I was the one with tears in my eyes. I choked up thinking back on the greatest wish I'd ever made for me and my dad and that was his acceptance. How many times had I wished for him to really see me and validate my work in film and photography.

I stood numb, not realizing my dad had taken my laptop up to the hotel staff who were helping with tech support for the evening. Things happened so fast, I didn't realize what he was doing. Soon, my documentary could be heard through the speakers. The video appeared on the large white screen at the front of the room. The title popped up on the screen. It was still rough as I hadn't finished putting in all the details. The IRB record and all the names involved appeared as did the university information and the fact that this was a master's thesis documentary film project.

And then I felt it. That shift in the air that happened when she was near. Lacie walked up to the screen. She stood and watched intently, not responding when I called her name. When I reached her side, her hand went up, and she shook her head. "Tell me what this is, Briggs, because it looks a lot like a thesis project. It looks like you made *my* film clips, and yours, into a documentary. It looks like you used my internship as your own little grad project. You exploited my work and the LeBlanc family."

I motioned to the staff to kill the video. When the screen went dark, she turned to me with tears in her eyes. Fuck. "If you'll let me, I can explain."

"There's no time to explain. We have to get focused on the fundraiser. I'll just be trying to figure out why you didn't tell me about one of the biggest projects in your life." She walked away with tears in her eyes. I couldn't explain it either, except that every time I tried to tell her about the project, something else would come up. There was never a right time. I wanted her to know, but in the end, I'd made the decision to proceed without her approval.

To be honest, it's not easy to show your work to people who are close to you. It's their opinions you care about the most, and the thought of her not liking or approving of my work sent me reeling, and that was just me on a hypothetical. I don't think I'd be able to process her rejection. I'd tried to do some pre-visualization of me responding successfully to her rejection of my work, and every time

I got to the end of the reel in my head, I lost it. *If she doesn't like my work, I'll trash my project.* If I did that, I would not be able to graduate. I also did not know if I'd hold residual resentment toward her.

I hadn't realized when wanting a relationship with her that she could be the one thing that could unravel me. The person I care about more than my video work, more than myself, is the one person whose acceptance means everything to me and is the one person who could send me spiraling into my old habits.

I had every intention of telling her about the documentary I'd made and turned into a thesis project, but my thought process had been weighing how to best manage her rejection. I knew if she didn't like the film, I'd stop all production immediately and I hadn't been ready to do that. I wanted to see this thing through. To be honest, it was a great project. However, I didn't even need to pause and think about it . . . if my thesis project meant losing her I'd drop out tomorrow.

She stood in front of the large screen. Frozen. I couldn't see her face, but her body language mirrored defeat. Fuck. I felt my whole world collapsing. I couldn't get air, only the shallowest breaths to keep me from passing out. Black spots danced across my vision. I tried again to engage my diaphragm, but it was no use. I stood behind her, still not wanting to see her face.

I placed my hands on her shoulders and said, "Lace, can I please talk to you?" My voice was ragged and cracked under the weight of so much at stake. She moved, turning toward me. Her face, a mess of smeared makeup. Tear tracks streamed down her face. "Lacie, talk to me." Please let her see the beauty of my work, I prayed to anyone who was listening. "I don't want to start the fundraiser like this."

"Then you shouldn't have lied to me." She pulled away and started walking.

"How did I lie to you?" I asked, confused. Here I was trying so hard to be true with her, and she was accusing me of lying when I hadn't.

"It's a lie of omission, and it's a pretty big one. You used my work, my internship, my family . . ."

"Your family?"

She leaned in and spoke through clenched teeth. "Penny, Steve, and the girls are like family to me now, and you used them so you could have a graduate project."

"They're like family to me too." I pounded a fist into my chest while her eyes narrowed. "And I didn't use them. Will you stop saying that, it hurts. I put everything into this project and it's good and I want the world to see how much this family loved one another and struggled through the losses and pain but still wouldn't have changed any of it if they'd known."

"Known what?"

"I asked Penny if she'd known how it all would end if she'd still do it."

"You asked her that?" Lacie looked surprised.

"Yeah, and she said she wouldn't change a thing."

I reached for her, but she put her hands up, issuing a warning for me to stay back. "Let's call a truce until the event is over. I can't go out there and mix it up with people if we are fighting."

Fighting? "I don't want to fight with you." *I won't fight with you.* I couldn't.

"We've got to go out there and present as a united team," she said as she swiped a finger beneath her eyes.

The thought of her mad at me tore my insides apart. I couldn't stand the way things were now. How could I move forward with the night? "How do we do that?"

"Do you really not know, Briggs?" She shrugged. "We just put it to the side. Us. We put *us* to the side, and we focus on all the good that we've done and are about to do for the LeBlancs and for ALS."

I smiled, relieved that she could see that what we'd accomplished was so good. "I can only do that on one condition." The topic of *us* was all I thought about. "I need to know that when it ends, I've got you in my arms for the night."

Her head started shaking. Her mouth formed words that were left unspoken. For a few seconds more she stood before me. I reached for her hands and she let me. "Lace, please, there is no other way I can put the thought of us aside and make it through this night. *Please*."

"Fine. Tonight. If we have a successful fundraiser, I'll meet you in the room later."

"And stay all night, in bed with me."

Her head shaking, she said, "fine."

She walked away, but not before turning back and looking me in the eye, giving me a genuine smile. She walked back to me and wrapped her arms around me. "I don't want you to worry. This is just a discussion. Your movie *is* a work of art. It's a gift to the world. I just wish you'd told me everything. I don't want it to be hard for you to tell me things. I'm mad, but not at the art. Let's call a truce for tonight, but tomorrow we get into a discussion about why you failed to trust me with the most important thing you've ever done."

She wiped away more tears and oh God. How was it possible that her vulnerability and acceptance made me feel worse than her anger? I tried to swallow around the hard lump in my throat. "Lacie, I'm so sorry. I never want to hurt you. I love you. Please don't give up on me." I pushed a rogue strand of hair behind her ear. "And you're wrong. The most important thing I've ever done is Briggs and Lacie."

"You can't say things like that to me when I'm in a full face of makeup." She kissed my cheek, and I stood frozen, watching her walk away with the most adoring smile on her lips. My belly warmed like I'd swallowed the sun. I wanted to go after her but couldn't. I had to focus on the task before me.

It was nearing seven o'clock. That meant it was go-time. But where the hell was Cash?

I walked onto the main floor of the ballroom and felt the excitement move beneath my skin, awakening my lovesick bones. Adrenaline kicked in, and my blood started pumping in double time. I could feel the success. This was going to be a night for the books.

A light and a camera were pushed into my face. "This is the host of the evening . . . Robert Briggs St. Martin, younger brother to Cash, the most successful poker player in history, having won $18.35 million in the Big One for One Drop live invitational poker game and with a name like Cashel Gray St. Martin, is it any wonder. Briggs, tell us what we can expect from your brother tonight."

"I was told to tell you to loosen up those wallets, folks, because Cash is coming, and he's ready to win big for the house tonight."

"That's interesting. So tell us, if Cash wins tonight, he's prepared to give all of the winnings away. Is that right?"

"That's right, Marla, from channel six, *Eyewitness News*," I said the slogan in that sing-song way the anchors do as I eased into my MC role. I'd grown up watching this woman. It was kinda cool to be talking to her in person. "He's donating the proceeds to the LeBlanc family and to the ALS Research Foundation."

"And a good cause at that. Well, we can't wait to see who the big winner will be. Interestingly, Cash has never lost a hand of poker in his career spanning almost ten years."

The local news blathered on about Cash. When I heard the screaming from outside, I knew he had arrived. Relief washed over me like a warm blanket. Camera flashes blinded, and it dawned on me that it might be the reason he wore the Wayfarers all the time, even when he played.

He finally entered the ballroom in his signature black leather jacket, white T-shirt, and jeans. He had a thousand-watt smile that he flashed around, which girls ate up like catnip. He paused to answer a question for each of the news cameras before taking his seat at the table.

He sat next to Johnny "The Grinder" Mott. "I see you came out of retirement for one night. Hope you don't crack a hip, old man," Cash teased.

"Funny, your mom said the same thing last night," Johnny retorted. Evidently, the trash talk had begun.

"Jesus." Cash removed his leather jacket. "I walked right into that one."

He waved a finger in the air and his table server answered the call. "Get me a Johnny Walker, neat, and a glass of spring water."

Once Cash was set up, I walked up onto the stage and welcomed everyone to the fundraiser. "Thank you for attending. I'd like to extend a special thank you to my brother, Cash, for being here today, without which this event wouldn't have been possible."

"It almost wasn't," yelled someone in the crowd.

"It's true, Cash is known for making an entrance." I laughed it off.

Cash raised his glass of whiskey in the air. "Go early to market and as late as you can to battle."

"My brother, ladies and gentlemen. Always ready with a one-liner. And I apologize for his tardiness, but I know we're all glad he's here today." I continued my welcome, including the history of the LeBlanc family that Penny helped me put together.

Once the game started, I felt like a wild boar had been lifted off my chest. There were still things to do. The accountant continued to need my help signing off on bets over the limit, and I helped Lacie take care of the players. Cash constantly had a gaggle of women hanging around him, but he held his cards close to his chest, and rarely looked at them. In the end, the participants fell like they lived in a house made of cards. It didn't take long.

Once it was down to the last six, the seating arrangement hadn't mattered. Dad ended up at Cash's table.

"So here I am, sitting across from the boy wonder who has never lost a game," Dad said.

"I'm twenty-six, Pop, old enough it's time you called me a man."

"I'll call you a man when you start to act like one."

Cash looked to the woman flanking his left arm and then to the woman on his right. He leaned forward. "In the morning, you can ask any one of these fine young ladies if they spent the night with a boy or a man."

"Okay," I interjected and motioned to the dealer to open the game for bets, "and remember this is airing on primetime, so can we clean it up a bit, please."

Once the game got underway, I searched for Lacie. It led me to the overflow staging that had been set up just outside the door of the ballroom. A bar had been set up out here too. It seemed unnecessary, and I didn't like that it had been set up without my approval.

It would cut into our fundraising profit. Cameras and media personnel were out here drinking and changing film and lenses.

"So, your brother has become famous." Slurred words over my shoulder had me turning and coming face-to-face with Tex, who was drunker than I'd seen him in a while.

"Tex, you doing okay, buddy?"

"Naw, man, I'm down for the count. Kenzie and I broke up." He shot another glass of whatever he was drinking.

I took the glass from his hand and set it on one of the tables. "What did you do?"

Tex laughed. "What did I do? *She* was in her car with her ex. All I did was exist."

"Why did she break up with you?"

"*I* broke up with her." He slurred and swayed. "The windows were fogged up."

"It's southeast Louisiana, the windows are always fogged up." Though this story wasn't looking good for Kenzie. "Did she say why she was in the car with him?"

"I didn't ask. I think it was pretty clear as to the reason." He motioned to the server for another shot, which I discretely called off.

"Did you ever tell her about yourself?"

"You mean the money?"

"Yeah." Tex was a billionaire a few times over. Make that five times over. He was a wiz at finance and had created some social investment sight that allows people to manage their own stock portfolios easily with the click of a button.

"No. And I know what you're thinking and I don't want to hear it."

"I doubt you do. For the record, I was thinking that if all you have to do to get her back is tell her you're rich then why not do it. You'd have her and you'd both be happy."

He shook his head. "You don't get it."

I shrugged. "I think it's easier than you're making it."

"You ever had to deal with an ex-boyfriend coming back and proposing to the woman you love?"

"Can't say I have."

"Then shut the fuck up."

He hadn't told anyone that he had money and he'd gone to certain links to keep Kenzie in the dark, even acting like he struggled with money at times. I could see where his lack of trust in her over the years would be a fight when she finally found out the truth about him.

"I wasn't sure I'd ever tell her. Don't see the necessity of it. Now it hardly matters." He wiped his face and then fisted a hand in his hair. Distraught as he was, he seemed to be holding back tears.

The kicker of it all was that Kenzie's ex was also very wealthy. Unlike Tex, Bradford was old money dating back to the pine industry. His family was responsible for the creation of Louisiana-Atlantic. The company produced pine that was made into pulp and used in everyday products like paper towels, toilet paper, and printer paper. Bradford was a stockholding board member and was driven around Baton Rouge in a Bentley.

I tipped a server to walk Tex to his room.

Back inside it was down to the last two standing. Pop and Cash. Well, I could have predicted that. I walked over to the table where security was having to get physical with the crowd who was closing in around the two players.

"You wanna go ahead and fold, old man? I got your nuts in a vice." Cash had kicked up the trash talk while I was away.

"Not a chance. In case you forgot, I taught you those moves."

"Yeah, well, I perfected them." Cash smirked. I don't know why he always liked to provoke the old man. Now he'd go for broke. Which is exactly what he did. In the end, and by that I mean, after two hours, we had a winner.

Cash won, but old Pop proved to be a worthy competitor. I met with the accountant who gave me a total of the night's pot. Cash presented the whole pot to me in a gesture of good faith. The accounting firm filled in one of those gigantic checks with the amount in black magic marker. The check was so big physically that it had to be held by two sets of hands, mine and Cash's.

In the end, the media was only interested in Cash and his generous donation. Fine by me; directors by nature wanted to be directing. I wasn't uncomfortable in front of the camera, but behind the camera is where I felt my soul.

I searched the room for a vision in seafoam green. When I found her, I walked over and placed my arm around her. She was talking shop with Finn. Trying to save yet another poor soul from communicative failure. She was so passionate. I smiled at Finn, and he excused himself.

"Hey, you."

She smiled, radiating all colors of blush that skin could, mixed with a lot of sex in her smoky eyes.

"Hey," she purred. Her cute shy smile didn't fool me. In about fifteen minutes, I'd have her begging for me to enter her.

"I think our work here is done."

"I think you're right," she answered.

"Shall we call it a night?"

"Sure. I know you don't drink caffeine but you're going to need to find your second wind. I'm not tired at all." Her brow arched suggestively.

"I think I can manage."

CHAPTER 23
LACIE

I told Briggs I was mad, but not about the art. That part was true. I was mad that he did not trust me enough to confide in me about making the whole ordeal of making the film into a documentary for his thesis project. However, what is it they say in Hollywood . . . *the show must go on.* We had a fundraiser to get through and I know Briggs. He would have obsessed over us if I'd not given him a little bit of grace. But this was far from over. And I was far from okay.

I'd been warm all night.

It had nothing to do with the temperature in the elevator and everything to do with Briggs in a fitted suit, every curve torture as he leaned into me, our curves fitting together, the long, thick line of his cock pressing into my stomach. Our kiss that I'd imagined as soft and sensual was anything but. Briggs was hungry, and I was ready to feed him.

When he pulled the key card from his wallet to open our hotel room door, my mind settled on Kenzie. Of all the times, but my mind was never off of her completely. I missed her and longed for our friendship.

I rubbed my eyes and shook my head to lodge our fight from my thoughts before Briggs could tell something was going on.

He walked over to me and lifted my chin. "What's going on, Lace?"

Of course, he figured it out. He'd been all kinds of attentive lately, seeing things he never saw before. "I'm fine." I looked down, away from his prying eyes.

"Are you thinking about Kenzie?"

What the hell? "And now you just know everything I'm thinking?"

"Watching you and her all night, glancing at each other with sad eyes, kind of gave it away. You should contact her. I know she's hurting."

I cried while he held me. It did hurt to be at odds with her, but I wasn't ready to reconnect and hear all of the reasons why my efforts to obtain the medical equipment Steve needs are futile. The tears were really going, and I think I wiped my nose on Briggs's shirt, but he didn't seem to care. . . at least he'd removed his jacket.

***

BRIGGS

Back in the room, my only goal had been to get naked with her.

But her needs at present precluded nakedness, so I pushed down my own needs to focus on hers.

"I just wish. . .Kenzie," she whispered.

I inhaled a ragged breath. "I know, Lace." I rubbed her back, not trying to solve but only sooth. She and only she would be the one to make the decision to forgive. In time, when she was ready, she would.

Snapping her head up, she wiped her cheeks and said, "I want to watch the documentary."

"Now?" I had hoped we'd be undressing each other by now.

"Yes, I didn't get to focus on it because I was so busy with the high roller tables."

I reached for my laptop.

"But first . . ."

I heard the telltale sound of a champagne cork coming out of a bottle and turned to watch her pour Marinelli's sparkling apple cider into two crystal glasses. "Here's to a successful night for us, the LeBlancs, and ALS research."

We toasted and sipped. "I couldn't have done any of this without you, Briggs. Thank you."

Her smiling lips descended on mine. This was the sensual kiss I'd expected in the elevator. Her lips were soft and teasing against mine. We broke apart, but her eyes lowered, lingering on me. Her slow, sexy smile had me melting into the floor.

We'd accomplished something big together and now we knew that we could do big things together, things that would make a difference in many people's lives. I pulled her over to the couch so that we could look out over the cityscape through the floor-to-ceiling windows, I fed her chocolate covered strawberries and we drank sparkling cider. It would have been perfect, but instead, it was difficult due to the video on my laptop that had us both holding back tears.

Working on the documentary project had put so much of my life into perspective. I'd watched hours of tape, the kids learning of their father's illness, Penny helping Steve walk to appointments, Lacie working with him. It was the footage of Penny that made me realize how love is wonderful and scary, devastating and whole. When Steve grimaced in pain, she grimaced. When his body tensed, so did hers. They were in tandem, riding the wave of his terminal illness as one. It was easy for him, he had her there to see him through. After though, she'd be left holding onto the life they'd shared, but only half of her would be there. Instead of two plates, one. No getting up early to beat him to the shower. What would she do with his car? His clothes? Would she slowly start to erase him from her life?

A person could go crazy thinking about it.

The sound of the computer talker speaking the words *I love you* had Lacie's hands going up to cover her face. Lacie does that move if she's about to cry. I took the laptop from her knees.

"She hasn't heard him say that in two years. He had done so well with therapy. He was so excited to tell her, and then he went to sleep, as he always did after therapy because he's completely exhausted. He slept for ten hours that night. When he woke up, his swallowing muscles were useless. Been that way ever since. One system shutting down at a time." She coughed her cries had become so hard.

The more I learned about ALS, the more I realized how cruel God above could be. I thought having bipolar disorder was a curse. The blackouts were a curse. You woke up only to come back to a place and find out you'd destroyed physical property and any relationships you'd had with those you loved.

She continued to watch the video. "God, Penny looks so sad in these."

"Can you imagine…?" I asked.

She anchored her focus on me. "No, and I've tried. I look at her and think how strong she is, but realize she doesn't even know she's being strong, she's just surviving. That's how it would be for anyone. You don't think you can do it. You'd rather die than to go through it, but you would find the strength to push through for your kids, for him, for everything." She looked away quietly, clearing her throat and the thick tears that she didn't shed.

"If you could know going in, would you still do it?" I asked her.

"Would you?"

I thought about my parents and all of their useless fights over the years. Their infidelity, the ridiculous threats they made to one another. One time, after Dad received a phone call from a woman, Mom went out to his truck and trashed it. Keyed the paint, broke any and all glass she could find, took a rake to the hood. It was brand new. He'd actually just driven it home. A beautiful F-450 Super Duty limited edition dually with running boards and every accessory they had to offer. It was a seventy-thousand-dollar truck. Turned out the woman called to remind him of a teeth cleaning appointment he had the next week.

They'd made up by dinner, and in the end, Dad didn't seem all that mad. He just didn't want Mom to be mad at him. He never wanted that. He went out of his way to make her happy. In her own way, she did the same for him, but their fights were just stupid.

If you knew going in that your time with this person was going to be limited, I gotta think you wouldn't waste it. You'd make the most of every miniscule moment. Even the things that make up the monotony of everyday life like washing clothes and paying bills would become spectacular because you only had ten years instead of, say, sixty in which to memorize every nuance of her voice, every line on her face, the position of every freckle, the way the hairs on her brows arched. You wouldn't want to miss any of it. And you surely wouldn't waste valuable time arguing about who left the freezer open.

"I would. Not that it would be easy, but I'd do it. Love for a person doesn't change when that person dies. If they die at thirty or eighty, it still leaves a hole, but to save yourself from the memories because you're too scared to lose them is like being dead already. Would I want to lose you after only having you for ten years? No, it would damn near kill me to say goodbye, but would I walk away from you now knowing I was going to lose you in ten years? No, that would also kill me. My only option would be to soak up as much of your love as possible and physically show you how much I love you. Try to pack what should be fifty years of life into ten so that we don't miss a thing."

Her eyes caressed me, and something intense flared to life inside of me.

"You mean any woman in general. If you only had a few years with a certain woman, you'd do those things…"

Her whole being seemed to be filled with waiting, the prolonged anticipation was almost unbearable. Did she really not get my meaning? "I meant *you*. *Always* you. *Only you*. I love *you*, you crazy thing."

My gaze fell to the creamy expanse of her neck, her pulse visible, and I knew her scent would be strongest there.

I took her into my arms and pulled us against the back of the couch. The warmth of her next to me comforted like a cozy blanket. She'd been missing from my side. "Lacie." I let her name caress my tongue, swirled it around my lips, enunciated every sound, my voice low and firm.

Her eyes caught mine, their color dark and smoky, exposing her feelings of desire. I wanted her too, but I needed to tell her one thing first. "I've loved you from the first moment I met you sucking on a grape Tootsie Pop and playing with that caterpillar. I haven't always been able to show you, but now that I can, I plan to never stop." My voice cracked, and my throat burned with holding back the love I wanted so badly to impart to her. "I'm sorry for the things I've done. I don't have an excuse, but I hope one day you can believe I've changed and even love me back." I kissed her neck and let my teeth graze her pulse, following the line of her lifeblood. "I'm especially sorry about Scooter, but most of all, I am truly sorry about your prom dress and ruining your evening. I would give my life to be able to go back to that day and do things differently."

I leaned into her, she smelled like apple juice and chocolate. I softly kissed the spot on her neck I'd been nipping. I absorbed her delicious moans of pleasure, and my cock hardened, her thigh pressed against my arousal; denial wasn't an option.

I had to lift my head and inhale outside of the halo of her scent to stop myself from taking more. Her eyes, which were lightly closed, fluttered open at the loss of me.

Her breathing was fast and shallow as she smiled warmly at me. "Either I'm having a really vivid dream, or this is real and you just told me you love me. Twice."

"It's not a dream," I answered.

"Briggs, I want you," she said, breathy and straining.

I found the zipper on the side of her dress and tugged it all the way down, letting her step out of it and admiring the view of her in a thong and strapless bra still in her Jimmy's. I walked around her in a circle, admiring all that she was. "How are you so beautiful?"

"Keep saying things like that."

"I'll never stop."

Again, I kissed her, but this time, she took control. Her hand came up and held my chin while she coaxed my tongue out and then sucked while I licked into her mouth. I was down with it. I'd let her take control of my body all night. She was hot and in control, using my body to meet her own needs. There wasn't anything hotter.

She started undressing me, and I let her. By the time I was in my boxers, I was ready to have my mouth on her. I reached up, and in one slick move, her bra fell to the floor exposing the most perfect set of breasts I've ever seen. She was made for me. That was it.

"Hey, that's a sneaky trick. How do you know how to do that?"

"Finn and I practiced."

Her eyes grew large. "On who?"

I started laughing. "Oh, babe, if I tell you, Finn will kill me."

"If you don't tell me, I'll think you've bedded half the county."

"We practiced on each other." Infidelity was definitely a sore spot of mine. It's what broke up my family. I wouldn't let Lacie think for a minute that there'd ever been anyone but her.

"Each other?" Her brows came together.

"We took turns wearing Mom's bra and practiced undoing the clasp."

A short chuckle escaped her throat. "You did not do that."

"I assure you, we did."

Her chuckle turned into deep belly laughter and had her bending at the hips, grabbing her stomach. "Oh . . . my . . . God."

I did a slight variation of an advanced tackle, going in and wrapping my arms around her waist and then dropping her down on the bed. Her laughter faded, and in its place was need. I slid down her underwear and then pushed her legs apart. "Show me where you need me."

Lacie spread her legs open further, showing me her most secret place. She was a goddess, and I worshiped at her altar. Her ripe fruit lay bare and glistening for me. I couldn't stop looking at her pinkness. I wanted to glide into her heat and live there forever.

I felt the animal instinct start to take hold of my tailbone and instinctively started a series of deep breathing exercises that tightened my core, lowered my diaphragm, and expanded my lungs. I held my breath for eight beats and then followed that up with an expertly timed exhale. I would need to go slow here so that I didn't hurt or scare her.

***

LACIE

Deep breathing.

I knew when he was doing it.

Like right now. He was breathing and going to his special place that calmed him. It made me so proud of him, watching him work so hard to stay in control. He was disciplined and followed a strict diet and supported lifestyle changes that kept him evened out. He did all of this for us . . . his friends and family.

But was he happy?

I took the time to really watch him as he settled between my legs. Sexy shoulders and upper arms flexed as he wrapped them around my thighs. His deeply male groan was appreciative, like the sound you'd make if you had fasted for two days and were about to sit down and devour a feast. When his hot tongue slid against me, I squeezed my thighs against his head in ecstasy. He took his time for a while, patiently waiting for me to get to that place just before I was about to unravel. Then, he became crazed for me, driven by getting deeper inside me; he seemed obsessed by getting as deep as he could go.

The noises he made were animalistic. Desire was more than evident in his eyes. There wasn't time for me to be embarrassed about this very base act. The energy he used to devour me helped me know that he found much enjoyment in what he was doing. He was so skilled and responsive to me; if I tensed, he eased; if I tugged his hair through my fingers, he gave more.

He was good at this. I tried not to think too hard about that. He'd said there had only been me, and I trusted that. Maybe he had practiced this with Finn, though I couldn't imagine how. I almost started to chuckle, that is until Briggs sucked the core of me between his lips and sensually massaged.

It was my turn to make animal sounds. I moaned around his name and squeezed his head with my knees so hard I thought sure he would push me away.

But he didn't; in fact, he kept up his worship of me until I started screaming out his name.

"Briggs, get inside me now."

He released me on a pop of his lips and then wiped his face against my inner thigh. So hot. I was about to internally combust.

He stood on his knees and produced a condom out of thin air. "Lace, I need you." He opened the foil packet with his teeth.

"Yes." I arched my back and stroked his thighs with my nails while I watched him pull out his hard length and roll on the condom. He was so thick and hard for me that my mouth was watering.

He entered me inch by beautiful inch.

I'd always thought those novels where the couples maintain eye contact during sex were so dumb, but now I understood it. Our connection was feral, body language was our only communication. I winced at his size, and he pulled back, taking the pressure off. When I pushed up for more, he gave me what I needed. His mouth moved, but instead of words, only moans.

His eyes closed, a pained look on his face. I watched his abs work like a bellows, his ribs expanding; he was regulating himself.

When he opened his eyes on me, I licked my lips, hoping he was ready to move and let me have all of him.

He watched me trace my lips with my tongue and a guttural sound escaped his throat. "Ready for me?"

"Yes!"

He drove home, thrusting in and out, his breath against my skin, hot and heavy. His elbows came down on either side of me, his hands gripped my breasts, and he rubbed my nipples against the scruff on his face until I fell again into his depths. I raked nails down his back and pressed my heels into his hips. Our eyes connected, speaking the words that we couldn't. Together we came, our connection making us whole again. Even as I was packing to leave my childhood apartment, it didn't matter because when I was with him. I was home.

***

BRIGGS

The next morning, I lay on my side, watching her sleep. She had the cutest little snore whenever she took in air. She was beautiful, and after last night, I knew that our future was solidified. Things had changed. I belonged to her and she to me. We could get through anything.

The vibration of my phone stole away my thoughts about our future.

> Tex: I'm dying without her.

> Me: You're a dumb son of a bitch.

> Tex: THE WINDOWS WERE FOGGED. You'd have reacted the same way.

In the past, absolutely. Now, not a chance. I wouldn't do anything to jeopardize my future with her, even if she had cheated. I couldn't live without her and was at her mercy.

> Me: Do you have a plan?

> Tex: I said some really fucked up shit to her. She won't return my texts, calls, or let me into her apartment.

> Me: Send flowers. Apologize.

> Tex: She won't open the door.

> Me: Singing telegram?

> Tex: Dude. How?

> Me: Acadian Extreme Talent, LLC. Dad used to keep them in business.

> Tex: She'd love it.

> Me: Let's hope so.

Lacie stirred, stretching her elbows up, revealing one perfectly pert nipple. Her shy smile and the blush that crept across her cheeks was something I would never tire of.

> Me: TTYL

"I need a shower." Her first words made sweet music in my ear.

"Yes, you do. Worked up quite a sweat last night. I'm surprised you can even talk."

"Oh God." She covered her face with her hands.

"Better keep it down; we don't want another noise complaint." I removed the covers and rubbed my scruff all over her neck and chest to her delighted squeals that had me getting harder than my normal morning wood.

"I can't believe someone called in a noise complaint on me."

"Let's see if we can get another one." I went down to her stomach and applied the same treatment.

"Briggs, stop, it tickles. Oh God." She tried to push me away, but I nipped at her most ticklish side.

Knocking at the door was like ice-cold water on a smoldering fire. I jumped up and put on one of the room robes. "Cover yourself up. If we're gonna get arrested, I'll tell them I was watching porn. Alone."

Her chuckles continued while I floated to the door, still in our afterglow.

I opened it to Kenzie's puffy face. I was immediately uncomfortable. I didn't know what to do here. I had talked to Lacie about reconnecting with her best friend, but she wasn't biting.

I decided to walk out into the hallway and shut the door behind me.

"I need her," she pleaded.

I nodded to the thick carpet beneath my feet. "I know."

"I can't go through this thing with Tex without her."

I didn't want to betray Lacie's trust and had no idea if she was ready for this reunion right now. "Let me ask her."

"You know, I always told her."

"Told her what?"

"It was always going to be the two of you."

I took a deep breath and entered the bedroom. "Lacie, get dressed, please."

"What is it?" She sat up, worried eyes pleading.

A few seconds later, she was standing before me in a robe of the same make and model. "Kenzie needs you." We both dressed, and then I opened the door and watched two friends reconnect.

"Lacie . . . I," Kenzie cried.

Lacie practically jumped into her friend's arms, bear hugging her with everything she had.

I turned around and went to shower, feeling happiness for my girl.

My. Girl.

CHAPTER 24
LACIE
January

Briggs and I never did get around to having a talk about his thesis project—the documentary feature starring me. I didn't like being on camera, but Briggs said he wanted me to approve of every aspect of the film or he would not use any piece of it. Every time he made a change he would send me that snippet of video. I thought that was enough. Plus, the film would raise awareness of ALS and fundraising dollars. How could I say no to that? However, we still needed to talk about why he didn't trust me enough to tell me about making the video he'd taken for Penny into a documentary for his thesis. We'd just been so busy with packing up me, mom, and Gramps, school, our projects, Sarah and Rylie, and working that we never had a spare moment alone.

"Did you want to keep all this candle-making stuff?" I asked mom.

"Oh! Keep my candles. I think I might start making them again. We will be living on the boardwalk; all I have to do is set up shop right on the front porch. I can envision selling many candles to tourists. Especially if I can get Cordelia to put a protective hex on them. People would buy them to protect themselves from the juju of Baton Rouge."

"I think you're onto something," Briggs said while I rolled my eyes and then admired my man's biceps as he carried the candle box to the trailer.

I'd be starting the new semester with a new home and a new man. Hopefully, my fresh start would rub off on Steve.

His speech equipment came in yesterday, and, of course, I couldn't wait, so I took it out and played with it all day, making Mom, Gramps, Theo, Kenzie, and Briggs try it out.

Penny said Steve was exhausted from all of the holiday family visitors, so she wanted to wait until after the holidays to get started on the device. I was a little disappointed, but if Steve was too tired to work with the equipment, that wouldn't work either.

In the end, we'd had enough money to get a new bed that had a mounting system for the computers and eye gaze equipment, and the OT and PT had already committed to helping me get everything set up.

I could already feel the confidence boost at the thought of being successful with Steve's communication. We would prove everyone wrong and show them just how far a little old fashioned ingenuity and a caring could go.

"Hey, hey, hey." Theo's sing-song greeting made me smile. "I brought the party. Mama Gulch made meat pies, just fried. And I've got beer for those who want it." Theo dragged a cooler behind him.

Finn, Briggs, Theo, and Gramps devoured the tray of meat pies. I turned to Kenzie and Mom. "It's like the hunger games over there. If you want a meat pie, you better grab one."

Mom watched them with delight on her face. "Oh, let them eat. I can always heat up some tamales." I'll say one thing about the South, you definitely won't go hungry.

"Oh my God, look what I found." Kenzie put her hand over her heart. "Briggs, it's your pictures of all of us when we were just babies."

Looking over Kenzie's shoulder as she flipped through a photo book, I saw the images from Briggs's black-and-white phase. Theo, Kenzie, me, Finn, Tex, Parker, and Briggs letting a lazy summer of lake frolic unfold. In every photo, Briggs and I were shoulder-to-shoulder. He'd had a tripod that he worked with and a little remote gadget he'd been excited about that could operate the camera from a few feet away. He joined us in looking over my shoulder at the images, bringing the meat pie in his hand to my mouth so I could take a bite.

I gestured to the photo book. "I want these."

"Done." Kenzie placed the photo book with my box of things to keep.

After the last load had been placed on the trailer, Finn came up to me and handed me a folded piece of paper. Unfolding it I read the words "follow me."

I followed him out the front door and into the grove of pecan trees. He started writing on the little notepad with the blue flap that he kept in his pocket, peeling off notes and handing them to me.

I don't want you to be mad….

You want me to use a computer talker…

I hate everything about it…

I have been taking ASL classes with Briggs…

I like expressing myself with my hands.

You said it was a burden on my comm partners…

And maybe I'll only have Dad and Briggs to talk to but…

It's what I want and that should be what matters.

Please stop harassing me about my communication.

This is what I want.

He'd said so much in those few lines. I couldn't talk, I could only process and try to organize my thoughts.

Harassing? Is that how he felt? It must be if he'd written it. I had harassed him about his speech. And then he'd made a decision on his own. The right decision for him. I'd been going about this all wrong. I wasn't listening to him, only pushing my own agenda. God, I was awful at this.

"So, you and Briggs have been taking classes together?"

He nodded and wrote.

Please don't be mad at Briggs…

I made him swear he wouldn't tell you.

Why would he think I'd be mad? "Finn, I'm not mad at Briggs

or at you for pursuing sign language. I'm so happy you found something that is perfect for you. I'm sorry that I ever gave you the impression that I'd be mad if you decided to go against my suggestions. That's what they were, just suggestions."

It seemed like more...

You were struggling with Steve and Gramps. I was the one project you really wanted to make happen.

I plopped down heavily on one of the benches. "God, Finn, I'm so sorry. I should have never made you feel like that. I should have listened to you. I can see now that I didn't. As your therapist, I should have spent more time listening to what you wanted."

Hey, don't do that. I didn't know what I wanted.

"Still, I should have afforded you the time to decide. Again, I'm sorry."

I'm sorry too.

"For what?"

I'm sorry I wrote those words to you the day after prom. I was worried about Briggs.

"Oh, Finn, have you been worrying all this time? I knew where you were coming from."

Still, I want to apologize and know you accept it.

"Of course I do."

A thought formed in my brain, a way to let Finn know that I supported him. "Can I take ASL with you? As a friend, not a therapist."

He smiled, and I realized he did that even less than Briggs, so when you caught a Finn smile, you needed to relish it because it happened less than a shooting star.

I'd really like it if you would though it'll make it hard for Briggs and me to talk shit about you.

Yikes, maybe I didn't want to know...

It's a joke.

He laughed now, and even that was silent, but I enjoyed the sight of him having some fun. I wadded up all the notes and threw them at his head. "Finn!" He caught the ball before it made contact.

Then I started to cry. Not a pretty, petite cry either but a big, ugly cry with snot and snorts, the whole shebang.

Finn's eyes got large, and he sat down next to me, scribbling in the notebook.

You ok?

I made a big, unladylike snort. "I'm not. Everything is changing and I just—" I couldn't talk from crying so hard, "—I just realized that I won't ever sit under the shade of this pecan tree again." I let loose a boatload of tears and whines. Finn was furiously writing in the notebook.

What makes you think you can't come sit.

Landry Plantation has been here longer than you have.

It will be here long after we are all gone.

You can sit here whenever you want to.

I happen to know this from experience.

I laughed. It was true. It wasn't unusual to look out the window and find Finn sitting in this very spot whittling on some wood.

"Do me a favor, next time you come to sit and whittle, text me. I'll bring a book and read next to you."

You got it.

***

LACIE

It really didn't take long to move us once everything had been loaded onto the trailer and into the U-Haul. Briggs drove and Theo and Finn helped him, while Kenzie, Mom and I unpacked.

My life was full of friendship and love. The people in my life supported not only me, but my family. I was very lucky to have such a strong network of friends. My eyes misted, but I'd been emotional lately about all of the changes, not realizing how much can be learned inside of those changes.

Finn had taught me that I need to listen to my patients. Kenzie had taught me, and continued to still, to have fun and not take things so seriously. She also helped me to not be such a dreamer, but to also look at reality and work within systems and not against them. Briggs . . . God, Briggs had taught me how to let go and live in the moment. He'd shown me that people can change if they really want to. All of these people had made me realize who I was and who I hoped to become. I realized that good friends make you become the best version of yourself.

While I sat watching Finn sign with Briggs and Kenzie and Theo throw wadded up packing paper back and forth, it seemed like everyone's phone buzzed or pinged at once. I reached into my pocket, pulled out my phone, and read the text from Penny.

Penny: Steve has passed.

CHAPTER 25
LACIE

Steve has passed.

Three simple words. I wanted to be the person whose immediate thoughts went to how to support Penny and the girls in their time of need, and in the past five days, there had been a lot of that. But now that Steve and Penny's families had descended on Whiskey Cove, she and the girls had more help than they could deal with.

Briggs hadn't left since we'd moved to the boardwalk. He'd helped unpack, clean, cook, and he had bonded all over again with Gramps. The two of them took walks at dawn and dusk together and talked for hours on end about craft beer, fishing lures, and even books they'd read. It seemed Briggs was going to take up fishing and Gramps was going to teach him.

I'd been absorbed in my own self-pitying thoughts. Thinking of all the ways I'd tried to give Steve his own voice and failing miserably to fill his one dying wish. Sitting on the edge of the bed, I held up the yes/no board I'd made for him. I'd tried to come up with some questions that would guide the development of a communication system for him. To do that, I had to think like him. And to think like him, I'd imagined myself in a hospital bed, sentenced to a life confined to a body that doesn't move, doesn't work. In the end he couldn't even eat anymore. He couldn't breathe on his own. But the brain, that brain worked like a champ right until the end. It was like being trapped inside your own body.

I could only remain in his world for so long, ninety seconds to be exact, before I had to break away and think of something else. Breathing was hard. How did he do it? I felt claustrophobic and panic settled into my bones. I couldn't breathe. How did he do it for so long? Did he welcome death?

Briggs walked through the bedroom door and came to sit down next to me on the bed. "How you doing?"

"I've been better. You?"

"I've been editing countless hours of video. I can't figure out how to *not* make Steve look weak in the end. I mean he *was* completely helpless, that fucking disease wasted him, but I don't want to make his life about that. I want people to see him for who he was to this community. In the end, everyone was treating him like he was made of porcelain."

I scratched at my neck, taking in his words. I think he was missing the whole point of community. "I don't see it that way."

"No?"

I shook my head. "I know it seemed like everyone who came to visit him in the hospital was quiet and reverent but that wasn't because Steve was weak. It was because it was what was needed at the time."

Crossing one leg over the other, I thought about how to explain what community meant to Steve in the last days. "I think community comes together when you need it most. They come to celebrate with you, like at graduations and weddings. But they also come to help and are concerned when concern is needed, like when Gramps was lost. For Steve, Penny, and the girls, the community came to support them with love. To wrap around them and be there, quietly waiting for any sign of need from Penny, or the girls. Mrs. Cordelia could drive them to gymnastics practice, or you could take the girls when Penny worked nights, or when we needed to raise money for Steve's equipment. The community is always there. Just like anyone else, it has feelings that change with the tide. Best thing about community is that it will always be there. Steve may be dead, but in time, his girls will give us a little part of his spirit, and he will live on in the community through his grandchildren."

Briggs regarded me with a sense of awe. "You are so beautiful."

I pushed at his chest and scoffed. "I'm so puffy from crying, I know that can't be true."

"Your beauty can't hide; it seeps out of every pore."

I rolled my eyes. "Wow, now I know you are full of it."

"No, I'm serious. I think that of Penny too, in a different way. Steve must have seen it. Her quiet strength during his illness. Most couples at thirty-two haven't gone through what they have—he witnessed Penny's resilience. There is this one video of him watching her, tracking her every move with his eyes. The doctors are telling her the worst news, and she is like an oak tree, taking the news and holding her girls, being a beacon of strength for them to cling to while they break down and cry."

A tear rolled down his cheek while he continued to speak, "when someone dies at the end of their life and they're old, friends and family are sad but it's different because they lived the years they were expected to live. You make it eighty, eighty-five, ninety years, then there is room for a mistake or two. There is a celebration at the end of your life of all of your accomplishments, the family you made. I want Steve to have his celebration, as dumb as that sounds. I hope my documentary captures who he was to the community."

"Of course, your video will reflect that. It already does."

In a flash, he was up and out the door. I knew when he acted this way it meant he'd been inspired and would need to be in front of his computer uninterrupted for hours. It was the creator in him.

***

LACIE

To know Steve was to love him, and reflecting that thought, the funeral was packed with everyone Steve had ever known. After the funeral mass, me and my crew made it through the crowd to hug

Penny and the girls and to support Mrs. Frannie, Steve's mother.
She held me tight, saying all the appropriate things one said, but I
saw a great relief in her. She wasn't up to her usual tricks of saying
or pronouncing the wrong thing or knocking things over. Instead,
there was a steadfast expression to her and an inner peace.

"He's not suffering anymore, Lacie. Our Steve will never know
pain like he knew on this earth. He's sitting at the throne of God
now, bright and free of that evil illness."

"You're absolutely right, Mrs. Frannie."

"Briggs, your video was beautiful. You captured everything
Steve was to this community and more." She reached out and
grabbed Briggs, holding him to her for several seconds.

Briggs's throat worked several times, but he didn't voice any
words, and I knew he was trying to hold it together. Like we all
were. His hand linked with mine, his eyes speaking to mine in a
language all our own. In his suit, freshly shaven, he looked like every
woman's fantasy. But he belonged to me. I leaned into his side and
whispered in his ear, excusing myself to the restroom.

Briggs had written Steve's eulogy and stood before hundreds of
people, cool as a cucumber, and presented the life of our special
friend. Then he played the video he'd titled *A Life Worth Living*. He'd
ended by saying all Steve ever wanted was to be surrounded by
friends, family, and community, which is something he had in excess.
To Steve, his life was completely full, and he'd want us to see it
that way.

I took a break from crying and walked toward the plantation
doors, the sunlight welcoming even though my eyes were sensitive to
the light. I stopped at a huge wall mirror, noticing how my eyes were
still puffy, but I couldn't blame the chandelier lighting in the fancy
Landry Plantation I'd been in so many times. The low glow was
perfect for hiding a number of blemishes.

I was joined at the mirror by one of Briggs's professors.

"Briggs is a very talented film maker," he mused while straightening his tie.

I smiled, agreeing.

"The ALS documentary he entered into the film festival is

making big waves, and he has not gone unnoticed by the big producers. If you want him to win and have a successful career, you should impress upon him the importance of finishing the damn thing."

I ran into the bathroom, vomiting into the first stall.

There it was, just like when we were kids.

A broken balance hung in the air. We would never be equals. He would always see me as something he could use for his amusement, using everyone in his path against me, and they'd eat it up, just as they had. I thought he had grown up and become a real man, a hero, but then he'd gone and entered a film festival behind my back.

I stood and leaned my cheek against the cool tiled walls.

I left the bathroom, walking mad as hell back to the reception area, but I had the fleeting feeling that maybe I shouldn't carry this anger into Steve's final goodbye. So, I decided to go home but not before I heard my name behind me. I turned ready to tell him off, but it wasn't Briggs.

"You're Lacie Ryan, the speech therapist from Briggs's thesis project."

Was it too much to ask for the universe to just put me out of my misery already. How many times was I supposed to forgive Briggs and give him another chance to gut me?

When I didn't respond he introduced himself. "I'm Professor Grabassy from Media Studies. Briggs has been one of the most successful students we've seen in our department. We are proud of his success, especially his potential to win a Jury award at the Austin Film Festival for his Documentary entry. If he wins the Polly Platt award for producing, we can all say we knew him when."

"The Austin Film Festival?" So he'd already won something and he'd kept it from me.

"Yes, isn't it something. He said he knew he had something big when he landed this project."

My stomach churned with acid. God I was gutted.

"Said it was the perfect story to tell. He has such a good eye and a sixth sense about what people want to watch on the screen. He has so much talent. Now the world will see that. What a great opportunity it was for him to collaborate with the communication disorders department. Well, it was nice to meet the star of the show." As he walked away, he said, "make sure you get your IRB paperwork turned in. If those releases are not completed, Briggs's project will get kicked out of the film festival."

I'd been rammed through by a Mac truck. I'd never felt so numb. Briggs had been doing all of this behind my back? Using Steve and me and Penny and the girls as a project, to make a movie, to get famous, to win a film festival.

On the walk to the parking lot, I let out a scream. I was fuming mad and hurt. How could he betray me after all we'd been through? Is the documentary project the reason why he's been around so much, so attentive to me and Gramps, even to my mother? He'd slept in my bed for over a week now, holding me tight and keeping me warm, whispering words of love and devotion–and it was all bullshit.

Suddenly images of Briggs came flooding back to me—the day he broke my heart on his front porch when I'd asked him to take me to the school dance, the day he pulled poor Scooter in two, the look on his face when we'd given ourselves completely to one another, the adoration in his eyes as I rocked on top of him in the barn. All of it was mingled together in some kind of grotesque papier mâché project.

And that's all I'd ever been to Briggs.

A project.

CHAPTER 26
LACIE

More knocking at my bedroom door irritated me.

"Go away!"

"Lacie, please let me in."

"I don't want to talk to anyone right now, Mom."

If I had extra money, I'd go get a hotel far away from here.

I'd come home from the funeral and set all of his shit outside on the porch that was right on the boardwalk hoping passersby would take what they wanted. I even put his laptop and video equipment in the box. I thought about taking a frying pan to it, but I lacked the energy. Anger and hurt depleted my reserves faster than running laps on the track. I'd locked my bedroom door. And, for an added measure of protection against those who care too much about me, I shoved a chair under the doorknob.

Briggs had come to my window and wanted to talk. I had no words to say, so I went into the bathroom and closed the door. I ended up taking a one-hour bubble bath.

When I returned to my room, he was still outside my window.

I just wanted to be left alone to sleep for hours, and then I'd wake up and decide what to do. If he wanted to sit outside the window for hours on end, so be it.

At this point, I vowed to never speak to him again.

***

LACIE

I woke up at one-fifteen in the morning to relieve my bladder and then was wide awake.

I lay back on the bed, and my mind was racing with thoughts. A whirlwind of the past semester of Briggs up at the hospital, Briggs with the girls, Briggs above me, his breathing hard, hips moving in a sensual dance.

I groaned and covered my face with my hands.

Why had I let Briggs back into my life and my heart?

I didn't know what to do, so I texted my ride or dies.

> Me to Kenzie/Theo: You up?

> Kenzie: I am now.

> Theo: Girl, what happened?

> Me to Kenzie/Theo: Can I come over?

> Kenzie: Why don't you guys come to my apartment?

I slipped out of the house. Upon walking to my car parked along the curb, I saw Briggs asleep on one of the lawn chairs twisted up like a pretzel. It would have been more comfortable to sleep on a cactus.

I felt zero sympathy and hoped he woke up with a wicked neck crick. He was lucky I didn't have a voodoo doll.

I was full of shit. Looking at him through my windshield caused an onslaught of tears. He was my one, the peanut butter to my jelly, the rice to my gumbo.

I couldn't imagine a life without him, but I also couldn't imagine a world where I shared a life with someone who hurt me and lied to me. Who didn't trust me enough to share important information with me. He'd changed, I'd give him that. No more blackouts and the violent anger was gone. In the time he'd been away, he'd become a man. Without me he'd been able to rid himself of those demons that haunted him.

And without him I'd grown into what? Had I even advanced at all? I managed to accomplish something big with ALS research donations but all of that had been done with and through Briggs. The whole thing had been his idea. Now it had me wondering if he'd wanted to do the casino night for even more publicity for the film festival.

Had he told Steve and Penny about the film contest?

Suddenly my mind drifted to the words I'd heard Professor Grabassy say: *make sure you get your IRB paperwork turned in. If those releases are not completed, Briggs's project will get kicked out of the film festival.*

***

LACIE

Theo and I hovered over Kenzie's shoulder. "I've never actually seen Tex that drunk. I mean, I've seen him drunk, but this is over the top."

"Damn, he still looks fly though, even with the slurred words," Theo said.

Kenzie and I shot Theo dirty looks. He put his hands up in surrender. "Sorry, it's just the guys you two date are really hot."

"Ugh!" I rolled my eyes. He wasn't wrong, but it was the last thing I wanted to hear after watching a video that Tex had posted of himself talking about Kenzie hooking up with her ex. He was plastered.

"I hit submit," Kenzie said.

I shook my head. "That's horrible."

"Hey, I'm not fucking around. You screw with me, you get to deal with my wrath."

She'd posted a video she'd taken of Tex serenading her, poorly, I might add, in his tidy whities. The unfortunate thing was that he sang *Like a Virgin* and then tried to complete a pirouette but crashed headfirst into a glass cabinet. Unfortunately, when he landed, you could see his eggs and his bacon, if you know what I mean.

The video wasn't even embarrassing, but I didn't have the heart to tell Kenzie that. Tex was ripped and as Theo had put it, had a beautiful cock.

Kenzie seemed pleased with herself and given what she'd been through over the last few hours, I didn't have the heart to tell her my thoughts.

"So what's a girl to do when her handsome ex proposes marriage, but her current boyfriend is a sizzling hot literal piece of shit?"

Theo cut eyes at her. "I think you mean, sizzling piece of hot ass."

Kenzie had gone over this story three times already. "So you're mad at him because he jumped to conclusions about you in the car with your ex *with* the windows fogged up." I summarized.

Her eyes grew large as she regarded me." He busted out the headlights in Bradford's Bentley. More importantly, he wouldn't listen to me! Wouldn't let me talk. He called me a whore. He thought we'd banged in the backseat. He doesn't trust me."

Kenzie was very tipsy and therefore worked up so this was not a good time to point out that Tex found her with Bradford's tongue down her throat. There were faults on both sides.

My phone chimed again, alerting me I had a message from the devil. "Ugh."

Briggs: **Where are you?**

"Is it from him?" Theo asked.

I nodded. I had told them how he wouldn't leave the bungalow and had spent hours outside my window and finally gave up and went to sit on the porch.

"You gonna talk to him?" Kenzie asked.

"I can't."

"I hear you." Kenzie pulled a bottle of Hampton Water rosé from the fridge and held it in the air.

"Nectar of the gods, yes, that's in order," Theo said.

"I hope you have more than one bottle," I added.

"Well, I only have one rosé, but I've got a shit-ton of hard seltzer."

"That's my girl," I said.

"Bring me one every half-hour until I pass out," Theo said.

Kenzie shook her head. "I'm not doing that."

He stuck his tongue out at her.

We drank, and I told them about the run-in I'd had with Professor Grabassy.

"Grab-assy." Theo held up a groping hand and wiggled his fingers.

"Eww. Of course, that would be Briggs's mentor." I wondered if all the rumors were true.

I finished filling them in about thinking things were one way, that he'd done everything for Penny, for Steve, for the girls. A truly selfless act. However, there hadn't been anything but selfishness in his motives. Everything had been done for his gain. For this film festival.

"It's sad." Kenzie scratched her chin.

"Maybe he should give the film to the family. Let them release it on social media and get a viral response," Theo suggested.

"How would that help?" I asked, genuinely wanting to know. I cringed at the word *viral* and my face and voice making rounds on the internet.

He shrugged. "I don't know. Guess it wouldn't that much. Unless the movie was picked up by Netflix or one of the big streaming services."

Getting some money for the family would be good but it sure wasn't going to happen with the film in Briggs's hands. I rubbed my face. "Ugh, I don't know what to do."

"Should you get your hands on the film at least? So you have the control and not Briggs," Kenzie offered.

"Sure, but how do I do that?"

"For starters, if you go to the Internal Review Board, he will have to take the film out of the festival." Theo topped us all off.

"He will?" Kenzie asked.

"Yeah, according to Grabassy, Briggs never did get my signature on the release form."

"Bam!" Theo said.

"I can go and turn him in and since he didn't obtain my permission, his whole project would be toast. That would include the festival entry."

"Do it." Kenzie set down a plate of fancy cheese and meat snacks.

I'd think about it. I definitely didn't want Penny and the girls to be exposed, their privacy taken away, and their lives used so that Briggs could gain fame and fortune. I remember learning Brittany Spears had been exploited by a queasy collection of documentaries that showcased her troubles with the press and the long-ignored abuse through her family's legal control of her estate. A shiver worked its way down my spine. I'd put a stop to Briggs's little project first thing in the morning.

I pulled up the IRB website and emailed to let them know I'd be in and that I would need to talk to someone about the documentary on Steve LeBlanc. "Hey, is it okay if I stay here tonight and maybe for the rest of the week?"

"Do you even have to ask," Kenzie replied.

I shook my head. He hurt me yet again and I let him do it. "He's never going to be someone I can count on to not hurt me. To keep me safe. Never lie to me. He's not capable of any of those things."

"I mean, in the past, this couldn't be said, but it can now so I'll say it . . . the lies seem off-brand for the new Briggs we've been falling in love with," Theo said.

I nodded. "I know what you mean. It's not really that he lied. It's that he didn't trust me enough to tell me the truth behind what he was doing."

"Maybe you could ask him about it," Kenzie broached.

I refused to discuss anything with Briggs. I wasn't the kind of person who could talk through my anger and hurt immediately after it happened. I processed everything slower than most people. Kenzie called me an over-thinker. Maybe I was, but I couldn't think with all the emotional hurt coursing through me. First, I needed to get through the numbness that had settled deep into my bones. Once I was feeling more like myself, then I'd let myself think through Lacie and Briggs.

No matter how many times he texted.

Or called.

Or fell asleep against my window.

CHAPTER 27
LACIE

The next morning, I left Kenzie on the couch. She'd drunk most of the wine last night. I'd had some, but I wasn't feeling like consuming anything at all except hurt and loss. I was so nervous sitting in the research office, my foot was tapping with a rapid pace and rattling the one-hundred-year-old flooring causing me to receive stern looks from the research assistant and receptionist.

The conference room door cracked open. "Ms. Ryan." My name was called by an older gentleman in a dark suit and maroon tie. "Right this way." He led me to the head of the table. "Please, take a seat."

He maneuvered around with impressive agility to take the first seat at the table. "I'm Professor McDonald, this is Provost Connor. We've read through your statement."

My stomach turned over and I felt sick. *Shitfuck*. I've never been this close to the provost. Why was the provost involved?

"The infractions you've listed are grave. The university does not tolerate research inconsistencies, and we sure don't tolerate breaches where human rights are concerned," Professor McDonald said as he straightened his tie.

Human rights?

"We feel it is in the university's best interest, and yours, to terminate the ALS film project."

God, did they have to say it like that. *Terminate* sounded ominous.

"We'll need you to sign this attestation saying what you've written is true and complete to the best of your knowledge and belief, and you understand that you subject yourself to disciplinary action in the event that the above facts are found to be falsified."

The provost passed the document to me.

What was going on? I couldn't think. Professor McDonald slid me a pen. I reached for it with shaking hands.

I thought about the video, all of the things Briggs had kept from me. I thought about my ruined prom dress. Graduation night. Scooter the caterpillar. How cute he was with Sarah and Rylie, his attentiveness to Penny. The morning after I'd given myself to him. He'd wormed his way into my life and stolen my patient right out from under me. He was a wolf. A wolf disguised as a sexy, Southern young man with ice-blue eyes and those sex muscles that could really get me going.

Without realizing it, I'd signed the attestation, and the provost was seeing me out. The door shut and there I stood wondering, hoping, I'd just done the right thing.

I ran down the corridor and made my way quickly outside where I puked in the shade of a nice little Camellia tree. "Sorry about that." I patted the bark.

I watched fast clouds roll in and let the blackness settle into my corner. At least the weather was cooperating. I called into work. I wasn't fit for much. Kenzie met me and took me to her home. I climbed straight into bed without passing go. I told Kenzie to leave the lights off.

With the shades pulled and the rain outside, I let go and cried. The pain oozed from every pore. It was a pain like I'd never known—even when I was seven and I'd had my eardrum lanced. One day it burst from fluid. At the time, I thought that was as bad as it could get. What a child I was.

My heart ached and I couldn't even touch it. I beat on my chest and yelled, "Get out."

***

LACIE

Hours passed. I was unsettled, bothered by what I'd done. I wasn't a revenge seeker. Not on my enemies and definitely not on someone I loved. I thought of all the things Briggs had shown me over the past several weeks. How he'd changed. He was an honorable man; I knew it deep in my bones. Except in keeping his ambitions and the film festival from me. I was so torn between the man he'd become and the man of his past who at times reared his head.

But he'd lied. And he'd hurt me. Again. I'd flat out asked him not to exploit the LeBlancs and he'd promised he wouldn't.

I wanted this pain to end.

How do you speed up a broken heart?

After several hours had passed, I tried to get up and eat cereal, but everything tasted like metal to me. He'd hurt me, but my body still wanted him. My brain on the other hand was ready for blood. I wish the two could come to some sort of a consensus so I could know what I'm supposed to feel. Broken hearts were so confusing.

I opened my motor speech textbook and pretended to study.

The only thing I could focus on was Briggs. My mind wouldn't go anywhere else. It was no use. I turned on the television and watched some stupid reality show on Netflix. I can't fault the show, it was so good I was able to stop crying. But it wasn't so good that I was able to forget about Briggs.

No show was that good.

CHAPTER 28
LACIE

I fell asleep to the sounds of rain. When I woke, it was still raining. My phone was ringing, buzzing, pinging, and in general driving me bananas. I picked it up and read the notifications . . . so many missed calls, texts, voicemails. My head pounded so I rubbed between my eyes. I started with Finn's text.

> Finn: I need to talk to you.

> Me: No, you don't.

> Finn: Don't do this. You really need to hear what I have to say.

When I ventured from the bedroom, I looked around the living room and spied empty bottles of wine and ice cream, a half-eaten pizza, and cereal boxes. I recalled Kenzie coming in and out. Though now she was passed out in her chaise as we nursed our wounds together.

> Finn: I can just talk to you via text but I'd rather come over.

Whatever. He could come over and tell me that Briggs had been under the influence of alien activity when he'd made the bet on me, and it would change nothing. I was done.

I was hungry and we'd depleted Kenzie's freezer stash. "Kenz!" I called.

She snorted a few times but didn't rouse. I set my phone down and leaned up to make a loud clap.

She immediately sat up. "What the fuck?"

"Do you still want Jack in the Box?"

"Yes, but I'm not using Door Dash."

Kenzie was convinced the last time she used Door Dash to get a pizza delivered the driver ate a piece and then pushed the remaining pieces together to make it look like a full pizza.

"Finn wants to come over. I don't want to see him, but I'll allow it if he brings food."

"Nice skills. Let's order the works. And tell him to check the order before he leaves."

> Me: You can come but there are conditions.

> Finn: Fine.

> Me: You have to come alone. You can't tell Briggs. You have to pick up and pay for my Jack in the Box Order.

> Finn: Done.

> Me: You have to check the order before you leave.

> Finn: OK.

> Me: Oreo shake, mini churros, egg rolls, loaded mini tacos, spicy popcorn chicken, 2 sourdough jack combos with curly fries and diet cokes.

Finn: DIET coke is a nice touch.

Me: Or just don't come.

Finn: I'll be there after I cash in some bank bonds and then swing through the drive through.

Me: LOL

Kenzie reached for a bottle of pinot noir that was half full. "You know Finn is the hottest St. Martin, right?"

I nodded. "It's hard to disagree." Although all of the St. Martin brothers were hot.

"Chris Hemsworth in the flesh. And he's so tall and built. Maybe I should let Tex know who's coming over." Kenzie drank straight from the wine bottle.

"Maybe you shouldn't. Finn doesn't need to be dragged into whatever is going on between you and Tex."

"Well, maybe I should seduce Finn."

I walked over to her and took the wine away. "That's enough wine for you. Kenz, what are you saying?"

"I'm saying Finn is hot and I need a man tonight."

"But you love Tex. You've loved him for years." I texted Finn the order number and told him it was under his name.

"Yeah, well, where has that ever gotten me?" She looked so small.

"Don't do something you'll regret before you sort your shit."

"You're one to talk."

What did she mean by that? "I'm not making plans to seduce a man." I picked up a trash bag and started filling it. "You know he didn't actually cheat on you. Plus, he'd broken up with you. Why were you in the car with Bradford anyway? You can't expect Tex not to jump to conclusions.?"

"Whose side are you on?" She looked at me incredulously.

"Always your side, babe, but you know he was just hurting from the breakup." I sniffed at some leftover king cake, deciding it needed to go the way of the pizza crusts.

Her mouth fell open as she stared me down. "What are you saying?" She stood and started grabbing trash from around the room.

"I'm not saying anything, I'm just pointing out facts."

She dumped trash in the bag in my hands. "I may have kissed Bradford."

"You what!" I couldn't believe my ears.

"It's only because Tex confused me." She reclaimed the wine bottle and took a large swig.

"Confused you how?"

"I'm ready to take a step toward our future together. I want him to commit something to me. I wanted us to get our own apartment together before next school year, but he didn't want to. He said things were fine as they are. And I know this may sound like I'm a totally batshit crazy gf, but I swear the man is keeping something from me."

"Like what?"

She shook her head in thought. "I don't know, he's been weird and off. Okay, it's going to sound really weird but the other day I was looking for his Voodoo Brewing sweatshirt which is my favorite of his to wear and he said he left it at his other place. Like Lace, he was typing on his laptop, something work related so he wasn't paying attention—he was distracted and it just popped out of his mouth."

"What's his other place?"

"Great question. He looked up when I asked him, his attention was back on me one-hundred percent. Then he back pedaled. Acted like he was joking but there is one thing I know for certain."

"What?"

"Tex never jokes."

***

LACIE

The Tex and Kenzie thing was in my head. I couldn't stop thinking about what she'd said. And she'd been right, Tex never joked. He made sarcastic comments, he made inappropriate gestures, but he was not a jokey kind of person.

My phone pinged.

> Mom: This boy hasn't left the bungalow. He goes from your room to talk to Gramps. They walked twice today for about an hour each time. It's great exercise for him but I'm worried about Briggs. FYI, he hasn't touched his computer, or camera, something I've rarely seen leave his hands.

> Me: Tell him to go home.

> Mom: Oh honey, he's hurting. I can't dismiss him while he's hurting.

Ugh! I couldn't even go home. This was getting to be a tad ridiculous. I realized I'd have to hear him out. That didn't mean I wasn't dreading it.

A knock at the door had Kenzie looking through the peephole.

"It's Finn," she said with enthusiasm.

As soon as he was through the door, he handed her a huge bag of Jack in the Box which she grabbed and then thanked him for.

He immediately planted a legal pad in front of my face.

I'VE BEEN TEXTING YOU.

"Sorry, I've been a little heartbroken."

Kenzie brought a big plate to the couch that she'd loaded with a sample of junk food. I guess she wasn't planning on giving me privacy with Finn. Though it didn't even matter because I'd be telling her everything.

You shouldn't be heartbroken about something you've created in your head.

"What's that supposed to mean?"

There is an explanation.

"And what is it?"

How should I know. He's being as frustrating as you are. He refuses to do anything until he talks to you.

"Well, that could take a while."

Finn sat, shaking his head.

"Frustrating, aren't they?" Kenzie said with a mouthful of food.

You know you could get the scoop from Tex. Finn wrote and passed the note to Kinzie.

"No way. I'm not talking to that asshole after what he pulled," Kenzie snorted.

I turned to Finn. "You know, last time this happened, you told me we couldn't be together. That it would kill him if we were, and you told me we bring out the worst in each other. You yelled it."

I yelled? Good one.

"No, I mean you wrote it on that yellow legal pad with a big black marker in all caps and a bunch of exclamation points. I can't unsee it."

That was before he changed.

"But has he changed?"

His every move begins and ends with you.

I sighed. "Okay Finn let me tell you the short version. Our project with Steve LeBlanc was about recording family videos and cataloging Steve's last moments with his family so the girls and Penny would have the footage to watch when they get older. They are so young and he wanted them to know him as their dad. When Briggs came onto the scene, he said he was there to shoot and edit the video. We needed him. We lacked equipment and editing skills. The videos were taking up too much space on my computer. Briggs helped me. He promised he would never exploit the family, and yet, at the funeral, I find out from his thesis professor that he's a finalist in some Austin Film Festival contest. That he's being scouted by big Hollywood producers for the story he's made."

You need to hear his side of it. None of this makes sense.

"That's what I said," Kenzie added while dipping a spoon into the Oreo shake.

"By the way, Kenzie is full of shit," I retorted.

"I meant after my initial shock I said it didn't make sense."

No, it makes no sense. Briggs thinks about every aspect of every move and how it will affect you. He doesn't make a move until he's thought through how you will react. It's exhausting, but he's determined to make things work with you. He's stubborn. No one can tell him this isn't how love works. It shouldn't be this hard.

Finn. God, he'd understood so much about us. Things I'd never considered. Of course, Briggs overthought everything surrounding me and him. He would have done exactly what Finn had said. He would not make a move until he'd thought through my reaction. How exhausting. *Oh Beautiful Boy.* Was that why he hadn't told me. He knew I'd have a bad reaction to the news.

Finn had me feeling things for Briggs. My chest felt heavy, and my eyes watered. My poor confused boy. I wouldn't deny all of the changes in him. He'd worked hard to make those changes, and he'd become a man. He worked hard on everything he did. I'd noticed it too. He was always engaged in quiet study. I guess he'd never really shown me his true self. He's guarded and unsure.

I want you to come to ASL class tomorrow.

"I don't know, I don't think I'm ready to see him."

His tattoo.

"What about it?"

It's lake ripples. The ripples are words. 'Under the silver moon, two hearts became one.'

I gasped, and the tears immediately fell. I had no control over my feelings. Finn had basically ripped my heart out and left it beating on the floor.

"Oh my God, that's so romantic," Kenzie added.

Finn stood. He tore off a sheet of paper with the words: *be there.*

Kenzie stared at me. "You okay, Beans?"

"I honestly don't know."

Down to the center of my lollipop, I let the frustration go into the chewing required to break down the chocolate.

What's a few cavities in love and war.

CHAPTER 29
LACIE

I arrived fifteen minutes early to the ASL class. Finn texted and said he'd paid for my courses. The little rat. He knew I would attend if he'd paid. Actually, I was planning on attending anyway. Since he'd chosen ASL as his communication medium, I planned to learn it so that he and I would be able to communicate using sign language.

I decided to make my way into the class and find a seat.

That was a mistake. As the seconds ticked by, my stomach got more and more nervous at the thought of seeing Briggs. I wanted to see him, but I was nervous he'd be mad about the steps I'd taken to undo his project.

But when I saw him, his lips spread into a big smile as he walked over to me.

"Lace," his voice broke with emotion.

He sat next to me, reaching for me. I hugged him back. "Please tell me this means we will be okay."

God, his plea was heart-wrenching. I didn't want to break this man. If only I knew that I could trust him with my heart. I took him in . . . the large and sincere blue eyes, the way he warmed when he sat next to me, the hitch in his breathing. This wasn't someone I had just met. God, I'd known him most of my life. Could I sit here and say that I didn't trust him?

And not even one word about the project and the steps I'd taken to ruin it. In that moment I hated myself.

But no, my heart wasn't ready to jump right in and pick up where we left off. For starters, his behavior surrounding the music fest had me going to the IRB board to ruin his beautiful video. I'm not saying my actions are his fault, I'm pointing out that maybe, just maybe, what Finn said was right all along.

We bring out the worst in each other.

The truth is I wanted him, *needed* him with a rawness that scared me at times. I nodded. "I really want us to be okay, Briggs." I took a fortifying breath. "The lack of trust you have in me hurts. It felt like the day after prom all over again." There were so many examples of that hurt. Our relationship was a mess.

He exhaled and then breathed in deep, closing his eyes. He grabbed my hand and squeezed. "It all happened so fast, I didn't know what had happened. The truth is, I didn't enter the film. Grabassy did. I'll admit when I found out how far it had gone, I was ecstatic and I should have told you, but I didn't even know about the festival until after the funeral."

His eyes were clear and open and solely focused on me, my reaction, my breathing, every nuance said he was searching for any answer that I understood what he was saying. My pulse beat hollow in my chest. "I believe you."

The breath he let out changed his posture from stiff to relaxed. He laced his fingers through mine. "I thought I'd lost you." He brought our linked hands to his mouth and placed a kiss there.

God, what had I done? Surely I could go in and explain that I had not known it was Briggs that had entered the film festival. Would the IRB Board reinstate Briggs's project? How could he not hate me for ruining his life, and yet he was here, holding me, seemingly relieved that we'd be okay.

The class ended, and we said a quick goodbye to Mr. St. Martin and Finn, who looked pleasantly surprised as they took in our body language with one another. Briggs had stayed close to me the entire class, our arms twined together like he was afraid to let go. Now I was the one afraid of losing him. I'd derailed his whole life. I had to make things right. He needed to know I would go back to the board and make things right.

I pulled Briggs out to his SUV, which would be a lot better for accomplishing what I had planned. "Get in the back."

"Going to be hard to drive from the back seat."

"You won't be doing the driving."

His heated gaze on me sent jolts of need to my core. His lazy smile and hooded eyes made me want to ravish him. "That right," he said in that southern drawl that could melt the panties right off of me.

I needed him in that carnal way a woman needs a man. I climbed in after him and shut the door. He sat on one of the bucket seats, and then I straddled him, letting my chest fall against him, getting as close together as we could.

***

BRIGGS

I grabbed both her wrists and pinned them down at my sides. I hadn't done anything wrong. I had no idea Grabassy had entered the documentary into the film fest. I'd only just found out when Grabassy himself told me he'd run into Lacie and revealed the news. When I found out she'd left the funeral without confiding in me I'd been mad. Then, when Grabassy told me the film was closing in on winning the top award I forgot all about being mad and felt like I was floating. It felt wrong to enjoy something when I knew that something was tearing us apart.

"Lace, wait. I need you to know. . ." It was hard to concentrate when she was rubbing her warmth against my cock. "I did *not* enter the film into the festival. I didn't even know until *after* the funeral. I looked for you, but you were gone." His voice broke. "I need to know you believe in me?"

"I believe you, but I need you right now. *Please*."

I groaned. I couldn't shift that quickly. "I-I can't." I thrust up into her core, stiff and awkward, needing to let out some steam. My body quieted when she crushed her lips to mine, plunging her tongue into my mouth. My hands moved down her body, along her cotton-covered curves that I longed to uncover.

"Lucky for us, the sun has set." I pulled her shirt over her head, and then unclasped her bra, letting it fall to the floor of the SUV. "God, I thought I'd lost you." I pressed my cheek against her skin, skimming her back with my hands. "I was sure you'd never forgive me." I kissed her deeply, my hands caressing everywhere I could touch her bare skin.

I groaned as she unzipped my jeans and slid her hand inside, wrapping her fingers around my cock.

"I hurt you again, just like when we were teens. I'm so fucking sorry." I groaned again when she gripped me tight, working me with her hands, and bending down to take me between her lips.

"I'm sorry for Scooter, sorry for your prom, I'm sorry for that day at Bayshore." My voice broke and a tear rolled down my cheek.

"Briggs, stop." She kissed my lips softly. "I love you. That's all."

She loved me. *That's all*. I could work with that.

I pulled her so I could hike her skirt. I removed her underwear and was hypnotized by her creamy skin.

I put my lips to her ear. "Spread your legs."

She complied.

"Spread yourself more," I told her, while pushing my jeans down further.

With her legs open before me, I slid a finger inside her, slow and deep. A guttural sound escaped my throat—she was warm and wet, soft and tight. I pulled out and pushed in two fingers. She gasped and whimpered as her body stretched to accommodate my fingers. I rested my head against her torso, wanting nothing more in this world right now than to be inside of her, connected to her. The significance of what it meant to become part of her, letting me know that we would be fine, that she loved me enough to invite me into her body and let us become one.

When I pressed my thumb to her center, she unraveled. I loved her responsiveness. She placed her hands on the ceiling of the SUV and pumped her hips, leaning into my hand with tiny little thrusts. Her moans filled the SUV that was already fogging up. "I'm close. Don't stop."

"Not a chance."

Beneath my thumb, she was firm and swollen, and I pressed in harder, swirling my thumb around and around. She cried out repeatedly, her fingers fisting tightly in my hair, her entire body going stiff except the rhythmic pulse of her orgasm around my fingers.

I pulled her onto my lap and then pushed into her tight, wet heat. She was made for me and I for her. Slowly, she lowered herself until she rested at the base of me. We were one, connected at our most vulnerable place.

She trusted me.

I loved her.

That was all.

She gasped and whimpered as her body stretched to accept me, arching her back and placing her hand on my chest.

Gripping her hips, I began to move, thrusting up and into her with deep, rhythmic bursts that made her cry out as she bounced her way to her second orgasm on top of me, her breasts swaying in a dance that hypnotized.

At her core I pressed in with my thumb, rubbing circles, calling for her release.

"Briggs, I trust you with my heart, my soul, and my body. I love you."

"Lace." Her words meant everything to me. Trust is what I had hoped she'd see in the new me.

"I need you harder," she rasped.

"Is this what you need, Lace? My hands on you, my breath on your skin, my cock inside you?" I thrusted hard and deep.

"Yes," she panted. "All of it. I need to be close to you."

"God, Lace." I inhaled her scent. "I've never needed anyone the way I need you."

"Use me, Briggs," she said, her voice breathy. "Stop holding back."

Fuck.

***

LACIE

"I don't want to hurt you," Briggs said.

"But I need more," I cried. I needed him to find that place deep inside of me that would connect us for the rest of our lives.

"Then take more. God, I'm so hard for you."

I took more of him, going down gently, wanting to get all of him inside. Once I hit the root of him, I rocked my hips, testing my ability to move. The slide and pull were addictive, and I enjoyed the control I had over him.

I was so close to him that I could feel his forced breath on my chin, born of his will to hold back and prevent a blackout.

With each plunge, his breathing was heavier. Sweat rolled from his hairline down his temple, and I knew he was trying his damnedest to hold back.

I pulled out and rode just the head of him, losing myself in slow, tantalizing fucks that rubbed against something inside of me, bringing me so close to climax that I closed my eyes, feeling every nerve ending with hyper-acute awareness. When I was about to come, he grabbed me and forced me down hard to the root of his length.

Groaning he apologized, but didn't change the angle of his cock as he devoured me. He growled as a drop of his sweat rolled across my breast. His pounds were relentless and those same nerve endings from before exploded, and I climaxed around his hammering cock, milking him and riding the detonating waves. His hands slid beneath my ass, his fingers digging in—fingernails scratching across tender flesh as he emptied into me.

Spent and exhausted, I collapsed on top of him, not wanting to move and wishing we could move through life as one.

Closing my eyes tight I decided it was time for us to talk about things. I worried he'd get mad. Worried he'd not want me to be close to him, but he was here and I had no doubt in my mind he knew that I'd gone to the internal review board. "Briggs, you haven't said anything about what I've done. I ruined your whole life. I feel horrible. How can you still want me, let alone love me?" I cleared my throat, as tears flowed down my face.

His fingers swept the hair at my temple behind my ear. "Lace, you still don't get it.

God when he called me Lace, I swear my heart quivered. "Professor Grabassy approached me at the funeral and said you were in the Austin Film Fest. I didn't trust that you hadn't exploited the whole situation with the family. I went to the IRB. I told them I hadn't signed the papers." I swallowed down the dry lump in my throat.

"Lace," his hand gently caressed my cheek, "none of that matters to me if I don't have you. You are my every why. Without you I have nothing."

I made an ugly, audible sob. "But you want my trust, what about my trust of you."

He closed his eyes and let out a breath, his hands caressing my back through it all. "I do want your trust, but do you remember me telling you that I've always loved you, but I haven't always deserved you?"

Oh God, not that. How was I going to keep it together? I felt like a newborn colt with shaky legs. I couldn't even speak so I nodded.

"I've got a lifetime of hurt to make up to you. I'm never going to go against you. You deserve everything. Even if you take, but shouldn't, I'm not going to fight you. Not anymore."

My brain scrambled to translate what he was saying. "You won't tell me when I'm wrong?"

He shook his head. "No baby." He placed a sweet kiss on the corner of my mouth. We were still connected. He was giving me back all that he'd taken. For that, I should have been ecstatic. It was sweet and his way of showing that he truly and deeply loved me. But I was alarmed.

It was my turn to take his face into my hands. "Briggs, a relationship cannot work like this. I need you to tell me when I've done wrong so that I can become a better person. We can't live in the past. I forgive you for everything that happened. Now we move forward together. You catching me when I fall, when I mess up, when I do the wrong things. In turn, I will catch you. That is how we become better. That is how we make this last. You can't be the one always giving."

He was crying. "But I was horrible to you, Lace. I want to make it up. I need to be able to make it up to you. I want you to treat me bad."

I smiled at him. My beautiful boy still didn't understand relationships. "Oh honey," I kissed his lips, "we are not going to play that game. I don't want that kind of relationship. I love you. I never want to hurt you either. I don't want to get back at you. I'm not moving from this spot until you agree to let that thinking go and put your eyes on our future."

He chuckled. "That might be okay. I know I'd stay right here in this spot forever if I could." His body tensed with so much force I could feel him hardening inside me.

My lips met his and against them I said, "tell me."

"My eyes are on the future."

"You'll let go of the past?"

"I will let go of my past transgressions, but I won't forget them. I need to remember them to know how far I've come."

"Fair enough. Now tell me how much trouble I've caused by going to the IRB. Tell me like you would have told me if you had not been thinking about the pain of the past."

He frowned. "I don't want to."

"I need you to tell me how you really feel."

His eyes burned through me. He sat up, and I scooted off of his lap. While he pulled his jeans up, I adjusted my skirt. He sat with his head in his hands. I let him sit there and come to terms with everything. When he sat up his expression was more distant like he was deep in thought.

"Talk to me Briggs. How do you really feel? What did you want to say to me in that moment when I told you what I'd done?"

He swallowed. "I guess I would have said, Lacie what have you done?" His voice was low.

This was going to hurt. "Keep going."

He grimaced. "I can't believe you called off the project. That project was going to help so many people. It wasn't about you or me or even the LeBlancs anymore. And you just killed it to spite me."

God, his words were killing me. "And I would have said. . . *you lied to me yet again!*"

"What? I've never lied to you."

This was harder than I thought. Hard to fight without having a fight. "Yes, you did. You took my internship and turned it into your little playground. You only ever said you were making videos for the family, you never said you were making a documentary, doing a thesis, or that there was a film festival."

He let out a long, slow breath. "If that's how you and Penny feel, then that's fine. I don't want to proceed with the project. I have a lot to learn about production. If I can't motivate the key players around my project idea, and if they don't trust me, then the project is dead anyway. I got carried away. I'm sorry I let you and Penny and the girls down. The documentary means nothing without you anyway."

Gutted. That's what his words did to me. I knew he had not known that this thing would get so big as to be entered as a documentary into the Austin Film Festival. "Can I ask you something?"

"What is it?" His demeanor was low energy and unfocused.

"Were you excited when you found out how well the video is doing?"

He shrugged. "I was, but I don't want to go through with it so I'm not going to. I only want to raise awareness and help research efforts. I am not interested in fame and fortune at the expense of those I love. I would never want you or Penny to think I was in this for any other reason but love." A tear slid down his face.

It's official. I'm a bitch and I totally hate myself.

CHAPTER 30
LACIE
February

The argument between me and Briggs had escalated into something that we both never imagined it would. He said some things. I said some things. We agreed to give each other some space so he went back home. We agreed it was not a breakup, but he said he'd need time to think things through.

Briggs thought he hadn't done a good job managing his project.

He'd sat me down and interviewed me regarding his management of the whole thing. He even had a rubric and a critique sheet for me. It was an assignment he had to do since he'd messed up the IRB releases.

I kind of felt bad but I knew he hadn't told Penny about the film fest, nor had he obtained my release.

He was hard on himself, and he wasn't even mad at me a little bit. I couldn't help but wonder how I would have responded if the situation had been reversed. Had I shown that I trusted him where his project was concerned? Had I supported him?

"Ugh, I'm so confused."

Kenzie carefully walked over to me with a mug of something steaming. "Here, drink this."

"What the hell is this?"

"Mushroom tea."

I pushed it away. "I'm not drinking that."

"Gimmie." Theo slid the hot drink to his side of Kenzie's dining table. I watched him take a small sip. Then a larger sip. "Hmm, I'm not getting any mushroom."

"Of course you're not. It's cut with chai and cacao and loads of other things that bring clarity and focus," Kenzie educated.

"I can feel it working."

I rolled my eyes. "*Please*, that's not even possible in three seconds."

"You're a bit cranky; you should have some." Theo pushed the offending concoction in my direction. He had come to Kenzie's apartment to check on us and to feed us. He brought Mooyah's burgers, and I devoured one.

"When I was thinking of becoming a vegetarian, it was Mooyah's that stopped me." Theo hoovered three fries.

"A Cajun vegetarian is an oxymoron," Kenzie offered.

"I'm Puerto Rican." He licked his fingers. "We know this." He snapped his fingers in the air, diva style.

"So, what are the plans tonight?" Theo asked.

"I'm going to meet Tex. He has something to tell me that is going to change everything." Kenzie rolled her eyes.

"Penny's dropping the girls with Briggs, and then she's coming over so that I can talk to her about the documentary." I sipped Coke, something I tried not to drink but lately I craved.

"Is this something she set up?" Theo asked.

"No, I set it up. I want to explain Briggs's project to her now that it's a documentary feature film and is," or was, "entered into the Austin Film Festival."

"Briggs should have kept up with Penny about the nature and use of the film. Well, he should have kept up with everyone involved, but he didn't," Theo said.

"I thought you nixed the project," Kenzie said.

"I did but I'm having a change of heart." I made the equivalent of the yikes emoji. "I feel confused about the project."

Theo pushed more mushroom water my way.

"I don't think he was maliciously careless. I just think Briggs dives into things headfirst and figures them out as he goes along," he took a long sip of mushroom tea.

"If Penny is fine with the project being a film fest contender, will you be too?" Kenzie asked.

"I don't know." I reached for the mushroom tea about to take a sip when there was a knock at the door. I stood, setting the tea down. "That'll be Penny."

Opening the door, I had expected Penny, but it was Mr. St. Martin. I didn't know if I should curtsy or call Briggs. "Erm…hi."

"Mr. St. Martin, to what do we owe this pleasure?" Kenzie said, hugging him and shooting me the eye. "Won't you come in. Can we get you anything?"

"No, no, I don't want to be any trouble."

"You wouldn't turn down a Southern lady's hospitality. I've got Coke, Corona, and bottled water."

"I'll have a Coke."

I sat on the couch, and he took the recliner caddy-cornered to me, our knees nearly touching. He was a tall man, filled out in the shoulders and chest, and about six and a half feet tall. He looked uncomfortable in the Kenzie-sized chair.

"One Coke." Kenzie passed him a Coke wrapped in a napkin.

"Thank you kindly."

"You're welcome."

He sat and sipped his Coke with not a care as to the time or getting his mission accomplished. I liked him. He had an easy way about him, he always had.

"Theo, your mom tells me you got an internship at WCAM. That's impressive. You do your best and they'll see your shine. We sure our proud of you around these parts."

"Thank you, sir. I'm hopeful. I feel like it's what I am supposed to do. I don't know. It may sound silly but when I'm at the studio, there's no place else I'd rather be."

"Listen to that beacon, it'll guide you right into an anchor position one day."

He checked in with Kenzie and then turned his sights on me.

"How are you settling into the new place?" He sipped Coke as daintily as Tinkerbell.

"It's so nice. We can't thank you enough for letting us stay there."

"Oh now, stop that. How is Larry finding things? Was he able to transition okay?"

I had to think for a second, no one ever referred to my Gramps as Larry even though that was his name. Mr. St. Martin was quite proper in his demeanor. "He's doing well with that. I put up some pathfinding notes around the bungalow and he seems to enjoy his long walks with Briggs twice a day."

"Family is real important to Briggs."

"I know it is. He takes care of me and my family like it's his own."

"Maybe it will be one day." He smiled. "Let's talk about Briggs's thesis project for a minute." He shifted his weight in the chair. "I'll be the first one to tell you, I had hoped Briggs wanted to work at the family business, but he flat out is not interested." He chuckled but I felt sad knowing how much it would mean to him if Briggs had been interested in what he did.

"Everyone has free will, but he took a one-eighty from the family biz. It's fine now but at first, I know I drove him crazy suggesting that he major in a trade, as well as an art. Good thing he didn't listen. That boy's got a gift. Can I ask…have you watched the documentary?"

"Not all of it." My face heated. We never could get all the way through it without ending up entwined in one another. And it was still a sore subject between us, to be honest. I still wanted him to get mad at me. We were working our way through it.

"Hmm, well I highly recommend it. You know sometimes things start out one way but then they morph into something better, organically speaking. With art, you have to follow where it leads, even if you don't know where you're going. Trust the process kind of thing. The documentary highlights one family's story with ALS. The ups and downs, the beautiful way Penny and you and the girls processed the ever-changing foundation. It was a beautiful fight. Briggs captured it perfectly. He stands to win one of the biggest awards in film, for documentaries that is. It could push the film into the hands of the general public. That'd be great for fundraising money that could go to research and one day for a cure. Imagine. And it all started here with six people."

His words warmed my insides. Six people who were connected by love. My beautiful boy was a caterpillar who had morphed into a beautiful butterfly. My love for him in that moment bloomed into something so great I was having a hard time breathing.

"His first mission was to tell the story of a young family's struggle and the beauty of that family lifting up their patriarch in the biggest gift of all: celebrating life. His second mission was showcasing a therapist with a heart of gold and her marathon to keep up the quality of life in her progressively ill patient. His final mission was to increase awareness and fundraising. He accomplished all three."

I knew that. He was a brilliant filmmaker. "I have seen some of those scenes. They are beautiful."

Mr. St. Martin stood so I followed suite. "Is there someplace we can talk in private."

I led him to Kenzie's bedroom. I sat on the bed, but he stood. To say I was nervous about what he had to say would be an understatement. I was terrified. My heart raced, my body felt like it was on vibrate, but I wouldn't be giving Mr. St. Martin the ole' *what for*. He wasn't someone who sought a person out to talk and then didn't get to have the talk. When he spoke, people listened. That much I knew. I'd have to endure this and for some reason, I didn't think I was going to come out of it smelling like gardenias.

He took a metal box from his pocket, which he opened and took out a cigarette. The homemade kind. St. Martin land still yielded a lot of crops. One thing they were known for was organic tobacco. "Nineteen years is a long time." He looked at me, a nice warm smile on his face.

Eighteen years . . . it was the length of my history with Briggs. I internally rolled my eyes. Nodding, I leaned back on the bed, pulling my knees to my chest and hugging them.

He didn't light the cigarette, just fiddled with it, smelled it, rolled it between his fingers. "I love all my children, but Briggs . . ." his voice quivered with emotion, "Briggs is the one whose needs I could never meet. It wasn't until I could admit those words that I was able to understand him and ultimately help him. I think you must know he suffers from classic bipolar disorder with psychosis. When he's high he's untouchable, godlike, can take you all the way to the top. It's a wild and risky ride. When he goes low, he leaves this world and enters into an abyss that almost no one can pull him from.

He knew his son very well. Funny, Briggs always said he didn't.

He fiddled with the cigarette. "Sometimes parents don't have all the answers. I surely never did. But I was wrong to not believe in him. He's incredible. Not only did he overcome the darkness, he conquered his art. He's a visionary." He chuckled and shook his head in wonderment. Leaning forward, he sniffed the long side of the cigarette. "This project of yours has already raised hundreds of thousands of dollars for ALS."

How had it done that? Were people donating money?

"Thing is, the film can't be entered into the festival even though Professor Grabassy says he has a good chance of winning in his category. Something to do with the internal review board and a hang-up about ethics with one of the parties involved." He tapped the cigarette on the case. "Be a shame if this thing got kept from the world." He turned his eyes on me. Eyes that were so much like Briggs's I didn't think I'd be able to tell them apart in a lineup. "I know he hurt you. He hurt a lot of people, but I've seen a change in him. How could I not? I know you must see it too. He's worked hard for a lot of years. His life shouldn't have been this hard, this soon. He had no semblance of a childhood, but I've learned about his disease and mental illness isn't something I'd wish on anyone."

"Sir, you can light that. I don't mind."

"But you know why he's lucky?" He continued, ignoring my suggestion. "Because he had something to live for, the hope of

someone waiting for him if only he could be stronger than the darkness that pulled him under. And he was. *He is.* It was never going to
be easy with someone like him. And he's always going to give you
big, sweeping gestures of love because that's who he is. With Briggs,
you'll never have to wonder if he loves you. Loving him will be
hard, but I hope you will give him the chance."

I leaned forward on the bed. "Mr. St. Martin, it's not that I don't
love him. It's that I lose myself when I let him sweep me up and I
don't know how to have an identity in our love." Not that it would
keep me from loving him. I'd figure out a way.

He laughed. It wasn't a subtle chuckle either, it was the deep
belly kind of laughter that was loud and rumbled around the room.
"Perhaps Mrs. St. Martin could have served you better today. I
reckon she knows a thing or two about that kind of love." There was
a twinkle in his eye that fell to his cheek. He swiped the tear away
with his finger and stood. "I've watched the film. What I saw were
two people who came together to aid a family, putting all their
differences aside to serve and I've never been prouder of my son, *or
my daughter.* You really do bring out the best in him."

What he said shredded my heart. But I was confused and
thought maybe he was so wrong. How did I bring out the best in
him? He didn't find his way out of the dark until he was gone. He
found himself *when he wasn't around me.* Without me, he was able to
become this new Briggs who keeps his cool. Plus, there is the fact
that I destroyed his film career, the one thing I knew he'd loved for
almost his entire life.

He stood, towering over me and passed me Briggs's laptop.
"The password is LACIEBEAN." His hug was warm and lingered.
He smelled like mulling spices, and it stuck with me how someone so
tall and so manly could be so warm and gentle. He comforted me,
letting me revel in his embrace, and for a moment, I wished to never
leave his side. For so long I had dreamt of a father to hold me. I
didn't want to lose him, and oh how it would be so easy to slip into a
relationship with Briggs and his family and just lose myself.

I wanted Mr. St. Martin to stay with me and protect me forever.
I watched him through the window. He met up with Finn, who had

waited outside. I watched them until I could no longer make out the color of Mr. St. Martin's truck. The scene faded away, and I was alone in the darkness with only the memory of his recently uttered words.

I went back to Kenzie's room and typed the letters into the computer, hitting play on the video file.

The video started with a description of ALS. Medical specialists explained the disease's progression. After a brief history, including the manifestation of the disease in its namesake, Lou Gehrig, current research in the field was explained. Briggs had interviewed countless specialists, neurologists, and pathologists and clipped together segments about disease management and about the research still being done and the necessity of funding to keep that research going.

Twenty minutes into the documentary, clips of Steve were introduced. Still pictures of his early life played across the screen while facts about the disease ticked across underneath them—average survival time once diagnosed, average age at first diagnosis, percentage of people diagnosed each year. The facts were staggering. The effect of pairing a man's life and his experience with the disease *with* those facts was even more dramatic. Toward the end of the film, video clips of Steve in the hospital, with his family, played out.

Several moments of me teaching Steve and his family to use the communication devices were included. My voice filled the room. The ticker on the bottom of the screen read: *Lacie Ryan, Speech Language Pathologist, giving Steve a voice where otherwise he wouldn't have one.* The OBI Robot scenes of Steve using the feeding device described the increased independence during mealtime that Steve communicated using the EMG tracking solution, relating that it made him feel somewhat human again. There were happy moments of shared success, and moments of teary-eyed frustration.

Briggs had detailed the expense involved in keeping up with Steve's disease progression. He'd explained, as I had explained to him, what happens when insurance companies get these types of patients with progressive neurodegenerative diseases and their lack of willingness to put money into the devices that a person needs to communicate in their best and most effective and efficient form.

A voiceover spoke the words: "Are we not a country that can provide those who are dying with comfort and dignity? How have we come so far in technology that we've taken a step backward in patient care and basic humane treatment? This man was dying. He wanted to talk to his family, to say goodbye, to express his love on his last breath. We must do better. "

The documentary ended with video of Steve using the boards I had made to tell his family he loved them. Using eye gaze, he communicated to each of his girls to give him a kiss and a hug. The video zoomed out on the image of Sarah and Rylie, smiling, tenderly kissing Steve's cheeks.

It ended with a dedication for Steve.

What have I done? The tears gushed; my heart pounded. Was there anything I could do?

"Oh my God."

"Honey, are you okay?" Theo was at my side.

"Penny's here," Kenzie announced.

I ran out of the room and straight to Penny. "I have to get the documentary re-entered into the film festival."

***

LACIE

It was a long shot, but Professor Grabassy thought there might be a way to save the documentary, and he even said a last-minute entry would be considered based on the sensitive facts surrounding this film. What he meant but did not say was, the main character had passed during the making of the movie.

He got on the phone with Austin while Penny and I went to visit the IRB. We had to get the college to reinstate Briggs's thesis, and we needed to file all the releases with the board.

Penny was actually not aware of how big the project had become. But she'd seen the documentary and was excited by the prospect of increasing awareness and funding for ALS. Plus, she said that Briggs had given her some paperwork earlier today. Turns out he'd made her the rightful owner of any and all film proceeds. If this thing did well, she could have a new job as a non-profit organization director that she always had the hopes of starting right here in Whiskey Cove.

CHAPTER 31

LACIE

February-March

I'd been so busy I'd not realized Valentine's Day had descended upon us. Kenzie was so distraught over her breakup with Tex everyone tiptoed around her. Theo was busy working on his big break for his journalism project and I was still trying to dig Briggs's project out of the hole I'd put it in.

I deserved nothing from him, but he came through anyway.

The doorbell rang but I continued to towel dry my dripping wet hair hoping Mom or Gramps would answer it. No such luck. I wrapped my hair in the towel and opened the door to a dozen, deep purple Gladiator Alliums.

"Delivery for Laciebean."

"That's me." I reached for the flowers, wondering how in the world he'd managed this. My favorite flowers bloomed in the fall and not anywhere within our growing zone. The best thing about them—they are bulbs. If I plant them, maybe indoors under a grow light, they'll grow for multiple years. "Thank you."

"And one more," the delivery guy held up a large bag of take out. I inhaled the rich Italian sauce and my stomach responded with a grumble. I set the flowers down and took the food. Then I tried to tip the delivery guy, but he told me he had already been tipped and very well. "Enjoy."

I texted Briggs, thanking him and asking him to come over and share the food with me and to plan on spending the night. He said he was way behind on the project and couldn't spare an extra moment, even for me. He said he wanted to see the project through even if it wasn't going to work for his thesis. He wanted to see it finished and put into Penny's hands.

February turned into March. I emailed the Provost and Professor Grabassy and asked to meet with them. After a lengthy meeting with both of them, they suggested another meeting with the IRB.

As it did the last time I was in the research office on campus, my foot tapped wildly on the floor, rattling the boards. Unlike last time, Kenzie and Penny were here with me for moral support. Kenzie placed her hand on my knee, and it stopped bouncing.

I'd come today to do what I had to do. It wouldn't be easy, but it was what was right and, in the end, doing what was right was the only way I could live with myself.

"Miss Ryan, we're ready for you."

I walked into the room on shaky legs, leaving Kenzie and Penny behind. I did a double take when I saw the president of the university in the first chair. My knees went weak, and I thought I might even faint. The provost placed his hand on my shoulder, moving me along. I plopped down ungracefully in the same chair as last time, heart thundering like a freight train. Looking around, I counted three additional people.

"Miss Ryan," the provost addressed, "may I introduce President McDonald and Professor Grabassy. Additionally, we have Dean Thompson from the College of Communication and a representative from your school, Professor Marks." I nodded. Yeah, I guess. I'd never met the dean of my college. Because we were in communication disorders classes, we were lumped in with mass comm, which was part of the College of Fine Arts.

President McDonald put tiny glasses on his nose. "Per your

email you stated that your last report was entirely provoked by a lover's quarrel and that it was completely false in nature."

I'd said some semblance of that, but I definitely had not used those exact words. "Everyone has a copy of your sworn statement and the attestation that you signed." He removed the tiny glasses. "Miss Ryan, this is a grave infraction of the highest order. You've compromised the integrity of university research and another student's program. An admission of this caliper would have you expelled from the university. Are you absolutely certain that you wish to proceed?"

Did I wish to continue? I wanted to clear Briggs's project. I was a terrible therapist. It had been hard to admit but it was the truth. Kenzie had been one-hundred percent accurate about my inability to separate my emotions from my job as a therapist. Cordelia said I was an empath which I'd recently learned was someone who is highly attuned with the emotions and feelings of others and it may even become impossible to separate my feelings and the feelings of others, or even that of patients. This individual would make a great therapist if they could handle it. Alas, I was not someone who could.

Lately, I had been yearning to create—mostly floral arrangements, but I was becoming interested in the sowing process as well. This would be something Mom and I could do together. The only hitch is that it would take money. If I saved like mad, we were looking at five years before we'd be able to open a store front. So yeah, I'd been sitting and dreaming about a floral shop on the boardwalk while I'd been studying.

I took a deep breath and looked across the table at all the learned men sitting before me. "I made the whole thing up because I was mad at Briggs. He made a bet on me. Two hundred dollars that he could get me into bed. It's on social media now. It pissed me off, so I shredded him." A full admission on my part was the only way to fully exonerate him, no questions asked—project back on. There was no other way to do it. This was a white lie and an okay one. It didn't hurt, only helped.

God, I felt sick and hoped I could make it out of here without puking.

Professor Grabassy slid a paper to me. "Read and then sign if you agree everything is as it happened and has been recorded correctly." I didn't have to read it. I signed it and then stood. President McDonald stood as well. "We'll be in touch. As I said, this is a grave infraction. We will set up a jury, and you'll be called in to determine your future at this institution."

I nodded and ran out of the room. I had to keep running, but I made it out to my puking tree in just enough time to hurl my guts onto the ground. I patted her bark again. "Ah, we meet again, and again, I'm sorry."

Kenzie's face was scrunched in pain. "Lacie, you okay, hun? You were talking to a tree?"

Penny passed me a Kleenex.

I raised up from being hunched over and got a gut cramp. Uh, I was a mess. "She and I have become friends. Let's just say, I may have puked on her before."

Kenzie's lip curled in a look of disgust. "Can I get you a ginger ale?"

I shook my head. "I'll be fine. Well, I'll be expelled and lose everything I've worked for, but I had to do it." Kenzie and Penny's arms came around me. "Only thing to do now is sit and await my fate."

Kenzie and Penny started walking, and I followed. "That is one thing to do all right. Or . . ."

"Or?"

"Or we could get those tattoos."

I stopped abruptly. Kenzie and Penny followed suit but ended up running into one another. "You know what, let's do it."

"Shut up! Oh my God," Kenzie squealed and ran to grab me in a bear hug.

Penny joined. "I don't know what's going on, but I love hugs."

"I've been trying to get Lacie to get a commemorative tattoo, designed by yours truly." Kenzie pressed her fingers into her chest. "I don't mean to brag, but it's the perfect little drawing of a heart created from our thumbprints with our graduation year flanking the right sides.

"Ooooh. Does she get your thumbprint on her heart and you get hers?"

Kenzie reached for Penny. "It's like you're in my head."

"I have five tattoos. All of my ink is personally created. Two by my best friend, three by Steve. I'll treasure them always."

Wow, that is sweet. She bears his mark, for always, he'll be part of her. Shit now I was crying, but so were they.

"Let's go get tatted up." Kenzie held up the artwork.

"Do you carry that around?" I asked.

"Yes, it's important to always remain hopeful.

***

LACIE

It turns out we couldn't get tattoos until a week later because Kenzie had to be off of her acne medication for a certain amount of time.

During that week, things happened fast for Briggs. He was back in the film fest and was working around the clock on his project with Professor Grabassy. He also hadn't been back to the bungalow, nor had he asked for my help when I offered. Twice.

Things felt off, and it wasn't just me getting kicked out of school. Things were different.

I had plenty to think about so the fact that a needle was piercing my skin a bazillion times was okay. Not great, but tolerable.

After tats, Kenzie and I walked down the boardwalk. I wasn't ready to go home.

"You should go to the festival."

I looked through the windows of an empty storefront. I had not told anyone what had happened regarding myself and the future of my program. I was called in for a hearing and had to sit in front of a board of three, including one student. They may give me the opportunity to resign from the program. I typed up a resignation letter yesterday. "He hasn't really asked me to."

"When has that stopped you?" Kenzie stood next to me, staring through another window.

"I don't Kenz, I feel like things are different now. I acted horribly. He's been perfect since he came back. He didn't deserve my reaction and I know it didn't come from a place of being mad at him. I was mad at myself, for all the things I was unable to do and what I failed at. I may resign from the speech program."

Her jaw dropped, "you what?"

A cool breeze blew hair across my face. "To reinstate his thesis project, I had to say that I made everything up to get back at him. I acted like we were fighting. They told me I would probably get kicked out, but they may let me resign instead."

"But that's not true. We can get you back in good standing because that's not true."

I took her hands in mine. "No Kenzie. I don't want to continue. I suck at being a therapist. You were right, I can't separate my emotions from my job. Besides, I didn't even like it. I know what it is I was born to do and for the first time I feel relieved."

Kenzie moved in and gave me a big, comforting hug. "Oh honey, I'm glad you took that leap. I'm dying to know what your destiny is."

"I want to open a floral shop. I want my mom to be able to grow some flowers on St. Martin land. You know how she loves the dirt and I love arranging. It's a perfect pairing."

She held me by the shoulders, her eyes wet with moisture. "I love it. It's perfect."

I chuckle-cried. I cried for Steve, for the horrible thing I'd done to Briggs, for Gramps, and for not listening to Finn when he'd tried to tell me how he felt about speech generating devices. I missed Briggs terribly and I desperately wanted to be at his festival, celebrating his creation and success, but would he want to see me. We hadn't talked a whole lot. There was a kiss two days ago, but then he was gone again, working hard to finish his project. "I'm just so sad about the mess I've caused and I really, *really* want to see him and support what he's doing." I cry coughed.

She put her arm through mine. "Come on, I'll drive you home. Then you're going to pack and get ready for Austin."

CHAPTER 31

Inside the bungalow, I poured a glass of iced tea and sat at the table to go through the stack of mail my grandfather had left with a Post-it note. *Glad you're feeling better, Bee.*

When I was little, he used to call me bee all the time because he said I buzzed around so fast I reminded him of one. I loved him so much. I pulled off the Post-it and opened the first padded mailer. I had accumulated a lot of mail during my meltdown. I pulled out a long, narrow velvet case. When I opened it, gold shined in all its pristine glory. A long, delicate chain was attached to a locket. I opened it to find my favorite picture of me with Steve. It was before he lost the use of his limbs. I assumed Penny had sent it. I couldn't find a card.

I put on the locket and continued going through the mail and found a letter from Briggs.

Hey Lace,

So much has happened. I don't even know where to start. Two things seemed to make the most sense: finishing the video and giving you the space you needed to mourn Steve and also to figure out if you still want to be part of my life. I can't seem to make you happy, I keep letting you down. I don't want to push you away like so many times before so I'm asking you to decide what happens next. I am truly sorry that I did not tell you about the film festival.

I don't want to think about a life without you in it, but I have learned that it's not up to just me. I have also learned that trust is more important in a relationship than any one thing that I want. Initially I thought I wanted to make you fall in love with me. Now I know that I want you to fall in trust with me. If you'll let me, I'd like the chance to try.

I thought if I tried hard enough, I wouldn't make any more mistakes. I failed you again. If you think you might ever forgive me, I will spend the rest of my life making it up to you. I have always loved you; it started the day I met you, holding that ridiculous caterpillar. I guess that's why I teased you relentlessly. I'm sorry. It was never my intention to hurt you.

I don't want to upset you or your grandfather, so I won't come over, even though it's killing me to say goodbye in this way.

I love you Lacie Bean.

Briggs

(FYI . . . there is something on your google drive that you need to see.)

I was numb. I dropped my head to my arm on the table as I thought about my relationship with Briggs. The date of this letter was from weeks ago.

Weeks ago!

Had he been waiting on me to read it and make a determination about our future? He must think I no longer want him, but God I missed him so much.

I went straight to my room and booted up my laptop. Clicking into my drive I found a file that hadn't been there before. *My Why.* The title intrigued me.

I clicked the icon. Aqualung's *Thin Air* played as pictures of me flashed on the screen. Images of my childhood played before me, pictures of us together: a fall hayride, a Christmas parade, and one of my birthday parties. I remembered that picture. He'd given me a Polly Pocket, and I'd been ecstatic. There were pictures of me on his eighteenth birthday, wearing a black strapless dress. He'd taken them on the front porch of his home. One showed me on the swing with my legs drawn up underneath me, a favorite position of mine then—there were eight candid shots of me from that night. I hadn't known he'd taken them. He'd added captions.

The one on the swing: *The moment I knew Lacie would be burned into my memory forever.* There was one of me walking barefoot in the high grass, carrying pumps wedged between my index and middle fingers: *Genuine beauty comes in one form—Lacie Ann Ryan.* There was a picture he'd scanned in; one he'd taken with the novelty camera I'd given him that night. It was a close-up of our heads together. He'd held the camera in front of our faces and taken the shot: *The moment Briggs knew he loved Lacie.*

He'd been right about that camera, it was shit.

I cried like a baby. The pictures changed to more recent ones. He'd included pictures of me with Steve and the girls and of me teaching them how to communicate with their father.

The song's crescendo accompanied the footage of us together under the silver moon on the night I'd given myself to him. This was rough video, from the Super 8 he loved so much. My hair, the light colors of my torn dress, and my light skin were in stark contrast to the dark colors of the night sky and his bronzed body and dark hair. The video was tastefully edited and showed no objectionable nudity, just unbridled passion. I saw myself through his eyes and I was beautiful.

I writhed beneath him, and my eyes were darker than I'd ever seen. I wouldn't have recognized myself. I was sexy and passionate, and for the first time, I realized why he could have been attracted to me. I was desirable. I saw it in myself but more than that, I saw it in him, in his eyes. They held admiration and reverence. They held love.

There were more pictures. There was even a picture of me asleep. In fact, there were several pictures of me in various sleepy poses. The video ended with me telling the Mr. Mouse story to Sarah and Rylie above the melodious hum of Matt Hales.

I plugged in my headphones and listened to the Aqualung song over and over until I fell asleep. The words begin to seep through my skin, and I felt them deep in my bones. I held no doubt that Briggs had always been in love with me. His videos were not exploitative. They told a story just as clearly as if he'd written out the words.

CHAPTER 32
LACIE
March

It took a week for everything surrounding my confession had been process and the IRB to make a decision.

In Briggs's favor and against me. In the end they let me resign which meant I could leave in good standing and not be blacklisted.

When the email of their decision came in it was the twelfth. The same day as the festival.

I texted Finn.

> Me: Are you driving to the festival?

> Finn: Fam's already left. We are landing in Austin in five minutes.

> I couldn't miss this! I had to make this right.

> Me: I'm going to try to book a flight. Don't tell Briggs.

> Finn: Thank fuck. Text me. I'll wait for you.

> Me: I will.

I immediately went online and booked the next flight to Austin, using two credit cards to pay the exorbitant last-minute fare. I had thirty minutes to pack so that I had the recommended time to spend getting through security and reaching the gate. I didn't really care about much, except my green chiffon dress and sequined gold sandals. I'd be changing at the airport, so I'd need to pack it in carryon. I didn't have time to waste in baggage claim. Lucky for me, I owned a travel steamer.

Four hours later, I was dressed, wrinkle-free, and getting in an Uber. "Paramount Theater, please."

Fifteen minutes later, I stood outside of the theater under a huge lighted marquee that read Austin Film Festival. The light fabric of my ankle-length gown blew in the breeze, tickling my skin and opening up the thigh high slit.

The theater's blade sign extended vertically past the roof of the building in what must be a hundred feet and was capped by a star-burst design, its colors of maroon gold cast a warm glow against my skin.

I walked inside, my feet padding over plush carpets. The theater was beautiful with its rich mahogany wood, wall sconces, and light fixtures. I sent a text to Finn.

Me: I'm here.

Finn: We're in the auditorium. Come in.

I walked toward the noise and applause. Soon, I was standing at the auditorium doors. My heart pounded against my ribcage. I took a deep breath. Though I'd stepped up and made it right, I'd caused Briggs a lot of worry and anxiety. I didn't know how he'd regard me. When we talked, and I'd made him admit how he felt, he'd said

He'd be pissed I'm sure, but I wanted to apologize and that needed to happen in person. I had no way to know how he'd react upon seeing me, and that had my palms sweating. He'd asked me to trust that he'd changed, that he'd show me, and make me believe. I believed it now. I twisted the handle and pulled the door open.

I was unprepared for what lay before me. Hundreds of people, cameras, video recorders, flashes of light. Speakers projected a man's voice, but I couldn't see who it was. He sounded older. To my right a hand flagged me. It was Finn, and boy was I glad to see him. He pointed to his phone. I pulled mine out and read his text.

> Finn: It's looking good for the project. The other features only had a few people in them.

> Me: Incredible. He deserves it.

> Finn: As do you.

> Me: Where is he?

> Finn: At the table up front with his thesis advisor, Grabassy, and the girls.

I smiled up at Finn. He was so tall, like his father. And then I heard his voice . . . Briggs's voice was all over the room. It wrapped around me like a warm, cozy blanket. He spoke about the many hours of editing, comparing the process among different genres. Slowly, I walked forward, searching through a sea of people until I saw him. Our eyes met.

"Get up here."

Did I hear that right? Maybe I was hearing things. Before me, the sea of people parted, dozens of heads in the room turned toward me. The room went quiet. I cleared my throat, and it reverberated around the auditorium. I walked toward the stage on shaky legs. I climbed the steps, and Briggs's hand was there to guide me over to the table. We sat amidst all the flashing lights and hot spots from above.

He leaned into me and whispered, "You're famous."

I watched him, not believing he was right there beside me. He was at home in front of all these people, answering their questions, calm, cool, and collected. It was mesmerizing. This is what he did. This is what he needed to do.

Me on the other hand. . . "I don't know what to do."

"Just smile. They already love you," Briggs said, smiling toward the audience. But I couldn't take my eyes off him or turn my face away. I was frozen, memorizing every line of his face, the way his Adam's apple bobbed up and down, his jaw line, the sweep of his lashes when he blinked. "Smile at them, not me," he said, all while looking out at the sea of people that I could no longer recognize. It was just him and me.

"I can't help it." I smiled away like a little fool in love. "I love you."

His face turned toward me, lacing with concern when he saw my tears. "Me?" He pointed to himself, asking in a way that was like a child on Christmas morning finding out the big gift is for them.

"Yes, you. I love you, Robert Briggs St. Martin." He took me into his arms, hugging me and whispering my sentiments over and over in my ear.

We were both shedding tears. At the same time, it dawned on us that we were in public and there were many cameras pointed at us. We both turned toward the audience and giggled.

Briggs leaned into the microphone and said, "She loves me. I'm celebrating."

Flashes of light went off all over the room, it was a headline in the making.

CHAPTER 33

LACIE

In this little theater, Briggs was famous. I became famous. Suddenly, people wanted to ask me questions. I felt kind of bad taking the spotlight off Briggs.

"Lacie, will you continue to focus on communication for people with neuro-degenerative disease?" a woman in the audience asked.

I wanted to but didn't know if I'd be able to get a license without a degree. "I would like to be a support system for families and caregivers."

"Treating this population must be difficult given their prognoses. How do you prepare yourself for the inevitable?"

I looked at Briggs.

"Do you want to answer that?"

I was so nervous I just wanted him to take over. "Help me."

"You're right, it's difficult. Lacie is honest, honorable, and above all, she does what she does with kindness and love. You won't find a better person caring for your loved ones."

He raised his brows at me and tilted the microphone in my direction, squeezing my hand for support. I could do this. With him at my side, I could do it.

Looking out at their expectant faces, I knew I had to say something, so I adjusted the mic, pulling it toward me. "It's not an easy job. There was never a day I didn't think about losing my patient. I'm close with my families, who are also thinking about when that day comes. I strive to give my patients and their loved ones the highest quality of care and life possible given the circumstances. I advocate for them and their needs. In that way, I'm their voice, guiding them through and hopefully making life a tiny bit easier during the process."

When our time had ended, we stepped down from the stage, still holding hands. We walked in silence through the theater and out the front doors. Limos lined the curb. Finn was there, along with the rest of the St. Martin family and Penny and the girls who were chatting amongst themselves. I couldn't talk at the moment; my throat was full of unshed tears as I tried to keep my emotions in check. Briggs walked to a different limo than the one the family was boarding. I followed.

I got inside and then Briggs got in beside me. He immediately rolled up the privacy glass. We sat with our cheeks against the cool leather, looking into one another's eyes, calmly breathing and with light smiles on our faces.

"I'm so sorry," I whispered, closing my eyes as the tears fell.

Briggs's hands on my face made me to open my eyes. "Don't do that."

"But I almost ruined this moment for you," I cried.

"Get over here." He pulled me onto his lap so that I straddled him, our foreheads touching. "This moment belongs to both of us." He held my hands in his. We existed in that space for several moments, the limo gently rocking us.

"This moment belongs to Steve," I whispered.

Briggs's lips took mine in the softest, sweetest kiss ever given from a man who loves a woman.

It didn't take long for the kiss to go from sweet to intense and then much more. His tongue caressed mine, and I drank him down into my soul. We were, after all, soulmates to one another, and I never wanted to live another day without his sweet taste.

The windows fogged up as I rode him, feeling his hardness

against the barest of silk panties. His hands on my hips guided me where he wanted, his fingers dug into my flesh, bruising my skin, lost in passion. A pinch and a snap against my skin had my panties falling away.

"Lace," he said, raspy and deep, full of need.

My hands found his zipper and pulled him free. I needed this, he needed this; there was no reason to wait. I lifted my hips, he helped guide me, and we came together. After so long apart, it felt good to be connected again. I rode him, driving us both to that place we longed to be. The strength in his arms and core lifted us higher, his powerful thrusts giving us the satisfaction we desired. We reached the top together, and then I fell against him, spent and exhausted, but glowing with a warmth that was spreading all over my body.

His hand banded around my upper arm, pulling me back. He willed me to look him in the eye. "I submit to the film festival. I need to say that again, Lace."

I smiled, closing my eyes. "I believe you."

His throat made a funny little noise, and his hands held me firm to his chest. I sat up so we could see each other. "I need to say a few things and I want you to let me."

"Of course," he said.

I took a deep breath. "I'm sorry I left you naked in the barn. I'm sorry I didn't trust you or let you explain about the festival. But the one thing I can never make up to you are the actions I took when I thought you'd kept things from me." I paused and took another deep breath. "I deliberately tried to sabotage your beautiful project." I was ugly crying now. He tried to wipe my tears, but his fingers couldn't keep up. "And I said," deep breath, "I said you were exploiting the LeBlancs." I couldn't breathe. I took a series of tiny breaths. "But I was so wrong," I cried. "Your story was beautiful. I wanted to get kicked out. I don't deserve my degree or you or your family or anything good in this world."

His hands were on my cheeks, his lips kissed my tears. "Baby, baby, baby, what are you even saying? You fixed it when you went to the board the second time. I don't give a shit about any of it. I only care about you. I need you to breathe." He continued kissing away my pain. "All that other stuff is just tertiary bullshit. We are going to be okay. We're part of the *could be's*."

"We are?" I asked with a crack in my voice.

"Yep. It's a hell of a lot better place to be." He smiled and kissed my lips.

"Better than where?"

"The *couldn't be's*. We've been there too. I never want to go back."

"I don't either."

"Then we won't." He kissed my lips again, still holding his mighty hands against my cheeks. "And my dad spoke with the provost. You're going to get reinstated. And you know my family loves you."

I couldn't believe his dad had done that for me. I had a dad now. A dad who did things to help me. Fresh tears pooled in my eyes.

Briggs's hands moved to my ribs, and he kissed me deeply, but then pulled away. "And you deserve *everything* good in this world, and I'm just the man to give it to you."

I shrugged. "Thank you, but I don't want to be a therapist. I can't handle it."

"No?" He looked adoringly into my eyes.

"Does that make you think I'm weak?" I was actually worried about his response.

"Because you want to change your course in life? Lace, you have free will. You can be or do whatever you want and tell anyone who dare cross you to fuck off. Say it."

"Fuck off."

"I knew you had a filthy mouth in there somewhere." We laughed.

When the limo stopped, I realized he was still inside of me. I blushed. He chuckled. We righted ourselves and our clothing and emerged, but not before he saw the tattoo of Kenzie's heart.

"Hey, what's this?" He lifted the skirt of my dress. "A heart?"

"Kenzie's design, it's her thumbprint, and she has mine, with the year we graduated."

"That's really cool."

"Finn told me what the ripples on your arm say."

"Oh yeah?" He looked a little embarrassed.

"Our moon. I want a tat of that."

"I want that on you too." He smiled.

We exited the limo and were greeted by his waiting family, who embraced us. I was going to have a huge family now. That thought had my smile stretched as far as it could go. We were the *could be's*, and if anything could be better than it was right now, I couldn't imagine what it would be. Then, I realized we'd just done it without protection. Images of beautiful dark-haired babies with ice-blue eyes came to mind.

I smiled warmly.

Yeah, that'd be just a little bit better.

EPILOG
LACIE
Two Months Later

I left my delivery van parked in the lot and headed toward the food truck. Bayou Tacos had the best tacos in town and both Kenzie and I agreed we needed a fix.

> Kenzie: On my way! Had to do a last-minute intubation.

> Me: OMG!

I ordered and then sat at one of the wooden tables, under the shade of the umbrella, and pulled the invitation out of the pocket on my overalls. I'd received it three weeks ago, reminding me to save the date. That date was today. The party was tonight, but I didn't know anything much else about it other than it had Briggs written all over it. It said as much on the card: *Big party. Top Secret. RSVP through the sexy, handsome guy who still has your sea foam green, lace thong panties from the limo ride.*

God, what is it about limos?

Kenzie walked up to the table looking super cute and super official in her navy-blue scrubs and stethoscope around her neck. "God, it was so cool. There I am saving this guy's life and feeling like a fucking god. Whatever," she shrugged, "it's what I do."

I chuckled, accepting the taco tray from our server. "Thanks," I said.

Kenzie grabbed one before I could set the tray down.

"So, are you really not going to tell me about this invitation?" I asked.

She motioned as if she was zippering her lips. Chewing and then swallowing, she said, "I'm your best friend, of course I'm not going to ruin your surprise."

"I hate surprises."

"You'll love this one." She chomped down, devouring her second taco.

"If Briggs is there, it won't matter. I'll be happy."

"See there," she said, wiping her mouth with a napkin. "Are you wearing green?"

"You bet I am. Mom was able to fix my prom dress, so I'm wearing the same dress I wore to prom. Shoes too." I haven't had time to do any shopping anyway. Since we got back from Austin, things have been crazy. So is Tex bringing you tonight?"

She chewed, but her eyes met mine, and she smiled. "We are engaged."

"What?" I grabbed her left hand, but there wasn't a ring. "How could you not tell me?"

"Actually, we promised not to tell anyone, but I can't keep anything from you."

"Except whatever the hell's going on tonight."

"That's Briggs's story to tell, not mine." She picked through her tacos, removing chunks of tomato. "We are going to get ring tattoos."

I gasped. "Oh my God, I love that!"

She nodded. "I know."

"I'm so happy for you."

"Right back at you, Beans."

***

EPILOG

LACIE

The note Briggs left me said to be outside on the sidewalk at 8:00 p.m. It was 7:55 and there I was in my sea foam green chiffon gown and Chuck Taylors. Not sure what was going to happen inside, my stomach was nervous, so I took a deep breath and told myself I didn't have to worry. Whatever was waiting for me inside was something that Briggs had worked hard on for me, and I knew it would be special.

He walked out, looking fine enough to eat in a light gray three-piece suit with a sea foam green tie and pocket square.

My stomach fluttered as I took him in, his flirty smile, his every hair in place, with something that had him looking like a greaser bad boy of the fifties. "Wow, you look super hot."

His arms came around me, and then his lips softly met mine. He smelled divine. "And you're a vision. I'm so glad you wore this dress."

I stuck my foot out from under the dress. "And the shoes too," I added.

"You're perfect." He kissed me again and then led me, holding both hands, toward the door. Once inside, my eyes took a moment to adjust.

White chiffon, lighted from beneath tablecloths that were sea foam green. The seat covers and napkins were also sea foam green. White, translucent drapes hung from every beam, back-lit with white twinkle lights. Frank Ocean's remake of *Moon River* hummed through the sound system.

But the most impressive thing I've ever seen was the entire ceiling covered in white hydrangeas lit by a smoky pink color. It felt like I'd entered my very own fairy tale.

"Welcome to your senior prom. We've got punch, fruit, nuts, cake, friends, DJ, photographers to capture every little move we make, the arch of balloons for making a memory, a photo booth, and chaperones." He lifted a finger and everyone I had ever known —correction, everyone I'd ever known and enjoyed, seemed to be there, even Sarah and Rylie.

We danced and loved each other, the way I'd wanted to five years ago. Only this time we had our families and friends there to share it with us. Cash and Camp came in for the event. Finn looked most handsome in his black and white tuxedo. My beautiful friend, Kenzie, wore a deep purple gown that Tex matched to the perfect shade reflected in his tie and pocket square.

Mom and Mr. St. Martin danced, and Gramps enjoyed himself dancing with all of the beautiful ladies, but his favorite dance partners were the Sarah and Rylie.

The last song of the night was by Adele, but unlike *Set Fire to the Rain*, in *Remedy* she spoke of Briggs as my remedy for anything that could ever hurt me.

"I love you, Lace. Thank you for taking a chance on me."

I closed my eyes and set my cheek on his shoulder. "How could I not, my beautiful boy? Life is nothing without you."

THE END

Leave A Review

Reviews: Ratings and reviews are the lifeline of the book. Please leave book reviews, short or lengthy, all are appreciated.

The Lies We Tell

BLURB

LACIE: My story is about forbidden love. I'm 19. Jackson is 29.

My parents pseudo adopted him when he was seventeen because he'd lost both parents in a plane crash. Even though I was eight years old at the time, I knew from the first moment I met him that we'd be together forever. I just didn't know how much we'd have to fight to stay that way.

After my accident, I needed Jackson and he needed me. Our friendship grew into need and need turned into desire. Our all-consuming love has blossomed behind closed doors, even as it betrays the trust of my family—the ones who took Jackson in when he was orphaned.

Fast forward ten years, and we've been together secretly for the past two years. We said when I turned 19, we'd tell the family. The time is now but with Jackson working as a firefighter EMT and completing his hospital residency, our time together is a luxury. Plus, I'm not ready to tell my brother Clay, Jackson's best friend and boss, about us because I know he's going to go all kinds of crazy.

For the life of me I can't understand how our love, a devotion that is beautiful and pure, can be considered wrong. For me, there is nothing I want more than to be consumed by Jackson's protective embrace. Even if it means I'll have to sacrifice my family to get it.

JACKSON: I can't let Clara make the choice that will cause her to lose her family. I've made the anguished decision to let her go for her own good. My heart is bleeding for us, but I'll deal with that tomorrow. The only thing that matters now is that she has the love and support of her family. I'll figure out how to survive without her or her family.

Thing is, Clara won't surrender so easily. She's willing to fight against familial and societal scorn for our once-in-a-lifetime love, even if it means sacrificing her family's acceptance.

If I have to fight Clara to save her, I'll do it. For two broken souls who found wholeness in each other's arms, giving up seems impossible. I'll keep fighting because I know what it is to live without family. Even if it means pushing her away from me.

The Lies We Tell
CHAPTER 1 (EXCERPT)

The scent of fresh pastries and brewing coffee lingered in the air as Clara bustled around the large plantation-sized kitchen, her mind swirling in a vortex of the double wedding plans of her brother and his BFF Auggie. Plus, never far from her mind was her concern for Jackson, the poor overworked love of her life.

Even with all her responsibilities, it was hard not to smile. Today was the perfect day for a double wedding. The early morning sunlight streamed through the kitchen window, casting a golden halo around her, while the soft rustling of her khaki shorts echoed in the otherwise silent room. The sharp ping of her phone broke the tranquil silence, and she glanced down to see Jackson's name flashing on the screen. His message was simple yet filled with an unspoken tension that tugged at her heartstrings.

Jackson: Where are you?

As she began to type a reply, she couldn't help but reflect on their shared world—a chaotic mix of medical residencies, paramedic shifts, her work and college, and now, wedding preparations.

It was a world spinning too fast for Jackson, yet he refused to slow down.

Today was no different. It was supposed to be a day of celebration with Clay marrying Eve, and Auggie marrying Mia. The two women were sisters so that meant Clay and Auggie would become family—a fact they didn't wax on about but a fact Clara knew meant a lot to both of them. But as Clara stared down at Jackson's text, she knew it was more than just another wedding day—it was a test of strength, love, and patience.

She typed a reply text using just her thumbs.

> Clara: Be there in a bit. Had to get brides b-fast trays.

She'd told him to sleep in. Figured she'd be busy as wedding coordinator extraordinaire—she added the flair to her title.

> Jackson: Hurry, I need you.

She whispered, *Oh Cracker Jack, I need you more.* She smiled at the use of his nickname. He gorged on bags of the stuff while he completed endless mountains of paperwork and reports during his hospital residency.

She'd known he wouldn't stay in bed without her, but he had been behind on sleep and so she'd hoped. She grabbed two mimosas from the kitchen and made her way out to the pool house where the men were staying. She'd done her hair and makeup but hadn't put on her bridesmaid dress yet. There was still a lot of work to be done. After all, the stakes were high: a fancy wedding to organize and a sleep-deprived lover to take care of. And all she had in her arsenal were khaki shorts, a white tank top, two mimosas, and her unyielding spirit.

She opened the door to the pool house and found him slouched on the couch, a frown on his face.

She dangled the breakfast drink in front of him, just beyond his grasp. As she kissed his lips, his pout began to soften. "You can have it," she teased, "if you promise not to be such an Oscar the

Grouch." She mimicked an exaggerated pout herself, her eyes catching the shadows under his and the deeper wrinkles beside them, a little deeper than she'd remembered.

His frown was back with a flicker of something more—impatience and maybe even a little fear.

"Come on Cracker Jack, it's a most glorious day." She presented the mimosa to him.

"I'm on call. I can't have it." His bottom lip jutted out in a pout, though his eyes betrayed the act with their weariness. They held back words he'd rehearsed endlessly. She understood what he longed for, but they had to wait.

"I told you to sleep in. You look tired." She felt her face morph into a little frown of concern.

He traced a hair back behind her ear, his fingertips lingering at the spot where he'd first kissed her when she was seventeen and they'd needed each other more than their next breath. "I missed you, Bug."

The nickname had started as a joke about how she'd gotten under his skin, impossible to extract; now it carried the weight of all they weren't saying.

She giggled. "I think we were apart for about an hour."

"I don't care. I don't like waking without you." His eyes narrowed, jaw tightened, that same muscle twitch she'd noticed the first time they'd discussed telling her brother. "And I'm not happy about today either. It's been two years. We should be the ones getting married."

She took a large sip of the champagne and orange juice before setting the glasses on the couch side table. She kissed him and smiled against his lips. "We will be, baby. Soon."

Marriage to Jackson was the thing she wanted most in the world and so she hoped but wasn't sure herself. "But we can't move forward until we tell my brother and your best friend. We can't do that until you finish your residency." Her fingers found their way into his thick, wavy hair.

"Why not?" His hand covered hers, stilling her anxiousness.

"Because that's what we decided." Their eyes met, and in that moment of silent communication, they both acknowledged what remained unsaid; her fear that her brother would make her choose, and her greater fear that Jackson would push her to choose family. How many times had he said he wouldn't dare come between her and her family?

"I want to revise the decision. Anyway, I'm almost done." The words came out light, but his knuckles whitened as he gripped the couch cushion.

"How about I kiss you here," she nipped at his lips, tasting the salt from his breakfast, "and when we're done with that I'll kiss you down here." She fisted between his legs. "See if we can't turn that frown upside down." Even as she offered the distraction, a sudden raw honesty escaped her: "Sometimes I'm afraid we're waiting for a perfect moment that might never come." She blinked, surprised by her own admission before returning to the safer territory of seduction.

Jackson's lips brushed hers with a tender intensity, their breath mingling as a soft, involuntary sound escaped from the depths of his throat.

One of his hands slid up the back of her neck to grip her hair—always at that same spot where her curls gathered in a whorl—while the other cupped her jaw, his thumb tracing the scars from her accident at sixteen. His kiss was demanding and needy. He explored her deeply and alternated rough and soft strokes, as if he couldn't decide whether to worship or devour her. She loved his kiss, his touch, his everything—even his brooding that cast shadows between them on their brightest days.

He was ten years her senior, but that didn't matter because she'd loved him since she was seven years old. Since that summer afternoon when he'd shown up at their home, moved into the room next to hers, one bathroom between them. Even then, she sensed something broken inside him. He'd lost his parents. Hers pseudo adopted him. In the St. Martin family dynamic, they were connected as siblings, but were anything but.

Her Jackson. As the seasons changed, and the years passed, their connection grew into friendship and then into something more complicated—something that made her heart race with both longing and fear. They'd started getting intimate when she was seventeen and he was twenty-seven. It was part of the reason they hadn't told her family. Sometimes, in moments like these, guilt and desire battled within her—the thrill of his touch against the weight of their secret.

She was now nineteen. Still too young in modern times to marry. But she'd always felt older.

Her hand fiddled with the hardware on his jeans as she made a production of slowly undoing the button and pulling down the zipper. The metal was cool beneath her fingertips, a stark contrast to the heat building between them.

She knew how it sounded—their admission wouldn't paint a nice likeness of Jackson. The world would see predator and prey, not two souls who'd grown together across boundaries of age and propriety. A love born of need, her body broken and scarred, his heart shattered at the loss of so much so young.

She knew Clay had suspicions and had even alluded to their relationship, his sideways glances carrying judgment she pretended not to see. They'd thrown him off the hunt numerous times, each lie another brick in the wall between their private world and everyone else. Luckily, Eve had kept Clay exceedingly distracted.

She pulled his hardness free. He smiled at his readiness, but his eyes held vulnerability she rarely glimpsed—as if even now, after all these years, he feared she might find him wanting. His deep blue eyes shimmered like sunlight on the sea, the same gaze that had held fury when her brother once called him "damaged goods." She shimmied down his legs to kneel on the floor.

He grabbed a pillow, "Here Bug, don't kneel on the hard floor." The childhood nickname slipped from his lips—the one thing he'd carried forward from those early days, a reminder of what they'd been before they became this.

She rose and he slid the cushion under her knees, his calloused fingers lingering at the sensitive spot behind her knee. In that small gesture lay everything unsaid between them—his tenderness, her surrender, and the unspoken question of if what they'd built could survive the storm that was brewing and promised to destroy them.

Grasping his weight in her hands, she placed her tongue on his most sensitive part, and then took him between her lips, her heartbeat quickening in that familiar way that made her feel seventeen again—terrified and invincible all at once. He palmed her head and aided her efforts, his fingertips trembling slightly against her scalp. "God, Bug, I love being in your mouth." The words hung in the air between them.

She couldn't respond, not with words, but her eyes fluttered closed as something tightened in her chest—that old ache of needing too much. She loved it too, perhaps more than she should. Their connection had always been powerful. Their energy had been too potent to ignore. That's what had happened when she was seventeen—the first time his hand had brushed hers. Her skin had remembered it for days afterward. And once they'd connected on a physical level they couldn't stop, like addiction, like gravity, like breathing.

It was as if one could not exist without the other. Sometimes that thought woke her in the night, cold with sweat. She took him deep, loving the feel of him and the groans he made for her, while somewhere in the back of her mind she cataloged this moment—storing it away like all the others, a shield against the times when his job as an EMT and his long hours of residency at the hospital kept him away from her. Her fingers dug into his thighs, leaving half-moon impressions that would fade by the afternoon, unlike the marks he'd left on her that no one could see.

"Christ. Your brother's coming."

Her mind was disoriented, but Jackson pulled her from the floor, the momentum throwing her forward and onto him. Her heartbeat thundered in her chest, a metronome of guilt that seemed to broadcast their deception across the room. His hands at her waist moved her onto the couch. While he fastened his jeans she lifted the pillow from the floor, her fingers trembling slightly against the fabric. He'd barely finished containing himself when they heard the snick of the door opening.

The air in the room seemed to thicken, making it harder to breathe naturally.

Clay's wide ice blue eyes met her own before they narrowed to slits. His gaze migrated to Jackson and back to her.

"Clara." He frowned. "What are you doing out here?" His deep baritone reverberated around the room.

"I was looking for you." Each word of her lie seemed to scrape her throat raw, even as she maintained the bright smile. Jackson's hand started to rub against his denim-clad thigh. She knew he hated the lies they sometimes had to tell to hide their relationship. His smile didn't reach his eyes as they exchanged glances—a silent conversation of panic and reassurance.

"I saw you walking out here fifteen minutes ago. What have you been doing?" His eyes darted between her and Jackson, carrying the same skepticism they'd held since they were children and he'd caught her stealing cookies.

"Been talking with Jackson." His hand rubbed faster against his thigh. "I brought mimosas, but he told me about being on call at the hospital." She jumped up and skipped to Clay with practiced light-ness, while inside she was sinking under the weight of her deception. She threw her arms around his neck and kissed him square on the lips. As she wrapped her arms around her brother's neck, she caught Jackson's scent still clinging to her skin and wondered if Clay could smell it too.

"Such a wonderful day. I love you. I'm so happy my big brother is getting married to his one and only love." The words tasted both true and false on her tongue—she loved him completely, which made the betrayal burn all the more. Her cheeks ached from the forced smile—the same smile she'd perfected over months of hiding.

He squeezed her tight. "Love you too, Clara Bear," he said, using the nickname her family had given her.

"Are you being a good boy?" She smiled up at his six-foot-five frame, breathing in the familiar scent of his woodsy cologne. Clay could be intense but nobody beat Jackson in that department. Truth told, Jackson reminded her a lot of her brother. Clay was fiercely loyal and protective, something she sensed Eve needed. They'd be so happy together. She wasn't jealous but it wasn't lost on her that she and Jackson were as equally perfect for one another as Eve and Clay.

"Auggie's the one you should be worried about. He's in Mia's room."

"Are you serious? That's not allowed." Her voice shed exasperation but deep inside she knew if Auggie wanted to be near Mia, nothing would stop him.

"She was crying."

Mia's eyes grew large, her hand instinctively rising to cover her mouth. "Why was she crying?"

Clay shrugged. "Auggie made her cry."

"What?"

"Bug—err—Clara, you better go check on her."

She turned to Jackson on the couch and couldn't help the slight smile that was forming at the corner of her mouth. As an EMT and emergency room doctor, Jackson was good at maintaining a tight control on his words and emotions, except when it came to her.

She kissed Clay's cheek. "Text me if you need anything."

"Will do."

She looked back at Jackson. He was always so serious. She'd seen him laugh just a few times and it was usually at something she'd done or said. She wished she could think of something now that would bring him relief. His downturned eyes and stiff body held so much pain it radiated across the room, coiling in her stomach with the familiar heaviness that had become her constant companion these past months. The weight of his silence pressed against her chest, making each breath a conscious effort.

Clay's head was turned away, so she held up the universal hand sign for *I love you*—three fingers extended, the silent language they'd developed during the days following his parents' death.

His grief had left a dampening effect on her entire family. Those days words had felt too loud, too inadequate for the emotion and pain coursing through him. Then she blew him a kiss. The right side of his mouth lifted ever so slightly—that precious micro-movement that had become her sustenance, the smallest proof that somewhere beneath his grief, her Jackson still lived.

The Lies We Tell
AVAILABLE NOW!

**Available Now
Scan the QR code**

About the Author

Gina Watson writes steamy, small town romance novels with lovable characters. She published her first novella in 2014. Since then, she has published over twenty romance novels and novellas in many sub genres including small-town, forbidden love, new adult, and action-adventure.

Gina makes her home in Vermont with her husband, Brian. They married on Valentine's day and celebrate Valeversary every year while trying hard to live out their very own HEA ending. With hot cocoa and snowy picture windows it is practically perfect.

Connect with Gina Watson online:
https://www.facebook.com/ginawatsonauthor
instagram.com/whiskey.cove
http://ginawatson.net/

Email List

Keep in touch: Join Gina Watson's email list at ginawatson@ mac.com to receive alerts regarding sweepstakes, contests, give-aways, and upcoming book releases.

www.ingramcontent.com/pod-product-compliance
Lightning Source LLC
Chambersburg PA
CBHW031152020726
47499CB00002B/339